ACCLAIM

"Fans of C.J. Redwine's *Rise of the Vicious Princess* and Tricia Levenseller's *Daughter of the Pirate King* will swoon at Chavis' fast-paced debut! With a rogue pirate, a prophetic quest, and a heart-wrenching bond of sisterhood, this high seas adventure is clean pirate fantasy at its finest!"

—BRITTANY EDEN, author of the *Heartbooks* series

"*Heart of the Sea* is a lush tale of familial love, a longing for home and what could be, all packed with adventure, danger, and a particularly chilling siren. With a dollop of romance, *Heart of the Sea* delivers all the right pirate vibes!"

—AJ SKELLY, bestselling author of *The Wolves of Rock Falls* series and *Magik Prep Academy* series

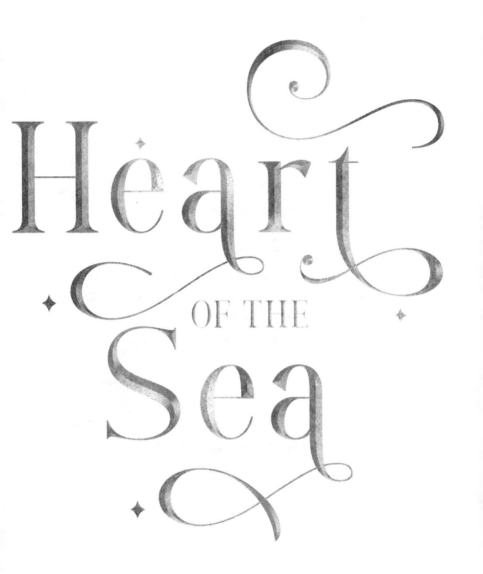

# Heart
## OF THE
# Sea

OTHER STORIES BY MORIAH CHAVIS

Exquisite Poison ("The Assassin's Kiss") - Phantom House Press
Sharper than Thorns ("Thorns of Winter") - Twenty Hills Publishing
Masquerade ("Swan Song") - Selected short stories and poems by Kelly
Dowswell and Adella Quick
What Darkness Fears (2nd. Ed. - "Ghosts at Midnight") - Twenty Hills
Publishing
Tide & Scale ("Sea of Sorrow") - Twenty Hills Publishing
Never Tales Vl. 2 ("Timeless Love") - Twenty Hills Publishing
Magic & Mistletoe: A Quill & Flame Christmas Anthology ("The Last Dance")
- Quill & Flame Publishing House

MORIAH CHAVIS

# Heart
## OF THE
# Sea

Quill & Flame
PUBLISHING HOUSE

## Quill & Flame
### PUBLISHING HOUSE

To my family—those by blood and those I found.

the FIVE King
The Edge of the World
Lake Mercy
Highland Woods
Icelandic Nation "The FOX"
Deadlands
SKRACAE SEA
KINGDOM OF ECBARHOT
Dead Sea
Narrow Wood
QUEENDOM OF
KINGDOM OF FLAVIUS
PERMA SEA
Dragon's Keep
Islands of Perma
FYRIAN OCEAN
Dragonlands
Fiore Lake
Dragon's Pass
ABHOR SEA
OCEAN OF TRANQUILITY

**nd Queendoms of**
**NE**

OCEAN OF ICE

Thistle Mountains **Cardon**
Lord of the
**MOUNT**
"The Bear"

Bow Lake
Halivaris

Lady of
**Halivaris**

"The
Wolf"

**UEENDOM OF MONTAGNARD**
**DOM OF EASTERLY**

s of
LY

Queen's
Lake

The Hills

**Teraceron**
"New kingdom"

**Brevlyra**
"Old Kingdom"

Aquisitionery
Island

Siren's
Cove

Acma
Lake

Claymore Channel

**BHERASUS**
**SEA**

OCEAN
OF
NEWNOS

Islands
of mechelonia

# part one

"Eighteen revolutions around the sun

Will reveal the chosen ones.

The power of the sea

Shall either tempt or make him flee.


One fair, the other scarred.

Down their paths will they begin.

A chosen journey to the end.


Two captains, one motley crew.

A bleeding dawn, the darkest midnight, too.


The alliance, most crucial it will be,

For while one conspires, so does the other bleed."


— "The Prophecy of the Sisters" From Ballad of the Seas

author unknown

# PROLOGUE
## NERISSA

*Acubay*

I can never escape the water for long. On land, I can almost forget the part of me tied irrevocably to the waves. But a yearning grows with each passing moment I'm away, clawing at my skin and demanding my attention. The desire to be amidst the foam and salt fills my veins, beating stronger and faster with each thump of my heart.

"Hello, sea," the witch hisses as I wait in the doorway to her hut. Her thick, otherworldly accent slices through me. With one greeting, this woman reminds me of my harsh reality—of my gift—my *curse*. Anxiety, sharper than the current, rolls through me, and I'm struggling to catch my breath above water.

Deeper in me still rolls the truth I have come to accept: to save the one person who matters most, I must embrace my burden.

I step inside the shadowed room.

Candlelight shines through the witch's paper-thin skin. A film coats her eyes, making the pale, sickly blue even more challenging to see. I'm amazed she has eyes; scarring around the edges hinting at the reason the few pieces of furniture are organized to make a path, not to complete the space.

"She's from the highest corner of Northwest Penreine, the Kingdom of Ice," Claudette, my second, whispers in my ear. Her long black braids tickle my arm, and I leave the familiar comfort, taking a step closer to the witch.

The witch shifts in her leather chair, smoking a pipe and flipping lazily through the pages of a book. Her scarred milky eyes are trained on the blank, smooth surface as if words cover it from left to right. When I'm inches away, she tilts her gaze in my direction.

"Witch, I have the payment your mercenaries requested I bring," I say, bowing my head slightly. Frustration hovers at the back of my throat. It hadn't been easy to find her; it was even more difficult to schedule a meeting.

She smiles. White curls trail down her back and over the arm of her chair. Even with her scars, her youthfulness is alarming. Stories of her power date back before even Father was born, though her skin is as smooth as porcelain, not a wrinkle in sight.

"I've been waiting for you, lovely. So has this." She holds up a rolled piece of parchment, and my fingers itch to yank it from her hand. "What did you decide to bring me?"

I pull the satchel off my belt and hand it to her. "A pearl necklace," I say, a lump forming in my throat—my mother's favorite necklace, the one she wore daily. But it was either this necklace or my father's timepiece, and I knew which one I would rather give up. My mother left me plenty of memories, many of them sour, and the necklace only pulls those things to the surface.

She takes the bag from me, motioning for me to sit. The plush leather chair bends around my body as she places the book on the table next to the fire and deepens her smile.

"You couldn't find what you seek, mhmm," the witch says, and there's a silent chastisement in her tone. "If you had come to me sooner..." Her voice trails off, all singsong and jest. "Rumors only take you so far. Sometimes you need something more concrete."

"And where will *your* rumors take me?" I ask, fingers itching to rip the truth out of her.

"You've not been across *all* of Easterly yet?" she asks, tilting her head as if listening for an answer before I give it.

"I've been everywhere a map can lead us—every inch of charted water. My sister is nowhere to be found."

My mind whirls around the many failed leads, the endless hearsay I've followed to try and find the next piece of the puzzle. None of them worked. Except the suggestion I come here, the queen's armory, barely five leagues from my home of Helene.

*Less than fifteen miles from my island.*

"Yes, this map is special. Quite difficult to find," she says, tapping the roll of worn parchment.

I narrow my eyes on her. "And you are a difficult *woman* to find."

She smiles wickedly, all sharp edges and malice. "But not as difficult to catch as you. Shame about your ship. The storm season does like to rip through those smaller vessels. At least no one was killed."

I gulp down the anger rising sourly in my throat. "I can find another ship."

She leans closer. "You need more than a *ship* to go where this map will take you." Her voice is a taut—a challenge whispered into the smoke curling above the candles. I grit my teeth, and her grin widens.

"How much *more* will it cost me?" I ask, not sparing Claudette a glance.

Without a word, the witch slides the map across the table, and I hurriedly unfold it.

Anger rises in me as I rip my gaze from the parchment and focus my eyes on the witch. "What is this?" I squint my eyes, trying to focus on the constantly moving figures on the map. No matter which way I turn it, it refuses to stay still. "How am I supposed to get anywhere *safely* if I can't read the map?"

"Do you know where it's taking you?"

My hands tighten into fists. "If I knew, I wouldn't be here."

My sister is out there. A tugging in my middle tries to pull me closer to her, but no matter how hard I search, I can't find her.

She leans closer, her blind eyes somehow settling on mine and burning into me. "It's taking you to Brevlyra."

"Brevlyra?" I ask, throat dry. "It's been cursed for the past fifteen years—people have forgotten how to even get there."

"Have they forgotten? Brevlyra still touches Teraceron, but when people try to head south, they meet disastrous fates." Her lips curl up in a malicious grin. "No one can touch it. Not even an inch."

I grit my teeth. "It's cursed. No one wants to touch a cursed place."

"Cursed? Protected? Seems a matter of perspective. Either way, the Light and the Darkness fight over it." She leans back, tapping her long nails on the top of the closed book. "That's how it began. The Darkness captured the land, and when the Light fought for it—and won—the only way to keep the Darkness out forever was to make it impossible for either side to step on the land. That's if you can get close enough to it. It would be a fight the entire journey."

"And a silly map knows not only how to get there, but—" I bite the inside of my cheek.

"Exactly what you need? Sea, it knows more of what you need than you do. You are exceptionally bright, but the map knows. It knows everything."

I don't give her the satisfaction of a response.

The witch leans in closer, *"Eighteen revolutions around the sun, Will reveal the chosen ones."*

"Stop," I whisper.

She continues. *"The power of the sea, Shall either tempt or make him flee."*

"I said stop," I snap. "I know the prophecy."

The witch's smile turns lethal, happier than a cat with a mouse between its paws. "The map requires two captains to work. And as for the *more* you seek, lovely, I'll give you that slice of information for free as it is more of a burden than a tool. You need a ship, a good ship able to survive these waters, not the ones you have been asking after on the docks the past few days. While there are plenty of ships in our seas, there's only one you need—the *Red Dawn*, captained by none other than Cyrus Crow. He's the price you have to pay."

"Why?" I ask, the name rolling over my skin. Crow—the queen's man who calls himself a pirate. As handsome as he is dangerous.

"Crow's ship is the fastest in Penreine," she replies, milky gaze settled on me. "But the captain is your treasure."

"I don't need a captain. I *am* the captain. I trained for over a year, scoured Easterly for a crew, a ship. They respect me—"

She clucks her tongue and rests her chin in her hand. "Then what's the problem, lovely? You have the Gift of the sea. It will help you get to where you need to go, but only with *this* map. And to read it, you need Crow."

A growl rolls off my lips, and a satisfied laugh fills the room. "My *curse* hasn't helped me this far—"

"Your mother did you a disservice. Truly, she should have trained you from the moment you showed promise. Instead, she hid you away in the dark. Tore you away from the sea—your one true home."

"And if my mother had remembered she had two daughters to take care of, maybe I wouldn't be headed to Brevlyra," I say, heat rising to my cheeks. "My inability to control my powers now has *nothing* to do with her training."

The witch snorts. "Feisty one, aren't you?"

I let loose my pent-up anger through one long breath. "By the sea, why do I need a monster-hunting pirate to read this Light-blessed thing?"

She leans back in her chair. "You aren't the only one trying to find Brevlyra. Which is why, my dear, you need Crow. But forget this not, Crow needs *you*, too."

# FOUR
# WEEKS
# LATER

# CHAPTER
# ONE
NERISSA

***Pirate's Bay (Rogue Territory, Previously Part of the Isles of Levimeer)***

My eyes narrow on the massive ship before me, watching Cyrus Crow and his men load another barrel of supplies.

*Fully stocked. Perfect. Thank you, Captain Crow.*

The sound of men's drunken laughter from the tavern nearby hides the waves rushing against the docks not even a quarter league away. Salty spray hangs in the air, sending goosebumps across my flesh. I grit my teeth against the magic threatening to take charge.

*Not right now,* I think. *Blasted sea!*

*Focus on him.*

My eyes find Crow again in the darkness. As soon as he disappears up the ramp, I take my chance.

"Excuse me!" My heart roars in my ears, louder than the black birds cawing in the night sky above.

Crow's men turn to face me. The one with an eye patch settles his hand on his sword. They're typical pirates, rough around the edges and reeking of bad booze. The brisk night air buffets the sweat dripping down my back, causing shivers to snake down my spine, reinforcing a coyness I lack.

"I'm sorry to interrupt, but I'm needing safe passage to Helene," I say, swishing my skirts, getting their eyes to look anywhere but my face.

Lucia always did say I was a horrible liar; she could see it in my eyes.

*Lucia.* Thinking about her causes my heart to race, pain stealing my breath.

"Your ship," I say, nodding toward it. "Is there room for one more?"

Captain Crow isn't in sight, and these men have two options: say no to a woman in distress, or say yes and risk the ire of their captain.

Their jaws go slack, and they don't immediately answer.

*You've got them!*

"Below deck. You won't even know I'm there!" I say, taking a step closer, close enough to lay a hand on the arm of the man nearest me.

The man with the eyepatch harrumphs. "I don't think—"

"I have money." I take out my purse of gold—the only gold on me.

*Please be worth it.*

He studies me, eyebrows twitching. "Follow me."

The man grabs my arm and doubt flickers in my mind. Bad things often happen to delicate girls.

But I'm more than a pretty face.

"No need to drag me there," I say, voice squeaking. I clear my throat and yank my arm free. "I can walk."

The ship is a frenzy of activity as the crew gets ready to set sail. The waves welcome my footfalls, lapping hungrily against the bow, but I push them away. The rocking of the boat eases. If there's one thing strangers cannot know about me, it's the power flooding my veins. A few men glance in my direction, whispering to one another at the sight of me. "Bad luck," one says, and I hold in a smirk.

*They have no idea.*

"Keep up," Patch hisses, and I rush to follow him, each footfall thudding in my chest.

He raps his knuckles on the captain's door, my throat tightening the longer we go without an answer. He glances back at me, mutters, "Stay here," and walks inside. I listen to his footsteps grow fainter, the soft sound of his voice calling out for his captain. A murder of crows flies around the masts, and a shiver races its way down to my toes. A crow with white-tipped wings flies overhead, landing in the crow's nest and staring down at me.

"Come on," Patch says, and I jump. He tugs me inside, and my eyes flash around the room. It's a decent space with a drafting table—a cat snoozing on top—on one side, a bookcase bolted on the opposite wall, and an open chest. A small bed and an extra cot sit on the far wall. The fanciest things about it are the stained glass window behind the drafting table and the sword hanging above his bed. It's almost...comfortable. "You'll wait here."

I glance over my shoulder and see a flash of my cousin's—and first mate—hair as she slips between the supplies waiting to be loaded. The door creaks closed enough to hide Britta from view, and I'm clenching my sweat-soaked palms tight in my skirt. My mercenaries position themselves at various lookouts, ready to board the ship as soon as Britta gives them the go-ahead.

I spent precious days finding out when the *Red Dawn* would leave the port at Pirate's Bay—nearly two weeks calculating the best time to find the pirate and convince him to let me on his ship. Crow came into the tavern every night, making sure he never noticed me. I hunted him, and he didn't even know he was prey.

"Captain's up top, but he's interested in hearing your *request*," Patch says as he eyes the room.

"How did you speak to him—"

He smirks. "Lass, I don't tell all his secrets. Now, sit there and wait." He motions to a chair in front of the drafting table. "Touch nothing, unless you want your chances squandered for idle curiosity."

"Oh, I'm never curious, sir," I reply, flashing him a smile. "Only grateful."

He narrows his eye on me, as if thinking all women are as pesky as the cat jumping from her perch and slipping out on deck. I'm left alone, only the sound of the waves lapping against the wood to entertain me—with all the captain's things. Silvery light shines through the stained glass window, creating a colorful dance on the planks as I search for weapons.

They've made this almost too easy.

Moonlight glints off the sword over his bed, though moving it would be too suspicious. I make a note of it and search the rest of the room. A few moments later, after I've had time to hide as many blades as I can find and locate stacks of journals and correspondences with Queen Weylan herself, Cyrus enters his quarters. He takes off his sword and jacket, and I'm a little offended.

*Never underestimate your opponent, Captain.*

I study the way his back muscles stretch against the worn cotton shirt, imagining where to land my dagger if needed.

*"Right here," Kip said, brown curls resting on his brow. His pointer and middle finger pressing on the small of my back. "You'll hit a kidney and kill your opponent." His hand slid up. "And here will just hurt like an isler."*

Cyrus Crow glances at me, and surprise sparks in his eyes, half obscured by his raven hair. He tugs at a crow feather half-hidden beneath his bandana and glances away, staring out the porthole next to the stained glass. "Well, what is it, miss? Why do you need to board *my* ship to go to Helene?"

I swallow the nerves twisting in my belly and ask, "Don't you have the best ship in Penreine?"

He glances up, eyes startlingly blue. His grin widens, though he's anything but amused. For a pirate, he's beautiful. His teeth are white as pearls, and his face is tan from years in the sun. A scar escapes his bandana and disappears into his brow, another at the corner of his mouth. It distracts from the perfect contours of his otherwise handsome, devilish face. Or perhaps, it adds to the attraction.

"Of course. I'm Cyrus Crow. But you're a lady—why are you consorting with the likes of me?" He exudes arrogance, the sickly taste of it settling on my tongue. "You must know the things people say of me—*hunters* like me."

A blush rises to my cheeks, but not for the reason he suspects. I clench my fist and use it to my advantage, casting my gaze down.

If Mother were alive, she would praise this look.

*"Men don't want strong, Nerissa," she said in exasperation. "They want someone with a pretty face—someone who needs them."*

I am not modest as my mother had hoped, but Cyrus wants to believe I am. I can give him a show.

Because I need his ship.

I need *him.*

"You're *the* Cyrus Crow—Captain of the *Red Dawn*, Keeper of the Crows, and the queen's chosen hunter," I whisper, turning my eyes to him at the exact moment, fluttering my lashes a few beats before peering through them. "A lady needs protection, does she not? The queen protects this ship."

Crow turns to me and leans back on his desk. "Not everyone appreciates my relationship with Queen Weylan *or* the work I do for her," he says.

Hot determination rises in my chest, but I push it down and smile.

"A girl can never be too careful in this current climate, and the queen is who I stand behind."

*Liar.*

I change the subject, clearing my throat.

"You're fair, treat your crew well," I say, pausing to chew my lip for effect. "Can you guarantee me safe passage?"

He leans back, arms crossed, cerulean gaze emotionless. "Why should I? It's a few leagues south."

The storm season has passed, but the waters are murkier than ever. If Crow is who I need to make the map work, then I'll do whatever it takes.

"Miss?" Cyrus Crow asks.

Convincing him to align with me will be difficult, so I'm forcing his hand. "Because, Captain Crow, I have something you need."

He opens his mouth to respond when a sound clamors outside. He turns, and I grab a book from his desk, hitting him over the head. It doesn't knock him out, but it does send him to his knees.

I reach for my dagger and try to rest the blade at his throat, but he grabs my ankle and yanks me to the deck. A low, guttural scream escapes my throat, and the dagger falls from my fingers. I scramble to make contact with the weapon, but Crow yanks on my leg, adding too much space between the knife and my hand. My boot connects with his face, sending blood spurting from his nose and splattering the skirt of my dress.

The captain lets out a slew of curses as he releases me. One of my mercenaries comes charging in, and I have enough time to yell, "Don't kill him!" before a blade sinks in the wall next to Crow's throat.

I grab the weapon at my thigh as a woman with blazing red hair rushes through the door. Before I can utter a warning, my mercenary falls to the floor with a thud, the bitter tang of copper assaulting my senses. I scramble to my feet, grabbing the sword Crow left with his coat and lifting it up in time to block the redhead's next deadly blow.

She glares at me, putting all her weight into forcing me back. My feet slip in the blood pooling on the floor, and the air escapes my chest as a dozen crows fly into the space and lift Cyrus in the air, causing me to lose the girl in the melee.

I try calling the sea, but it doesn't listen.

Almost as if to say, *Not now, Nerissa. You've got to be kinder first.*

"Blessed Light," I curse under my breath.

Britta rushes into the room as Claudette and a few other mercenaries fight the rest of Crow's crew on the deck. Britta charges into the murder of crows, blade slashing through feathers and loud caws, but soon her screams reach my ears.

The birds scatter, and I find my cousin and Cyrus locked arm-in-arm, covered in feathers and blood, pure fury painting both of their faces. Their weapons lay out of reach, barely visible past the crows filling the space. The redhead raises her sword and sprints toward me. Our blades clash, the force reverberating up my arm and causing my teeth to clack together painfully. Cyrus's blade slips through my hand, leaving me with only a dagger.

She's stronger—a lot stronger.

*Fine. Let's try going under instead of over.*

I slide beneath her, wood splintering into my knees through the thin fabric of my dress, and yank her by the waist. Her knees crack against the ground, and she reaches back, yanking at my braid. A grunt escapes my lips, and my fingers fumble to keep hold. I yank at the band of her breeches and grasp her shoulder with my free hand. Lifting the dagger to her throat and biting back a hiss of pain, I scream over the caws, "Enough! Unless you want her blood on your hands, call off the birds!"

A heavy silence settles over the room, and the birds land on any available surface, waiting for their master's next command.

"What do you say, Captain?" I ask, panting.

The girl releases her hold on my hair, my scalp tingling.

*Keels, my knees hurt.*

Britta raises her sword to Crow's neck.

"That's what I thought," I say.

His eyes are hard, bluer than the bottom of the sea.

The sounds outside cease, and Claudette enters the room. She brushes her long, black braids over her shoulders, her umber skin glowing in the moonlight.

"Cap," she says from the doorway. "We're ready."

The woman beneath my blade spits at my feet. "Don't do it, Cyrus," she says, and I press the sword in farther.

*I've never killed someone.*

*Liar,* hisses the voice in my head. The sharp tang of bile slides against the back of my tongue.

"He's not the captain of this ship anymore, are you, Crow?"

He glares at me. "You want my ship?" he asks, and Britta rests the tip of the blade on his chin.

"There's no *want* about it. I have it," I reply.

Then he laughs at me.

The sound boils my blood. "It would take one thought—one breath—and my crows would destroy you," he says.

"One slice, and she's dead." The blade cuts into the woman's skin, but she doesn't squirm.

Bile rises in my throat from my empty threat and death's essence permeating the room.

*Could I do it* again? *Take another life?*

My palms start to sweat, and I fight back the edges darkening my vision.

*Stop, Nerissa,* I chide myself. *This isn't him.* But I can't get the image out of my head, the blade sinking into his throat before he fell to the ground—

I tighten my hold on the weapon.

Crow's eyes follow the redhead, his gaze softening. This is someone he loves—someone he would die for.

Her breath quickens, and she stops struggling.

"What'll it be, Crow?" I ask, voice mocking.

The birds leave, one by one, flying out of the room and back out into the night air, moonlight glinting on their feathers. The prickling sensation leaves my skin as the last bird disappears from sight.

"Claudette," I say over my shoulder. "How many? How many of Crow's men are on our side now?"

"All but four, Cap."

Relief floods my veins. I hide it behind a smirk.

"All but four, Crow. All but four of your men are on *my* side now. The others vow to call me captain."

"You're dead," the woman spits. "The second you turn your back—the moment you—"

"Bec," Crow says, and she stops. "I'll play. Most of my men. What about the others?"

Claudette answers. "The four left are already tied up, Cap." A breath of relief fills my lungs.

I turn to Crow with a smile. "See? Do as I say, and no one gets hurt. Leave them tied up on the docks—"

"No," he snaps, eyes flashing. "Abandon my men, and I will have my crows end you. They stay on this vessel."

"An empty threat. If you kill me, you kill *her*," I say, my eyes dropping to where my blade rests on the throbbing vein in her throat.

"She's one member of my crew, *one*." He runs his tongue over his teeth, a fine sheen of blood turning the white of his teeth pink. His expression blanks. "I sacrifice her, and I save my entire ship."

"Lies." A smile twists on my lips. "She matters more than you say, Crow."

He doesn't say a word, meeting my gaze, testing me. He doesn't believe I will do it. I grit my teeth and throw the woman to the floor. Claudette rushes to tie her up as the girl curses her with every breath in New Kingdom slang.

Something in me weakens, and as much as I shouldn't, I find the words forming on my tongue. "Fine. They stay on board," I say. "Until we have this,"—I motion between us —"ironed out."

I pull the map out of the sling around my waist. Cyrus's eyes flash with something hot, his jaw clenched, but it's iced over in an instant as his gaze rises from my middle to my eyes, where I wave the map.

"You've been looking for this, or so I've been told," I say, tilting my head.

His eyes never leave my face as I slide the parchment back in the sling.

"Do you understand?" I ask, but he remains stoic.

Cyrus's stare lingers as I make my way toward him. His nose still drips blood, curving around his lips and into his mouth; the smile he offers me is bloodied and malicious. My stomach churns at the sight, the stench of copper filling my nostrils. "Do as I say, and none of your crew will die, even the ones you're forcing me to keep. Do we understand one another?" I ask.

His shoulders relax, and he leans back, arms hanging loosely at his side. "Of course, milady," he says.

Anger boils my blood, and I raise the hilt of the sword, knocking him out.

"East," I say to my crew, standing stoically behind me. "We head east."

I stand on the quarterdeck, staring at the sea as the sun begins to creep over the horizon. My knees sting from the alcohol I used to wash away the blood and clean the wounds. Luckily, none of my injuries needed sutures. The waves crash against the ship, rocking us into the morning. Britta sidles up next to me.

"Six crew members left against us, Issa," she says, using my name for the first time since we boarded this ship, her entire body buzzing. "Can you believe it?"

"Including Crow and the redhead?"

She nods, teeth taking hold of her bottom lip to reign in her smile.

I fight the urge to roll my eyes. Britta might see this as a little adventure to distract her from the life she left behind, but it's anything but a self-validating quest for me.

"We can send the crew loyal to him away whenever you like," she says. "They're going to be mad as islers—"

"We still have a lot of sea ahead. Is the map secure?" My nails dig into the side of the ship.

She rolls her eyes. "Can you be excited for a moment?" I give her an exasperated look, and she continues, "Fine. It's safely secured in the hold until we move Crow and the redhead to the brig," she says.

"Good," I say. The word gets caught by the wind and disappears into the waves. Now I have to convince him to listen to me.

I stare at the ship, the red-tinged wood and the beautiful sails, clearly funded by the queen. At barely nineteen, Crow has made a name for himself, but it piggybacked off the queen's influence. It's what separates us, but it's also one of the many reasons I need Crow on our side. If the queen hears we have taken over Crow's ship, we will never escape. If we make it to Brevlyra, it will be nothing short of a miracle, even with the fastest ship in the five kingdoms. The land is untouchable, but with this map, there's no way we won't succeed.

*Please let this work.*

My eyes drift close, and I breathe in the salty air. The wind whirls around me, and the magic of the sea lifts up the bottom of my ruined dress.

*Nerissa...*the sea whispers.

*Now* it wants my attention...

I open my eyes. Britta won't look at me, but she doesn't have to. I know she sees. Britta always sees and was the first one, besides Mother, to ever witness the water take me. When my power consumes me, it's like being caught in the current, not riding it. Above the water enough to not drown but still out of control. When I began testing my powers, I didn't know what to expect. The sea responded angrily.

*An anger you still haven't been able to control.*

The sea rolls beneath my fingers, begging to be called. An ache builds between my ribs, magic undulating through my veins. I ignored my powers for too long, and my ability overwhelms me.

It terrifies me. I don't know what to do with this power; I don't know why I have the ability or where it came from. My mother knew, but she kept those secrets to herself. If I ignore my power, it takes and takes and takes until I pay attention. If I submit to it, I still get pulled beneath the undertow, unable to ride the wave and instead succumbing to its raging depths.

I chew on the inside of my cheek, squinting into the sunrise.

*Watch the horizon, Nerissa. It's always faster than you.*

The witch's warning sits bitterly on my tongue.

"We spent too long in the bay," I say.

*Eighteen revolutions around the sun.*

The sisters of prophecy.

*No. You're more than a prophecy. We both are.*

But are we?

Eleven days until Lucia turns nineteen—until my time is up, when she'll become an adult in Penreine, and her fate will be sealed. November 2nd, her birthday, with mine the day before. Being so close in age, 364 days apart, most would have assumed we were close our entire lives, beyond childhood. But our friendship ended where my powers began.

Even though Lucia and I fought, she is my sister. I will stop at nothing to save her. However, for the past two years, something has disrupted my journey. My powers, the storm season, no ship or crew—even now, the one thing standing between me and saving Lucia is Cyrus Crow.

"We have to move," I whisper.

"We shouldn't let any of them live, Issa—" Britta begins, and a shiver runs up my spine at the hostility on her face.

"We're not murderers." *Except for me.*

"You had Cyrus Crow fooled." She sneers, bloodlust thick in her words and the silent accusation a match igniting the flame of guilt in my gut. "You almost sound like a noble."

The words prickle my skin. My father had been a noble, but I never lived that life—thankfully, even if my mother did try her hardest to make a lady out of me.

I glare at her. "*I'm* the captain of this ship. Hold your tongue, Britta." My voice lowers, shared only between us before they're lost to the waves. "I don't care if we *are* family."

Her jaw clenches, and she nods, brushing a blonde strand of hair out of her eyes. "My apologies, *Captain*," she whispers and walks away.

Claudette comes over to me. "There are some breeches in the supplies below. Want me to find you something less...constricting?" she asks, her Mechelonian accent rich and low, like she's singing.

"Yes." I groan, giving her a smile. "For the love of the Light, get me some breeches."

She salutes me with a soft chuckle before walking away.

The ship is stocked, and the water is relatively calm, even if it does whisper to me. I check with everyone as we continue to sail, making my way to the forecastle deck. My nerves settle as the ship cuts through the sea.

I glance behind me, taking a deep breath of salt air, and then look at my hands. The black pearl ring, the last thing I have of Lucia's, glints in the morning light. Sized for someone smaller, it's too tight, a noose around my left pointer finger. Part of me wants to throw it to the sea, to head west toward another kingdom, instead of heading east, where Old Kingdom waits—it would have ruled Easterly if it weren't for the war.

A crash behind me breaks me out of my reverie.

"What's going on?" I demand, twisting around.

One of my mercenaries slides down the center mast and shakes his head. "Sound came from the captain's quarters."

He turns his head, but I'm faster, yanking my skirts up and breaking into a run.

# CHAPTER
# TWO
CYRUS

**Abbors Sea**

"That's no seabird. It's a crow," I told Becci, five years old and still enamored with the idea. "They talk to me when Mum isn't listening."

"Cyrus, wake up," Becci says, but I can't pull myself from the memory.

"We can't keep hiding, Cordelia," Aunt Gianna said.

"Cyrus! I swear to the Light, if you don't wake up…"

"Brevlyra is no more," Mum snapped.

My heart thunders in my ears.

Mum screamed, pushing me back, and my breath rushed from my lungs. The sickening thud of steel slicing through her chest rang in my ears. I fell to the ground as my eyes found Mum's back, metal clean through her dress where red bloomed. The slick hiss of the weapon pulling away ripped the scream from my throat.

"Cyrus, wake! Up!"

"My sweet boy," she said, her words a soft whisper. "I did it all for you. But there will be another who will come—someone who will save you."

Weylan stared at me, my mother's blood on her cheek. "Aren't you precious, Cyrus Crow? Welcome home."

"Blessed Light!" Becci, my cousin, screams, and there's a sharp jab next to my spine, finally pulling me back. "For the love of the sea, please stop talking in your sleep."

I startle fully awake. My neck aches from the imagined weight of the crown Weylan placed on my head years ago.

"Your dreams suck seaweed, sleep talker," Becci says, her voice tinged with faux amusement, hiding the panic underlying her words. The memory of our mothers' deaths shadows her gaze.

My eyes adjust to the muted light, noticing we're still tied up in my quarters.

I grunt, wiggling my wrists against the prickly bindings. "Everyone did tell us we were tied at the hip."

"I wouldn't wish it on my worst enemy," she says. "Hey! Stop yanking against the ropes, idiot. My wrists are sore enough." Her voice catches when I shift.

The ship quakes beneath us, and my eyes dart around the dark room.

*Master?*

Relief floods my chest. My connection to the crows is a family trait, magic passed from father to son. Besnick is my familiar, speaks to me like no other, though the rest of the murder would protect me at all cost.

*I'm all right, Besnick. Keep a lookout.*

Air rushes over my skin as my crows take flight, and my vision flickers, adjusting to seeing through Besnick's eyes. I watch the ship for a few moments. Nerissa stands at the helm, arguing with the blonde woman from before, worrying the ring wrapped around her forefinger. I'm jerked back by Becci jabbing her elbow under my third rib.

"Well," Becci says, her shoulders knocking into mine. "Any bright ideas?"

"I thought you boasted you were always the brains between us." I catch our reflection in the mirror across from us in time to see her scowl. "You look a right mess, by the way," I say. "Ow!"

She digs her thumb into my back, where her tied hands rest near my spine. "Ow!"

"Cyrus Crow, by the sea, I will end you before anyone else gets the pleasure."

"Apologies. Where's the rest of the crew?"

She shrugs. "Keels if I know. Dead, shipped back to our fair lady, locked below deck. Take your pick."

I clench my jaw. "We didn't have a choice," I whisper.

"Actually, you newk," she says, using the word we used to call the visiting dignitaries when we lived in the castle, "we do. She has the map, Cyrus. The girl—this creature daring to call herself a captain—got the map before *you*. She must've found the witch, the old bat. Wonder where she's hiding now? Remember when she used to torture us with her little spells at Weylan's parties?"

"Don't remind me. If we want to go back home—"

"Who says I want to go back home to *her*? Did you hear what I said? Torture. At Weylan's parties. And I know Weylan did worse to you. I got off easy when she'd throw me in the tunnels with her cats. You had to spend time with *her*." Her entire body shudders at the memory. "I can't go back there; I would rather die, Cy."

Weylan's power over her animals, while similar to mine, is more about control than connection. The magic she shares with her beasts comes from a different, darker place. We always hoped they might turn on her, though it hasn't happened yet.

"Our crew could be rotting below deck," I say through gritted teeth. "They *might* be alive—"

"Or dead," she drones, and I catch the grimace on her bruised face in the mirror. "It's an option!"

"Becci," I groan.

"*Becci*," she mocks, lips pursed.

"I understand you're upset," I say, and she huffs. "We can sit here tied up in my quarters, or we can untie ourselves and see what we can find out. She left us here, alone. Duncan can—"

"What about him?" Becci snaps, her voice taking a defensive tone. She's been more and more sensitive when I mention his name, and I wonder if she's realized exactly why.

I smirk, and she huffs again.

"He can take care of the others," I say. "I don't want to return to *her*, but I do want peace, and we'll never have it, unless we give her what she wants. Home is where you are, Becci, where we can finally rest. We need this girl."

She pokes me with her bony elbow again, but this time not in anger, almost like she's checking to see I'm still there. "She'll blame us both if this goes badly, you know. It doesn't matter who newked it up, as long as someone did," Becci whispers.

My face warms. "Look, I know I *newked* it up," I say.

She snorts.

"You finished?" I ask, and she mumbles, "Yes."

I take a deep breath, saying, "I was supposed to get the map and use it to bargain with the girl. I can't help what happened. We need her now."

Becci lets her chin hang to her chest. "Fine. If we must, but I don't understand it, Cy. I don't. Two years on the sea, risking our lives hunting those creatures for Queen Weylan's most recent power play. I say you should've told her to stick it right up the back end of those cats of hers. We should've run while we were little," she whispers, and my heart aches with the impossible idea.

I shake my head. "Weylan would've sent someone after us, or her enemies at court would have had to get on her good side." A humorless laugh falls from my lips. "You forget, Becci, you were her ward, too. Still are. By the Light! Stop poking me with your thumb! I'm doing this for the both of us—running her routes for *the both of us*."

"Stop being an idiot!" she says. "Is this the life our mothers wanted us to live? To chase after our own freedom like common court rats?"

I remain silent. "Do you not trust me, Becci?"

She's quiet for a long moment before whispering, "Of course I do, Cyrus."

Our eyes meet in the mirror. "Then stick to the plan. Nerissa needs us as much as we need her."

"At least fight for the crew. Make *her* fight for you. Just a little bit," Becci says. "Maybe if we break out of these ropes she'll actually listen to us."

I smirk. "Don't worry," I say, fiddling with the small knife hidden in my sleeve. With a little effort, I'm able to slide it under the ropes and free myself. "The map is only one piece to the puzzle. She'll soon realize why she needs us."

*Half-truths, Crow. When will you tell someone the whole truth? If not Becci, then who?*

Becci grumbles under her breath.

"The lady captain has the advantage, for now," I continue, and Becci's posture stiffens at the word *captain.* You'd swear she lost the title and not me. "But *we* know these seas. She's looking for something, doesn't matter what. This is the best and easiest way to get what we need."

"Which is why we're bowing at her feet when we know—"

"Becci," I hiss, pinching the bridge of my nose to try to lessen the throbbing in my skull.

She rolls her eyes.

*I* need her for something else.

"But she's done us a favor. She has the map—now we need her to read it."

# CHAPTER
# THREE
## NERISSA

***Abhors Sea, Near Acubay***

By the time I throw the door open to the captain's quarters, the ropes are a pile at Crow's feet. He barely spares me a glance as he fumbles with the knots around the redhead's wrists. He abandons them and rushes to the desk, hitting a button we missed on the side and producing a knife from a hidden compartment.

"Do we have to do this right now?" I ask, hands on my hips.

He throws the blade at my head. I dodge to the side with ease and roll my eyes. "Seriously, pirate? At least give me a challenge." I reach back, gaze still trained on him, and pull the knife from the wall.

"The only pirate here is you," he says. "Stealing my ship and imprisoning my crew."

He circles me, but I'm not worried about him escaping. I have his weapon now, and honestly, I'm disappointed in how he decided to use it.

"And what would you do if you escaped?" I smirk at him. "We're near Acubay."

His lips tighten.

I twirl the blade, pursing my lips. "I could barter you away. I could get a good price for you."

Crow stops circling and stands tall. He towers over me, blue eyes sharp beneath his overgrown hair. "Stop playing games."

My breath catches at the intensity in his look, and I know he could easily toss me aside. He wouldn't get past my crew, but I need him alive. I don't just need his ship. I need him.

*Think, Issa, think.*

The woman—Becci—continues to struggle against her bindings.

We're a few days from Brevlyra, and I will stop at nothing to get there. We've left free waters, entering where he doesn't want to go, and he knows it. Islanders don't trust the queen, and they don't trust those under her thumb. Everyone knows Cyrus Crow is her lackey.

His eyes shift to the windows. He can't step foot on Pirate's Bay because the people who live there are loyal to no one. The closer the ship drifts toward the outlying islands, the worse off his situation becomes. He has nowhere to go.

"Are you a privateer?" His voice is like velvet, smooth with a hint of a New Kingdom accent.

*New Kingdom.* Teraceron, whatever it goes by.

Those who don't live in Teraceron call it New Kingdom, but Brevlyra held more power before the fall, giving it the Old Kingdom moniker. It would have been the land of our monarch, if it hadn't been for the war.

"Not a privateer," I say, grabbing an apple off the nearest table and taking a bite. I throw it at him, hitting the wood with a hard thwack where his head was moments before. I slam him against the wall, whipping out the blade he carelessly threw and resting it at the base of his neck. "I do not work for any king or queen."

He snorts. "Then what?" he asks, still looking around for another weapon.

"Brevlyra."

He flinches. "You're going *there?* To the Light-forsaken land, *milady?*"

"Captain, my lord," I reply. "From what I hear, you're wanting the same."

He scowls, and I know I've hit a nerve.

"You're not my captain," he says.

"She's no one's captain. She's nothing but a common thief," the redhead says, spitting the words at my feet.

I turn to his first mate, raising my eyebrows. "Aren't we all common thieves? Nothing but pirates?"

Her disquieting violet eyes blaze with anger, shoulders stiff. "Keeling *newk*. You know nothing about us, *Captain*. You don't deserve the blade in your hand."

I tilt up Crow's blade, the tip hovering over the thrumming pulse at his throat. "Sit back down, Crow," I say, "before your lady here makes me mad."

"At least let us join our crew below deck," he asks, arching a brow.

"How about a bargain? You and *her* stay aboard. We'll send the others out on the extra dinghy."

"Cyrus—" the girl starts.

"Becci," he warns, voice low.

"You can't send them on a *dinghy*! The waves'll rip right through it," she says, but he raises a hand to silence her. He eyes me, cocking his head like a bird.

I think of his crows, their black eyes staring intently at us as we sail across the sea. An uneasiness settles in my stomach. Even though we would probably win in the end, it would be a nasty fight and seriously deplete our resources. Something has stopped him from attacking.

But what?

He wraps his leg around my ankle, and I fall on my butt with a surprised cry. My blade skitters across the floor, and he grabs my arms and holds them above my head, straddling my waist. He presses his thumb into the pressure spot on my wrist, and my heartbeat echoes in my ears. He squeezes his thighs tighter, the pressure of his body making it impossible to wrench free. A blade appears in his free hand, and he rests it at the base of my throat, the metal cold.

"Keels," I mumble.

Curse Britta. She forgot one—or never found it. What I know of animal magic, his crows had eyes on my cousin the moment she stepped inside.

*I should've done it myself.*

"Let me go, give me back my ship, and I might let you stay on as a...what do you want to call it? A passenger? Or maybe a not-so-honest hobbyist?"

I spit in his face, and he presses in closer. He smiles lazily at me, and I knee him in the groin. He falls to the ground with an *oomph*, the blade slipping from his hand and disappearing under the desk in the corner. I roll to the side and jump to my feet, fumbling with the blade at my ankle. As soon as it's in my hand, I lunge toward him, but he dodges to the right. A growl builds behind my teeth, but I manage to hold it in. We face one another as I straighten my shoulders and grip the handle of my blade tighter.

He breaks one of the chairs and brings up the broken leg, blocking my next blow. The wood whistles in the air when I duck, and I throw the blade at his thigh. He sidesteps it and reaches for the fallen blade.

We circle each other, looking for weaknesses.

His eyes glaze over for a second, and before I can realize what he's done, the door flies open. His murder of crows flies around the room, and I block my face from their beaks and claws.

As soon as they come in, they're gone. The distraction allows him enough time to shorten the distance between us, his weapon inches from my throat. I swing my blade, but he slides across the floor, going under my dress and pulling the fabric out from underneath me. I fall on my face, tasting copper. The point of the blade tickles the base of my throat as he holds my head up by my hair.

"Nice try, my lady. Maybe next time, know your opponent."

"Oh, I do." I twist my arm, biting back a scream of rage, and roll over on my back. Once again, Cyrus Crow straddles me from above. I slam my knee upward, hitting the perfect spot. He doubles over in pain, and I wiggle my arm free. My elbow meets his chin, and he topples to the side, the blade skittering away. I reach for it, wrapping my hand around the handle and pressing my knee into his middle as he struggles in pain. I position the blade against his throat, the flesh giving way to the sharp tip. "Do we have a deal?"

His eyes dart to Bec. "Cyrus," she warns.

"Why do you need me?" he asks.

I bite the inside of my cheek, letting out a long breath. "The map needs us both. Not your crew. I promise no harm will come to them."

He mulls over the words for a moment.

"Cyrus—" Bec starts to say.

"I can handle this, cousin," he tells her. "I keep Bec, but the rest are free to go?" he asks.

"You have my word," I say. "We'll send them on a dinghy. We're not far from the shore."

He glares at me. "Deal."

# CHAPTER
# FOUR
CYRUS

*Abhors Sea*

Queen Weylan's endless reminders of my role in her court repeat in my head as we wait on deck, the whispers of my crew echoing in the wind. This lady captain is trying to put me where she thinks she wants me, but Weylan's plans settle into place. Nerissa's shipped off my loyal crew members, Duncan included, bringing us to a skeleton crew of mercenaries and those she needs.

"What are you looking at, yeah?" I ask the furry creature purring against my legs.

Piper, the black cat I never wanted, blinks one eye at me, the other gone by the time I found her in the Hills' port city.

"At least we get to keep you on board, right?"

She purrs in response, rubbing her body against my leg before trotting off. I stare out at the sea and search the deck for Becci. She's fussing at someone, the woman with the long black braids and rich accent. While Becci's hands flail wildly around her head, the other girl remains calm, a look of ease on her face when she shrugs. I bite back a grin when my cousin joins me.

"This is ridiculous. Are they waiting for us to keel over?" Becci asks, slouching against the rail.

"Becci," I sigh, rubbing a knot in my neck.

She catches my eye. *Relax,* I say through my glare.

She grumbles her irritation, listing ways to kill everyone around us. "Angry mob, decapitation, poison, blade to the jugular..."

I drown out her voice by focusing on the ship. It maintains a steady rhythm, the sun high in the sky, bathing us in a warm winter wind. My skin prickles with every movement around us, waiting for her to exit *my* chambers, the ship in a sort of stasis as the crew waits for their orders.

*"It was never rightfully yours. Brevlyra."* Weylan's voice taunts me from years before. *"And now, you'll win it back for me. Only this girl can break the curse on the land, but I need something else from you. A secret between you and me."*

I sense the new captain moving behind the doors of my stolen cabin. The staccato of the crows' wings moves this ship across all Penreine, but she has shifted the dynamic. They wait in the wind for my next command, but the second Nerissa joined the crew, the ship shifted under her weight, as if deciding whether or not she belonged. As the Queen said, the waves respond to the girl, her ability driving the ship toward our final destination. With her, my crows don't have to work as hard.

I blink a few times then call out, *Besnick. Let me see.*

*Yes, Master,* he says, and my vision flickers, the sea expanding around me as he flies to the cracked port window, poking his head in.

*"Has anyone checked on them?"* the captain asks the dark-haired girl.

*"I checked a moment ago. They grow restless."*

*"Grab Britta, would you? Tell her to get them in line."*

Nerissa's hair travels down her shoulders, stopping slightly above her backside. The dress she wore before is gone, replaced with black breeches and a white shirt made for a man. But instead of making her look less than what she is, she looks more. My heart roars in my ears. I rub the stubble along my chin, tongue running along the edge of my mouth as I'm reminded of the look in her eye and the redness rising in her cheeks as she thrust her blade under my throat. Her gaze lands on Besnick, and a flash of determination lights in her eyes.

She walks to the window and shoos him away.

My eyes snap open.

"She's coming," I blurt out, interrupting one of Becci's numerous ways to kill the girl in her sleep.

The new captain of my ship walks out, casting her shadow over the light of the rising sunshine peeking through the clouds kissing the waves in the distance. Her hair waves around her face in thick honey-brown curls. I clench my fists against my side the closer she draws near.

Her eyes tilt upward to meet mine on the quarterdeck above.

*Issa,* her name is like whispers in the wind. It sends a chill through me, and I push it away and walk to the center of the deck.

Her boots clack against the wood, meeting me halfway. Issa's lips quirk at the glares my crew shoots at her. She has the power here—she has the people. The largest man I've ever seen waits behind her, eating an apple to the core. Two women, garbed in men's clothing, flank her on both sides.

"Hello, Cyrus," Issa says.

I move closer, and the blonde to her left shifts closer to her captain.

"Call down your bodyguards, Issa," I whisper.

"Nerissa," she says. "*Captain* to you."

"Nothing but a pirate and thief to me, milady."

She grits her teeth, the ebbing and flowing light coming through the gaps in the clouds, dancing over her sun-kissed skin.

"You'll speak to your captain with respect," the blonde girl says, fists tightening.

"One of a matching set?" I ask, gaze angling toward the women at her sides.

The map wrinkles in Nerissa's fingers as she leans down and spreads it on the deck. It can tell me how to get back to Brevlyra.

I squat and study it. A perfume of ink and wood wafts from the parchment as I lower myself to the planks and spread my hands on each side. My head begins to ache from the continually moving shapes dancing across the page.

"I can't help, milady. Unless you like seeing me in pain." I glance up and tap my temple.

I look back down, squinting at the picture as the wood creaks beneath her. My body stiffens as Nerissa lowers herself to my level, bending on her knees across from me. Her face clenches, a wrinkle forming between her brows and her lips pursing. She rubs her temple and rips her gaze from the map. My heart stutters and veins run cold.

"You can't read it?" I ask, trying to hide the fear threatening to bubble over.

"I can't read it." She looks up. "Because of you. Together, it will make itself clearer. It takes two to make the map work—two people going to the same place. Two people wanting the same thing. You don't want to play by my rules, so how could we be on the same side?"

*My rules don't interest you either, milady,* I think, swallowing the words.

She stands, chest rising as she looks behind her. "Neither of us will get where we need if we don't agree with each other."

"Says whom?" I ask.

"The same person who gave it to me," she replies, tossing me a tight smile.

"Not going to offer me a name?" I ask.

She drops her gaze. "Doesn't matter now, does it?"

*Fine.*

"What do you—or don't you—see?" I ask, while rubbing the ache between my brows.

She runs her hands through her hair and stares down at the parchment. "Right now, nothing. Something will appear, but it slithers like a snake when I try to focus on where it's headed. This part," she points to the bottom of the map closest to me, "stands still." Her hand moves up a little higher. "This is where we are now. I got what I came for and know where we need to go, but I don't know how to get there without..."

I glance up. "I thought we were both after Brevlyra?"

Her jaw tightens. "There's something I need so we can get there, but it will require a trade. This map should lead me to—"

She stops, and I ask, "How do we get to Brevlyra, milady?"

Her tongue runs over her teeth. "I need your help, Captain Crow. The next leg of the journey isn't safe, which is why this map can tell us how to get there alive, *possibly*. Not even luck can get you there."

"No such thing as luck when it comes to Brevlyra," the blonde says, and Nerissa throws her a glare.

"Hmph," I snort. "And where exactly are we going first?"

Nerissa's gaze settles on me. "All you need to know is I'm going alone. Everyone else stays on the boat," she says, voice like steel, prepared for my fight.

"And where exactly are *you* going but we cannot?" I ask again.

*You've got her, Cyrus. Stop asking questions. Make a deal. Do what Weylan wants one last time. Earn your freedom.*

"*I think*...based on the few blips I've seen, the map is taking us to...Siren's Cove..."

An unamused laugh bursts from my chest. "You're joking," I say, but her gaze doesn't waiver. "You're mad then."

"I think you and I have to be on the same path in order for it to work. If that is where it's taking us, everyone but me stays on the boat. I need something off the island, and this map will tell us how to get there safely."

"You don't know what you need?"

Her eyes flash upward and meet mine. "It hasn't told me yet."

I shake my head, not comprehending what she's saying—how could she be so careless? "It doesn't matter how safely we get there if we never make it past the island. There's a reason you can't find it on any map. Why it's never been on a map."

She stands, her shadow stretching over me and obscuring her face. "Look, if we agree, then the map will tell me *where* we're going and *why*. But *we* need it to get to Brevlyra. Are you with me or not?"

I shorten the distance between us, forcing her to look at me. "I don't make deals in front of the whole crew. I make them captain to captain," I say, sitting back on the deck and crossing my arms over my knees.

"Britta, Max, leave us," she says, her eyes never leaving mine.

"But, Nerissa," the blonde—Britta—says.

Nerissa throws her a glare. "Claudette stays," she says, begging me to disagree. "Max, take the prisoners below deck. They've had enough air."

"Duncan stays," I counter. "He should stay on board, too."

She studies me for a long moment before shaking her head. "No. Her." She nods toward Becci. "And he's not staying. For the third time."

"Very well, milady," I say, irritation burning in my veins. However, I would still rather have Becci.

The darker woman, Claudette, speaks with her captain as they round up the crew. I pull Becci to the side, the words already forming on her lips.

"Cyrus," Becci says. Her piercing violet eyes burn my skin, but I shake my head. "Are you sure about this plan?"

"It's the only one we have. It's me and you, Bec. No one else. Say your goodbyes. Make sure Duncan knows what to do. Tell them to not come after us."

She looks ready to argue, but I say, "Bec, please."

Finally, she nods.

Once all but Claudette and Becci are left, the captain joins me on the floor, crossing her legs in an unladylike fashion. A smirk tugs at the corner of my mouth. I wish I could get the crew to understand I need Nerissa as much as she needs me. The simplest mistake, and everything I've done over the years, all the voyages I've sailed, the bidding I've done to earn a name for myself, won't matter.

My freedom from a madwoman hinges on Nerissa.

I have to start playing the game she doesn't know she started.

"I'll help you. On one condition." I look at Claudette; she's strong. Her hand hasn't left the hilt of her sword since she set eyes on me—so she's smart, too. Loyalty beams off her. I lock eyes with Nerissa and tip my chin toward the darker woman. "She becomes your first mate."

Nerissa flutters her lashes at me. "How do you know she isn't?"

Impatience festers in my bones, and my muscles tense.

"Don't patronize me," I say. "I can see, and what I see is how *she* responds to everything you do. The blonde shows too much hunger. She would take your ship from you the first chance she got. She worked her way into your heart a long time ago. She's your first mate—most likely the truest friend you have." I look down, pausing and picking at a hole in my breeches. My gaze slides back up to Nerissa, and I can see I've disarmed her with my accuracy. "Until she stabs you in the back."

Nerissa does not contradict me, muttering, "Cousin."

I chuckle. "Even worse."

She lets out a small laugh.

"It's all I ask," I say, eyes locked on hers.

"Claudette," she says, not looking over her shoulder. "Fetch us something to write with. We'll make this a true deal."

"Captain, I do not think—" the woman begins.

Nerissa waves away her concern. "It's fine." She turns back to me. "You trust her but not Britta."

"As should you. Though I am curious: what's a highbred islander and a common Mechelonian lass doing together?" I ask, tipping my chin to where Claudette disappeared.

"We're pirates," Nerissa says, her brown eyes flashing gold. "Not upper or lower, not Mechelonian or Levimeerian. Women. Pirates. What else do you need to know? You've got a Hillsman in your crew. Don't think I don't know you're New Kingdom to the core."

"We're no different than you, Nerissa," I say. "Just pirates. Don't separate yourself based on where you're from. Pirates need not worry about the basic rules of etiquette. If you're good to us, we treat you in kind."

"I think we're on the same page then," she says, and my heart races at the softness in her voice.

Before I can reply, the Mechelonian pirate reappears, zeroing in on Nerissa. She glares at me as if she expected to return to find her captain buried under a murder of crows. Tempting, but to do what Weylan's asked, I have to be smart *and* patient.

For now.

"Here you go, Cap," Claudette says.

"Thank you," Nerissa says with a nod. Her eyes meet mine, filled with fire. "We have a deal." She holds out her hand, and I take it in mine. Her grip is strong, palms rough and calloused—unyielding.

"It appears we do."

*Take me there, Crow, and you'll be free.* Weylan's words echo in my mind.

We both glance down.

The map appears.

# CHAPTER
# FIVE

### NERISSA

*Abhors Sea*

The map works—and I know exactly where the mysterious Siren Queen hides her shiver, the other sirens, and what I need from her. I'm itching to set sail. I can't tell if it's from the thrill of finally being close to finding Lucia or the sea rushing through me.

"How are the supplies?" Cyrus asks, walking into my new quarters.

I cross my arms over my chest and arch a brow. "I know how to run a ship, Crow," I say, pushing away from the desk.

He copies my stance and stares down at me. "Of course, *Captain*," he says. "Then lead the way."

The one named Duncan is upset with Bec. They argue, standing next to the rope lowering the rest of the crew into a dinghy. I catch bits and pieces on the breeze as I walk toward Britta. His anger has little to do with him not staying onboard.

"Come with me," I say, and Britta follows me to the forecastle. I wrap my hands around the edge of the ship. Soon, the last of Crow's men are nothing but a blip on the horizon.

I look out onto the crystal blue water. Anxiety gurgles in my core being so close to the thing calling me home. Yet I'm comforted by the lulling of the ship over the waves. It's a bittersweet taste on my tongue, salt and sea begging to be understood and welcomed in. I don't trust the sea, but it's the only way I'll reach Lucia.

Britta shifts from foot to foot, uncomfortable with the silence. "What is it, cousin?" she asks.

"Crow's cooperation came with terms, to which I agreed."

"Like?" Britta huffs, pursing her lips, arms crossed.

"Claudette is now first mate."

Her jaw drops. "How dare you! I've been your first mate since we started this journey, *Issa*," she says, her words filled with unspoken threats as her eyes flash.

I clench my fists and glance over at her, my muscles tightening. I love my cousin—what I know of her. Cyrus's words ring in the back of my mind. Britta was born and raised in New Kingdom, a different world than the Island of Helene.

"I don't understand," Britta says, eyes round and watery, breaking me from my thoughts.

*I don't either*, I think.

Her words cause my stomach to roll with unease—unsure if this is acting or real. "Have I not always been loyal to you?"

"In order to make this journey, we have to make sacrifices," I say with a shrug. "I will still seek your guidance. Crow insisted—"

"We can't trust any of these people!" she says, slamming her fist onto the lip of the ship. "If it weren't for the Light-forsaken map you can't read alone, we know how this would all end!"

I grit my teeth before saying, "If we want this to work, Crow and I have to be on the same side."

"You will never be on the same side," she spits. "He sits at the Queen's feet. I heard him and the redhead discussing her. Father says—"

"Watch your tongue," I snap, my body tensing. "*Rumors* do us no good. And your father is a noble—he reports to *her*."

Rumors are the primary reason my parents left New Kingdom. My mother was a foreigner and brought a magic to Easterly she passed down to me. It wasn't welcome in a place used to a corrupt royal family.

Britta glares at me, the feigned sadness hardening. "I can't help my Teraceron upbringing."

I sigh. "I know."

Teraceron nobles are notorious for how stoically they treat their children. They hold their children at arm's length, and the lower class can barely support theirs. It's the second reason my father and mother moved to the Island of Helene, southwest of New Kingdom. The third reason was my father's abdication of his title—one he never talked about or shared with us.

Father never spoke of his family. Britta wrote me a letter after his death, or I wouldn't have known about her either. The rest of our family is a mystery to me. I know the life my cousin lived before couldn't have been easy. Guilt burns in my gut, and my fingers brush her elbow. She jerks away, crossing her arms defiantly over her chest.

"He used to dine in the castle, I bet," she says. "Why is he sailing the seas now, hmm? I have been around Easterly more than you have, Nerissa, beyond Teraceron. You need me."

The anger lights in my chest, and I count each breath. If there's one person on this ship I can count on the most, it's Britta. Crow claims to glimpse something in her he doesn't like, but most people do. She's crass, sometimes rude, and says what she thinks. For many, noble blood signifies training and decorum. Not Britta.

I wait until the knot in my chest loosens before saying, "I do. I know I haven't been around the kingdoms like you, cousin."

Her eyes soften, and she touches my arm. "Trust me on this. We can't put any faith in him. He bows to *her*."

"How are you so sure?" I study the redhead and Crow as they whisper on deck, the girl's face slowly turning the same shade as her hair. Bec's hand flies around her face, and Cyrus stands rigidly with a pinched expression on his face. An unwanted smile quirks at the corner of my mouth at the sight. Apparently, I'm not the only one with family issues.

Britta's hand tightens around my arm, and I turn back to her.

"While Father might not care much for me," Britta says, voice cracking, "he does take an interest in the royal court. He was at the palace more than he was at home, especially after Mother left."

A shiver runs up my spine. "Why was he at the palace?"

"It's what you would've done too, if you'd been raised in New Kingdom," she says, but something about her tone doesn't settle right against my skin.

"Britta—"

"You have to trust me, Issa," she interrupts, voice softening and the tension falling from her shoulders.

I place my hand over hers. "I do trust you, Britta, but I also need to get to Brevlyra."

The clouds move above, blocking the sun, and an island comes into view—an island appearing on no map but the one in my possession. "Cyrus Crow is the way," I say, the words a whisper of wonder at the sight before us. "The witch said so. His ship is the fastest and strongest in the seas. I need him."

She pulls away, her voice cold. "You didn't even blink when he said to get rid of me and to give Claudette my position, did you? You trust her more than me?"

I steady my gaze on hers. "Hatred is never useful, Britta. I never said I trusted her more than you."

"You've known her for how long, exactly?" she asks, crossing her arms.

"If I remember correctly, I've only known you for a few more months than I have Claudette. She may not be a long-lost family member, but she's *like* a cousin to me."

Britta looks over my shoulder. "I came on this journey with you to be your first, to be the one you trusted most. I know what happened to Lucia." Her words end in a whisper. "I know you want to save her, but this is madness. She may not even *want* to be saved."

I shorten the distance between us, nostrils flaring, a growl coming over my lips, "How dare you?"

Britta is undeterred, and she steps into my space. "We don't even know what they want! For all we know, they could be here to, I don't know, kill us or something."

"Don't you think they would've done it already?" I ask, arching a brow.

She purses her lips. "Look, anything might be waiting for us in Brevlyra, including an ambush. I would expect nothing less. It's no man's land, Issa. No one knows what awaits them there."

"A lot of hassle for nothing," I say. "They could end us here and save themselves the trip." I shake my head, stepping back. My next words are slow and measured, "And what do *you* want, Britta?"

My cousin looks away over the rolling ocean and grips the side of the ship. Her motivations have never been clear, and she remains unwilling to share. Anxiety prickles my skin, and I fiddle with the ring around my finger. Maybe using Claudette as my first instead of Britta was a wise decision, though it makes me wonder why Cyrus would *help* me. What does he get out of it?

"We don't have time to worry about Crow and his crew," I say, interrupting the silence and turning away from my cousin. "There are bigger monsters out there. Claudette," I call, and she's at my side in seconds. "Grab the box from my quarters—the one with sand and the queen's insignia—and the whole crew. We're almost at Siren's Cove."

*At least I thought to bring it*, I think, imagining the worn black box.

"Crow," I say, my words catching on the wind and reaching him where he stands halfway down the ship. I nod to the captain's quarters. Britta's fury burns my back as I meet him at the entrance.

"Milady," Crow says with a bow as he holds the door for me. "To what do I owe this pleasure?"

I roll my eyes as he closes us in, the tumbling waves fading away.

"I was going to bring it to you, Cap—" Claudette begins, but I cut her off with a wave of my hand.

"It's fine. I needed to speak to Crow." I look up at him. "We're approaching Siren's Cove. The men must be...tied down."

"There are other ways to get to Brevlyra." His throat bobs as if speaking the name of the fallen kingdom causes him physical pain.

"But not to get what I need," I say.

Claudette holds the box in her hands, eyes going between us as if watching a chess match.

"I'm sure there are other ways to get whatever you need," he says. "Do you even have anything to protect yourself from them?"

"I know what I'm doing."

He scoffs. "Magic sand, hmm? You'll need something else, too."

"I would not be so sure, Crow," Claudette says, glancing at me. I grit my teeth, and Crow looks at me for one more moment before relinquishing my gaze and focusing on Claudette. "Thanks to you, your queen has nearly driven mermaids to extinction. The sirens are almost as unlucky."

His body tightens at her words. "Not much surprises me. I don't think you realize what you've gotten yourself into," he says, turning his attention to me.

"Go ahead and get them ready, Claudette. This won't take long."

She glances between us once more before walking outside, softly shutting the door behind her.

I tilt my head to the side, studying him, before saying, "I've scoured countless documents about sirens. When I go on the island—"

"You've *read* about them. But you've never faced them. I have. They're one of the many beasts the queen has had me hunt the past two years. You don't know what you're doing," he says, stepping closer, real concern coating his tone and prickling my skin. *You're going to let him talk to you like that, Issa?* Kip's voice rings in my mind, and unexpected sadness washes over me.

Cyrus studies my face, the crystal blue rolling over my skin. He smells of leather and salt, sweat and seaweed. Crow appears to be equal parts human and bird—divided and connected in conflict.

Like me.

It's been over two years since I've been this close to a man—a man who questions me, makes me think. Speaks to challenge me and not belittle me. Shivers dance down my spine. Something rises in my throat, my cheeks reddening, but I shake it off with the ashes of remembrance.

*Get it together, Nerissa. He's not Kip.*

*Kip is gone.* The sudden burst of attraction is chased away by the icy cold truth.

Crow quirks a brow before continuing. "Reading about a place isn't the same as experiencing it. You need to experience the earth between your toes and the sun on your face before you truly know a place. If anything, reading about it will do you more harm than good."

I take a step back, heart pounding. "It will be fine."

"What do you need on the island?" he demands, coming back into my space, eyes searching my face.

"Something from the Siren Queen. It's none of your concern," I say, lifting my chin. The map told us where to go. With two people in agreement, it wouldn't lead us astray. "I'll take Britta and Claudette."

He tenses. "Leave Britta. Take Becci...take *me*," he says, gaze fierce. A lump forms in my throat at the thought. The thrill of someone who's awakening emotions I haven't felt in so long boils my blood. Cyrus Crow would be too much of a liability. Kip became a casualty in the war between Lucia and me, and I won't have it happen to anyone else.

I shake off the thought and plaster a smirk on my face.       "Becci? The one who tries to kill me with a look?" A laugh falls from my lips. "She won't listen to a word I say."

A ghost of a grin tugs at the corner of his mouth. "For now," he says.

I scoff, hiding the way my eyes are drawn to the corner of his lips. "And *you*? A man? The sirens *hate* all men, want nothing more than to end you all. You *especially*," I say, my voice harsher than stone. "I wouldn't risk my crew or yours if there were any other way."

He's silent for an eternity before, "Fine."

I bite back a laugh and nod. "Thank you."

He runs his tongue over the inside of his cheek. "Lead the way."

The waves crash against the ship, and a heavy silence settles in the air. Cyrus's crows circle overhead, and I walk down the hatch as Claudette readies the men. They're tied to the masts as she walks around with the box of sand.

Claudette stops in front of the first male, a mercenary who didn't come cheaply, and levels the open container with the tip of his nose. From the look on his face, I can tell he's regretting his decision to join a crew of female pirates.

The black sand creeps over the edge. Like a steady stream of water, it glides over the box, traveling up his shirt and across his chest. The man's throat bobs, and he clenches his eyes shut as the sand dances across his face. Small grains stick to his skin, cascading over his eye patch. His breath hitches as it settles in his ears.

He opens his panic-filled eyes and looks around. "It works," he says. Then louder. "Can you hear me?"

Claudette touches his chest. "Do not fret," she says.

He reads her lips and nods.

She moves to the next male, repeating the task.

The hair on the back of my neck rises with unease. I glance back at Cyrus, his blue gaze unwavering. Our eyes meet, and his lips quirk at the edges, a whisper of wings fluttering in my stomach.

Why is he not tied up yet? I flick my eyes upward and count to ten.

He walks up to me and stares at me down his nose. "This won't work," he says. "Your plan won't work."

"It will," I say, and the emotion fades into irritation. "My plan or no plan."

*At least the crew can't hear.* Though Claudette, Becci, and Britta watch us, hesitantly glancing between each other and waiting to see what will happen. I force a smile on my face and he does the same. He lets loose a deep breath, and his tongue traces his bottom lip. "I've encountered the creatures before. Whatever you need on this island isn't something you can get on your own. And you need someone who knows what they're doing. You need *me*," he says. "I go with you, not Claudette."

Before I can argue with him, he continues. "We have to be in one accord for the map to work, don't we? This is me disagreeing with you. Take me with you."

"You cannot ask to go with her. Cyrus, those *things*—" Bec starts, breaking away from her darkened corner.

"Will leave the ship alone if I'm on the island. They know who I am; they want revenge. It's no secret what I've done."

"I am responsible, too," she replies, something unspoken passing between them.

"But the blood is on my hands, not yours," he says, picking at a piece of invisible lint on his sleeve. "Which means something."

I chew the inside of my cheek, hating the rightness settling in my chest. Trust blossoms warmly in my center. He's willing to sacrifice himself for his crew or, at least, lower his defenses. This agreement might not be what I imagined, but the idea does settle some of the worry.

"Fine," I concede.

"Cap," Claudette says at the same time Britta says, "Issa!"

I shoot Britta a hard look. "He's right, Britt. If we want this to work, we have to work together. He knows these creatures better than anyone else."

part
two

Sail away, sail away

On the winds of an ending day.

The sun no longer shines,

the water's deadly with invisible eyes

Watch your stern and row your boat,

The things that lurk in the darkness

can hurt you the most.


— "Waves of Darkness" from the Ballad of the

Seas, author unknown

# CHAPTER
# SIX
### NERISSA

**Abhors Sea**

Father used to tell Lucia and me stories of the sirens.

*Before.*

I swallow as the memory washes over me, a reminder of better times.

*I crawled over into Lucia's bed, snuggling beneath the sea of pillows and blankets. Our toes battled for the warmest parts of the covers.*

*"What story do you think he'll tell tonight?" I asked.*

*Lucia giggled. "Maybe it'll be the one about the five princesses of Penreine!"*

*I shook my head vigorously. "No. He's told us it too many times. I know it by heart. Besides, Mama doesn't like when he talks about the princesses. She says princesses are not all sweet and nice. Most of them are mean."*

*Lucia's brow furrowed, and we snuggled closer together. "It's fun to play princesses, though." And we had. For hours we had played at the shore, pretending to be from anywhere else but Helene. I had witnessed Father's smile as he watched us from the blanket, but Mother never relaxed.*

*"Are you girls ready?" Father called, peeking into our room.*

*We stifled our laughter and nodded.*

*He leaned on the edge of the bed closest to Lucia and began. "The sirens are the most dangerous creatures in the sea," Father said, brushing back my hair and wiggling his eyebrows at Lucia.*

*We glanced at each other, sharing a giggle and burrowing into the sheets.*

*"What makes them so dangerous, Papa?" Lucia asked, her voice a high-pitched squeak of excitement.*

*"Well, my dear," he said, tapping her nose. "When my father was a boy, he used to sail these waters, back and forth to New Kingdom, and everyone knew never to travel past Siren's Cove."*

*My brow furrowed. "But there is no Siren's Cove," I said, picturing the map above his desk. "Your ships never have to worry! It's not in our waters."*

*His laughter rolled over our skin, a smile still lingering though his words turned cold. "The Cove isn't meant to be seen. It's meant to devour. But it doesn't devour little girls like you!" He reached out and pulled down the covers, burying us in tickles.*

*"All right, all right, that's enough, Ranulf. They'll be awake all night," Mother said, coming into the room and grabbing the candle on Lucia's side of the bed. She hovered behind Father with the ghost of a grin on her lips.*

*"But he didn't even start the story!" I whined as he tucked us back in. "Is there an island, Papa, truly?" I imagined exploring the caves around Helene with Lucia, pretending to be pirates in search of lost treasure.*

*"Yeah!" Lucia added, bouncing in the bed and causing the blanket to pool around our waists. "How does it end, Papa?"*

*"It didn't even begin, silly," I said, and Lucia prodded me in the side.*

*Mother shook her head, walking back to the door, "Tomorrow, girls."*

*Father leaned over and brushed a kiss on each of our foreheads. "Sirens don't want little girls, my darlings. They want cruel men."*

*My eyes widened, and Lucia gasped. "But not you, Papa?" she asked.*

*His eyes glazed over, and for a moment, the words were lost on his tongue. "I would never leave you," he replied, following Mother out the door and taking the candle with him.*

*"Do you think they're real?" Lucia whispered, excitement lacing her words.*

*I gnawed on the bottom of my lip. "There's one way to find out!" I said, and we started planning our next adventure.*

The memory cuts me deep. We'd wake in the morning, almost unable to tell whose limbs were whose. Back then, we were more than sisters by blood—we were constant companions, best friends, with not a secret between us. By the end, it was a constant battle. A shiver runs up my spine, and my stomach swirls.

Claudette's voice brings me back. "It's time, Cap."

Claudette, Britta, Bec, and I go above deck and stare out at the island. Bec glowers at me, but she doesn't say anything to her cousin when he joins us, ears covered in black sand.

"Make sure the men stay tied up," I tell the women. Father might have told us sirens desire cruel men, but in truth, they don't discriminate.

They want all men, no matter their disposition.

"Whatever you do—" I begin, but I never finish the sentence.

"You're not my captain," Bec snaps, eyes darkening. "Cyrus may be an idiot, but I follow his orders. If he trusts you enough to risk his life, then I will do whatever it takes to protect this ship."

I try to thank her, but my mouth has barely formed the words before she hisses, "Don't thank me," and walks away.

We drop anchor far enough from the Cove the siren sounds are a whisper on the wind, but I know we're not far enough. The sand is no guarantee of their safety.

"Don't you think I should go with you?" Britta asks.

I straighten my shoulders and shake my head.

"I'm taking Cyrus," I tell Britta. "He wants to do this to himself, then so be it. My decision is final," I say, witnessing the argument rise in her.

She clenches her jaw but nods. I hand her the small telescope I found in the captain's quarters. "Watch for us."

"Yes, Captain," she says and brings it to her eye, looking out over the waves.

Claudette walks up to me, a rope slung over her frame. "Here is everything you need," she says. "Though the raw meat offering is disgusting."

"At least they don't want a live sacrifice."

She gives me a satchel and helps tie it securely with a leather band around my waist. I wrap the waterproof skin Claudette offers me tight around my torso until the slab of lamb clings to me, the blood weighing down the meat shifting beneath the leather.

The skin cost a large portion of the gold I brought with me when I started my journey. Father left us money before he went on his last voyage to the Lady of Halivaris, but I didn't want to use it. When I return home, I'll have to. Instead, I had used the little money Mother left us, even though it didn't compare to the funds Father had accrued through his business.

*You girls will always have each other.*

His voice rings in my mind, even now. He would be ashamed of the last few weeks my sister and I spent together. I am. If the sister that shared her bedtime stories and her pillows with me can be saved, I owe it to Father—to the little girls we used to be—to try.

"Why lamb?" Claudette says, curiosity painting her tone.

Britta answers for me. "They say it tastes like male children." Her words are sharp with truth.

I glance over to her as she looks through the telescope. She jerks it away from her face and gives us a solemn look. "Don't let them take you with it."

"Cap—" Claudette begins, but I raise my hand to stop her.

"You ready, Cyrus?" I ask.

He trains his gaze on the island. I go up to him, lightly touching his arm to draw his attention away from the swaying palms and tumultuous waves crashing against the shoreline. He turns to me, the sand securely in his ears, and reads my lips before nodding. We climb over and swing onto the rope ladder bumping against the side of the ship.

"Don't worry. I won't cut you loose, Captain," Bec says. "Either of you."

I grit my teeth before slipping into the water.

The shock of cold pierces my flesh, but I move fast to get out of Cyrus's way. The water recognizes me, even if my mother did everything to create a rift between us. Dropping into the waves is like coming home. The water welcomes me, swirling around me as if I'm the director of the current, guiding it instead of the other way around. I surface, treading water, and wait for him to do the same. He pops up, and we begin the swim.

We don't get far before the water's kindness dissipates. The waves begin to rock and knock against me, rougher than any waters I've ever encountered. I want to curse Mother again for failing to teach me what I was born to do and instead instructing me how to be a lady. She hid the person I was destined to become. Instinct only goes so deep, and there are still waters left uncharted. If I had been allowed to accept myself as who I am—if Mother had—maybe Lucia and I wouldn't be where we are now.

I push away thoughts of Mother as anxiety threatens to burst through me. I keep going, glancing back once to make sure Cyrus is following.

Finally, my feet scrape against the wet bed of sand, and I walk the rest of the way. The siren song dances on the wind—not tempting but sending shivers across my skin. I fling my hair out of my eyes and tie it back with a leather band.

Cyrus comes up behind me, white sand sticking to his boots. He untangles a strand of seaweed from his inky black locks and flings it at his feet. I'm drawn to the curve of his chest, visible beneath the thin, wet threads of his shirt. The afternoon sun shines against the waves and the droplets of water cling to his skin, bringing heat to my cheeks. I look away and release a shaky breath. I squint up through the dying light at the island.

I turn back to him so he can read my lips. "According to everything I've read," I say, voice faltering slightly. "We need to go farther inland to find the ones we seek."

It takes a moment for him to process what I said before he gives me a stiff nod. The knot in my chest loosens. I don't bother to address why I'm relieved.

*The sand worked.*

"Lead the way," he says, voice a little too loud, and we break into the trees.

Cyrus's crows circle overhead as we go deeper inland. I swallow down the anxiety bitter on my tongue and take another step forward, the sound of rushing water pulling us deeper toward the island's center. A waiting waterfall pours into a crystalline pool, and all the sounds around us filter away. I glance up, and the crows settle in the trees around us, blinking beady black eyes in our direction.

"The map said through there," I say, pointing at the cave entrance peeking through the falls and speaking slowly enough for him to follow my words.

He eyes his birds. "They can't follow us there," he says.

*Good,* I think, but instead say, "They fly. We don't. They could follow, if you needed them to."

It takes a second, but his lip twitches at my words, tugging at his scar. "I'm trusting you," he says. *Don't make me regret it,* his gaze screams.

"And I, you. In there, we're a team. She's the enemy," I say.

"We won't be able to speak once inside, unless there's a splash of light," he says, and he digs in his ears. The sand falls away, and I don't have time to stop him before it puddles on his shoulders and drips down his clothes.

"What are you doing?" I demand. "Do you want to get yourself killed—"

"She knows we're here," he says. "I can take it, Nerissa."

"You can start planning your funeral!" My chest heaves, holding my anger at bay as I grind out the words. "Did you plan to do this the whole time?"

Cyrus shrugs.

"Fine, but this was *your* decision," I say. "Bec—"

"She knows. Don't worry about her," he says, nodding me forward. "Let's go. We don't have time to argue. The longer we're on the island, the more time our ship stays in dangerous waters. If she wanted me, I would already be hers. The song isn't for me—you would know. She's survived this long for a reason. We're wasting precious moments we don't have."

We walk around the edge of the water, careful not to touch the pool. A fine mist coats my face the closer we get to the falls. We duck under the steady stream, and I cling to the wall, grappling with the slick rocks. The cave consumes us, and I strain my eyes through the darkness.

"Give me the rope," I say, and he hands me one end after tying himself with the other. His muscles are wound tighter than mast cables in a storm.

"Is the song getting to you?" I ask.

"Nothing I can't handle," he says.

I tie the rope around my waist and secure it with a triple knot. He pulls his end, and I tug back.

"Hand on the wall at all times," he says, and I nod.

We start the descent.

Water dances across my palm, trickling between my fingers and running down my shirt sleeve in small rivulets. The jagged rock grates against my skin, the sound of loose rubble filling my ears as we make our way through the cavernous space. The farther we go into the cave, the colder the air grows. Chilled, damp air rushes through the tunnel, puncturing the late-October warmth. Inside this place, winter has arrived.

The path begins to slope upward. A glimmer of light breaks through the darkness, and I follow it. The path flattens, and we step farther inland.

The cavern stretches impossibly wide, and the walls angle upward before curving like the lip of a bottle. Something sinister waits for us beyond the sea circling the island. Whatever is there, it's at the edge, waiting to pounce like a cat.

I tilt my head back and let the panic roll down my spine. The fading light of the sun shines from the circular opening above. Red and orange clouds stir overhead, dancing around the edges of the harsh light.

"We need to hurry," I whisper, gazing up at the sky. The air crackles, and a roll of thunder echoes in the cavern. "We have to get off the island before the storm lands."

He closes his eyes, gaze flickering as they move back and forth beneath his lids. "I sent the birds back to the ship," he says. "They'll report if anything goes wrong."

We loosen the rope and slide out of the bindings, laying our supplies on the ground. I untie the package from my back and begin unwrapping it. I crouch down and splay it on the tarp. The putrid stench of raw meat stirs my gut. Cyrus bends down next to me and peers into the water. I study him out of the corner of my eye, but his gaze remains trained on the pool.

"Are you okay?" I ask, the vein in his throat throbbing.

"Yes," he says, voice strained, but I don't say anything else.

The aroma of meat and salt fills the whole cavern, and I know that, in a matter of minutes, they'll fill the space, breathing through the slits in their throats and smiling up at us like we're the treat.

"Stay here when I go down," I urge Cyrus. "If we both go under, neither of us might come back up. If one of us stays, then we have a shot at getting back to the ship."

"Not to state the obvious," he says, sensing the shift in the air and tightening his fists. "But we're both needed to get the map to work. We should do this together—"

"No. This is how we're going to do this. I let you come on this island with me, but I don't have to let you go down *there*."

Cyrus opens his mouth to respond but gets cut short.

"What a *glorious* bouquet! It's...hmm...blood and children?" The voice echoes around the cavern.

My head jerks toward the water where a siren bobs below the surface. Her scales shine in the weakening sunlight filtering down into the cavern. Her wicked grin reveals sharp, jagged teeth.

"Do you have a treat for me?" she asks, her voice a low purr. "And I don't mean the meat." Her hand slithers up the edge of the pool, and I move in front of Cyrus. He falls back into the sand with a curse.

"*This* is the thing we're not allowed to sing to? Why would our queen tell us to not drown him with our song?" another siren asks as she surfaces.

A third joins the group, eyes narrowed on my companion. "*Cyrus Crow?*" She jerks back with a hiss. "Get that monster out of our sight!"

One more beast surfaces, the water cascading down her skin like silk.

"Don't be so quick to send him away," the first siren says. "He holds no power here. We can play with him a bit. We don't have to take a bite, unless our queen allows it. She might *consider* the dish." The hatred oozing from her skin is heavy in the air.

"We should rip out his throat and let the sharks have them *both*," says the second. The third siren moves closer and touches the edge of the cavern. She leans her arms on the rock and exposes serrated fins running from her wrist to elbow. My eyes linger a moment before meeting her gaze.

Cyrus's jaw tightens as he rises to his feet. "I'm a fighter. I was fighting more than your sisters when Weylan sent me after your queen."

The sirens share looks with one another before going back under.

"Where did they go?" I ask, leaning toward the pool.

Cyrus snatches my arm. "Not so fast, milady. They'll be back."

I shrug him off. "We don't have time for this!"

"We don't have time for them to pull you under before you've taken a breath. Patience, Nerissa. They'll return."

An eternity later, they resurface. "Fine. We understand more than most that orders must be taken from one's queen regardless of our beliefs. We do not respect you, Cyrus Crow, but we will listen to what your girl has to say."

"I need to speak with your queen," I demand, lowering to the siren's level but staying far enough back to not incite Cyrus.

Their shrill laughs reverberate through the cavern like the screech of bats waking from slumber. Cyrus flinches and covers his ears.

"What a *thing* to say! You dare to walk on our island and make demands?" the siren asks.

She pulls herself even higher up on the rock and sits, flicking her tail in the water. "It's a long way down to where you need to go, Captain Eliott."

"Maybe we could go for a little nibble," one of the other sirens says.

"A small bite couldn't hurt," the last quips, staring at Cyrus instead of the offering. "Even if the meat is rotten."

"This isn't a buffet," I say. "He's not on the menu, but you can have half of the queen's share," I bargain. "Of *this* meat. You leave Cyrus alone, and you take me below."

The sirens' eyes widen in surprise. "You would risk giving half of what belongs to our queen to us? We're," —her lips form a sneer— "gatekeepers. No better than *him*."

I lean down, and our faces are mere breaths apart. The scent of dead fish and briny water fills my nose. The black soulless depths of the siren's eyes send shivers down my spine, but it's a familiar chill. "Every hand on a ship is valuable. Everyone has their part, even in a hierarchy. You are as important as the queen, even if you cannot give me what I seek."

She arches a brow. "And? What's your point, Captain Eliott?"

"Cyrus can't give you the justice you seek. Your anger belongs to another queen. He might have landed the killing blow, but he simply followed orders." She chews on my words, nodding for me to continue. "Take me to *your* queen."

Her malicious grin widens. She blinks once, then twice, and snaps her head back to the other three sirens staring hungrily at the meat. They shift to a sea language neither of us can understand, waiting for signs of an attack. Their shoulders relax with every word, and a staggered breath escapes my lips.

"One-third," she says, words hissing over her teeth. "Our queen will not be pleased you offered us any. If we take half, *we* will pay the price."

"You're sure?" I ask.

As one, the sirens study Cyrus. "We're sure," the one up front says. They all turn back to me.

My skin prickles, and unease settles in the pit of my stomach. I stare at them a second longer, looking for the lie. Unable to find any other way, I motion for Cyrus to cut the meat.

He slices a third of the lamb away with his sword and hands it to me, my hands shaking.

"For safe passage and an audience with your queen," I say and toss it to the siren.

She takes a hungry bite, and her eyes turn silver. Her lids close, and drool slips down the corner of her mouth as she chews. She passes it to the next siren and looks back at me, chunks of meat stuck between her teeth. "Come, Captain. Take a deep breath. It's a dark dive," she says. "Hope you're not scared of the shadows."

I wrap the meat up and secure it with the bag back around my waist. I stand on the rock where the siren waits, grazing her hands over the water.

"Feet first," she says, eyeing the sword at my waist. I don't dare remove it.

I dip my boots in first. Her talons wrap around my forearm in an instant, and a smile curls onto her face. I fill my lungs with air, and she drags me under, going deeper and deeper until the sunlight fades, and all I feel are siren tails hitting my flesh.

# CHAPTER
# SEVEN
CYRUS

*Siren's Cove*

My body goes cold as Issa slips into the water. I resist the urge to follow her, my fists clenching at my sides. The sirens' barely-contained fury bubbles to the surface. Their song dances over my skin, even though their mouths remain closed.

"Did you show any remorse when you slaughtered our sisters?" one asks, her hair hanging around her neck like wet seaweed.

I bore my gaze into theirs. "Your kind tried to kill me, too."

"You attacked first. We were happy on our island."

I clench my teeth. "You provoked the attack when you broke the twenty-five-year-old oath made to Teraceron to not hunt in the queen's waters."

The beasts lounge in the water, flicking their tails and spraying brackish water over me in a salty sprinkle. "Things change, Cyrus Crow. So do people. We made that oath with someone long past, gone to the Light, if you're a believer," one of them says, her voice like silk on my skin. A shiver runs up my frame and raises the hair on the back of my neck. I inch closer to the cave wall.

"Weylan is many things, but she does not break an oath," I say.

*It's the reason I'm here, doing her bidding. If she promises freedom, she will give it.*

The first siren moves onto the rock closest to me, hair hanging over her shoulders as rivulets of water drip down her chest. Her cheeks catch the fading sunlight, the skin made of something not human—a flicker of scales. Long, nimble fingers stretch over the smooth stone, and a flash of her red tongue slips from her mouth, slowly sliding over her full lips.

"Very well. Justify your guilt," the one farthest away says.

The one on the rock tilts her head. "We should have some fun while we wait, Crow, don't you agree?" She slides closer, and for the first time, I realize I'm hovering on the edge of the pool.

I jerk back and stumble onto the rocks behind me. There's a loud *rip* as one of the rocks cuts into my shirt and tears it open. Their laughter bounces off the cavern walls and ricochets in my ears.

The sirens we hunted were in our waters—on Teraceron shores—and isolated from their shiver. Now, in this enclosed space, alone, I'm the obvious underdog. I knew it would be safer for the crew if I came on the island, like drawing flies to honey. I'm too sweet a prize for them to pass up, even if the queen has banned them from hurting me.

For now.

The siren's laughter boils my blood. Her teeth elongate, the stench of stale water and rotten fish wafting toward me. The water around her begins to bubble, and my eyes widen as her tail disappears and two legs form.

The other siren squeals with delight as the woman stumbles onto the shore, her skin a sickly gray color. She grazes her nails over my cheek. A sharp burn travels over my skin as her nails sink into my flesh and draw blood. She reaches around me and caresses the cut on my back, sending shivers down my spine. Her hand comes away bloodied, and she sticks her pointer finger in her mouth.

"Delicious," she whispers.

"Stop playing with the food," a chilled voice says from behind.

Another siren walks into the cavern. Light from the hole above catches in her blood red hair and reflects off her blue-tinted skin. Her legs are unnaturally long, and her toes wrap around the rocks like an octopus's tentacles as she moves closer. A soaked and practically nonexistent dress clings to her thighs.

The siren closest to me pouts. "I saw him first," she says.

"Liar," the one in the water snaps. "Archaia did, but she took the girl to confer with the queen."

"Second!" the siren screeches.

I flinch, and the newest siren chuckles, the sound deep in her throat. The fear of what might come of this disappears, replaced with a tugging in my core. I glance at her. "I believe he belongs to our queen. She'll be ever so pleased to have the one responsible for our sisters' deaths." Turning her back to the others, however, she mouths, "*Mine*," and my body aches with need.

*Stop it, Crow.*

I breathe in through my nose and try to clear my mind. I focus on someone—anyone else. Nerissa pops into my mind, and I picture her smirk, her hand in mine as we made a deal. The siren runs her fingers over the collar of my shirt.

"You have a choice, Crow: listen to my song or let your crew drown." She forces me to the ground, nails digging into my flesh. "The queen has changed her mind. You should have never set foot on this island."

I don't care about myself. I focus on my crew.

"You're lying," I say, the hair on the back of my neck rising.

She smirks, yanking me closer. "Ask your crows. We'll wait."

My eyes shift toward the sirens. The one on the shore slides back into the water, and her tail reappears. I close my eyes and call on Besnick.

He lets me in, and the bright red sunset above ground burns my corneas. I find Becci kneeling on deck in front of a siren, face drawn in a silent scream. She covers her ears to drown out their laughter, but it echoes around her. A sharp kick in her back sends her sprawling. One of the shiver yanks her up by the throat, sliding razored teeth along her neck.

Becci's nostrils flare. They drag the men from the hold, half a dozen sirens walking like humans. But there's something otherworldly about them—the longness of their legs, the way their hair blows in the wind, and the wideness of their eyes.

I return to the cave and pierce the sirens with my glare. My heart races in my chest, and the one in front grins like we share a secret.

"Want it?" she mouths, plump lips making my mouth water.

"You'll keep your word?" A flicker of doubt settles in my core as she gives a slow, sensual nod.

"*Want me*," she says.

And I do. I yearn for the sound of her voice and her delicate caress. I've never been so close to the sirens without the sand in my ears, and even then, their song was intoxicating. Killing them would have been impossible without Becci. My cousin can't save me now, and I have no choice but to let this beast in. As soon as I do, my body relaxes. The sound of the ocean laps at my ears, but it's nothing compared to the siren song.

All I want—*all I need*—is her.

She opens her mouth and sings, and it's the sound I've been looking for. Warmth spreads through my veins, and why I'm here—*why am I here?*

"Can you swim, Captain?" she purrs. She extends one hand in my direction, and I reach for her with trembling fingers.

"Oh, my captain." She leans down, running a finger over my chin and down my throat. Her hand clasps mine, and my muscles tense in pleasure. "You're a vision—hair the color of your precious birds. What do you think of me, pirate boy?" Strong, willowy arms tighten around my waist. Her dress soaks my clothes, every drip of water like a soft caress.

"Lovely," I whisper, voice thick with passion. "You're the most—"

She laughs and kisses me on the mouth. Her teeth graze my bottom lip, and a shot of lightning pierces in my chest. I run my hands down her arms, fire igniting where our skin meets, but it barely satisfies my need. Her hands wrap around both sides of my throat, angling our mouths closer, harder. It draws a groan from my throat, and I tighten my hold on her.

Her laugh brushes against my mouth before she breaks away. She taps the pads of her fingers against the hollow of my throat. Fiery red ringlets brush against my shirt, and I reach my hand up and run my fingers through them. Her eyes are the most striking thing about her, an effervescent orange, like the color of coral.

My chest tightens when she pulls away.

"Please, don't—"

"Oh, my pirate boy, you're coming with me," she says, leaning in and nibbling my earlobe.

"I would swim across the sea for you," I say.

Her eyes glint in the fading light streaming from the cavern opening, and she traces her nails over the delicate skin around my wrist.

"Strong heart, this one. You were adorable with that scowl on your face. Shame it had to go away," she says, a purr underlying her tone.

"Let's go for a swim," I say. "Please, go for a swim with me. It would make me…" I raise her knuckles to my mouth and kiss them, tasting the salt from the sea. "Most pleased."

My breath burns in my chest while I wait for her reply. "If you insist, Captain Crow," she finally says, and the air rushes back into my lungs. Her laughter fills the room as she weaves our fingers together and pulls me under.

# CHAPTER
# EIGHT
NERISSA

**Siren's Cove**

Fire burns my lungs. I clench my eyes shut and hold on tightly to the back of the gatekeeper siren and—*by the sea, will this ever end?*

Suddenly, it does.

The siren throws me on the sandy shore. My chest heaves with each breath, a wheezing sound scratching at the back of my throat.

"Not all of them survive," says an echoing voice. "When my gatekeeper throws them ashore, sometimes they never breathe again. It's fascinating how little endurance some of your kind have."

I roll on my side and look up at the Siren Queen. She lounges in a small pool of water, separate from the others, her tail splashing water onto the sand around her. Like bees, the queen is the largest of the group, her fin almost too big to fit her liquid throne. If she had legs, she would stand at least seven feet. The fin makes her roughly eight feet long. Her blue-tinted veins stretch like tree roots, visible beneath her skin. Her arms reach across the lip of the pool, covering the whole surface of the gray stone. Thick, silky black hair cascades around her.

Also like a hive, they hide the queen in the darkest depths. The cave sparkles with rhinestones and gems, the small fraction of light managing to reach this far down glints off every available surface.

The Siren Queen sets her ebony and vibrant gray rimmed irises upon me, stealing my breath.

"There's fresh meat on you, girl," she says. "I detect my shiver on you, as well."

*We are so far beyond our depth.*

The queen smiles as if I said the thought aloud.

At the sound of their queen's voice, more heads pop up. Some of them are pale like the queen, the ones who have been in the caves the longest. Their skin, although various shades, are all tinged blue. Others look like they've spent time in the sun—a siren with tawny, brown skin here, one with vibrant red locks there. They don't spare me a glance as they wait for her to give them their next command.

I fumble with the water-logged tie at my waist. My breath echoes around the cave, and the dozen or so pairs of eyes land on me. I untie the sling, and the meat makes a sickening suction sound as it pops free from my skin.

I present it to the queen, and her eyes narrow in on the freshly marred edge made from Cyrus's blade.

"I see my shiver got the first bite."

I clench my trembling fists, and say, "My apologies. I offered them some to bring me here. Only your kind can make the trip."

The answer brings a smile to her lips, and she reaches out for the rest of the meat. She sniffs it, and her eyes close. "Smart. Some are not as wise, though you had some idea how to handle yourself, did you not? Was your sister as smart as you?"

Thoughts of Lucia rush around me, but I push them down. Flexing my jaw, I shake my head.

She smirks. "Two sides of the same coin, yet so different," she says, tossing the meat in the water.

I tremble at the memory of the same words from my father's lips.

*Two sides of the same coin. My priceless girls.*

The shivers' attack snaps me free of the memory. They claw at each other for a bite. It's a feeding frenzy like no other, with hands and talons flying and slicing. The water darkens with each cut, the shivers' claws slicing into one another as much as they do the lamb.

"What is it you seek, Captain Eliott?" the queen asks. I snap my gaze toward her. "That is your name, yes? The sea speaks of you. Please do not tell me you came all this way for no more than a moment with me?" She smirks, and I swallow the bile rising in my throat.

"Brevlyra. My sister is trapped in the abandoned kingdom. The map led me to you."

She tilts her head to the side. "Do you know why the map led you to me?" she asks.

I gulp down the anxiety rolling in my gut. "I can't go to Brevlyra unarmed. It told me I need the voice of a mermaid. I don't know where it's leading me next."

"Yet, you trust something without a mind of its own? Who do you think controls the map, the Light you believe in, or the Darkness you know to be real?"

I bite the inside of my cheek, tasting blood. "I trust the Light."

She chuckles. "You trust a rumor?"

"If the Light does not welcome my path, then I will not be successful. It's called hope."

"Some things are bigger than you and me," she says. "Hope, I'm not so sure of. Anyway, the destruction of a once beautiful land was tragic, but no one has been able to enter Brevlyra in almost fifteen years. Is the Light what makes you special? You are nothing but a girl. A prophetic coming, but a girl, nonetheless. What can you do that others cannot?"

"The Light works in prophecy as much as the Darkness. We can discuss our theologies all day, or we can trade."

She smirks. "Oh, darling, what fire you have. I wish I could be there to witness it. Fine. I'll bite: you're here for the voice of a mermaid. What do you intend to give me for such an item?" she asks.

I swallow. "What do you want?"

"Interesting." The queen taps an overly long nail against her lip, and the resulting smile sends a chill down my spine. "Anything I desire from you, then?"

Father's voice echoes in the back of my mind, *Sirens will tear you apart,* he said.

"Anything," I whisper.

She quirks a brow and murmurs something under her breath. Her tail shifts, turning into a pair of legs.

"Rather unwise to promise one such as me *anything*, but you are a clever girl. As was your father." She drapes them over the side of the pool before standing.

"You—You knew my father?" The words struggle to break free, but she hears them, and a satisfied glint brightens her gaze.

"Oh, yes. When he was a few years older than you, a freshly minted ship-wright. I see him in your eyes, but I think your spirit belongs to your mother." She grabs a sheet from a dark crevice of the cave and slides it down over her head like a dress. My head spins, trying to sort her words with the transformation taking place in front of me—sirens can *shift*. When—how—

"This ability," she says. "Was a result of some powerful trades. Don't worry—it's a gift bestowed to the select few. Besides, it's nothing you need to concern yourself with. We have moved past theology, have we not?"

She walks over to me and holds out a hand. "Come, child. Let me show you *my* collection."

Her scaled hand pulls me to my feet. She lets go, and I follow her deeper into the cave, my breath burning in my chest as it takes in the rot and decay. The ceilings arch upward, and small pockets of stones twinkle like stars. It's a path designed to catch a thief. One sleight of hand, and I might meet my end from some unseen safeguard.

Her bare feet resound down the path, rolling my stomach.

We step into another cave, and it's brighter than I would have expected, speckled with cages. Birds caw and creatures fight against their confines, each as unique as the next. I stay on the narrow path, as far away from the cages as possible, my hands wet with perspiration.

"You need something precious to trade, correct?" she asks. "But the voice of a mermaid—why that?" She spins around, and I almost barrel into her.

"I know the price of the voice is steep."

"It is. The Light sure likes to test those who believe in Him."

I swallow the lump in my throat. "I survived before. I'll live to watch the sun rise another day."

"Seems a steep price to pay for belief," she says before leading me farther into the cave.

"We all have to believe in something. The Light would not have to test us if the Darkness didn't try to tempt us."

She looks back at me, momentarily cut short. "You are quite extraordinary, Nerissa Eliott."

The shock from her compliment pales when we come upon the thick bars, covering a small pool of water. There's scarcely enough room for half a body to sit out of the pool. An almost imperceptible ripple touches the surface, and I lean forward. A beautiful face comes into view. The mermaid looks nothing like the sirens. Sirens belong to the sea, more creatures of the deep than those on land. However, the woman in front of me could pass for human, if it weren't for the tail barely visible in the dark depths.

Her face changes as soon as she realizes I am not one of her captors. She grabs the bars and starts yanking. "Please help me! I don't know why I'm here. I can barely swim," she pleads, tears filling her eyes. "And there's something down here. Please, please, help me!"

The queen waves her hand in the direction of the mermaid, and she stops talking, mouth opening and closing like a fish on land. She grabs at her throat, and then she begins clawing through the bars. Her face flushes and her eyes flash red. She glances in my direction, and her entire being changes. Her light, silky hair flies off her shoulders. Foam grows around the corner of her mouth, slinging silent insults in my direction. I take a step back, heart thundering in my chest.

"They're a fiery bunch. Not quite the appetite of a shiver, though," the queen says. "They prefer the dead. Scavengers, all of them." I glance at her, and she curls her lip in disgust.

My eyes continue to wander back to the mermaid. She twitches and bangs in her cage, but no matter what she does, she's trapped.

The queen studies the mermaid. "While they can't boast their brilliance, they are fast. She's been here for, oh, twenty-five years. Are you sure you're willing to forfeit what it takes?"

I grit my teeth, clenching my fists to keep from attacking her right then and there. I'm tired of these games and need to get back to the ship before the siren shows me more of her tricks—before she decides to use them on us. "What do you want?"

The queen's hand dashes between the bars, grabbing the mermaid's throat. A pearly mist escapes her lips and travels into the pendant dangling from a chain around the queen's neck.

She spins around and begins her trek back toward the cavern. I stare at the mermaid for a few moments, watching her ire grow red in her cheeks.

"Come, Nerissa Eliott. We have some things to discuss."

I rush after her, the sound of the mermaid pounding in her cell echoing the whole journey. Once we're surrounded by her shiver, the queen unties the string and dangles it between us.

She rubs the mermaid voice between her forefinger and thumb.

"What do you want?" I ask.

"An oath between you and Cyrus Crow, and the ring on your finger as a token to ensure you keep your word."

"W-what?" I clench my fist, wishing the gold band would melt into my skin. The ring was Lucia's, the last piece of her. The delicate band and simple black stone are icy against my skin, a constant reminder of the sister I lost—and the person who gave it to her.

She grins. "Do you know what power it holds—what you could do with that small piece of jewelry? That small stone," she says, her fingers tracing the cool gem. "Is from the Dragonlands."

I take a step back. "You're lying. Travel to the Dragonlands is impossible. Jewelry like this would be worth—"

"More than your weight in gold, but it has something more. It has a story."

"You want this for the story it holds? Why?" Fear curls in my chest, and I wish I had never stepped foot on this island.

"Stories carry their own magic," she says. "Especially from a land unchartable after they sealed off their borders to the rest of Penreine."

The western Dragonlands are impossible to touch, endless rocky terrain and powerful waters. The inhabitants there are mad, raising beasts able to destroy us all. The one thing keeping us safe from turning the rest of Penreine into a feast is the treaty they signed at the end of the war nearly a century ago.

"Don't tell me a little dragon story terrifies *the* Captain Nerissa Eliott? Or is it the fear of knowing how that ring ended up on your finger?" I clench my ringed hand, and she winks. "What would Cyrus Crow say? Speaking of which, back to that bargain. It involves a little something from both of you."

My blood runs cold in my veins.

"We wouldn't want you to leave without the thing you came for," the queen says.

From the shadows comes one of her shiver, standing tall on a pair of legs too long and too muscular to fit a normal body. She throws Cyrus Crow at my feet, and the whole shiver begins to laugh.

# CHAPTER
# NINE
CYRUS

*Siren's Cove*

"You could've killed him!" someone shouts—a woman. A modicum of familiarity rings in my mind, but it's a hazy recollection, like peering through a fogged glass.

"Poor thing." My attention snaps to the beautiful woman leaning across me. Her eyes flash over my lips, trembling as I try to breathe, and she swipes her finger across my mouth. My eyes roll into my skull at the pleasure racing through my limbs. "Such weak lungs."

I roll to my side, spitting salty water in the sand.

A whimper escapes me as she disappears from my view, body aching from the cold. The water burns my eyes and blurs my vision. Warm hands turn me on my side and pound the space between my shoulder blades until more water scratches its way up my esophagus.

"What of this bond you seek, siren?" the person snarls, and my mind searches for a memory of the voice to grab onto.

"A bond between you and Crow to replace his connection to the queen," replies a smooth silken voice—a perfect voice, yanking the memory away. "I don't blame him for the death of my girls, but I do blame the usurper queen in Teraceron. She took mine, so now I'm taking hers. I will remove the bond between Cyrus and the queen, but breaking a bond such as theirs can lead to death. A slow, painful death, unless replaced by another. Madness would creep in—"

"No," the girl says. I shake my head and train my gaze on the beautiful blue woman.

My chest sags with relief as the queen gives me a smile. "Move," I demand of the girl still holding me, elbowing her in the side.

"No. Not today. You are not dying on me," the girl says and digs her nails in my arm.

"Let me go," I demand and try to crawl toward the woman who brought me.

The girl blocks my view—who is this girl, the one dressed like a man? Her hands cup my face, and she spits on my cheek, causing me to jerk back.

"Pull yourself together, Cyrus Crow," she says, a fire in her eyes. "I'm not letting you go, so don't fight me. Got it?"

I nod, uncertainty settling in my gut. "Got it," I mumble. My head grows heavy as I stare at her. I grip her wrists, her skin burning beneath my touch.

"What did you do to him?" the girl asks, her gaze locked on mine.

*What is her name?*

"Nothing, my child. Simply what we sirens always do," the woman says. My eyes flick in her direction, at the smile residing on her face, and it sends a spike of fear through me.

*Fear?*

I shake the thought away and turn back to the girl in front of me.

"Come here, my pirate boy," my siren says, words a soft hum.

The girl's grip on me tightens as I try to stumble to my feet, only managing to say, "I—"

"No!" The girl in front of me yanks me to her chest. "Stop it, by the sea. Please stop!" She turns her harsh gaze to the siren.

*Siren?*

"I will stop, if he asks me to. I'm nothing if not fair," the redheaded siren says.

"He's part of the collection now," my captor says, her eyes bright.

*Captor?* No—nothing so sinister, though nothing else fits.

"The way to release him is through a *bond*?" The girl's light brown eyes land on mine. A sharp uncertainty settles in her irises, but she blinks, and it fades.

"Yes," the siren says, her voice barely restrained. Her fingers tap madly on her side as if she's ready to pounce and wrap her claws around the girl's throat.

I squint my eyes shut and shake my head.

The girl's nails dig into my skin.

"You're hurting me," I say, voice leaning toward a whine.

"What?" the girl asks, gaze landing on our clasped hands. Her gaze softens, but her heart continues to race. "Oh."

My face warms as I look at her, a deep connection sinking in my gut. I furrow my brow and stare into her eyes. "I know you."

Her name dances on the tip of my tongue—

She's yanked from my side. I fall back, and the beautiful redhead from the sea wraps her arms around my waist. She laughs, running her hands over my chest. I lean down to kiss her when a voice in my head screams, *Stop!*

I shake my head.

*Remember who you are,* repeats the voice, almost sounding like my own. My shoulders tense, and an angry snarl takes over the siren's features.

The woman whispers in my ear, words I can't distinguish, almost like lyrics. The voice in my head fades away, but my shoulders stiffen.

"Let me go!" screams the girl. Her feet kick at the rocks, the sound echoing around the cavern. "By the Light, I will end you, siren!"

The woman—*siren?*—smiles at her. "Tempting," she says. "But not why you're here. Do we have a deal?"

The girl spits at her feet. "No."

"Why not, my dear? Is a ring worth more than this man's life? Well, he is a *pirate*," she says, her smile turning my stomach. "A noble one, but still a pirate."

*Nerissa,* the name resounds in my mind. "Nerissa..."

All eyes turn toward me.

"Interesting," the siren, as the girl calls her, says, running a finger down my cheek.

She focuses on Nerissa—Issa.

"I can give you what everyone desires, my child—power," the siren says to Nerissa.

Nerissa's nostrils flare and her jaw clicks—it's a fierce look on someone so beautiful, even so dirty and ruffled. I shake my head, looking back to the red-headed siren—the most gorgeous thing I've ever beheld, but something fails to click. My eyes find Issa.

*Why are you looking away from the siren?*

I shake my head, trying to clear my thoughts.

No, Issa is the one who deserves my attention.

"I'll give you the ring, but you will not take it from me. You can't. If you do, it loses its power. It must be a gift willingly given. Let me go," Issa says to the siren holding her.

The siren flicks her wrist toward Nerissa, and she stumbles free. She frets with the ring on her finger and slowly slides it free. The redhead holding me pushes me away and slips it on her hand. She holds it up to the light, the surface shimmering.

"Perfect fit," she says, winking.

"Give me the voice and Cyrus, and be done with it." Nerissa growls the words.

The woman smiles, her grin haunting and unkind. "I can't *give* him to you. You have to do what I say—and that requires blood. From each of you."

Nerissa charges, but she's yanked back by a siren with long, curly hair. The smell of brine infiltrates my senses, and a hand slides up my back, grasping my shoulders. Sharp talons dig in, and a voice whispers, "There, there, little crow," in my ear. Goosebumps pepper my flesh, and my hand hovers in the air, inching closer to Nerissa.

"How dare you—" she begins.

Nerissa and I are yanked to the center of the room and thrown in the sand.

"I will not be butchered like a lamb," Nerissa says shrilly.

*Don't touch her!* I want to scream. The words never come.

"Let us go!" Issa shrieks. Panic slices through her words, and my heart thunders in my ears until it's all I hear.

Nerissa stumbles to her feet and reaches for the siren, but she hits an invisible wall. The shiver titters around us, and Issa presses her hands on something unseen. She begins to yell, but the sound is cut short. The shiver's laugh reverberates through the tunnels, bouncing back on them and vibrating in my bones.

The queen smiles, revealing all of her jagged teeth. She snaps her long fingers, and the sirens on legs leaps onto us, holding down first Nerissa, and then me. The sand flings into my eyes and mouth as Nerissa's screams rise higher and higher; the laughter of her captors drowns her out.

I fight against them, but they sink in their claws. Warm blood bursts from the new wounds on my arms, legs, and shoulders. A siren gags my mouth. High pitched laughter echoes around us. A willowy siren with tight black curls and dark brown skin straddles me, leaning down and caressing my face from my hairline to my jaw. I fight against her, my stomach twisting with distaste.

"I wish I could revel in this, Cyrus Crow. My sisters would want me to." She licks her lips. Flecks of spit hit my cheek. "It's said a Crow's blood tastes like sweet nectar."

The other sirens hiss and scream, and she snaps at them in turn.

"Hold him still," a siren above me orders.

One of them jerks my head to a stop, claws digging into the flesh behind my ears.

The siren takes a ruby-hilted dagger in her hand and draws an invisible line around my lips before sliding down and holding the knife over my forearm.

"Sorry, this is going to sting, but it's how these things must be done. Ceremony and all." She winks. "Tell me, what do you wish for in the dark of night, Cyrus Crow?" she asks, tilting her head. "Do you wish to be free of your queen? Or do you wish for a quick death?"

When the dagger meets my skin, I start to burn from the inside out. A pain builds behind my eyes, slowly intensifying until my body buzzes with agony. The world shifts beneath me, and a hollow voice booms, outraged.

*Weylan.*

She knows what's happening, even though I don't. Panic slices into me as she forces her way inside my mind, the memory rising like a tidal wave.

The putrid stench of the cavern grows, and vomit rises hot in my throat.

*"Cyrus!" the voice screamed—one of the girls Weylan tormented. "Cyrus, my love, save me. Please."*

"Get out of my head!" I scream, fighting the slicing pain. The pressure in my ear reaches a peak.

*"Sic him, Tybalt,"* Weylan had said, speaking to one of her cats. *"It's dinnertime."*

I hear thundering panther claws on the castle as the knife digs in deeper.

Someone yanks my arm from my side, and my skin meets Nerissa's beneath the forced fingers of the shiver. I imagine the feline's claws digging into my arm.

*"I'm sorry, my queen," whimpered the servant girl. "I didn't realize he was yours—"*

*"Now you do, and now he gets to learn what happens when he breaks an oath."*

The screams of the past mix with the present. The bond between Weylan and me severs. Weylan's rage washes over me once more before dying away. I'm left with the wreckage of my past—of the endless torment at the hands of our bond.

I remember how the girl's blood seeped across the entry hall. I can still taste the sharp tang of it dripping down my cheek and into my mouth.

I pass out to the sound of laughter.

# CHAPTER
# TEN

**Siren's Cove**

The pain is blinding, but I know I have to stay awake when Cyrus passes out next to me. They drag him toward a cage, the sirens hissing and laughing, promises already broken. I fight back, the water coming alive around me. It builds in my belly and rises around me—through me.

Suddenly, an angry tendril of the sea shoots up from one of the pools surrounding us, throwing off my captors. The rancid stench of death hovers beneath the salty tang of the ocean. Thunder rolls overhead, and a harsh wind whips through the cracks of the cavern.

I rise to my feet, wobbling as blood continues to trickle down my arm. My nostrils burn, overwhelmed by the acrid stench of burning sand. The sirens holding Cyrus drop him and charge at me, but another burst of water breaks from the ground and throws them into the pools. Salty spray stings my skin, bringing me to life.

The high ceiling of the cave echoes with the queen's orders. "Destroy her! If I have to do it myself, the whole *sea* will pay!" she snarls, and her shiver begins climbing out of the pools, shifting between their two forms. It's at that moment I realize some of them don't have tails like the queen. Some have tentacles like octopuses, while others crawl and skitter over one another like the crabs at the docks on Helene.

I scurry back, keeping my eyes on Cyrus. A curly-haired siren hovers over his body, eyes shining black, a monster protecting her prey.

"You can't escape us, Nerissa!" The queen's voice booms around the cavern, louder than thunder and sharper than lightning.

One of the sirens grabs my arm. I jerk away, and the water rears up, flying into her chest and throwing her against the wall. Copper and rot explodes in my nostrils as her body falls to the sand. A moment of silence breaks out over the room before they attack.

*You're doing this, Issa,* the small voice whispers in my head, and I raise my arms.

The water responds, rising beside me. My body hums with power, the bitter bite of the sea burning the back of my throat. Hundreds of siren eyes widen. Some of them retreat to the water below, while others hesitate.

"If you go back under, it will be the last time you breathe air or water!" the queen yells. She snaps her fingers, and the remaining sirens attack.

I struggle to guide the water, and I'm tugged in other directions. My teeth clash together, and my arms tremble with exertion as it pilots *me.*

*Trust me,* it whispers, and I try to relax into the movement.

As soon as I do, my ability clicks into place. The water acts like rope and wraps around their throats, squeezing tight as claws grapple between the rushing waves. Power rushes through me. A siren is pulled into the waiting watery depths. Another tendril drags a second siren under. Her nails leave claw marks in the sand as the sea crashes her against the side of the cave, and it turns black with her blood. I push down the heat and bile rising up my throat and search for Cyrus.

An intense urgency spreads through me, and the water begins to swirl in the air like palm leaves during a hurricane. The queen spits orders at her retreating shiver, anger crackling in the air as one after the other disappears beneath blood and carnage.

My sword, ripped from me when they held me down, sits a few inches away.

"You think you can waltz in here and take what is rightfully mine? Think again, young captain," she says, her lips turning up in a snarl.

I straighten my shoulders and meet her gaze. "Give me Cyrus and the voice and let us *go*."

The queen's leg muscles ripple as she paces over Cyrus. "You don't come to my domain and make demands, little pirate," she hisses and attacks.

My heart thunders in my ears. The gash on my arm throbs as the blood continues to run freely, the sea diluting the red as I blast the queen with tendrils of water. My other hand reaches for the fallen sword. Finally, the hilt is in my hand, the handle warm and slick with death. The queen reaches for me, and I yank the blade up, slicing through her throat. Inky black blood speckles my face, each dot burning my skin. I roll to the side to avoid the torrent rushing from her fallen body. I gag on the scent of decay wafting from her. The last siren standing backs away from a still unconscious Cyrus, her jaw slack before diving in the water.

I walk to the dead queen's body and slide my ring off her finger, ripping the necklace from her clawed hand. The water around us settles and shifts back from the rushing waves to a calm, reflective surface.

Cyrus groans, and I run over to him. The world tilts, and my legs crumple beneath me. Blood pools in the crook of my elbow, and I rip off part of my shirt to secure the wound.

"Keels, Cyrus," I mutter, tearing off another ribbon of my shirt to tie around his wounds. "I told you not to come with me. *I told you!*" Urgency laces my words. I struggle to secure a knot in the bend of his arm with my trembling fingers, and fiery panic rushes through me.

He rolls his head to the side, his eyes fluttering open. He touches his head, pinching the bridge of his nose.

"Where are we?" he asks, his voice cracking around the edges.

"Still…" I have to pause and take a deep breath. I glance back down at my arm, vision blurring. My thoughts grow fuzzy. "Keels, that's…a lot of…blood…"

"Issa?"

"Still…here…"

"Nerissa?" Cyrus asks, hurriedly sitting up and cupping my face in his hands. "Stay with me."

Black waves dance in my vision.

"I think I need to..."

A strong hand catches my head before it hits the sand. My vision fades as feathers graze my cheeks.

My eyes slowly peel open, but the dull light is still more intense than the darkness underneath the island. Rain peppers the stained-glass windows of my quarters. I jerk upright, and the dull ache in my arm turns into a stabbing pain.

I let out a low whimper, and Claudette and Britta rush to my side.

"Don't move, Issa!" Britta urges me, pressing me back on the bed.

"Your hands are cold," I say. My whole body aches, and I throw off the covers to relieve the weight pressing down on me. I struggle to get the words out, my voice husky and low as if I haven't spoken in weeks. I try swinging my legs over the edge to stand, but the room sways.

Britta plucks her rain-soaked shirt away from her chest and brushes a strand of hair behind her ear.

I go to ask where Cyrus is, but I don't have to because I *know* where he is. There's a tugging in my core, and I try to follow it, but my head spins. I clasp my hand over my forehead and clench my eyes shut.

Flashbacks of our time on the island assault me, confusion furrowing my brow at the memory of feather soft caresses before the world faded away. Something about it calms me, brings me a sense of peace. The ship is balanced now, like the water and skies are in line with one another.

"If you'd settle, we'd answer your questions," Britta says, pushing me down.

"I can stand." I lose my balance, and my butt hits the edge of the bed.

"Cap," Claudette says, her voice soft and soothing. "It is best not to move too quickly. I do not trust the thread I used."

"I found that thread," Britta says, mouth tilted down. Moving over to the other side of the room, she leans down on the pile of blankets and feathered pillows.

"You realize I worked as a medic on Mechelonian ships, do you not?" Claudette asks, lips pursed and shoulders tight. "I can recognize quality, and what you brought me is not it."

Britta rolls her eyes. "You didn't stay, did you? Don't look at me like that, Nerissa."

"Then stop fighting. Where's Cyrus—" My sentence is cut short by Becci's sharp laugh.

Crow's cousin sits on the bed, checking the stitches in question. "Over there. Newk would have flayed me flat if I'd put you on the floor instead of him. The cot isn't much better."

*Newk?*

I glance around, the ship beyond the open doorway a flurry of movement. The rain distorts the crew as they fight the sea. I rise, pressing my back against the headboard. The rain begins to settle, shifting from an unyielding pour to a steady drizzle.

"How did I get here?" I ask—at least I try to.

Claudette and Britta fuss over me, but I push them away.

"How?" I repeat—nothing. I can barely speak.

Claudette sucks in her cheeks, and Britta gnaws on her bottom lip.

I claw at my throat and try to use my voice, but the words won't come. The more I attempt to talk, the worse it gets.

"Cap," Claudette says, but I ignore her. Panic chokes me, and my mouth opens and closes with unspoken words.

"Captain," she repeats, her hand brushing my wrist. I throw her off and grasp at my throat.

"I can't—" I try to say, but the words scrape against sandpaper. "Talk! I can't-" Tears pool in my eyes, hot as they fall down my cheeks.

"*Nerissa!*" Britta yells and rips my hands from my neck. Her grip is strong, fingers turning white. "Calm down. It's only your voice. It will come back. We have bigger things to worry about." She nods at my new first mate, the one who replaced *her*.

They share a look. Some kind of understanding settles between them. My head swivels back and forth as I try to comprehend what is happening, unable to articulate what I want to ask.

Claudette clears her throat and breaks me from my reverie. "Crow was not conscious when we found you, Cap. He was barely breathing. The only reason I was able to make it back with you both was because Bec went to the island as soon as they left our ship. The crows..." Her voice trails off, and she and Britta share a look.

"Go ahead," Bec says from the corner, placing a wet cloth delicately over Cyrus's forehead, cleaning his neck with another. "Might as well."

I arch a brow at my first mate and cousin.

"Claudette and Bec went to the island after the sirens left the boat. We were sure they were going to kill us all, but they stopped and screeched into the sky before diving over," Britta says. They share another look. "Then...the crows...led us to you. They were swarming the island and guided us to the cavern. It took a lot of rope, but we were able to climb down."

No one says anything, and I glance toward the open window. The flash of crow feathers blends with the night sky, storm clouds rolling west and away from our path. I sneak a glance at Cyrus and find Bec staring at me, sitting on the floor next to him and twirling a knife on the floorboards.

She stands. "I'm going to go see if anyone needs ordering around. I trust you'll make sure he doesn't stop breathing?" she asks, eyeing us.

I nod and swing my legs over the side of the bed before either of them can stop me. I steady my feet, hands outstretched, before attempting to stumble to Cyrus's side. They reach for me, but I shake them off, though the fog in my brain wishes otherwise. I sway and let a defeated sigh escape my lips as Claudette and Britta each grab an arm. I signal for Britta to continue, trying to get them to answer the questions I can't ask.

"Bec says it's dehydration, possibly, why he won't wake. We're not sure what the siren did to him," Britta says.

His eyes fly open, and I fall next to him. An intense pain claws at my chest. A scream breaks from my lips, and my hand claws at the fire building in my throat. I yank away the thin, corded necklace and throw it to the floor. The ringing in my ears accompanies the lingering pain, and a calloused hand cups my cheek.

My eyes meet Cyrus's piercing gaze.

An unfamiliar, gut-wrenching zing vibrates in my chest, making it difficult to breathe. I gulp before backing away. Claudette picks up the necklace I yanked away but drops it with a mumbled curse. "By the sea, what is that thing?"

On wobbly legs, I pluck the necklace from the floor. The oval medallion pulses with life. My hands shake as I weigh the warm leather strap. A vague memory of a crow tying it around my neck prickles my mind. The light catches, turning the pearly green liquid into shades of blue, purple, and pink—some shades I didn't even realize existed. I touch the pendant, and it warms with a heartbeat of its own, though it doesn't burn the same as before.

"The voice of a mermaid," Britta whispers as I tie it back around my neck.

# CHAPTER
# ELEVEN
### NERISSA

*Between Abhors Sea and the Bheragus Sea*

Britta's eyes dart between Bec and I as I sit behind the desk and study the map, head pounding with the continued effort of following the unpredictable pattern. The next location appears on the parchment, an island to the east of Siren's Cove called Amasse. However, what I need on the island isn't clear, flicking in and out of focus as soon as the words attempt to dance across the map. It's as if the dreams filtering behind Cyrus's fluttering lids are at war with the present predicament. As soon as Bec leaves, a mercenary with a medical background takes her place. I look at Britta.

"Out with it," I say, my voice a mere whisper. Anytime I try to speak louder, nothing. My lips twitch at the corners with unspoken words, and my eyes have to do the talking for me.

Britta pushes the broth Claudette brought me across the table.

"We may have a problem," Britta says, eyes darting to the door. "Claudette, she made a decision in your absence—"

I arch a brow, drinking half the bowl. "Duncan, the one with the eye patch—half-Hillsman and half-Mechelonian, by the look of him—is back." I think of the man with tanned skin and curly brown hair. "He swam back toward the ship in the middle of the night before we neared the Cove. When we dropped anchor, he..." She rolls her eyes upward, shoulders taut with frustration. "He helped us fight off the sirens. If it weren't for him, we'd be dead. As much as I hate to admit it." Britta slumps down in the captain's chair. "Claudette wants him to stay."

Her gaze moves to the mercenary treating Cyrus with some of the remedies we purchased from an apothecary on Pirate's Bay. I gulp down the rest of my soup. The man's eyes land on my throat. I turn away and move closer to my cousin.

"He's a liability, regardless of how he help—"

"Let him stay," I croak, placing my now empty soup bowl on the drafting table.

Her eyes meet mine, shoulders tense. "It's another mouth to feed."

I cut her off. "If he wants to be here so badly, let him stay. He can fish for his food."

"But you sent him away," she retorts. "Others will view it as weakness—"

I raise my hand to silence her, and pinkness rises on her cheeks. "Let him stay," I repeat.

Clenching her jaw, she nods and rushes back out, her shouts to Becci drowned beneath the roar of the wind. The sun is high in the sky, but the wind whisks thick white clouds across it, blanketing the blue in white. It shakes the ship and disturbs the waves, water crashing onto the deck and spraying the crew. I hold tightly to the drafting table and take a seat at the bolted down chair.

I study the jumbled mess of a map, the parchment rough under my fingers. The figures are clearer than when we first got back, so it makes me more confident Cyrus is getting better. The sea rocks against the ship as I study the map's movement. A thin line reads, *where the waters meet.*

I go to the doorway and study the waves lapping at the ship. Wind whips my hair out of my braid, slapping against my cheeks. The waves continue their onslaught, and some of the crew steadies themselves by grabbing the ship's side or the mast. Salty spray permeates the air and tastes bitter on my lips. The taller mercenary we brought from our crew, Max, almost topples over Claudette. She pushes him back up as we cross from the Abhors Sea into the Bheragus Sea. The gray water behind us dulls in comparison to the bright cerulean waves dancing in the sun peeking through the clouds.

As soon as we pass into the other sea, the waters start to calm. Still, I brace my hand against the door frame to my quarters, gritting my teeth. It's been two days since we left Siren's Cove, meaning we're seriously behind schedule.

*Nine days.*

Eight days until my eighteenth birthday, my sister's the next.

*November 2nd.* It hangs over my head like the constant presence of Cyrus's crows.

At the beginning of this journey, I planned to be in Old Kingdom with eight days to spare, but as the time continues to dwindle, I can't settle the unease in my belly.

Low murmurs rise behind me, and there's a prickling on my skin—an awareness I wasn't keen to before. I glance back. Cyrus sits up and shakes his head in the direction of the healer. His shoulders sag with exhaustion, and he glances up as I walk toward the drafting table.

"Thank you," he whispers.

"Light be with you," I mumble, the words hoarse.

He scrunches his brow.

"It's an islander thing." I clear my throat. "A phrase used by those from the islands. It's how we say thank you. A more profound thanks. It's also something you say when someone heals."

*You never said it to Lucia.*

*Stop beating yourself up, Issa,* another voice replies, sounding like Kip.

*You shouldn't spare my emotions. Not after what happened to* you, I reply to the voice in my head.

"What happened to your voice?" Cyrus asks, bringing me back.

I touch the necklace at my throat.

"Nerissa, take that off—" Cyrus begins, but I silence him with a shake of my head, wrapping my fingers around the pendant.

"It must be worn," I say, and the words are sandpaper in my throat. "In order to keep its full power, according to lore. An unused voice is as good as no voice at all."

He opens his mouth to say something else, but I shake my head and return my attention to the drafting table

He leans over my shoulder. His hand brushes my wrist, and I spin around to his blue eyes boring into me, raising the hair on my neck. My legs press into the tilted surface of the drafting table. The rough edge catches the smooth fabric of my breeches.

"I remember what happened," he says, his voice as low as mine. "Thank you for not leaving me there. But you have no idea what you've agreed to—what you have woken..."

I recoil from his touch, the items on the table clanking loudly against each other. "What?" I say, but it comes out as a squeak.

Heat radiates from his body, dancing over my skin.

"I told you not to come with me, but you didn't listen!" My voice is barely a whisper.

His eyes widen, and a small smirk edges up the corner of his mouth. My gaze lingers on that small curl of his lips, the heat in my cheeks turning into an inferno.

"You think you're so clever, Nerissa Eliott," he says, his eyes searching my face as his smirk transforms into a scowl.

It's so severe, I flinch.

"You don't even realize the disaster you've brought on us all by making a deal with that monster. We'll be lucky to even make it halfway to our destination," he says in a low, growling voice.

"She's dead!" I croak.

He grabs my arms, his hold weak but sure. Our eyes meet, and his pupils dilate so I'm staring into a sea of black.

"Captain Crow," the mercenary warns, and Cyrus releases me, staring at his hands for a moment, shocked at what he'd done.

I back farther into the table. My heart lodges in my throat, and I grip the side of the wood until it digs deeply into my palms, stopping the flow of blood.

*What have I done?* I think, and the fear is nearly overshadowed by a hot, sticky rage, sour on my tongue. "You're the one who didn't tell me what I was getting into by taking *you* on the island. If you hadn't gotten yourself involved, then maybe it wouldn't have ended like it did."

He chokes on a laugh, eyes flashing upward. "You're right, Eliott. Because you'd be dead," he says. "She knew what she was doing when she baited you. You kill her, but she gets the last word. Any creature in the menagerie belonged to *her*—was held captive because of *her*. With her gone, they have nothing holding them back."

I stagger at his words.

I've dragged innocent bystanders into my and Lucia's drama.

Again.

*Oh, Kip.* Sadness overwhelms me, icy and sharp like a winter storm. I want to scream until all thoughts of what I've done—who I've hurt, alongside those I continue to wound—finally let me go from this pain.

"I—you've..." He never finishes his thought, hands lacing behind his head as panic washes over him. His nostrils flare as he looks back at me and then walks out on deck.

*Pull yourself together, Issa. You're better than this. Don't think of me.* Kip's voice is like a salve on my fresh wounds, and I straighten my shoulders and swallow my fear.

"Cyrus Crow!" I yell, but my voice is barely above a whisper.

Still, he turns at the doorway.

"What have I done?" I ask. Liquid fire burns in my chest. The rest of the crew turns to us. "By the sea! I did what I had to with the crew and the choices I was handed. I saved you. I saved *all* of us."

"You doomed me," he hisses, the same potency blazing in his gaze. "You don't understand the game you're playing, and as long as you act like the pirate you *think* you are, you might as well throw the rest of us to the leviathans."

A hush settles over the ship. The eyes of the crew burn into my skin, but I can't look away—won't look away from Cyrus.

"How dare you?" I whisper. "We are *both* captains on this ship—"

"No, Nerissa. How dare *you?* You need *me*. When you took the bond with me, you freed me from Weylan. I have been her toy since I was a boy—she will stop at *nothing* to find me—to find *us*. You haven't saved me. You've put another target on our backs."

Something in me snaps. The necklace at my throat begins to burn. It lights a fire in my belly, begging me to say something. I open my mouth to speak, and a fierce wind rises around us. Cyrus goes flying across the deck, and Becci and Duncan rush to his side. Before they reach him, I jerk my head in their direction and glare.

They stumble back, the waves crashing against the ship. The sun hides behind bulbous, speeding clouds. White foam and salty spray rise over the lip of the main deck, stinging my cheeks. The waters that looked so bright seconds before turn wild. Every inch of my body sings; pinpricks of heat dance across my skin. An unknown strength rises between my bones, yanking back my shoulders, my chin held high.

Finding my voice, I take a step closer to Cyrus, then another, until we're nose to nose. Leaning down, I grab him by the collar. "Then help me. Help me find my sister," I tell him. "We can make this hard, or we can work together. What I did was stupid and reckless, and I shouldn't have even stepped foot on Siren's Cove, but it's what I felt like I had to do. One of the *only* choices that didn't end in our deaths. I'm sorry for being the only one—again—who takes responsibility for her actions!" My words don't even begin to match the anger roaring inside me, ready to shake the waves beneath me worse than a hurricane.

"Take your anger out on me, hate me for what I've said, but your anger isn't for me," he says, voice low.

His jaw tightens, and shame fills me, but I would do it again. And he's right—he's not the cause of all my anger, but he's here. He's the one taking the brunt as the waves swirl around me, uncontrollable after being held down for so long.

"Nerissa!" Britta yells.

I jerk my head back and notice the entire crew is down on their knees, unable to stand in the wind and waves of the sudden storm. They're all soaked, but the water never touched me. The mercenaries fight the sails with every onslaught of sudden wind. Britta leans toward me, reaching out her hand, fingers trembling.

"Call it off, Nerissa!" she screams at me.

I falter. My stomach rolls, and my hands tremble, still clutched on Cyrus's collar.

No one can look at me because of the wind and waves rocking the ship. When they do, they look away afraid, except one. Becci holds the main mast for dear life, but her eyes are open, flickering flames of darkened violet.

I drop Cyrus's collar and stumble back. The waves calm, and the sun peeks through the clouds once more, but not before I catch a glimpse of the crew members' faces.

What I did in the caves—what I did a moment ago—it's volatile, reckless. My hands shake, and tears threaten to fall, but I clench my fists shut. That wasn't me—didn't *feel* like me. It felt...

Horrible.

Wonderful.

*Deadly.*

My stomach rolls, and the little bit of food in my stomach rises in my throat. I run to the side of the ship and retch until my esophagus burns.

It's gotten worse since Lucia left—my powers. I don't know what to do with my anger, and it takes control of the sea, not me. This power may be Light-blessed, but it's my curse. Tears pool in the bottom of my eyes, and I press the back of my hand to my lips. The curve of Lucia's ring is cool on the edge of my lips, and I have to stop myself from taking it off and flinging it into the waves.

"Issa?" Britta calls, running over to me and hesitating before rubbing small circles on my back.

I jolt upright, and she jumps away. I hold my hands in front of me and stare at them for a long moment. Cyrus slowly rises to his feet, eyes burning with—what is that?

*Fear?*

*Uncertainty?*

*Pity?*

"Cap?" Claudette asks, her voice wavering ever so slightly. When I don't answer, she says, "Nerissa?"

I look up at her and drop my hands to my side. "I, uh…"

Bec walks up to me, a sureness in her gaze. Her eyes are clear but guarded. "What do you need from us, Captain?" she asks.

I stand straighter and let out a slow breath.

Nine days left.

I *can* do this, but not alone. I can't trust myself, but I can trust my crew. Most of them.

I glance at the sea. "Cyrus and I need to consult the map," I say, but my voice is back to barely above a whisper.

His eyes meet mine, and he nods. I attempt a smile, and he does the same.

*Together.* I can do this—with help.

"May I have a word, Captain?" Bec asks.

I blink, turning to her. She stares squarely at me and gives me a tight smile.

"Of course," I say and motion for Britta to stay put and Bec to follow me to my cabin. Britta clenches her jaw like she is about to argue, but I stop her with a look.

When we're alone, Bec steps closer and doesn't hesitate. "You have a curse around your neck," she says, the tips of her fingers grazing my necklace. "I imagine it doesn't help with your…powers."

"You think this could make it worse?" Part of me hopes that's the case, but I can't blame the voice for all of it. I need to be more cognizant of my abilities, less willing to let my anger win.

"A mermaid's voice—her song—is not a gift," Becci says.

I clench my fist around the voice. It thrums with life beneath my touch, almost as if it has a heartbeat. For a moment, it's as if the song does sing to me, a song for me alone—the mermaid's song. A distant melody hums in my ears, but it's so light and fleeting, it whisps away as soon as I drop my hand.

"It's how I save my sister," I tell Bec.

She tilts her head to the side. "The voice of a mermaid is harmful. There are other ways to get to Brevlyra—"

"Then why has no one been able to reach it in nearly fifteen years?"

Bec clenches her fists, but she doesn't back down. "If we can't get there, maybe there's a reason."

My gaze cuts into her, but she doesn't even react, her eyes narrowing slightly. "I have to get to Brevlyra. I don't care if it's stupid. I'm going. You don't have to stay on board."

She flexes her fingers, letting loose a slow breath. "Listen, why do you think sirens are so fascinated by the creatures? It's not for their looks but their temperament. Mermaids are rare, and they are not like sirens. They do not seek trouble; they *naturally* create it. Sirens call their victims. Mermaids will eat whatever is in their path. They're like barracudas, relentless when they hunt. Sirens only want men—it's a trait of their species, a fact of their lore. Mermaids don't care, and their appetites are insatiable. Whoever holds their voice will soon be much the same to a mermaid, if you live that long."

"This thing is how I get what I need," I whisper, forcing her closer. "The way I save Lucia."

She nods, eyes hard and unconvinced. "You carry a curse with you, Captain Eliott. Don't be surprised when it comes calling."

She goes to leave, but I stop her. "How would you know?"

"How don't *you*?"

I squirm beneath the words. "I read—"

"Reading gets you only so far, Eliott," she says. "You have to experience some things before you can know what they're truly like."

I gulp, clenching my fist. "And you know what exactly?"

"When you take a mermaid's voice, she will stop at nothing to get it back, and now you've freed everyone—*everything*—on Siren's Cove. You're in even more danger. A siren's voice attracts her food, but a mermaid's voice says who she is—where *she* is in the food chain. You're lucky you made it back to the ship without her tearing you apart."

"This mermaid was imprisoned—behind bars."

She gives me a sad smile. "You think bars could hold back someone who rips off the limbs of sailors? Her imprisonment will drive her to find you. And she will. A mermaid always finishes her hunt."

# TWO
# YEARS
# AGO

# CHAPTER
# TWELVE
## NERISSA

***Two Years Ago, Island of Helene***

"You can't go, Father," I say—I don't plead. I don't tell him how much I need him here, how everything has fallen apart since Mother's death.

The servants bustle about, carrying unfamiliar furs for Father to wear the farther north he travels. The luxurious wools and fabrics the maids keep bringing in for his approval don't match the sleeveless tunic he's currently wearing, his peppered brown hair pulled back from his face. Father's traveling outside Easterly and into Montagnard, the queendom in the northeastern corner in the Empire of Penreine.

His drawn ship designs are spread out in front of him, stacks on stacks of parchment, the sharp, soothing tang of New Kingdom ink thick in the air. The sweet infusion of lavender and a mix of turmeric from the southern Mechelonian islands has always reminded me of my father. If he leaves, the tenuous structure we have in our family will fade as quickly as the scent.

I've grown used to him leaving for months at a time, but this is the first time since Mother's death. It's also possibly the worst time for him to join his men back on the seas.

He could have been a noble, but he gave up his title for my mother. We never speak of his family—he won't even tell us the name he abandoned. As one of the leading shipwrights in Penreine, all five kingdoms turn to him for their new ship designs. If we're related to any of his employers, I am none the wiser.

All Lucia and I know is he grew up on the edge of New Kingdom, running around the docks and watching his father's business ventures from the shadows. But running the trade routes didn't interest him—the mammoths that carried silks and delicate fabrics, furs from the north, and the strongest ropes from the south interested him. He wanted to build something to last.

"What could be more lasting than concrete relationships and a sturdy ship?" he used to say.

He has tried to build something to last with us, but we're nearing our expiration date. Mother tried to teach me to ignore my tie to the sea, but all the lessons she forced me to take left a lasting separation between Lucia and me.

Father looks up at me, his sun-weathered face tired. He paints on a smile, his eyes wrinkling at the edges. "This is my job—my passion. The Lady of Halivaris does not trust many outside her kingdom, and she pays handsomely. You know I must go."

Curiosity stirs in my belly. His gaze won't quite meet mine, so I ask. "Why do they call their queen a lady? Isn't she more than that? What sort of place doesn't respect their queen?"

"They call her their lady *because* they respect her. You're lucky, Issa. The man you pick one day will be your choice alone, but she was not as blessed. She is the Lady of Halivaris because that's where she's from, but she's the Queen of Montagnard—a crown she earned. But she will always be their lady. One day, her daughter will fight for the crown, but she will still be their lady."

My brow furrows, not quite sure I understand. "It sounds dangerous."

"It's one of the safest places in the five kingdoms for me." He shakes his head. "Issa," he says, my name an impatient sigh.

"Father—"

"Your mother would know what to say to you in this situation, even when I do not," he says hurriedly. "Your sister needs you here, and I need you to trust me."

"Mother is gone." A stab of guilt shoots through me at the look on his face. For the past year, he's mourned with his daughters, worn black, and had his second in command talk to customers. But now, the Lady of Halivaris—their queen—will settle for nothing but Father designing and building her ships. According to him, it's time for life to resume, even though we placed more than one soul in the grave.

He wraps his arms around me. "It's only a few months. I'll be back before you can worry about me too much." He smirks. "You and Lucia can handle yourselves. I even have Nathaniel Wood coming over to check on you both from time to time. He told me you're welcome to stop by his home any time if you need anything."

The hair rises on my neck at the mention of his name. I will *never* take anything from Nathaniel Wood. Lucia may be charmed by his good looks and grace, but I know better. He's a wicked sort of a fellow and not to be trusted.

"Father, Kip told me he would be happy to let us stay at his parents' home while you are away—or at least check in from time to time so someone other than the servants know we haven't killed each other."

He cracks a smile.

"You needn't involve Nathaniel."

He releases me. "Issa, I know you don't like the boy—"

"I don't trust him, and you shouldn't either. He's not good for Lucia. Kip would be a much better choice." The pain of the words doesn't cut as deep as it used to, but I still rub the spot between my ribs when Father isn't looking.

"*Christopher,*" he enunciates, using Kip's full name. "Would be a fine suitor for your sister, but Nathaniel has already caught her eye. Let these things happen as they may. I will not be the one to stop your sister from following her heart." He rolls up his designs and throws them in his bag, gearing up for his voyage.

"Did someone try to stop you and Mother? Is that why you gave up your title?"

His hands still, and I think he's not going to answer. "Your mother was all I could've dreamed of. I loved her with my whole being. I still do. I would've given up the world to have her in my life," he finally says, meeting my gaze. "And I know you two have had your fair share of disagreements—"

"Then think of what she would say," I blurt out. "She and I fought a lot, but I know she loved me. She would tell you it's too dangerous, and you know it."

I mourned my mother for a few months, but I will never miss her like Lucia does—and never like Father. The sharp sting of betrayal rises to my cheeks when his face hardens before settling into a sad smile.

He tucks an errant strand of hair behind my ears, resting a hand on my bare shoulder, gently squeezing. "Yes, she would. However, Queen Weylan is a powerful ally. What do they call her? The wolf? The queen earned her title, and I will give her the decency of my presence."

"But Nathaniel? He speaks as if kingdoms bow to his every whim." I scowl.

"Nerissa," he says. "You watch your tongue. He is the son of the Lord of Helene and deserves your respect."

Anger wells up inside me. "He treats his servants as if they are animals. He punishes them for looking at him the wrong way. He's forced himself on one or two of the maids—"

On me.

*"Get off me," I said in the darkened hallway of Lord Wood's estate. The party guests are drunk with happiness and stumbling with laughter.*

*Nathaniel leaned in closer, his hand sliding over the blue silk of my dress. "I've watched you, Nerissa—"*

*I dug my elbow into his side—hard—bringing up my leg as Kip taught me.*

*He hissed in pain, cursing me under his breath. "Who do you think you are? You're nothing but common scum. Your father was an idiot to give up his title for a girl. I'm giving you a way out—"*

*"Cake, my lord?" a timid maid asked, holding the tray out between us and the venom spewing from Nathaniel's mouth.*

*He knocked the tray out of her hands. White and pink iced treats skidded across the floor, and a dainty fork tinkled against the smooth marble before stopping on the edge of a rug.*

*"What's your problem, cretin?" he hissed. The girl flinched.*

*"Nathaniel," I snapped, and he came to, realizing his mistake. He snorted before pushing his way back into the main room, fixing his too tight tunic and flexing his arms for the next girl to fawn over.*

*I bent down to help the girl, taking a massive glob of cake off the floor and placing it with a hard splat on the tray. A laugh escaped me.*

*"Oh, miss—"*

*I waved her off. "He's an imbecile."*

*She nodded, the moment of brave defiance slithering away. I glanced over my shoulder and then back at her.*

*"Does he do that a lot?" I asked.*

*She didn't answer and instead said, "I must go, miss—"*

*I brushed her arm.*

*She stared at my light touch before meeting my gaze.*

*"Only to certain girls," she whispered quickly and rushed away before I could ask anything else.*

"Nerissa," Father says, his voice low and demanding this time. "I told you once, and I will tell you only once more. Hold your tongue. It is not proper."

"Who cares what is proper? He is not the kind of man our Lucia should marry."

Father massages the bridge of his nose before placing his hand on mine. "Nerissa, she loves you, and I know you love her. Promise me you'll protect her while I'm gone." I open my mouth to respond, but he squeezes my hand to silence me. "She needs you, even if she doesn't know it. Promise me?"

I nod, pulling my hand away. "I promise. I won't let anything happen to her."

"Are we interrupting?"

I close my eyes and curse under my breath.

*Nathaniel.*

I spin around, clenching my fist. The hair on the back of my neck stands on end, and I shoot him a glare. Father steps around me, holding a proffered hand for Nathaniel to shake.

My sister's obsession stands in the entryway of our house, Lucia's arm slipped in his. She's wearing a blush pink gown with dainty straps. It's unfamiliar—a gown from her beau. It hugs her body and cascades to the floor.

Nathaniel smiles at us, my candid statements sliding off his back. A scowl paints Lucia's face, though she doesn't acknowledge me. From the day she met Nathaniel, she was under his spell. His smooth talk and effortless words charmed her.

We live beyond town, behind an iron gate. The open halls and wooden arches of our family home welcome the island breeze and sound of the rushing sea from morning until night. While Father renounced his title, his success brought almost as much profit as remaining a noble would have. We live more than comfortably. She doesn't need Nathaniel, but she wants him.

Nathaniel had done it all, sparing no expense to blind my sister from the truth. His fancy dinners, warm nights, and long walks on the beach romanced her like no other boy on the island of Helene could afford.

His tricks were blatantly obvious to everyone.

Except Lucia.

*And apparently Father.*

"Issa and I were discussing what to have for dinner this evening as I packed my things for the trip. Would you like to join us?" Father asks.

Nathaniel smiles. It turns my stomach.

"I couldn't impose," he says, and I have to hold in a snort.

"He couldn't impose," I say. "You're leaving in the morning, Father. Shouldn't it be the three of us? Our family?"

"But you already invited Christopher." Lucia turns to me. "He told me so when I was in town. I didn't realize he was family," Lucia says. "I would love for you to stay, Nate." She clings tighter to his arm and turns an adoring gaze on him. "It would be the perfect way to celebrate our engagement."

"What?" I whisper. My cheeks burn, and my nails dig into my skin.

Father exclaims, "Engagement!" sounding as surprised as I am.

*Think with your heart, Nerissa,* says the voice in my head. My heart thunders loudly in my chest. *Speak with your mind. Mother isn't here.*

"Why so sudden?" I ask, interrupting Father's repeated words of congratulations and Lucia's story of how Nathaniel asked her to marry him. Father holds Lucia's ringed hand.

*Mother's ring.*

Lucia must have given it to him, or turned down his ring in favor of Mother's. I'm sure it *thrilled* him.

The gold band with a black pearl glitters from the sunlight streaming through the windows. My blood runs cold at the sight of it; the same vision brings tears to Father's eyes.

A sign of Nathaniel's successful manipulation—not his love. The look on his face says she's something to own, and the ring says, "forever." She is the one he chose. His muscles ripple as he tightens his hold on her.

Lucia glares at me, sending shards of icy disdain in my direction. A wave of sadness overcomes me at the thought of the girls we used to be, sisters who loved our father's bedtime stories. Her tone drips with venom as she says, "We're in love, Issa. Not that *you* would understand."

Her words sting, though not as much as they would have last year. She might have turned Kip down, but he would have been a better match—a perfect match, even if the pain of his rejection of *me* took months to heal. Lucia continues driving nails in her coffin when she could have had more than money or status. A marriage to Nathaniel means a life of pain, of knowing your husband is unfaithful but unable to say anything.

It's a life of silence.

"If you'll excuse me," I say. Emotion wells inside me, and I can no longer separate my anger from my heartbreak.

I storm past her and out the door. The door slams behindme, and I run down the stairs and across the cobblestone walkway, the closed gate soon within reach. The soft sea breeze and March air washes away the fire in my bones. I stop in front of the gate, closing my eyes and breathing in the peace of the day.

"Miss?" one of the servants says.

"Going for a walk," I say, pushing open the gate and heading toward the docks.

I fiddle with the light fabric of my dress as I step into town. A flock of seagulls flies overhead, angrily cawing as they soar above the ships. The one out front dives into the water as soon as the land ends. I, too, imaging diving beneath the waves myself and getting lost in their coolness against my skin. A silent scream builds in my chest, but I fear letting it out would allow the water to rush in.

Footsteps chase after me, and Lucia grabs my arm.

"What is wrong with you, Issa?" she asks, tugging her shawl around her. Her eyes flicker back and forth to the people milling around us.

"Me?" I have to pause to swallow the resentment rising in my throat. "I'm not the one with the problem, Lucia. Nathaniel can't be trusted. He's not kind to women—"

I stop myself. The last way to get her to listen to me is by embarrassing her. Already a few islanders glance our way. "I won't allow you to spread rumors about my fiancé," Lucia says, crossing her arms over her chest.

I clench my jaw reaching for her, but she retreats. "You deserve better, Lucia Beth," I say, using her childhood nickname. "You can do *better* than him."

"You know nothing, Nerissa. You don't understand what love is. You've never loved anyone but yourself. You hated Mother, and you're jealous of me. That's why you don't want me to marry Nathaniel."

Tears burn behind my eyes, but I force them down. "I don't know what love is?" I ask, walking up to her and lowering my voice. "You got everything you ever wanted. I did whatever Mother asked of me even when it destroyed who I was." The anger rises in me, and the sea behind me crashes harder against the waiting ships. I take a deep breath, closing my eyes. When I open them again, Lucia glances at the sea.

"Was?" Lucia demands. "What could you have been?"

In a low voice, I say, "When Mother passed, where were you when she took her last breath? I was *there*—when Father was away, and you were too selfish to think of anyone's pain but your own. I know love better than you do. Nathaniel doesn't love you—he tried to hurt me, Lucia! He tried to force himself on me—"

She jerks back, stunned. "He wouldn't—"

I take a tentative step toward her. "He did, and you don't deserve that."

She shakes her head, unwilling to accept the truth. "He wouldn't," she says. "He didn't."

Her eyes meet mine, pleading with me to renege on what I've said, to tell her it was a joke, no matter how twisted.

"*I* love you, Lucia. Father and I love you more than anything in this world. We want what's best for you, and Nathaniel can't give you the life you deserve."

Tears stream down Lucia's cheeks, and she angrily wipes them away with the back of her hand. "Why?" she whispers.

"What do you mean—"

"Why are you telling me this now?"

"I-I—because Nathaniel doesn't love you. He never will."

Her slap stings my cheek, but I don't stumble. I don't regret what I've said.

"You've had all this time to tell me," she says, the hurt flashing in her eyes and tears trailing down her cheeks. "Why?"

"I didn't think you'd—"

"By the Light, you didn't think I'd fall for him! Why didn't you tell me?"

I grit my teeth.

*Because we didn't speak.*

*Because I didn't want you to have another reason to hate me.*

*Because I couldn't.*

*Because I'm a coward.*

No reason is good enough, so I remain silent.

She clenches her fists, words coming slowly from her lips. "You could have told me over and over again, but you didn't, and now I love him."

She waits for me to respond, but I don't know what to say. I don't know if there is anything to say.

"I hate you," she whispers, turns around, and goes back home.

*I miss you,* I think, but the words remain unspoken.

# NOW

# CHAPTER THIRTEEN
### NERISSA

*Bheragus Sea*

I study the map late into the night. Cyrus paces in front of me. He finally takes a seat when a particularly strong bout of wind rattles the ship, causing him to stumble.

We share a look. My face burns as I focus back on the map, one hand absentmindedly petting the cat currently sleeping on my lap. I try to focus on the parchment and ink instead of the man in front of me; however, he's difficult to ignore. I peer through my lashes, studying the angle of his jaw and the curve at the base of his throat. He raises a brow, breaking me out of my reverie. Embarrassment rises from my toes to my nose.

Most of the crew sleeps below the ship. Bec steers, determined to keep a steady pace for the remainder of the journey. I agree, not because of her reasoning, but because of the quickly dwindling countdown.

"This Duncan fellow," I begin, breaking the silence.

"What about him?"

I roll my eyes. "Why are you insistent he stay onboard? What's so special about him?"

A fierce wind rocks the ship, halting his response. "Why him?" he asks when the roaring gale has ceased. "He's a Hillsman to his core, a Mechelonian in spirit. You won't find anyone better for your crew than Duncan. Family is more than blood, and Duncan is more than family." He glances over me, flashing a grin. "Plus, he's in love with my cousin."

A laugh bubbles in my chest, but it's quickly stanched a whisper in my mind. *Eighteen revolutions around the sun.* The words prickle against my skin as if whispered in my ear by the witch herself.

"We're going into uncharted territory, Eliott," Cyrus says, gazing out the window.

*Not uncharted,* I think. *Dangerous.*

He smirks. "It might not be uncharted, but it's labeled dangerous for a reason."

I jerk at his response. His blue eyes snap in my direction, piercing through me like the hook on the end of a line.

My mouth forms the question, but he shrugs, leaning in a little closer so his breath, crisp from chewed mint leaves and tangy from the orange slices sitting near his elbow, mingles with mine.

"Tell me," he says, voice tickling my skin. "Can you hear me, too?"

I close my eyes for a moment and take a deep breath. Cyrus's hand touches mine, and a spark ignites between us. My eyes snap open, and I gape at him. I wish I could hide the surprise shadowing my face.

*Desperation.*

"No, but I can...feel you," I say.

His emotions seep into my soul and settle in the pit of my stomach. It falls over me like a blanket and wraps me in a different kind of warmth, an almost uncomfortable heat. It isn't like my intrinsic need to save Lucia but something else. It tastes like brine and iron.

He looks away, taking his hand with him. It leaves my skin cold.

"Why can't I hear you?" I ask, my voice barely audible over the waves beating against the side of the ship. Cyrus's emotions darken, a storm cloud so severe it would sink even the strongest vessel. Fear grows in my gut at his silence. "Cyrus?"

"Possibly because this isn't the first connection I've had. You might be able to hear me over time."

"With Weylan? She could hear you?"

He shakes his head. "I learned to fight it, and sometimes it's difficult to let those walls down. Maybe in time." He turns away, studying the map. "Anyway, we don't know what those markings are," he tells me for the tenth time, jaw tightening. He leans back and points at the almost imperceptible smudges to our left. "It doesn't matter how fast you get to the kingdom if you can't make it past here."

"We can go around, leave the ship in safer waters while we go on Amasse," I whisper, drawing a line with my finger. My finger brushes against his hand, creating a small spark, but I shake it off. I yank my hand away and meet his gaze. "It still won't tell me what I need—something keeps flashing, almost like the shape of a blade. I don't know, though. It's not as clear as the voice. When it appeared on the map, I knew instantly. It spelled it out and everything."

"Who is supposed to finish this journey if you never come back from the island? Who's to say you won't be slain with that blade?" Cyrus asks, emotion coating his voice. Genuine curiosity paints his brow and settles in my chest, heavy and dense.

"Why does it matter?" I ask. "This is my quest. No one else needs to finish it."

Something I can't pinpoint flashes between his curiosity and desperation. It settles on my tongue like soured milk.

*Guilt?*

He clears his throat. "You're not invincible, Nerissa."

I shake my head and look away from him to stare at the pattern on the stained glass.

"If you don't get back to the ship, there will be no one to save your sister."

I look down at the parchment beneath my fingers and grit my teeth. "Why can you hear me?" I whisper.

His throat bobs as he swallows. "This isn't my first bond."

"Queen Weylan—"

"Had full access to my brain until I learned to block her," he says, and the dark emotions cause me to take a deep breath. "But I only get bits and pieces with you...you're stronger than I was at nine."

"Nine?"

"Weylan took me from my home when I was five. I'm lucky to last so long without her influence." He clears his throat. "I've lived in Teraceron since my mother's death."

"And before that?"

"The Hills. We couldn't go beyond Easterly. Weylan has too many friends."

"The bond with Weylan is broken," I say. I inhale slowly after answering my next question.

*Why are you here?*

The words never make it out of my mouth.

"There are some, myself included," he says, clearing his throat. "Who believe we—those of us from...Old Kingdom—are cursed. To break that curse, we have to go back. To go back to...."

"Brevlyra," I finish.

Cyrus leans in close. His breath warms my cheek. He nods. Does he know about me, what people say about the Eliotts on the Island of Helene? Everyone thinks we're cursed, too. My mother's death, my father's, and then Lucia's accident. They all held their breaths when I walked by. What would become of me? What horror would I face?

*I know a thing or two about curses*, I think. Cyrus's eyes shimmer with understanding. I've seen magic—know what it does to a family.

Have I only made things worse?

"Don't believe me, milady? Worse, you do, and wish you didn't?" Cyrus leans across the table. "Think you're the only one who knows what a curse looks like?"

Embarrassment floods my cheeks, and my gaze lands on the map once more.

"You're not the only sailor on this ship hoping to find something in Brevlyra—in the Old Kingdom. That's what you islanders call it, aye? The kingdom that could have been?" His words puncture my skin, and I spare him a glance. "You have to trust us, Becci and me," he says when our eyes meet.

We stare at each other for a long moment.

"Give me a reason," I whisper, and his shoulders stiffen.

"No one but you knows how I am—*was*—connected to the queen. She was the one who took me. She was barely sixteen when she usurped her father's throne. We were supposed to marry as soon as I turned twenty, the age of manhood in Teraceron. The first day of the new year, in case you're curious." It's Cyrus's turn to look away. He fidgets in his seat and studies the crew moving on deck while the crows fly overhead. "The House of Crow needs to return *home*. And not as the queen's betrothed."

*Home*. The word is bittersweet on my lips. My home used to be my father and my sister. Father is gone, and now my sister is lost. We're not little girls playing hide and seek at the beach anymore. She isn't hiding behind the dunes, and Father's not coming to collect us for dinner, though his voice still carries on the wind if I close my eyes.

"Brevlyra is my home," Cyrus says. "My father was the king before it fell. I was a baby when they executed him in front of my mother. Weylan's father killed mine, and now she's trying to kill me, if not physically, then mentally. We've gotten rid of the bond, but the race for Brevlyra is on. She cannot force me to rule beside her, and she cannot take what is rightfully mine."

"I'm so sorry, Cyrus," I say.

Cyrus smiles sadly, trapped in the memory. "I've always had Becci. Weylan is a monster, but at least she doesn't kill children."

A shiver runs down my spine.

"Anyway," he says. "I trusted you enough to hand over my ship and when I followed you on Siren's Bay. The least you can do is return the favor."

I get to my feet, and the cat who had climbed into my lap yowls in protest.

I brace my hand on the doorframe and peer out at the deck. The ship runs with a smooth efficiency, my eyes tracking the movements to slow the rapid beating of my heart.

"Milady…" Cyrus says slowly, wary. I don't turn around to face him, and I sense him come up behind me, the heat from his body mingling with my own. His arm brushes against my side. His muscles tense.

"Do you understand what awaits you in my wasteland of a kingdom?" he whispers. "I have no other option, Issa. I will have no peace—no freedom if I don't go. She will find a way to control me. But you—you can have whatever life you choose."

I turn, my throat and eyes burning. "Two years—I couldn't find Lucia for almost *two* years. The Darkness destroyed Brevlyra, right?"

"The crown in Teraceron destroyed my home. My people's saving grace was we had the Light on our side."

"Then the Light trapped the land and ran out the Teraceronian army," I whisper. "All of us know the stories of the three endless days of Light. No one has been able to step foot on the land since."

"Cursed or blessed. You pick," he responds, his gaze on something beyond my vision.

"What can the Darkness do to someone as powerful as a queen?"

"Then you know this is a suicide mission," he says, breathing the word. "Some tales say there is nothing left. Others think a world awaits. We don't know if it's a prisoner to the Darkness or protected by the Light. We won't until we get there."

"The Darkness," I explain, "has Lucia. This map says she's in Brevlyra. I'm going to get her."

Cyrus nods slowly, and I realize he's after the same thing.

"You seek freedom for yourself—and possibly your people," I say. Our eyes meet. In them I don't find the need to run. I glimpse a glimmer of hope. "When Lucia was offered a way to change her fate, she took it. I could have been there, but I wasn't. She turned to the only hope she knew. I should have been there. I'm going there now."

Things can't get much worse—

"Don't jeopardize the tenuous ground we're already standing on, Eliott," Cyrus says, laughing, a hand tangling in his messy locks.

I arch a brow.

He smirks, reaching forward and tucking a strand of hair behind my ear. "Don't ever say—or feel as if—things can't get worse on the sea—don't even think it," he says. "*That'll* be when they do."

# CHAPTER FOURTEEN
## CYRUS

*Bheragus Sea*

For the past two hours, I've embraced Nerissa's every emotion as they whisked through her while she reads. The soft sea breeze from the open doors catches loose strands of hair from her long, thick braid. She brushes them aside, and her irritation prickles my skin.

Issa looks up at me with eyes the color of fresh coffee. "What are you staring at?" she asks.

"That book," I reply. "It's probably the best one on this ship. An account written by someone from the north, an unbiased history. As unbiased as they can be; though, it's missing the most important thing."

Heat floods her cheeks. "What's it missing?" she asks.

"History books hardly tell the whole truth," I say, taking the book from her. I flip through the pages until I find the one I need. "Look."

"The Three Days War?" She looks up, brows knitted together. "Everyone knows about this."

I let out a low chuckle. "Do they? Do you know why the war started?"

She glances over the pages, flipping through them to catch what she missed. Her eyes lift slowly.

"Queen Weylan—she's augmented the truth. Left out pivotal points of information." My eyes go far off, memories darkening the color to almost black.

"All rulers do. The truth is she started it. She's left it out because she lost. Because she lost me."

"And because she lost you...she lost Brevlyra? Or her father did?"

I swallow the lump in my throat. "Yeah."

Nerissa pulls the book toward her. The spine crackles with the turn of the page. Her hands dance over the dark ink as her brow furrows in concentration.

"Thanks for telling me," she mumbles, biting on her bottom lip.

I pop a piece of orange into my mouth, the sharp tang flooding my tongue. "It's the best way to get you to trust me," I say.

She narrows her eyes. Her emotions wrestling inside her, acrid on my tongue.

I slide to the edge of my seat, the chair creaking against the boards. Issa eyes me, tapping her nails on the book. The quill shakes between the forefingers of the other hand.

"There's no need to be so nervous."

She stills, shooting me a scowl. "I'm not nervous."

I smirk. "You can trust me, and you don't know what to do about it. You wouldn't have let me be in here with you without Claudette if you didn't. Plus, I can sense you. Like you can sense me."

She looks down and rubs her eyes with the back of her hand, shaking her head sharply to chase away the sleep lingering on her face.

"We don't need to talk about this. The Siren Queen did something to us. Fine, but it doesn't have to be a whole—" She waves her hand between us. It tremors slightly. My own fingers itch to take it between my own, for the pulse at the base of her throat to beat in time with mine.

"A whole what?" I ask, popping another piece of orange in my mouth to stop myself from reaching over. Faux amusement lifts the corner of my mouth, slightly puckered as I take another bite of fruit.

Her eyelashes flutter, and she looks away. Uncertainty weighs heavily on her, and it forms a knot in my gut.

"Nothing." She swallows hard. "That's what it is. Nothing. Besides, you appear to know exactly what I'm thinking."

"You need rest," I say after a beat, fighting the urge to touch her once more. "I know you're not thinking straight."

*I'm* not thinking straight—not with her near. Knowing what I have to do—what Weylan has demanded I do—turns my stomach.

She shakes her head. Frustration rolls over her like the tide, threatening to pull both her and me with it. My shoulders tense. Her thoughts don't assault me, barely slipping through every now and again. My gaze drops to the voice around her neck. I know we need to get it off Nerissa's neck as soon as possible.

Her eyes are dark as they lock on mine.

"I'm not thinking straight?" She throws her hands up. "I don't have time to talk about *my* feelings, let alone *yours*. No time."

I place my hand over the page, my fingers brushing against hers. "You're no use to anyone if you're dead."

*You're going to have to kill her.*

I swallow the bile rising in my throat. Issa looks at me as soon as the emotions hit her, so I fight against them. She has enough weighing on her mind.

"Take the bed." I nod over my shoulder. "Half the crew is below in the hold, already claiming a room or a cot. You want them at their best, and they need you at yours."

Issa looks at me, eyes steady, before giving me a stiff nod. "If you insist. But get out. I need to change. Not that I don't trust you, but I'm not showing you any part of me hidden by these clothes."

The tease washes over me in a warm wave, and I'm not sure who feels what. My cheeks flush, and I raise my hands in surrender. "Understood, milady."

My cat, Piper, slips into the room before I shut the door.

"Traitor," I mumble.

Becci and Duncan take turns at the helm, and my cousin waves her arms wildly trying to catch my attention. Duncan slumbers behind her on a bed made of old blankets and a flattened pillow he must have stolen from one of the cabins below.

"Come up," she mouths, lips visible in the waxing moonlight, to not wake Duncan.

"You're doing fine without me," I call softly. "I'm going to..." I motion to the crow's nest, and Becci shrugs. She stares at me for a beat longer before turning back to the sea.

Besnick caws in the night, swirling around the mast until my feet land in the small space.

"Ouch," I say through a hiss as his talons dig into my shoulder. "Either I should wear thicker shirts, or you should get your talons trimmed."

Besnick caws in my face, tickling my chin with the end of his white-tipped wing.

"Okay, okay. My fault. I should have thicker shirts," I say, chuckling. "Weylan is coming for us, isn't she?" The bird's wings flap once, hitting me in the ear as if to say, *"I tried to warn you."*

"I'm going to have to kill her," I whisper, and my throat tightens at the thought—another girl's blood seeping between my fingers. I'm glad Issa can't read my thoughts. Dread washes over me, and I run my hands through my hair, tugging on the ends.

*You can try,* the bird whispers in my head.

I laugh, but it falls flat. "Yeah, I can try."

"It's here on the map. In black ink. His name, the man we need: the Acquisitioner," Nerissa says, voice a breath away from a whisper.

"It's not about him!" I argue. "It's about what he can give, and that isn't something we should take lightly. That—"

"Stop," she says. "The crew doesn't need to know what we need. Only that we're going to get it. Now. Are you coming or what?"

"Of course, I'm going with you," I say, clenching my fist to squelch the rising irritation.

*I have to keep one eye on you and one hand on my sword,* I think, grinding my teeth. If the mermaid is coming after her, then we might need more than a sword. Anxiety rolls in my chest at the idea, and I rub my fist against the tightness.

She glares at me like she's been doing it her entire life. "I don't need help or guards. But I will take the extra set of hands." She looks over my shoulder at Becci and Duncan. Her voice is low, almost lost at this point.

Duncan winks at her, and Becci rolls her eyes.

There's a tug in my chest whenever I look at Nerissa. How am I supposed to kill the one person strong enough to go up against the Darkness feasting in New Kingdom—*keels*, probably all of Penreine if I do what Weylan wants.

*It's the only way,* I tell myself. How I get my life back—taking hers.

*You care about her.* The voice hisses in my ear, sounding like Weylan at my shoulder, studying me as one of her victims writhes. *You care about her, and it'll kill you as much as it will breathe life into your lungs.*

"We won't get in your way," I say, voice thick. "Consider us insurance. If things go wrong fast, then you get to keep every appendage."

"Both eyes, too, and both eyes is best," says Duncan, pointing to his patch with a smirk.

Becci elbows him in the side. "Do you *know* when to keep your mouth shut?"

He smirks. "Not really."

"You better not slow me down," Nerissa says, never looking away from me.

"You act as if I could." My fingers brush her wrist. "No unnecessary risks, okay? We will get whatever it is you need on this island."

*Seas, what are you doing, you stupid newk?*

She recoils, quickly masking her confusion, and throws her hands in the air. "You once said I had no right to call myself a pirate because I wouldn't take risks, *my lord.*" she says, the formality in her tone mocking.

"There's taking a risk, and there's being an insufferable know-it-all!" I shout back, following her foot for foot. No matter what I do, I can't stay away. Like a compass, I'm the needle, and she's my north, always dragging me toward her.

"Great, now they're shouting," Becci mutters.

"Shut up, Becci," we say at the same time, though Nerissa shortens it to Bec. We look at each other in shock. A ghost of a grin tugs at the corner of Nerissa's lips, and I struggle to dampen my own.

"They got you, Bec," Duncan snorts. "Ouch!"

"Don't you start," Becci says, holding up her hand to hit his arm again.

"I understand more than you think," Nerissa says, eyes blazing.

*And I have to do this alone.* Her thoughts jam into me, filled with desperation and confusion, and I clench my jaw.

"Why won't you take a moment and let what you're asking sink in? Going on an island by yourself..." I whisper, letting my emotions roll over her. We're nearly nose to nose, my traitorous eyes stopping on her lips as they search her face. "Please, Issa."

Her shoulders sag, and she lets out a sigh. "I don't have time for this," she says, falling back into herself. "Especially with this noose around my neck. We have to go to this island. There's something waiting for us." Her voice is almost gone by the time she finishes speaking.

She absentmindedly traces the vial filled with the pearly voice of the mermaid.

"Fine. Lead the way." I pause, our gazes locking. "Captain."

part three

The Light that brings;
A Darkness that looms;
The hardness of heart even wise men choose.

Balance can't be found,
And weakness settles in.
Look toward the Light
Where goodness begins.

The shadows that hide,
What you must face and see
The Light and the Darkness,
Only one will flee
When faced the choice between goodness and harsh deed.

The truth you seek,
Only one knows the way
The Light be your anchor,
Hope,
The only true way.

— From "The Proverb of Hope" in The Chronicles of the Light

# TWO YEARS AGO

# CHAPTER
# FIFTEEN
### NERISSA

*Two Years Ago, Island of Helene*

I abandon Father's latest letter to answer the soft knock at my door.

"Lucia," I say, and she smiles timidly at me.

She holds up the tray in her hands, a plate of treats and two glasses balanced on either side. "I brought cookies," she says. "Your favorite, chocolate chip with caramel drizzle."

My heart soars in my chest, and I open the door wider to let her in. She sets the tray down on my desk over Father's letter.

"And milk," she adds. "Chilled but relatively fresh from Jennie."

I rush over and take the cookies off the tray and sit on the edge of my bed, patting the seat next to me. Her foot catches on the carpet, a splash of milk popping over the edge and running down her hand. I take the glass from her.

"Do you remember," she begins when we're both sitting on the bed, "when we used to sneak into the kitchens and steal dozens of cookies?"

A surprised laugh bubbles in my chest, and I take a gooey, chocolate-filled bite. "And remember the time Father caught us, six or seven cookies in, our faces covered in chocolate?" I ask.

"And we insisted," she says between gasps of laughter, "it wasn't us who stole the cookies. We *happened upon* them."

We struggle to keep our glasses of milk from spilling all over us as we burst into fits of laughter. Marybeth, my maid, rushes in at the sudden noise, and we wave her off, breathing so hard we can't form the words.

"My apologies, milady and Miss Lucia. If you need me, I'll be in my room," she says, but her words are buried beneath our laughter.

As soon as we control ourselves, we go for the cookies again. A groan passes over my lips as soon as the melted chocolate hits my tongue, and I lean into my sister. She takes a bite, and a sigh of pleasure escapes her.

"These are better than I remember," she says.

I laugh. "I think I had a few last week. Jalinda made them for me after..." My voice trails off. Jalinda, the cook, made them because I was so upset after the most recent fight between Lucia and me. "She knows I love these cookies. She even got some pink salt from Kip's bakery to add," I finish lamely.

Lucia nods, chewing slowly. "I bet those were good."

I nod, taking another bite so I don't have to come up with something else to say.

"Issa—" she starts at the same moment I say, "Lucia—"

We laugh awkwardly. "I'm sorry," Lucia and I say at the same time, laughing again.

"Me first," she says before I can say anything else. "I'm sorry for snapping at you the other day—any day, really. I know I haven't been the easiest to live with, especially since Mother died." Tears shine in her eyes. "I know you had a special relationship with her, and I've always been jealous of that."

"Lucia, we weren't trying to push you out." I want to tell her we were trying to protect her. I would have gladly given up my time with Mother. She wasn't teaching me anything. She was taking away who I was made to be, ripping away pieces of my soul, and all it did was breed resentment. I hated those lessons, taking the tonic, and Mother making sure my powers were properly stunted. She tried every emotion, anger, sadness, envy—anything to try and bring the sea to the surface. But then she would stifle it as soon as it rose.

When those lessons were done, she attempted to tame the *wildness* in me, replacing it with a lady. She coached and prodded until my bones ached with exhaustion. It came naturally to Lucia, but not me. While I loved our mother, I also felt a sick sense of relief every time she canceled one of our lessons, whether it was controlling the sea or controlling my unladylike tendencies.

However, the guilt still stings when I think about *why* she canceled, those days—she was too ill to get out of bed. Lucia isn't wrong: we had a *special* relationship, if special meant her screaming at me when I couldn't control myself or her disappointment when none of her coaching worked. I could never be the proper young lady she wanted.

Lucia looks down at her glass of milk, almost empty now. "I know," she says. "I shouldn't have taken it out on you, but now—" She stops, tears falling freely down her cheeks. "Now, I think about this wedding. Mother won't be here. And you and I can't even think about it without getting angry with one another."

My fingers graze her shoulder, and she leans into my touch. Tears burn in the back of my eyes, and I ache to tell her what I know she wants to hear, but I can't. I can't tell her I approve of Nathaniel, because I don't. He's not someone who deserves my sister, and lying to her would not be taking care of her like I promised Father I would.

"Lucia, I want what's best for you," I say. "I love you. You're my sister, and I want you to have the world." I wrap my arms tightly around her, but she struggles free.

"So, you've changed your mind, then?" she asks, wiping her tears.

I clench my jaw and swirl the milk in my glass. "Lucia—"

She jumps up, sitting her own glass on the table next to my bed, not waiting for my answer. "It's all I ask of you, Nerissa!" she says, voice strained, tears coming even more freely down her face. "I want you to stand up there beside me when I marry the man I love. You don't have to help me with the wedding. Light knows Nathaniel's mother and sisters are plenty of help since you refuse."

I flinch, but she doesn't stop. I place my glass on the ground and cross my arms over my chest.

"I want you up there to represent the women in our family," she argues.

"Lucia, I love you more than anything, but—"

"Don't!" she shouts before I can finish. "You should want to do this for me *because* you love me."

"I can't," I shout back. "*Because* I love you, and you deserve better than him, Lucia! You deserve the world. It might look like he can give it to you, but he can't."

She shakes her head. "You're just jealous," she whispers.

"Of that? How could anyone be jealous of *that*! He controls you, Lucia!"

"Every girl on the island wishes she had Nathaniel," she says.

"Every girl has had him," I say, and the pain in her eyes cuts deeply. "Lucia, I didn't—"

"Can you not be happy for me?" she asks before running out of my room.

I glance at the cookies still sitting on the plate and the remnants of milk waiting to be drunk.

*Go after her.* The words slip into my mind, but I push them aside. *No.* She needs this time alone, to think about what I said. A part of me doesn't want to confront this, not tonight—not again. An ache settles in my chest, but even when I try to apologize, it somehow turns into an argument.

I move the tray and pick up Father's letter. The cracked blue wax seal mirrors the impression on the ring he wears on his right pointer finger. I used to try to figure out the creature at its center, but it was damaged too badly. I flip the letter open, and tears threaten my vision at his familiar handwriting.

"Do you need anything else, miss?" Marybeth asks me, coming not long after Lucia stormed out. She gnaws on her bottom lips, cheeks flaming, feigning deafness to another argument with my sister.

"No, thank you," I say, turning around before the tears fall.

Pulling myself together, I read Father's letter by flickering firelight.

*My dearest daughter,* Father's letter begins, and the first tear splashes onto the page.

*Since I departed, I hope you and your sister have made amends. It isn't right for you not to have each other. I understand your frustration. Christopher is a dear friend, and when he hurts, you do, as well.*

*However, I must plead with you to consider your sister's heart. She loves
Nathaniel. I read your last correspondence and understand your unease.*

*If I know you, Issa, I know I have your attention for only so long before you grow
weary of my pleading. You are as strong-willed as your mother and twice as brave
as I am.*

*I hope to return soon. I had forgotten how beautiful the mountains are, rising
in shades of blue and purple in the distance. I wish you were here to see it. The
architecture is stunning and so different from the Isles. You would thrive here. I
miss you both terribly, but the Lady of Halivaris has been wonderfully accommo-
dating and even paying me over the guaranteed price to do some other work for
her. I almost wish I had brought you and Lucia with me—started anew.*

*Kiss your sister for me.*

*All my love,*

*Father*

I sit back on my pillows with a sigh. My arms ache from sword practice with
Kip after he closed the bakery, but my heart stings from the hollow hole left
by my father's absence. From his past letters, Halivaris sounds like a beautiful
place.

He hadn't been wrong in his letter: Mother would know what to say. She
would tell Lucia the positive and negative aspects of her relationship with
Nathaniel, whereas I focus on the bad. She would know what to say to me, to
calm me down. Even though my anger at her over my abilities is still a gaping
wound, she alone understood it. It's why we fought so regularly.

*"The two of you have a secret language,"* Lucia said. *"And no one else has the
ability to translate."*

I fall asleep with my father's words resting in my hands, the ink from the letter
staining my fingers. A sweltering heat against my skin yanks me awake.

"Nerissa!" Marybeth screeches, tugging me out of bed. Soot covers her face,
and her hair hangs sweaty and limp against her cheeks. Her gown is singed at
the edges, blue eyes shining with fear. "You have to hurry. Fire!" she shouts and
tugs me harder.

I stumble out of bed and slip on my shoes, but one snags on the carpet and falls back to the floor. My maid doesn't relent and drags me down the hall without it. Smoke fills my lungs, and I gasp for air.

"Lucia," I say between breaths. "Where's Lucia?"

"Sybil will get her. We have to *go.*"

We speed down the staircase and out the front door of our house. The flames lick the sky, the crackling pop of wood splintering the eerie silence as people congregate on the cobblestones. An earth-piercing scream cuts through the silence.

"Lucia!" I cry.

Marybeth holds me back. I fight free, running with one shoe down the walkway and back up the steps.

Before my fingers can wrap around the door handle, I'm snatched back and dragged down the walkway. Sparks tickle my cheeks, and a few men rush up the stairs and into the building. I gently touch my face, and my fingers come back wet with gray tears. Marybeth settles down next to me.

"Where is she, Marybeth?" I whisper.

"She'll be fine," she whispers back, biting her bottom lip and bruising my arm.

Suddenly, an older man from town rushes out of the house with my sister clutched in his arms. I scramble to my feet and run to her. The stench punches me in the gut. I touch her uninjured arm tentatively. She sobs, and the man holding her puts her slowly on the ground.

"She was in the library," he says, coughs wrecking his body. "I barely made it out before the shelves collapsed."

A shrill hiss of pain escapes her lips.

"Thank you," I whisper.

Marybeth hurries to place a blanket underneath her. Sybil pushes through the crowd and breaks out into sobs.

"I didn't think to look in the library, miss. She never goes in there. I looked everywhere else, but there." She presses her hand over her mouth, cutting short a sob. "I'm so sorry. I thought she must've been in your room. Mrs. Moore told me we had to go before the flames engulfed us. I should have looked in the library," she finishes.

"Sybil," I say, but it's unnecessary. Marybeth shushes Sybil with gentle coaxing and wraps her in her arms.

"Hush now," she whispers, her eyes meeting mine over Sybil's shoulder.

# NOW

# CHAPTER
# SIXTEEN
### NERISSA

*Island of Amasse*

Rocking in a small dinghy between midnight and dawn terrifies me—but I won't allow Cyrus to see what I know he can already feel. The sea reaches for me, and I can sense the voice's need to return to a different master.

Claudette slides into the boat next to me, squeezing between me and Cyrus. He insisted Bec join us, plus Duncan, who wouldn't leave Bec's side. Duncan sits less than an inch away from her, body humming with tension, his hand on his sword the entire time. His one good eye never stops watching the horizon, unless it's to glance in Bec's direction. If it came down to where his loyalties lie, even Cyrus wouldn't stand a chance against his cousin for Duncan's affection.

I tilt my head to study Duncan, and he copies the movement, smirking at me. My cheeks burn, and I look away.

I glance back at the ship and think of my cousin keeping it afloat while we are on the island. She didn't even wait for me to tell her this time.

She looked at me, nodded once, and walked away without another word. She and I got along as well as fire and flint when we met, but as soon as a spark ignited, it was difficult to be in the same room together. She and Lucia would have been the best of friends, and our relationship settles a sliver of the ache in my heart left behind by the absence of my sister.

Britta and I fight because we pull the best and worst out of each other. Cyrus made a good point when he suggested I choose another second. Choosing my cousin had been a comfort; she reminded me of Lucia, and I yearned for a sisterly connection again—even if it was strained in a similar way.

"Cap," Claudette says. "Why did we bring them?" Her eyes train on Duncan.

"I'm good with a harpoon, lass," Duncan says, tapping the deadly looking object tied to his back. "I've fought sirens, mermaids, and other beasts."

The boat glides across the waves, and the echoes of the night fall around us. Cyrus's fingers brush mine, and I snatch my hand away and grasp my seat. Bec eyes us curiously, balancing her dagger over her knuckles. Claudette leans forward and stares ahead.

"That sound..." she whispers.

Duncan turns his head in the direction of the noise coming from the island. I strain my ears to hear, closing my eyes and blocking the sounds of the waves around me.

*A story to tell, a soul to sell,*
*Where wishes call, and princes fall,*
*Come to the island where all must share*
*And if you dare*
*You might make it back to the water.*

"The island comes alive at night," Cyrus explains. "Or so I've heard."

We decided it was safer to travel under the cover of night and face whatever comes alive. The water starts to shift. Droplets of the sea splash against the side of the boat from a rogue wave a little farther out. I squint into the night. Suddenly, a hand shoots from the sea and grasps onto my forearm, pulling me from the boat and dragging me under.

Water burns its way up my nose. Fiery pain licks my eyes, and the current slaps against me the farther I'm tugged down. My mouth opens, and the water rushes in, but instead of choking, the water goes through me, filtering the oxygen into my lungs. Every muscle tenses, and I struggle against my captor. The burning in my eyes begins to lessen, and the darkness grows brighter.

The mermaid, whose voice I hold, hisses at me and digs her sharp, talon-like nails into my skin. My blood seeps into the water and obscures my vision. I press my heels into her stomach, and the bottom of my boots cut into her skin. The water swallows her screams as her purple blood blossoms around her and dilutes in the waves, swirling lavender around me. I turn, looking for the stars flickering in the sky and the shimmer of the moon. The mermaid drags me closer to the ocean floor, clawing at me as she does. The salt hisses into each new wound.

I kick as hard as I can, the blow landing in her face. She releases me, and I swim swiftly to the surface.

My eyes meet the icy blue gaze of Cyrus as he ducks half his body beneath the waves. His determination is strange juxtaposed with air bubbles slipping through his lips. I grab his arm with both hands and hold on tight, my fingers bruising his skin. Suddenly, I'm tugged in the other direction. My grip loosens, and I'm pulled another few inches. His muscles strain to keep hold, but with one fierce flick of her tail, I'm yanked away.

The loss of his touch, coupled with the mermaid's sudden tug, knocks the air from my chest, and I take in another lungful of water. I wince but focus on breaking free. Once I'm loose, she hisses, grabbing at where I was before darting toward me. She bares her teeth, and they elongate into sharp points.

I brace for impact, crushing my eyes shut. The resounding thud in my ears grows louder as the waves shift around me. Power coaxes up my arms, and I recall those stories Lucia despised.

Stories about *me*—about what I am.

I open my eyes to find the mermaid mere inches away, and I hold out my arms, willing the water to do the same thing it did on the cove. The force of the wave sends me back, throwing my legs over my head. Once I've stopped moving, I spin around to see the mermaid still catapulting through the water, twisting fin-over-head. My legs slice through the water, body yearning for the light of the moon. I break through the surface, the cool night air a shock to my skin. Air crashes into my lungs, and small black dots prickle the edge of my vision.

"Cyrus!" I cry, eyes scanning the dinghy.

"He went below for you!" Bec screams, pointing at the water. "He hasn't surfaced!"

Bec strips off her sword and prepares to jump in. Duncan clutches her arm, but she turns her wrathful gaze on him, yanking her arm from his grasp.

I hold out my hand, and a wave shields the boat from view. I go back under and search for Cyrus. He and the mermaid twist in the water, and I ride the wave I created. I yank him from her hold and swim to the surface as fast as my legs will allow. The dinghy rows closer, and as my hand reaches for the edge of the worn wood, the mermaid buries her claws in my leather boots, near my ankle.

My chest warms as power fills me, and I call upon a wave to toss Cyrus back into the boat.

I spin and face the mermaid, narrowing my eyes. The mermaid pulls back her lips in a snarl. The sea swells, an invisible cord yanking at my middle and connecting us. The dinghy moves back to safety with a flick of my wrist. She goes for my throat, and rage contorts her features. Her fingers wrap around my neck, and I dig my nails into her scaled hands. Black spots edge my vision. The waves swirl and create a wedge between us. Her grip loosens, and I push away, using the water and the power in my blood to propel me to the surface.

The mermaid's eyes narrow as she shoots like an arrow in my direction. There's a loud whoosh, and the harpoon lands in her chest with a thud. The water blooms lavender before a new wave drags her under.

The boat is a short swim away, and Bec grabs my arm and pulls me up. Coppery drool drips down my cheek, and I slump in the bottom of the boat.

"Cap," Claudette says. She won't meet my gaze.

"What is it?" I say, or try to, but my voice is completely gone.

"That was..." Bec whispers. I rub the back of my neck, unable to manage anything more than a stiff nod and a shrug of my shoulders.

We spend the short distance to shore in silence. I touch my throat, searching for an outward change, but there's nothing. A calloused hand brushes against the back of my neck, scaring the air from my lungs, and I grab Cyrus's wrist. He twists his hand, looping our fingers together. My heart races in my chest, and the steady cadence thunders in my ears. I focus on his touch, my heart slowing. His thumb rubs the spot on my wrist where the pulse begins to slow, and it threatens to speed back up. I wish I could tell Cyrus to keep his hands off me—but in truth, his touch comforts a gaping wound left in my chest by Kip's death.

But I can't depend on him like I did Kip. Cyrus is a pirate I barely know. Relying on him is as dangerous and deadly as the salt and sea singing in my veins.

"You could breathe under there, couldn't you?" he asks, the lapping waves trapping his words.

I grit my teeth.

Cyrus leans in closer, my hand looped through his. A strand of hair falls into his eyes, slipping from the maroon wrap.

"Be careful, Nerissa," he says. "If the man on this island realizes what you can do, he might not be so willing to let you leave."

# CHAPTER
# SEVENTEEN
## NERISSA

*Island of Amasse*

Unlike Siren's Cove, this island is flat, and the palm trees stand tall and sway around us, bending in the dawn breeze. My hand never waivers from my sword as I walk behind Cyrus with Claudette at my side. Duncan follows behind me with Bec next to him, almost as if they're finally accepting my position as captain.

I pull out the map to calm my rushing thoughts. It has shifted again, smaller and focused on the island. Five little dots cluster at the edge of the sand signifying us, a small trail leading to where we need to go.

"Follow me," I tell them, voice husky and low. In the silence of the island, though, it sounds louder than thunder.

We wade deeper into the island forest. My eyes stay trained on the map, struggling to see in the darkness, and something prickles at the back of my neck.

"I don't trust this," Cyrus mumbles under his breath at the same moment.

*Neither do I.*

Cyrus and I share a curious glance. Emotion overwhelms me, a sense of unease not my own. My breath catches in my throat when I realize it's Cyrus—his emotions.

I stumble, caught off guard by it, and he grabs my arm to steady me. Warmth travels over my skin, and I yank away from him.

We walk until the map stops, the moon lighting our path. The dots signifying Bec and Duncan hover behind us and around a small 'x.'

"This is it," I say.

We all look around.

"Is what?" Becci asks. "A scam?"

I purse my lips, looking closely at the parchment between my hands. "No," I say. "Let's, I don't know—maybe there's—"

"A hidden door?" Duncan says smirking.

I throw him a disgruntled look.

"It would not be the strangest thing, Hillsman," Claudette says, sweeping her foot across the ground.

We all do the same, some bending and brushing hands over the island debris.

"Got something," Cyrus says, voice echoing in the growing night. If it weren't for the clear skies and waxing moon, it would be impossible to see anything. My eyes struggle in the darkness, but his anxiety rushes through me, hot and fierce.

His fingers catch on something, and a smile crawls over his face. Adrenaline floods him, flowing off his body in a tidal wave and settling on my tongue. He stops and wipes away the debris to reveal a round trapdoor made of brass. Our eyes lock and my relief transforms into excitement. His nostrils flare, knuckles going white against the handle as he lifts it; the remaining brambles shift with a soft rustle of palms and sand.

We circle the opening and stare into the dark depths.

"Who wants to go first?" Duncan asks, laughing nervously.

"There's a ladder," Cyrus says, squinting into the darkness. His emotions go flat, and it leaves me dizzy. "I'll go first and call up when I'm down."

He doesn't wait for a response and begins the descent. An eternity later, he whistles, the sound echoing around the opening. My muscles relax, and I follow after him, the rough rope of the ladder digging into my palms as I struggle in the darkness for the next rung.

"Behind you," he says, and his hands wrap around my waist. The heat from his fingers cuts through my shirt and into my flesh. As soon as my feet hit the ground, I back away.

Something digs into my waist, and I fumble through the dark while the others climb down. My hand wraps around a handle, and I turn to face the door, my other hand sliding over the rough wood. I yank it open, and the creaking hinges echo around the small, dark space, punctured by a tentative light that appears.

The light illuminates Cyrus's features, catching his blue eyes and the scruff on his chin. "Lead the way, Captain," he says.

I step past him and into a tunnel made of rock and root. My heart thunders violently as I step across the rocks and water marking the path, breathing in the salt and sea—and something more familiar, almost like roses.

*"Oh, be serious, Issa," Lucia said to me. "It smells pretty."*

*Mother chuckled from her vanity as my sister and I sat on her and Father's bed, playing with the makeup brushes from New Kingdom Father bought during his last visit. I giggled, and Lucia tickled my nose with the end of one of the brushes.*

*"Please don't torture yourself like the Teraceronians, my love," Father joked and went to tell us about mouse skin and fake eyebrows as Lucia and I listened in rapt horror. Those on the island were either islander by blood or Mechelonians, and we didn't dress or mess with ourselves the same way those in New Kingdom did—destroying our natural beauty.*

*"You don't need the brushes to make you any more breathtaking than you already are," he whispered in Mother's ear, pecking her gently on the cheek. He didn't mean for us to hear.*

*Lucia sprayed the perfume in my face, causing me to cough. "It tastes like death!" I exclaimed, and Mother looked over at us with a smile.*

*"One day, darling, you'll learn men tend to like it."*

Roses still remind me of death. Mother never wore any heavy perfumes—except one. Mother's rare hugs wrapped me in rose and ocean breezes at sunset, as if she had her feet in two worlds—that of New Kingdom and that of ours. The aroma overwhelms my senses, and I inhale through clenched teeth to avoid it.

It's here now, on the island, though I can't see through the foliage. The trail closes around us, bringing it closer. There's something not right about this. It's too easy.

I understand why when we break into the light.

The cavern is larger than two of our homes on Helene. I can't believe we walked so far beneath the earth and a place of this magnitude waits beneath it. Moonlight hits small gems embedded in the cavern walls from an opening above. A glassy pool of water stands serene in the center. The moon's reflection blinks in and out of view by the circling clouds. Our breathing breaks the silence, accompanied by the *drip-drip* of condensation trailing down the walls. Duncan walks from the back of the crowd and stares at the water.

"Well?" he asks no one in particular. "What now? Are we supposed to jump in and hope for the best? What exactly do you think is *underneath* that water, aye?"

It's as if Lucia's laugh hangs in the air, asking the same thing.

*"What do you think lies beneath the waves, little sister?"*

My chest aches at the remembered smiles. We're closer than ever to finding her, but I've never felt so far.

I focus on the pool to try and stop the tears stinging behind my nose. Cyrus reaches into his pocket and tosses something into the water. As soon as the object makes contact, a snakehead the size of a mountain caps the surface. This beast isn't like the garden snakes our servants used to find from time to time in the flowerpots under the bottom story windows. *This* is a beast. Webbed claws brace the edge of the pool and land near Cyrus's feet. Its eyes are yellow and milky, the black slits in them wide in the dark. A tongue thicker than my arm slithers out of its mouth, tasting the air.

My heart thunders in my chest as we plaster ourselves against the wall. Someone's screams echo around the cavern as the beast crests the narrow ledge. Its scales flake and peel, almost as if there's another body beneath the one in front of us. Bec's breathing deepens, and her eyes go wild and bulbous. Cyrus's hand wraps around mine, and I glance at him.

"Blind," he mouths, chin jutting at the reptile. "Don't. Move."

A sharp slice of air cuts past my braid, its tongue flickering in and out of its mouth faster than my eyes can catch it. My back digs into the jagged rock of the cave wall. I gently touch Bec's hand to warn her, but it frightens her. She lets out a small squeak, and the beast unhinges its jaws, revealing razor-sharp teeth.

The air catches in my throat, and I grasp her hand. Bec glances at me, lashes fluttering. "Blind," I mouth.

She nods sharply and clenches her eyes shut as the beast comes closer. With each whip of its tongue, rocks cascade around us as it searches for its prey.

As fast as it appears, it disappears. Something flashes in the corner of my eye but vanishes as soon as the beast goes back under. Our heavy breathing fills the space.

"What was that?" she asks, voice trembling with anger and fear.

"I believe," Duncan says slowly, "that was a Leviathan, lass."

Claudette snorts. When I glance over at her, she's worrying her bottom lip between her teeth, hand gripping the harpoon at her waist. "Of course it is," she mumbles.

Amusement rolls off Cyrus.

"One of its kin," Cyrus says, voice not revealing his true emotion. "It's nothing compared to the real thing, trust me. It's looks young."

"Are you saying that is a *baby*?" Claudette says, accent thick.

Cyrus doesn't hold in his chuckle. "Exactly."

"And what are we supposed to do? Go down there?" Bec asks, snapping her head in the direction of her cousin as she rights herself. "Are you mad? Did you see that—that...thing?"

"There has to be a way," Cyrus says, noticing his hand still wrapped around mine.

I look around the cavern, trying to find something to tell us how to go down into the pool of water without ending up serpent food. If nothing disturbs the water, the monster stays under, but as soon as something messes with the surface, it rears up. Finding a way to go beneath the water without disturbing it would be impossible.

Unless we empty the pool.

I tug Cyrus's hand and whisper, "No water, no monster."

We share a knowing look, and he gives a tight nod.

I close my eyes and release a breath. My fingers begin to twitch, almost like the reverb from swords clashing—the sea beckoning me. I drown out all the sound around me and focus, dropping Cyrus's hand and searching for the sensation of magic traveling through the water.

*Nothing.*

*Keels.*

My eyes snap open, and I stare at the pool. It shimmers like melted silver, the same as before.

Cyrus studies me, but I shake my head. Frustration floods my core, and I fist my hands at my side.

"It must have to do with the magic controlling...it," Bec says, shuttering. "Beasts of that size can't live in a place like this. It's a protection of sorts. You want to get down there, you have to play by the rules of the island."

"Risky little *isler*," Duncan says. "What's his name again?"

I roll the word on my tongue before saying, "The Acquisitioner."

"You'd think this Acquisitioner would want to make trade easier," he replies.

"It's not about an easy trade," Claudette says.

*It's not about a simple bargain—it's about a trade of the heart and soul.*

I clear my throat, pushing the words through my teeth. "There has to be a map to show us how to get there. If not a map, something," I say.

Cyrus alone hears me. Our eyes lock, and my thoughts are acknowledged in his eyes.

"Look for something to empty the pool. The entrance to the Acquisitioner's lair needs a path. Without it, he wouldn't be able to barter and trade fine goods," he says.

Bec pauses for a moment before tugging Duncan in the opposite direction to look. Claudette studies the room, looking high and low for something we might have missed.

"It can't survive outside the water so young," Cyrus says. "It's already shedding its skin and can't see us. Without water, it will slink away to find a source."

My hands glide over the wall.

After the minutes pass with no one finding anything, Duncan says, "This is hopeless. Searching for an idea."

"Not helping," I croak, shooting him a glare over my shoulder.

He raises his hands in surrender, and I move to the edge of the pool. I move to the corner, searching for the flash of something I'd noticed earlier. I squint into the dark depths of the water. There, right beneath the surface, is...something. I can't tell what, but I *know* it's what we need. I tilt my head, trying another angle.

"What did you find?" Cyrus asks, his voice low and velvety beside my shoulder.

I daringly stretch my hand close to the water, pointing where some sort of—

"It looks like a—maybe, uh, maybe a shell or something? I can't tell what it is, but it's not rock or sand," I explain, my throat screaming with every forced word.

Duncan comes over and squats down, squinting in the direction of my outstretched hand.

"I knew you were ambitious, Captain Eliott," he says. "But going into the pool with a Leviathan is suicide." He shakes his head in disbelief.

"It's the only option we have," Cyrus says, lowering himself down next to me.

"This *Acquisitioner* made sure of it," Bec says as we stand and turn back toward the group.

"There is no other way," Claudette says, coming up behind me. "But, Cap—"

"It is the only way, Claudette," I interrupt.

Cyrus looks up at me. I sense the unease flooding through him, and it mirrors the apprehension settling in my bones. But as far as options go, we don't have any better to choose from.

"It's the only way," he repeats. "Got any ideas?"

I pick up a rock and toss it in the air once. Cyrus looks at me, understanding flooding his gaze.

Duncan groans, and Bec lets out a nervous laugh. Claudette glances nervously around us, mouth parting slightly like she's ready to argue.

"I don't like that look," Duncan says, shaking his head at Bec. "Never have liked that look, and I don't like it now. And it's on *her* face, too." He nods to me.

"It wasn't you I had in mind," Cyrus says, taking the rock from my hand and tossing it in the air—once, then twice. "When we're all ready?"

He waits for our group to nod before throwing the rock toward the uninterrupted surface.

The pool erupts, spraying every corner of the cave and soaking us all. The monster hisses hot seawater and saliva, thrashing limbs reaching for the walls through a salty shower. Cyrus helps me lower myself on the edge of the pool, and I reach for the shell against the wall.

With a terrifying scream, Claudette releases the harpoon. It lands in the rough hide of the Leviathan, and it lets out an ear-splitting screech. I lean as far down as I dare into the water, but my fingers barely brush the shell. I slide farther down. Cyrus grasps my weight as I shift precariously closer to the remaining liquid, the steep drop off cutting into my torso. His fingers and the jagged rock dig into my ribs and cause me to gasp for air.

"I've got you!" he yells.

At the sound, the Leviathan turns toward us. Duncan raises his sword and shouts in the direction of the beast. It whips its head around and opens its jaws to reveal its sharp teeth. It lunges at him, and Bec shrieks, raises her sword, and swipes at its forked tongue. It tosses her aside, and she hits the wall with a sickening thud before splashing into the water. Duncan throws aside his sword without a thought, diving in after Bec. Claudette grabs his fallen weapon and draws the beast's attention.

"Eliott, you have to reach that keeling shell!" Cyrus shouts.

Fear, metallic and strong, races down my body from his grip, pumping adrenaline into me. I slide farther, my hips digging into the ledge. Water splashes into my eyes, burning them with salt and whatever magic resists my call. I force my eyes to stay open against the pain and scrape my hand against the rock. Something gives way beneath my touch, and the ground quivers. Water rushes out of the pool in a thunderous exit as Duncan grabs on to the side of the pool with Bec plastered against his chest.

Claudette helps pull them out as the beast screeches and slithers after the water.

Cyrus holds on tightly to my waist, and the fear gives way to intense re-lief—both his and mine. He pulls me back up and loses his balance, toppling onto me. My breath rushes from my chest. A spark ignites where our bodies align. Cyrus pushes up on his hands and gazes down at me, his ruffled hair framing his face. The rolling in my stomach increases tenfold, and heat spreads from my core, burning from the spots his fingers recently caressed.

A glimmer of a grin pulls at the corner of his lips. I want to reach up and brush my fingers over them, to have his breath trace my skin. A blush rises in my cheeks.

*Please.*

The meaningless thought slams into me, but a yearning matching my own unfurls in my core before coming to an abrupt halt. Cyrus lets out a nervous cough before jumping up and out of my way.

Duncan smooths Bec's hair from around her face, tapping her cheeks lightly and mumbling under his breath. "Wake up, Bec. Wake up."

Suddenly, her whole body shudders, and she jerks upright, nearly colliding her forehead with Duncan's. She spews a stream of water onto his chest.

He doesn't notice and pulls her against him, brushing his hand through her hair.

"I...hate...snakes," she pants, leaning into his embrace.

"Technically, that was a Leviathan," Duncan says. "I think they're of the dragon species."

Bec shoots him a glare and feebly pushes herself to her feet. He lifts his hand to caress her cheek, and I look away. Cyrus does the same, and we stare at the emptied pool. Water droplets drip between the rocks, an eerie symphony.

"The rocks form steps," Cyrus says. "A bit of a drop down."

Claudette slings her harpoon back over her shoulder, a trail of blood dripping on her bare shoulder. "Who wants to go first?"

I move to the edge of the pool and brace myself for the descent. The rocks are slippery and I stumble, landing on my hip. A hiss of pain escapes my lips, but I dust myself off and look up at the others. I slide my sword out of its sheath and

hold it ready at my side. Cyrus follows close behind, but Duncan calls down
before we can go much farther.

"She can't make the jump, mates!" he says, helping Bec to her feet. The color
drains from her face, and she sucks in a harsh breath. "I think she and I should
head back."

Bec shakes her head, wiggling out of his grasp. "I'm fine," she says, catching
herself on the wall. "I can go with you."

"No," I say, but she glares at me.

"You're not my captain." Her voice trembles. "Some of the crew might have
accepted it, but when it comes to helping out my cousin, I'll only listen to him."

Cyrus shakes his head. "Becci, go back to the boat with Duncan."

"Claudette, help them," I interject.

"Aye, Cap," she replies.

"No—" Duncan begins, but Cyrus quickly cuts him off.

"I know you can do it without her," he says. "But please try working together.
We don't know what waits for us and might need to make a quick escape."

Becci looks ready to argue but finally acquiesces. "Be careful, Cy."

"Always am." He throws her a wink.

Duncan begins helping Bec back the way we came, Claudette on her other
side.

Cyrus breaks off from the group and joins me below. Our steps echo around
us as we make our way down the steps. A screech comes from the corner, and
my entire body stiffens.

For once, my dying voice means I don't have to think of something to say.
The cries of the young Leviathan chill me to the bone. A steady sadness comes
from the screams, a difficult tune to ignore, reminiscent of Lucia's cries after the
accident. I force the thoughts away and continue forward. Cyrus's presence is
a soothing balm in the bitter dark the farther we go. My fingertips glide against
the rock.

"It's getting colder." The words are passed from my mind to his, rather than
from my lips.

My teeth begin to chatter. I ache to turn back the way we came—even if a monster does wait at the end.

A beam of light from a lone candle pierces the dark, the flame flickering in a soft breeze brushing my cheeks when we're a few feet away.

As we step into the cave, I'm overcome by the beauty and sound of the fountain at the epicenter. We stop, the edge of the monument extending to the doorway like a pool. It stretches high into the ceiling of the cave, not leaving room for much else. Water glides down the front, cascading down a variety of colorful stones and gems. The glistening turrets fill the space with a steady stream of sound that drowns out our footsteps. Candles cover every rock surface, flickering in and out as trails of wax bead down to form claws, frozen in time.

"Beautiful," I mumble.

Cyrus breathes out, and his awe floats over me, matching my own. "Stunning."

"You've found the fountain," a voice, deep and rich yet as inky black as the darkness we left moments before, says. A chill dances down my spine, and I fight the urge to grab Cyrus's hand for comfort.

A man emerges from the doorway on the other side of the cave. He's wearing worn breeches and a weather beaten tunic. A long maroon jacket hangs over his shoulders and swings around his knees to complete the ensemble. The neck of his shirt stretches wide with each step to reveal trails of tattoos across his skin. They dance over his frame and create moving pictures up to his hairline. His close-cropped white hair is slicked back on his head, the look almost as sharp as the blade at his side. It doesn't compare to the smile curling over his lips.

"It takes a certain person—*people*—to find this place," the man continues. His eyes land on each candle before settling on the fountain in the center of the room. "The prize of my collection."

"We've come to trade," Cyrus says.

The man holds up his hand. "Don't tread on the water unless you are willing to pay the price."

Cyrus stops with his foot hovering in the air.

The man walks barefoot in the water. It splashes his ankles and shins, spraying the mist on his clothes.

"What is it you seek?"

His eyes settle on me. My hand instinctively grasps at my throat, and the man's lips curl into a smile.

*"Mermaid got your tongue?"* he asks, the words wrapping around my thoughts. *"The map sent you for the sword—a Light-blessed blade."*

I glare at him, holding back my surprise.

A sword. We have gone through this for a *sword*.

*"Ah, Lass, this is a sword like no other. This sword allows you to defeat the Darkness holding your sister. It is Light-blessed, and only a true heart can wield such a weapon. A weapon that does not even harm its owner."*

There's a hint of laughter in his tone, and I clench my teeth, fearing they might crack. My voice remains locked in my head, truly gone unless I give him the voice burning at my throat.

"What are you doing to her?" Anger paints Cyrus's tone. He grabs my arm and cups my face in his hands. "Issa," he whispers, eyes racing over my face. "Are you all right?"

"She's fine, Captain Crow," the Acquisitioner says. "An easy fix."

The necklace rips away from my throat and sharp pain slices on the sides of my neck. The pressure releases, and a cry falls from my lips as I gasp.

"Eliott?" Cyrus says, brushing back my hair with his fingers.

"I'm...fine," I say, turning back to the Acquisitioner.

"Now, about that trade," the man says, dangling the necklace between his fingers. "The price is high. It's higher than some people are willing to pay."

"The voice isn't enough?" Even with my freedom, the words are scarcely above a whisper.

The candlelight flickers in response.

He tilts his head toward me. "Captain Eliott. You are everything I expected you to be—even more. The light in your eyes, milady, you could bring down entire regimes, but you use your power...for what? A hopeless quest to save someone who doesn't *want* to be saved?"

I look at him, clenching my fist. I promised Father I would protect her. I take a step forward, letting the water cover my boots. "You underestimate what I'm willing to do for a sliver of hope."

# CHAPTER
# EIGHTEEN
CYRUS

*Island of Amasse*

The Acquisitioner dangles the mermaid voice between them. It swings back and forth like a pendulum on its leather chain, and Nerissa's eyes follow each sway.

"Quite the determined one. I must know: how did you acquire such an item?" the Acquisitioner asks, his voice sliding over my skin.

I reach for her, but a voice in my head stops me.

*What are you doing?*

I've been asked to end her—no, ordered to *kill* her. Nerissa constantly puts herself in harm's way, and yet I can't stop myself from wanting to reach out and save her. My orders might have been clear, but some part of me, the deepest part, can't carry out the simple command. I may no longer be bonded to Weylan, but every inch of me screams she is tailing us.

And if I don't finish the job, I'll end up dead, too.

Either way, someone dies.

I shake the thought away and study Issa—the way she moves, how her chest rises and falls with each breath. The steady beat of her body slowly moving farther away with each step, taking a part of me with her. The tether between us pulls taut, begging me to step in front of Issa, separating her and this monster disguised as a man. My hand tightens into a fist as the Acquistioner's eyes meet mine, his lips quirking in amusement.

*Stop it, Crow. Remember your place.*

Nerissa looks up at the man in front of her. "The Siren Queen," she says in answer to his question.

"Ah," he responds, his brow arching.

"I need that sword." She stands impossibly taller. "The map told me I need it."

"*Liehtan* is a particular beast," he says, running a finger near to her cheek. "However, it's why you had to come here in the first place. Tell me. Did a piece of you die when you lost her?"

"My sister...she gave herself over to the Darkness," she whispers.

The Acquisitioner isn't wrong—*Liehtan* is fabled to have killed every person who wished to acquire its power. Forged in the darkest part of the sea, in the Kingdom of Ecbarhot in the Northwestern part of Penreine, to bring Light in the Darkness, when all hope appears to be lost. Pride blooms in my gut—this is the girl who has fought against storms and sirens to get to her sister. She raises her chin, her hands loose at her side, with her feet set apart like she's ready to spring into action.

She's the truest heart I have ever met.

The Acquisitioner's eyes slowly meet mine, and he nods once.

*What she seeks is possible, young king,* he says, voice like silk in my mind.

I flinch.

*Are you going to give her enough time to reach it? The whole picture isn't clear yet. Can you see it?* he asks before turning back to Nerissa.

"You can't return so easily from the Darkness. Why would a rich shipwright's daughter give herself up to Death himself?" the Acquisitioner questions aloud. He walks around her, and she turns with him.

"She didn't see any other way," Nerissa replies, her lips pulled taut, though her voice seesaws with each word.

"Hm," the Acquisitioner says, his back to me. "Pray tell, why didn't *you* help her?"

Nerissa flinches. "I thought—"

"You thought the accident was what she needed," he finishes. "You assumed she would come to the same conclusions you had months—maybe even so much as a year—before. She didn't, however. Your sister was weak."

"She has never been weak," she snaps. Her eyes burn brightly in the low light.

He walks up to her, leaning over and whispering loudly enough that it echoes around the room. "And yet, you are here, and she has succumbed to the Darkness."

"Enough," Nerissa hisses, clenching her eyes shut. "Are we going to play games, or are we going to trade?"

He laughs, lifting a strand of hair off her shoulder and rubbing it between his fingers. "You mess with things you do not understand, girl. It's a little obnoxious."

Nerissa's eyes flash open, and she steadies her glare on the Acquisitioner. "I am no girl. I am a captain and a sister. I am a daughter of the sea—a daughter of the Light. I am going to get my sister back. I have to."

He snaps his fingers, and the voice disappears. Clasping his hands behind his back, he stares down at her. "I will help. But for *Liehtan*, you will have to offer me something a little more."

"You have no right—" I begin to say.

Nerissa whips around, her glare stinging against my skin. The Acquisitioner smiles. I clench my fist, nails digging into my skin and threatening to draw blood.

"I have every right. You came to me," the Acquisitioner snaps before turning back to Nerissa.

Her eyes flicker toward me.

*Don't do this, Nerissa.*

She looks away, but I know she felt my discomfort, my warning. "What do you want?" she asks.

The Acquisitioner smiles. "Simple: a memory," he says. His lips curl into an innocent grin, but it doesn't match the hunger in his gaze.

"Nerissa—" I say, trying to step forward but finding I am frozen to the spot. "We can find another way—"

"The map is the only way." She takes a step, and that tie between us snaps whatever magic holds me in place. The Acquisitioner laughs, and somewhere in my head he finds the shocking truth—I'm falling for the girl I've been sent to kill. The dynamic between us shifts, shock filtering off his body as the chuckle dies on his lips.

"Well, well," he says, but I ignore it as I close the distance to Issa.

Water seeps into my shoes.

My fear rushes off of me in waves, ebbing only with her touch. "*Liehtan* can save Lucia."

I inhale slowly, and she nods. "Why are you afraid for me, Cyrus?"

"He's afraid for himself, lass—"

I cut the man off by pressing my hands against her ears and her forehead to mine.

The words flow from my mind and into hers.

*Forged in flame and bitterness blue,*
*The sharper the blade, the aim more true.*
*A heart that is pure, a blessing posed to last,*
*Few souls are up to the task.*

Liehtan *by name, but cursed by mistake*
*The greater the risk one must take.*
*But Darkness shall fall and Light reign supreme,*
*Unless the hands on the pommel are unworthy, he or she must concede.*

Her eyelashes flutter against her cheeks, and she places her hands on my wrists. *Is my heart strong enough?*

I press my lips to her head, flooding her with the truth in my emotions. *Yes.*

She swallows hard and steps away. "This is my bargain to make, Crow," she says, before nodding to the Acquisitioner. "I will give you a memory."

"Excellent," the Acquisitioner says. "It is most uncomfortable. I'm taking a part of you. As soon as the memory is mine, you will experience phantom pain, but you won't remember why. Memories are a strange thing. They are what makes us who we are—who we become. Are you sure you want to continue?"

"Nerissa—" I start, taking a step forward. *Let me do this,* I think, but she doesn't react. I need to do this for her, but her determination is bitter on my tongue. There isn't any way I can convince her otherwise, even if there are memories I would gladly trade.

*Look at me,* I plead inwardly.

But she won't, even when she flinches.

"I'm sure," she says.

His hand hovers in front of her forehead, and a beam of blue light circles around her. She cries out, her head jerking back as the memory flies around her. Suddenly, a sharp pain shoots through me, and I fall to my knees. The memory the Acquisitioner reaches for envelops my mind.

*Nerissa was twelve or thirteen years old. Her hair fell in a long braid down her back. She ran in front of her parents through the market, and a woman, nearly identical to her except for a pair of blue eyes, called out, "Nerissa!"*

*The woman wore a cerulean gown of soft satin, her shoulders bare except for delicately draped pieces around her arms.*

*"Issa, slow down!" her mother chided.*

*Nerissa halted in the middle of the street, the bottom of her orange dress already covered in dust, the white slippers a lost cause. A rainbow of beads hooked the dress around her neck and fell across her collarbone. When she looked in the mirror that morning, she felt as if she were staring into the sun. Now, her joyful countenance fell, and she turned to look at the woman. Her mother tapped the bottom of Issa's chin with two fingers, and she raised her head higher, plastering on a forced smile.*

*"Lucia, catch up with your sister," her father said, patting the arm of the girl next to him.*

*"A lady does not run," the girl—Lucia—replied.*

*A calming wave fluttered in Nerissa's heart at the sight of her family. Their nanny, an older woman, trailed behind them.*

*"I'm so glad we're all here together," she said. "I can't help my excitement!"*

*Lucia smiled, her hair two shades darker than her sister's, but her eyes the same shade as their mother's.*

"*Market day is Issa's favorite day, Mother,*" *Lucia said, flattening the folds of her yellow dress. Her voice rang like the tinkling of bells.* "*It has nothing to do with us.*"

*Nerissa looked up at her mother, tugging on the end of her braid.*

I wish I could run away, *she thought.* But she'd find me, or someone would tell. I wonder if the bookshop...

*No, it was too difficult to hide when she was a mirror image of Mother.*

At least I have Father's eyes, *she thought.* If people only looked at my eyes, I might have a moment of peace.

"*Nanny?*" *she asked in a low whisper, turning to the older woman.* "*Did you bring a scarf?*"

"*In this weather, Issa?*" *Lucia asked with a laugh.*

*Their eyes met. Lucia's eyes, no matter how warm her smile, were distant. They had been recently, ever since Mother increased her time with Nerissa, taking her places Lucia couldn't go. If only Lucia understood why—that Mother was taking part of Nerissa, distancing her from the sea and teaching her the proper way to be a lady.*

Ladies listen, Nerissa.

Ladies do not speak when not spoken to.

Ladies do not show emotion.

*Now, instead of finishing Nerissa's sentences, Lucia would stop and think, mouth open. Nerissa would catch Lucia whispering to Mother later in the day, and confusion would overwhelm her. She and her sister never kept secrets before.*

*But that was before.*

"Your sister cannot know," *Mother told her.* "She will not understand. This," *she motioned between the two of them,* "is something between us."

*Today was market day, and Nerissa wasn't going to let her sister's mood deflate her.*

"*I promised Kip I would meet him after we explored the market,*" *Nerissa said, ignoring the question.*

*Nanny tucked a strand of blonde hair pierced with gray behind her ear, laughing, and said,* "*Child, you've got to leave him wondering. Keep him guessing!*"

*Nerissa walked up to her and linked their arms, leaning her head on Nanny's shoulder. "The heart cannot stop beating in the direction it chooses," she said to her. Lucia ran up and giggled, taking Nanny's free arm in hers and smiling at her sister. For a moment, she was the sister she knew not too long ago. "Kip is a silly merchant's son, Issa. Why do you love him as if he were a lord?"*

*"Why do you think of him as less than the gentleman he is?" Nerissa asked. "He's not merely a merchant's son. His father owns half the island!"*

*"You are trouble, little sister," Lucia said. "And you act too old for your age."*

*Nerissa raised her head high. "I can love whom I choose. Father doesn't mind," she replied, throwing a smile over her shoulder at her father, who studied the fruits and vegetables her mother selected. He didn't catch her eye, but her mother did.*

*Nerissa looked away, her cheeks burning with indignation. "Besides, we're not from New Kingdom like Mother and Father! So I choose Kip."*

*"Christopher," Lucia insisted, "is awkward and doesn't even pay attention to us."*

*Issa shrugged, not bothered by the correction. "He has to pay attention to* one *of* us."

*The market day swirled around them, and they begged their parents to let them stay with Nanny, even after their parents were ready to leave. The sun dipped low on the horizon, and Nerissa still hadn't been to the bakery. Nanny was tired, and Lucia had already walked into what she said would be their last shop. The older woman grasped Nerissa's arm, stopping her from making her escape.*

*"The best bread is in the morning, Issa," she mumbled to Nerissa, who barely spared her a glance.*

*"We can buy one loaf and come back for more tomorrow?" she asked. "His father lets him take a break before they close the shop at a quarter until five. Please?"*

*Nanny nodded. "All right, but don't you dare complain tomorrow about stale bread."*

*She kissed her cheek. "Not a peep."*

*"We can at least eat a slice on the way back," Nanny said, holding back a grin.*

*"Whatever you think is best," Nerissa said, already starting to walk away. "I...think I will go visit with Kip."*

*"Very well," Nanny said with a wave of her hand.*

*Nerissa stopped herself from running to the back of the shop and slid her hand between the curtained doorway. She lifted it enough to slide through as the sunlight pierced the windows. Intricate shadows danced on the doughs and bread rising and setting on the tables.*

*The Browns owned many shops on the island, but their eldest son worked in the bakery more than any other shop. Her heart raced, thinking back to Kip describing how to make bread, a simple task but one he loved. He wasn't like the other boys. Sure, he was decent with a sword, but he much preferred his hands covered in flour rather than blood. Nerissa breathed in the scent of first love and freshly baked bread, and a thrill traveled through her.*

*Voices whispered from farther back, and she walked on the soft sides of her shoes so as not to disturb any of the other workers shifting things around the bakery. The voices got louder, and she stepped around the doorway that led to the alley between the bakery and a dress shop. Nerissa stopped dead.*

*"Mr. Brown—Christopher—" Lucia said.*

*"You can call me Kip," he said, looking at her sister. His cheeks flushed red, and Lucia's hands fiddled with something.*

*"Mr. Brown," she said. "It is beautiful, but I cannot take this."*

*She slipped something into his hand, and Nerissa's stomach wrapped around her spine. She couldn't force herself to look away. She knew Kip was fourteen years old, like Lucia, but he hadn't ever paid attention to her either. When they came to the bakery with Nanny, he always smiled in their direction.*

*She had always assumed he was smiling at her.*

*"It does not mean a thing, Miss Eliott. It's a gift, nothing more," he said, clearing his throat. "I made it in my free time. I have earned an apprenticeship with a carpenter on the island. I will work on many of the new residences on the island, some of the businesses as well. In a few years' time, I will manage many of my father's establishments. Hopefully, by the time I'm eighteen, I'll be his partner."*

*He peered at her through his eyelashes, and Nerissa felt the beginning of tears stinging her eyes.*

*"Mr. Brown—"* Lucia started, but he wouldn't let her finish whatever it was she wanted to say.

*"Take it, please. It doesn't mean a thing,"* Kip said, wrapping his hand around hers.

She nodded. *"I have to go find my sister,"* she said, her voice breaking on the last word.

Nerissa rushed back out of the room and into the main bakery. Her heart lodged in her throat, and her blood ran cold.

*"Nerissa?"* Nanny called, waiting outside with a now-full basket. *"Nerissa, what's wrong?"*

The fading day shone brightly around her. She took a deep breath and let it out, a few tears forcing a trail down her cheeks.

*"Nerissa?"* Nanny asked. *"What is the matter, sweet child?"*

Though taller than the woman already, she felt small next to her for a moment.

*"Nothing,"* she said. *"I'm fine."*

*"Did you speak with Mr. Brown?"* she asked.

She shook her head. *"He was occupied,"* she mumbled, the words as hollow as her chest.

*"Have you seen your sister? I don't know where she went. I know you girls are outgrowing me, but I still cannot help but worry."* She patted Nerissa's arm and opened her basket. *"Look, cinnamon rolls."*

*"Are we ready?"* Lucia asked, walking out from the shop and smiling. She hid her hands in the pocket of her dress.

*"What do you have, Lucia?"* Nerissa asked pointedly.

Why did you ask? What's wrong with you, Issa? *she screamed inwardly.*

Her sister glanced down at her pocket as if she forgot she was fiddling with the item the whole time, wishing it would disappear. *"Nothing."* Her hand slid out, and she smiled at her sister. *"Did you buy cinnamon rolls?."*

My lungs plead for air, coming out of the memory in an instant.

Nerissa is on her knees in front of the Acquisitioner. Her head rests in her hands, and sobs shake her body.

"What did you do to her?" I yell, reaching for him, but an invisible force pushes me back.

"Nothing she didn't agree to," the Acquisitioner replies with a wicked grin, looking down at Nerissa—*Issa*—for a moment before walking over to the fountain and reaching in. Her despair roots in my core. I can't tell which emotion belongs to her and which belongs to me anymore.

The Acquisitioner pulls a sword from the fountain. It blinks in the candlelight, the metal dripping water back into a puddle. He goes back over to Issa and sets it across her lap.

"The payment for a piece of ourselves is never cheap."

Issa's hands fall from her face. She wraps her fingers around the blade's pommel and holds it up in the light. He daringly brushes the bottom of her chin but snatches his fingers away when a spark of light catches his skin.

He studies her, his eyes glinting with...*respect.* "The person in that memory was gone years ago, and now you don't even remember her. Be careful how you speak of who you will become. She might surprise you." He leans in and whispers something in her ear. Her shoulders tighten.

"I'm prepared," she says.

"Do not speak of the person you don't yet know," he tells her. "For the person you were yesterday is already gone."

Her cheeks are flushed red, trails of tears sliding down her neck, eyes almost unseeing.

Suddenly, the ground begins to shake.

# CHAPTER NINETEEN
### NERISSA

*Island of Amasse*

My chest aches. The pain seizes me and wraps its gnarled fingers around my middle—the memory is gone, but the pain sears me to the core. My eyes blur with tears, and I reach out—for something.

Someone.

With the sword *Liehtan* in my hand, everything is clear. I know what I have to do and where I have to go to find Lucia. *Never trust a pirate, Miss Eliott,* the Acquisitioner had whispered in my ear. *A gift from me. If you don't know what treasure your companions are truly after, they have something to hide.*

Cyrus let me take his ship.

*Why?*

The water begins to cascade around me, splashing onto my shins, and I realize the Acquisitioner is gone. Cyrus's and my eyes lock as the walls begin to cave in, and he reaches for me at the same moment I throw out my hand. Water from the fountain breaks free and snatches his hand, listening to my call to pull him to safety. I follow after him, letting the water carry us toward the ceiling of the cave. I can sense the sea flowing through me like the blood under my skin.

We rush quickly on the waves through endless tunnels, and I'm not sure anymore if I'm controlling them or if they're controlling me. The hollowness in my chest fights against the power surging through me. I push it down and focus on the rushing sensation beginning at the tip of my fingers that spreads the longer I hold on.

We speed through the last bend, and the waves launch us into a pool of water—the pool which we entered through. My eyes don't sting against the salty spray, but I find Cyrus, eyes clenched shut, struggling to find me past the rush of the current. I throw myself in his direction, realizing the breath I took when we went under has yet to start burning in my chest. I am who I was when I started this journey, but I'm also someone new—someone I haven't fully met yet. The sea and I have made some sort of agreement, melding into one being.

I gave up a memory and got *Liehtan*.

But I don't remember the part of myself I abandoned. Whatever it was, the sea makes up for it. Something about the loss of the memory—whatever it was I forgot—tugs me closer to my powers.

My fingers wrap around his wrist, dragging him with me as we shoot for the surface. We hit the air, and Cyrus gasps for breath.

I look around, my feet treading water. "Do you know which way to go?" I ask.

He sweeps his hair off his forehead and glances around the cave. Suddenly, he looks down and shouts, "Is—" before he vanishes beneath the water.

I dive after him. Beneath the waves, the child Leviathan holds him between its webbed claws and screeches. The sound echoes in my head. I cover one ear and fumble for *Liehtan* with my free hand. I grasp the hilt and strike the chains holding the beast to the cavern wall. I refuse to let this monster remain chained, connecting to it like I am connecting to the waves around us.

The beast releases Cyrus, and he appears beside me, tugging at my arm. I shake my head and hit the bindings harder. Cyrus scrambles to my side and folds his calloused hands over mine. He shifts the blade, and together, we press the tip of the sword into the space where the chain meets the rock wall. We yank the blade down, and the rock begins to crumble. Within a few seconds, the chain breaks free from the wall, dust and debris polluting the water.

There's a loud screech, and we both tense, sliding as far away from the sound as we can until the debris settles. We swim as fast as we can in the direction Cyrus had been trying to take me earlier, expecting at any moment for the beast to wrap around our ankles and pull us back under. We break through the narrow tunnel into a small pool above ground, and the stars blink in greeting.

I swim until my boots scrape against the rock bed.

"You are completely insane," Cyrus says, gasping for air as he stands. He sloshes through the water and lands in a heap on the ground, propping his arms on his knees. Cyrus shakes out his soaked locks with a disbelieving grin. "We rode a wave out of the cave."

Our eyes meet, but he breaks the look and gazes up at the sky.

"It'll be morning soon," he changes the subject. I hold my hand out for him. I expect some sort of emotion to flood through me when he takes it, but everything is carefully masked again.

Then he drops my hand, and we fall in step, heading to the shore. Cyrus looks at me, eyes racing over my face. "I—My mother mentioned someone..." His voice fades into nothing.

*Longing* leaks out from him, thick and heavy, a bottle unable to be capped. For what, I'm not sure. But it settles in my bones.

"Told you what?"

He shakes his head. "Not important right now."

I grit my teeth, wanting to argue but decide against it. "I can't remember what he took," I say. "But I know something is missing. It's this hollow ache in my chest." I hit my fist against the beat of my heart. "It won't stop."

He doesn't say anything for a long moment. "I know."

We continue walking, our boots shifting in the sand, dirt, and debris as we make our way closer to the others. Neither of us speaks until we're almost through the trees, the dawn rising over the seas.

"Memories aren't always good," he finally says. "Sometimes, they're better forgotten."

I remember his offer to take my place, and there's something in his look—as if he knows the memory that was taken is better lost to the waves. I nod as we break past the palm trees. The others wait for us near the water's edge. Claudette turns her sword in my direction at the sound of our footsteps but soon relaxes.

"We were starting to worry," she says. "Are you all right, Cap?"

"Yes, I'm fine," I respond, voice level. "Any trouble getting out?"

She shakes her head. "Almost too easy," she replies with a humorless grin.

Bec sits in the dinghy, holding a cloth to her eyes and cringing with each movement of the boat. We all climb in, the entire thing shaking beneath us. Bec groans with the small movement, and Duncan leans over her, rubbing her neck. She mutters something to him, and his attention doesn't sway as he sits down beside her.

I look away and join Claudette, handing her an oar. A calm settles over me, knowing I'm one step closer to saving Lucia. We head back toward the *Red Dawn* as the sun begins to wink over the horizon, painting the sky orange and red.

The sea turns rough, splashing water into the boat, and we fight to steady it. Cyrus yells orders for Duncan to hold Bec close as Claudette stands in the boat, pointing in the distance where the waves originate.

The Leviathan breaks the surface, water running off its glistening scales, and the waves calm the closer it gets to our boat. It stops at the edge of the small boat, its blind eyes staring deeply into mine.

"It's still shedding its skin," Cyrus whispers.

The creature tastes the air with its tongue and leans toward me. Cyrus and Claudette start to unsheathe their swords, but I raise my hand. The monster's ghastly head hovers as it waits. I stand in the boat, ignoring the crew hissing at me from behind. Slowly, I reach out my hand and wait. The monster leans the full weight of its snout into my palm, its tongue flicking around my wrist.

Then it slowly moves away before diving beneath the surface.

"Keels, what was that?" Claudette whispers.

"A 'thank you,'" I say back and sit down. "A blessing from the Light, I think."

The crew is ready to leave as soon as our feet hit the deck of the ship. Everyone heads to their stations, and I go into the captain's quarters and study the map. The next destination appears, the shores of Brevlyra—a line telling us the path we need to take.

*Finally.*

"Maps only show half the picture, you know," Britta says, leaning in the doorway.

"How did you all fare while we were gone?" I ask her, ignoring the negativity rolling off her.

"Fine. A *real* first mate keeps a ship running properly in the captain's absence."

I look at my cousin and try to rein in my anger. Whatever the Acquisitioner took from me bleeds in my chest, an open wound that continues to fester. My eyes are heavy with exhaustion, and I haven't changed out of my blood-stained and salt-crusted clothes. Sand rubs against skin I wasn't even aware I had.

"Which is why you stayed on the ship," I say. "Your father might not have approved of your activities back in Teraceron, but they serve those who aren't as handy with a blade as you."

She rolls her eyes. "And what would your father say if he could see you now, Nerissa? Would he be proud? Would he be happy with what has become of his daughters?"

The guilt rips through me. I will find my sister, not merely because I love her but because of the promise I made to my father. Protecting her was my job—my *only* job, and I couldn't do it.

My dagger is at her throat before I can stop myself.

A flash of fear pierces Britta's gaze. The morning sun shines behind us, and those on deck stop and stare at the exchange at the door to my quarters. "This is why you're no longer my first, cousin—because if I can't trust my first mate, who can I trust?"

She slaps the dagger away, and I let her. My pulse pounds in my ears, and I walk back inside, slamming the door shut behind me. I find a chair in front of the map and fight the fresh tears threatening to fall on the old parchment. I grind my palms into my eyes to stop their descent.

There's a soft knock at the door, but Cyrus doesn't wait for me to respond before entering.

"Where to, Captain?" Cyrus whispers, walking over and looking at the map instead of me.

*Why did you let me steal your ship, Crow? Is what the Acquisitioner said true? Are you here to kill me?*

I stare at him for a moment, but he doesn't look my way. The pain in my chest starts to weaken, and I notice Cyrus clench his jaw.

"What day is it?" I ask.

"The twenty-sixth of October," he replies, glancing at me. "Why?"

Seven days.

Seven days to save my sister.

"We're on a schedule, Crow," I say. "Time is running out."

He winks. "You don't have to be fast," he says. "Just quicker than the sun."

"North-east, to Brevlyra," I say.

# part four

There once was a blade that cut true and fast
It shone brighter than the sun and cut scars to last

The skin of its master, it dare not harm
No challenger bothered to disarm

If truth you seek, but cannot obtain
Destroy the lies with the end of the blade.

— *"Psalms of Liehtan, the Blessed Blade," from The
Chronicles of the Light*

# TWO
## YEARS
## AGO

# CHAPTER
# TWENTY
### NERISSA

*Island of Helene*

"She won't speak to anyone," I shout at Kip. "Nathaniel broke off the engagement, and she acts like it's my fault he's a heartless pig."

Our blades clang against together. Sweat drips down my face and into my eyes. Kip's cheeks are red from exertion, and he raises his hand.

"Issa," he says.

"No, that's an insult to all pigs!"

"*Issa*," Kip repeats.

I drop my blade. "What?"

"You're...have you been practicing?" He leans over his knees, huffing.

My cheeks burn. "A little."

"With what, an entire armada?" he asks, looking up at me through his brown curls. I sheath my blade and sit on the hay-covered floor, burying my face in my hands. "I don't know what to do," I groan. "I told Father I would take care of her, but have you seen her? She won't even leave her room. Why me? Why do *I* have to take care of *her*? I'm younger!"

The fight drains from me, and tears pool in my eyes. "He would be disappointed," I whisper.

Kip sits down, stretching his arm around me. "Issa, you've done as well as can be expected. You didn't cause the fire, and you certainly didn't cause Nathaniel to be, so—"

"Spineless? He makes a jellyfish look dense." I pick at the hay at my feet.

"Stop worrying so much, Issa," he says, shaking me. "You'll destroy yourself with it." I rest my head on his shoulder. When the Browns offered us their spare bedroom after the fire while they rebuild our home, I was thrilled to have a place to go. With them, I could be myself, not someone pretending to have it all together.

But Lucia didn't want to go.

*"Nathaniel will come for me," she whispered in the cabin at the edge of the island.*

*I sat close beside her and tried to wrap her hand in mine without hurting her. "You are not yet man and wife," I said gently. She didn't even flinch. "Your wedding date is not until the fall. We can stay with the Browns until then."*

*"I'm staying with Lord Wood's family," she argued, voice shaking with conviction.*

*She wouldn't listen to reason, and we had overstayed our welcome at the healer's home. The healer never pushed us away, but even after the three weeks of necessary treatment, it was nearly impossible to get Lucia out of bed to pack her things.*

*"We can't stay here any longer, Lucia," I finally said after two more weeks—over a month of being in one of the beds someone else on the island most certainly needed.*

*"Nathaniel will come for me," she whispered, staring out the window at the sea.*

*My last letter from Father was almost two weeks prior. I didn't know if he even knew of the fire. How could he have known our home lay in shambles or that Lucia's invisible wounds were worse than her physical pain?*

*I walked out of the bedroom and into the waiting area where the healer, Mrs. Chastain, allowed me to sleep. My mat sat in the corner already rolled up and wrapped tightly with ribbon and rope. I went through the remainder of my things one more time.*

*On the night of the fire, we were lucky to be hit by a rainstorm that smothered the remaining embers not long after we took Lucia to the healer. Once I knew she was out of immediate danger, I returned to the house, needing any distraction from knowing my sister was permanently changed. I tried to tell myself Lucia hadn't* been dealt a fate worse than death, but I didn't believe it. Soot covered every inch of me as I scoured for anything of value, loneliness aching in my bones.

What would I tell Father?

I found Father's safe, containing a few pieces of silver and gold, beneath an empty basin in the wreckage. It fell through his study floor and straight onto my bed. If I had still been inside, and by some miracle of the Light the fire hadn't killed me, the safe would have.

With tears silently dripping down my face, I continued my hunt, finding all of Mother's jewelry and tossing it in a satchel Kip gave me. I sold many in the coming days—diamonds, pearls, and gold. Some of the silver paid for our board and Lucia's care. The gold needed to be saved to rebuild. I picked up the pearl necklace and rolled it between my fingers. It was the one piece, besides the ring on Lucia's hand, I hadn't parted with. Not yet.

"That's lovely," one of Mrs. Chastain's assistants, Taavi, said, walking in with a fresh pitcher of water.

Taavi's coarse curls were pulled back with a colorful band of fabric, dyed in deep indigo. My own hair was tied similarly, a gift from her when I came to the healer, covered in soot, hair flying in every direction.

Mother used to bring us to Mrs. Chastain. I remembered the hunchbacked older woman. She had methods spanning back centuries and even allowed input from her assistants, like Taavi. It was unheard of. Assistants were supposed to silently provide small aid. Instead of shunning Mrs. Chastain for her strange ways, the islanders realized she knew more about remedies than other supposed healers.

"It was my mother's," I said, holding the necklace of pearls between my fingers. "She had these pearls and the clothes on her back when she came from New Kingdom with my father. Her family wasn't happy with her decision to marry a disgraced noble." I shook my head in disbelief, rubbing the pearls beneath my fingers.

"May I?" Taavi asked and sat down beside me.

I handed her the pearls.

"And may I...?" I asked, nodding toward the water.

"Of course! Let me grab you a glass."

"*Please, let me.*" *I went to the cupboard and got a clean glass. I filled it with fresh well water and drank the whole thing.*

*Taavi stared at the pearls, rubbing her hands over their strange shapes and sizes.* "*They don't look like I imagined pearls to be,*" *she said, handing them back.*

"*They're in their natural state. The few alterations have been made by the sea,*" *I said.*

"*Shaped by their circumstances. That happens to the most beautiful things,*" *she commented as I sat back down. She handed me the necklace, and I tucked it back in my satchel, wiping my sweaty palms on my skirt.*

"*I'll go check on my sister. Hopefully she's ready to go. I've got more papers to show the bank.*"

*Taavi stood up and headed into the kitchens, but as I neared my sister's door, Taavi stopped and turned back.* "*Only the passage of time can heal some wounds. And some wounds,*" *she said even softer,* "*are too deep for any remedy to reach.*"

"*I don't know how to give her the time she needs.*" *I ran my hands through the ends of my hair, thinking of what Mother would do and, for once, wishing she were here.*

"*There is a way,*" *Taavi said.*

*Standing in the doorway to my sister's room, I studied Lucia's face, scars still raw. Mrs. Chastain's remedies only did so much.* "*How?*" *I whispered to Taavi, voice cracking.*

*Lucia valued her beauty more than she should, and she refused to look in the mirror.*

*Thank goodness she didn't know—truly know how much she was physically changed. I gripped the door frame, looking over at Taavi.*

"*The Darkness,*" *she whispered, hands gripping her skirts a bit too tight.*

"*Is not something to be tampered with,*" *I said, hand wrapped around the door handle.* "*And my sister doesn't need to start getting ideas about it.*"

"*He can give life back to things which have passed. He might be able to help her.*"

"Do you think she'll ever be okay?" I ask Kip now. "It's more than Nathaniel; it's the way everyone looks at her. The way they look at both of us. I just—I don't know how to help her. So please tell me it will be okay."

He stands and holds out his hand. I grasp his forearm and hop to my feet. "I hope so, Nerissa."

"Hope is dangerous," I mumble, grabbing my sword and readying my stance.

"Hope is like a bird. You have to let go of its wings before it can soar."

Kip's words ring in my ears as I toss and turn in the bed Lucia and I share. Her breathing is heavy, but I can't tell if she's faking it for my benefit or fell asleep when I wasn't paying attention.

When I walked in, she was already in bed, facing the wall with the covers pulled tightly under her chin.

Tonight, I didn't try. I'm exhausted from being Lucia's sister.

Around two, I slide out of bed, grabbing my robe on the way out.

"Issa?" comes her whispered voice when my hand twists the handle. "I'm sorry, for being like this. You were right about him."

"Lucia—" I say, slowly spinning around, but she's turned away from me, breathing heavily once more.

With my eyes burning, I walk down the staircase to the entryway, my robe wrapped tightly around me. The light emanating from the parlor draws me forward.

I find Mrs. Brown with her granddaughter in her arms, rocking in the chair shipped from New Kingdom. "I'm sorry," I say as she startles.

She laughs under her breath and waves me in. "No worries, darling. I heard you tossing and turning for at least half an hour. I expected you at any moment."

I give her a wan smile and plop down on the settee near the window, staring out at the streets of Helene.

"Why couldn't you sleep?" she wonders, and I turn around. The baby in her arms slumbers peacefully, eyes fluttering beneath the lids.

"I'm worried about her."

She smiles. "I think what you meant to say is you're tired of her."

I open my mouth to respond, but she shakes her head with a smile. "It's okay to be angry, Nerissa. Everyone has their limits. I've reached mine a time or two."

"She's—" I start, but Mrs. Brown interrupts me.

"She won't listen to you. She doesn't appreciate what she does have. She wants things to go back to the way they were before," Mrs. Brown supplies. "No matter how many times you tell her to appreciate her life, to appreciate the ones who *do* love her, and to look forward instead of behind, until she figures it out on her own, it will never happen. At some point, you have to live *your* life."

I stare at her, eyes bulging. Part of me assumed no one else noticed my sister's attitude. Another part is relieved.

My mouth opens to respond, but there's a small knock on the door.

"Ma'am," one of the maids says, still in her nightgown. "There's an urgent message."

Mrs. Brown's brows furrow, and she extends her hand.

"It's not for you, ma'am. It's for Miss Eliott."

I stand and take the letter, ripping apart the wax seal. My feet fall out from under me, and the air escapes my chest.

Somewhere in the distance, someone says my name. A hand cups my cheek and pries the letter from my fingers.

I hear nothing.

I see nothing.

Father is dead.

# NOW

# CHAPTER
## TWENTY-ONE
### CYRUS

*Bheragus Sea*

The sun beats down on the ship, though the air has started to cool the farther north we travel. I climb up to the crow's nest, the wind slicing through me. Becci stands in the wind, gusts blowing against her. She stretches out her arms, and I have to hold in a laugh.

She jolts, almost toppling over the edge.

"Be careful, Bec!" I say, pulling her closer to me and setting her feet solidly on the wood paneling of the nest.

"Don't sneak up on me," she mumbles, cheeks reddening. "I followed Besnick up here. My ankle was up for the challenge."

In response to his name, the crow caws loudly, flying up into the air and circling us a few times before landing in his regular spot on my shoulder.

"Why'd you follow him up here?" I ask.

Her face turns serious, and she fumbles with her pockets. "Because of this," she says, holding out a small piece of paper. "He almost beat a carrier bird to death. All evidence was quickly snatched by that cat of yours waiting in the corner. I found this...um, near a pile of feathers where she was sleeping."

Besnick nibbles my ear as I unfold the note.

"I never did understand why you kept Piper. She's a *cat*."

I pat the bird before slipping my hand in my pocket and feeding him a piece of bread. The bird flies off, but Becci won't look at me.

"She reminds me not all creatures of the same species are evil." I study the note. "You read it?"

"Yes," she says, voice chilling me more than the wind. "Someone is working with *her*."

*Update?* the paper reads.

I curse under my breath. I would know that hand anywhere, which means Weylan has been sending messages to someone on this ship.

Thank goodness for my crows.

Weylan has always tried to manipulate them for her ways; but unlike my family line, which has a *connection* with our namesake, her talent with animals is limited to training them. She teaches them to obey by breaking them. I remember the day Besnick came to me. Before I was taken to Teraceron, my connection with crows was fleeting. None of the birds belonged to me, but they spoke to me.

Besnick was different. He was a new chick, flying wings freshly minted, and had fallen from his nest—in the middle of the menagerie. Besnick's panicked emotions came to me, and I could suddenly see through his eyes. For the first time, a crow wasn't merely speaking to me but allowing me to be one with him. I ran into the middle of the menagerie and nearly lost an arm as a result.

*"What in the five kingdoms have you done, little crow?"* Weylan asked, stomping into my bedroom. *The windows were open, letting the springtime air waft into the room. Two dozen crows covered every surface, twenty-four pairs of eyes turning toward the queen.*

*She took a step back, bumping into her guards.*

*My tongue stuck to the roof of my mouth, and every muscle in my body tensed, waiting for her to pounce.*

*"Send these birds away* at once," *she ordered, eyes flashing around the room one more time before exiting in a rush of fabric and fury.*

Father had one crow, his constant companion, who died when Father passed—Weylan never expected I'd have nearly thirty. Or that the birds would not leave, no matter what she did. They always had a way of coming back, even when she tried her best to rid the castle grounds of everything with wings. I smile at the thought, but the emotion is buried by the knowledge that she got to one of my birds, convincing it to fly across the seas for *her*.

*My birds.*

She has found a way to turn things in her favor—again.

*Who can you trust if not your queen?* Weylan had asked, trailing her fingers over my shoulder. *Do this for me, and you're free.*

"We'll never be free, will we?" Becci whispers.

"Becci—"

"Don't." She raises a hand. "Don't, Cy. I love you, but I don't need lies right now."

Weylan never believed I would do this, that I would follow through. So she made sure we would make it to Brevlyra by planting a spy in our midst. Besnick took care of the rogue bird, but it was delivering messages to someone. Judging by the missive Becci and Besnick found, this isn't the first time.

Now I have to figure out who.

# CHAPTER
## TWENTY-TWO
### NERISSA

*Bheragus Sea*

I mull over the Acquisitioner's whispered words.

Cyrus Crow wants something, and my heart threatens to harden. We didn't happen upon each other by accident—or by the witch's encouragement. Cyrus was looking for me as much as I was looking for him. The witch told me about him, but who told him about *me*?

Is she on his side, too? Whose side is he even on?

*You can't handle this,* whispers the voice in my head. *You're the daughter of a shipwright masquerading as the captain of a ship.*

*You're a disappointment. You've failed Father.*

I scream, grabbing the closest thing I can find and throwing it across the room.

It shatters against the wall. I stare at the water basin and try to do what I did in the caves and when the mermaid attacked. Closing my eyes, I let my hands hover over the water, breathe in through my nose, and concentrate on the ship shifting on the waves.

"Is something the matter, Cap?"

*Can't a girl get some privacy?*

My eyes snap open. Claudette stands in the doorway with a bowl of something steaming. The wispy smoke curls and dances in the air, stomach rolling when with the promise of fresh food captures my senses.

A sharp pang starts in my forehead, and I press two fingers against the pain, squinting my eyes.

"Nerissa?"

I open my eyes and blink up at her. She's only a few steps away, the fresh oatmeal with apple slices sitting on the table next to me. Concern etches her face, and I have to stop myself from taking a step back. A fresh wave of...anger runs through my body, causing tears to build behind my eyes.

*Keels.*

I gulp down a bout of nausea and stare back down at the water. "I'm trying to control it," I say. "The water. Tap into it like I did before," I finish in a quiet voice.

The gnawing in my stomach intensifies. I stare over Claudette's shoulder. The clouds shift in the sky beyond the open doors, creating wispy paintings in the sky.

I know why I am here. But everyone else? Claudette is here because she needed a captain and I needed a crew. They've trusted me with their lives, and all I've done is risk them at every turn.

"Why are you here, Claudette? Why not join a Mechelonian ship?" I whisper.

She steps forward and puts a hand on my shoulder. "Because this life is better than the one I had. Change is the best gift I could have given myself."

My eyes blur as the stolen memory settles back in my soul. It's a broken piece, missing and leaving a gaping hole in who I am—why *I* am here.

"Do you ever wish you would've chosen differently?" I ask, thinking of myself and the girl I've become in so few years. I wrap my arms around my middle, trying to stay whole. I want—*need*—this pain to stop.

Mother and Father's deaths and Lucia's betrayal have forced me to become someone who has had to rescue and restore the life she so callously threw away. It all swirls around me like the steam from my forgotten dinner.

I had no choice—Lucia made it for me.

"I cannot say," she finally says. "I have never been given much of a choice."

Tears prick at the edges of my eyes. Our paths are so different—but all leading to the same end. I grit my teeth, suddenly possessive of the people I've met, whether willingly or not, since I started this journey.

"I've met some of the most genuine people in the last two years. Now I'm leading them to their ends."

Claudette remains silent for a long moment. She walks over to the map and squints at it. I rise to my feet and join her. "No one can tell you what to do, Cap," she says. "Sometimes you have to trust yourself to make the right choice."

"Thank you for dinner, Claudette. I appreciate your company more than you know, but I haven't got much time to prepare for what lies ahead, and—"

"Of course, Cap," she says, tilting her head. "But, Issa, you are never alone as long as you have your crew."

I nod once and look away, clenching my fist to stop from rubbing the physical ache in my chest.

She begins to leave through the open doorway and pauses, turning back to me. I meet her gaze and wait. "You have a connection with the sea, but you didn't have to let me in today—the sea has a choice to make, too. Maybe the problem isn't you but the water," she says and then walks out of sight.

# CHAPTER
## TWENTY-THREE
### CYRUS

*Bheragus Sea*

Nerissa sits in the middle of the deck, legs crossed and eyes closed. The light of the waxing moon shines brightly over the water and dances over the boards of the ship. One of her hands fiddles with a new hole starting on the left knee of her breeches, and a smile tugs at the corner of my lips. My fingers twitch at my side, and I walk over to her, feet gliding over the deck trying to surprise her with my presence.

"What are you doing?" I ask, leaning down to whisper in her ear.

She jolts, and a rush of panicked emotions flows off of her in a wave. It's enough to knock me off my feet, and she physically finishes me off, hooking one leg around my knees and slamming me to the deck. Suddenly, she's straddling me, a butter knife at my neck, the dull blade resting in the hollow of my throat. Her eyes, wide and darker than the wood beneath us, stare down at me, lips parting slightly.

"What are *you* doing?" she asks, her chest heaving, emotions confused. The panic bubbles into irritation and then something more potent and harder to ignore.

"Are you going to butter me to death?" I ask, hands raised at my head.

She winks at me, and something stirs in my middle. "You only wish you could be so lucky as to die at my hand, Cyrus Crow," she whispers, the words dancing across my skin.

I swallow the guilt bubbling up my throat and manage a laugh. She jumps up and offers me her hand. I take it in mine, relishing in the lightning traveling up my arm.

"Duncan's ship-day is coming up," I say, letting go.

She arches a brow. "Ship-day?"

"On my ship," I explain, "we celebrate the day a crew member becomes part of the ship. In many cases, there is too much rum and not enough of us to remember what happened." I cross my arms over my chest, tossing her a carefree smile.

"You've been a captain, for what, two years? The likelihood of this being a 'tradition' are slim," she says, blinking in disbelief.

My smile falters, and I take a step closer to her. "We need a break, Nerissa."

She studies my face, gnawing on her bottom lip. Unease settles in my stomach, both hers and mine. Her fingers flex, and mine itch to reach over and loop them together.

Doing so would be another bad decision to add to my pile of transgressions.

"We don't have time for a," she pauses, measuring her words, "party."

I smile at her, hooking my thumbs in the top of my breeches and leaning back on my heels. "Course we do. Look up." Her eyes find the stars. "That star probably died a long time ago, and we don't even know it. But we still look up and make wishes on something that doesn't exist anymore. While we can, we might as well celebrate the good things we have rather than the bad. It's one night, Issa."

"Cyrus—"

"You know," I interrupt. "We have a fine crew, especially considering how this all started."

*A fine crew for a woman you've been sent to kill, Crow.* I swallow the thought.

"A crew most captains would jump at the chance to share the seas with, and I trust the whole lot of them. When you can't even trust the sea, you can always trust *this* crew. They're my family. Let's wish on some stars while we still can."

Nerissa crosses her arms over her chest, tucking her hands under her armpits. She's changed out of the daring outfit she donned when we went to find the

Acquisitioner. Gone now is the dark shirt and tight breeches, replaced by a soft brown tunic that falls above her thighs and worn tights. Her hair is wet and flying loose in the wind, and I breathe in the fresh herbs and soap she must have used to get the island off her skin.

"Fine," she says, interrupting my thoughts. Despite the lack of amusement in her tone, her emotions are coated with relief—she wants to escape from what's coming as much as I do. "We'll have a party, but if it delays us—"

"I've already spoken with Becci," I say, excitement bubbling into my voice. "She's agreed to man the helm while we enjoy a night under the stars."

"Wouldn't that be *woman*?" Nerissa asks, cracking a smile. I have the intense urge to press my mouth against it.

I can't hold back one of my own. "It's only dancing, milady. It's not like we can find a five-course meal in these conditions."

Her shoulders relax, and she nods. "Only dancing, then," she says. "But don't expect me to participate."

"I would never," I say, raising my hands in surrender. I stuff them in my pockets and nod to her. "So, are you going to tell me what you were doing?" I ask.

"No," she says, sitting back the way I found her and closing her eyes.

I turn and walk toward the helm, and Duncan shakes his head with a smile.

"Not funny," I say, joining him.

"She agreed to the party?" Duncan asks.

"Aye," I whisper. "Issa agreed to some dancing, but it's enough."

"Still won't tell me why?" he asks.

I snort. "Yeah, if I don't tell Becci and I do tell you, there'll be a whole glitz of things I have to worry about."

Issa's hair moves in the wind, but she stays completely still. Water climbs above the ship, though it doesn't make a sound, and a gigantic wave curls over the side, hovering in the air. Sealife swims by us, and Duncan almost loses his grip on the helm and sends the ship careening into it.

"By the sea..." he mutters under his breath.

What will happen if I follow through with what Weylan wants? Will I even be able to kill Nerissa? Weylan has the backing of an entire army as well as her trained cats.

If I say no, then she comes after me.

Again.

After the family I have left.

*Again.*

But killing Nerissa isn't even an option anymore.

She gives me hope and peace, something to fight for—something worth saving. Weylan sent me to destroy Nerissa and give Brevlyra over to her, another land for her to conquer. But Brevlyra is mine to claim, and I am no longer tied to Weylan. My bond now ties me to this fierce woman, and where I wouldn't kill Weylan for fear of what it would do to me through the bond, I won't kill Issa because I simply cannot.

Issa opens her eyes. The water comes rushing toward us, along with the sea life dangling among the waves.

The wave knocks Duncan and me to the deck, water seeping through my clothes, in my mouth, and burning a trail up my nose. Fish flop around us, and an amused laugh travels across the whole ship. She walks up to the quarter deck and stares down at the pair of us, picking up a fish and throwing it back over.

"Looked like you two needed a good washing," she says, amusement flowing off of her like a wave. She turns on her heel to disappear out of sight.

# CHAPTER
## TWENTY-FOUR
### NERISSA

**Bheragus Sea**

"I hate dancing," I mumble under my breath, watching the crew from my spot at the stern. My foot taps to the steady ringing in my ears, and I keep glancing at the horizon.

*Tap. Tap. Glance. Tap tap. Glance.*

"We have better things to do than dance."

"Do not be so grumpy, Cap," Claudette replies, a light laugh in her voice.

I glare at her, and she sucks in her lips to hold back her grin. My hands grabble for my telescope, and I pull it from the hook around my waist. I lift it to my face and pray for land.

"How far can we be?" I mumble.

"Your sea legs already tired?" Max, one of the mercenaries, asks as he joins us. "An islander like you should be familiar with the waves."

I yank down the telescope and slam it into the mercenary's chest. "I'm tired of nothing but the sea. Find something different, preferably land." He chuckles under his breath, and Claudette shakes her head, mumbling something in Mechelonian as she follows me across the ship.

An energy buzzes around the ship, laughter falling around us like rain. The wind is high today, whipping the sails, and the crew handles the masts and sails from high above. The joy and the upbeat mood guide the ship as much as the breeze carrying us.

*You're allowed to have fun, Nerissa,* says the voice in my head, sounding like Lucia. The guilt twists in my gut. She adored dancing—always the fun one—she would spin me around until I gave in and joined.

"I, for one, agree this is a waste of our time," Britta says, coming up beside me and crossing her arms over her chest.

The sun begins to disappear beneath the horizon, and my skin prickles with anticipation.

*Four days.*

I can work with four days. I can find my sister in time to save her. The wind is high, pushing us north. Giving us a chance—but not if we don't *keep moving.* Throwing a party is the definition of coming to a complete halt, even if Becci does man the stern.

An echoing crescendo comes from the crow's nest, and we all stop to stare at Duncan, holding a lute in his hand.

"Attention all scoundrels and scalawags!" he announces. "Today is a most special day! A day to celebrate what we do have, the stars that still guide us to our destinations, and the people who make it worth the journey." He glances at Becci on the other side of the ship, but she's focused on the water below.

I study the crew. There's so much about these people I don't know. I'm leading them to a deserted land and searching for the sister I pushed away, all in an effort to break the curse she brought upon herself. Suddenly, I'm ashamed of all I've asked these people to give up. A knot forms in my chest, and the air in my lungs sours.

Duncan grabs a rope and swings down with his lute strung behind his back. He lands in a crouch, pops up, and begins to strum a few chords. Soon, the entire ship is dancing, swirling around each other and joining in on the music. Another lute joins the tune, and the song swells around us.

I walk around the outskirts of my shipmates. The atmosphere shifts and glides around us. Cyrus rushes up to me and holds out his hand. "Dance, Eliott. Throw all your cares to the wind."

"I have too many cares that need to be attended to. I can't lose them in the wind," I reply, body tense with want and anxiety—a lethal cocktail.

He takes a step closer, his fingers teasing the skin on my wrist. The light on deck is muted, growing as each lantern is lit for the party as the moon rises. Cyrus's eyes glow blue in the surging starlight as they meet mine. Desire. The singular thread of emotion cascades over me.

"One dance," he says, voice thick with it.

"It never ends with one dance," I counter, but I let him weave his fingers through mine. "One dance is always the precursor to two more. In any respectable dance, if you danced more than once, you were announcing something." My stomach does that traitorous thing it has become accustomed to whenever I'm around Cyrus Crow. "So, what are we announcing to the crew, Crow? Is this something other than a captainship?"

He grins, rubbing his thumb over the inside of my wrist. His emotions are more potent than Father's whiskey. "I am from respectable society, milady, but we're not part of respectable society right *now*, are we? The crew can pretend not to understand, too."

I crack a smile and let him pull me close, my heart and mind warring with one another. His touch ignites a spark in my chest, warming my skin. I struggle to breathe as my lashes flutter against my cheeks, getting caught in a stray strand of hair. He brushes it back with a light caress, his face masked with seriousness. A blush rises up my neck.

Unlike the dances my mother forced on me, the endless hours of wearing uncomfortable shoes and learning how close and far to stand away from a man, this comes naturally. These dances chase away the autumn air and bring forth the rush of excitement. I fall into step beside Cyrus and spin and weave through the rest of the crew. Bec observes from the steer, keeping the ship on course as we celebrate. Someone else takes over, and I look up. Duncan corrals Bec into a spinning dance, her laughter ringing through the sails.

The night feels meant to be, even on this strange journey. Laughter drowns out the sounds of the ocean at night, and the stars blink as if they are dancing with us. A deckhand takes Britta's hand and pulls her into the song, and she relents with a smile. The girl I used to know, the high-born lady with dreams bigger than her father's plans, makes an appearance. Soon, someone drags Claudette into the circle.

Cyrus and I are swept in, too, spinning faster and faster.

Then, it appears.

Land.

No one else notices, and I stumble, breaking the chain and backing away from the group.

"Nerissa!" Cyrus calls out, but I raise my hand against his words.

The music rushes to a halt—silence echoes around us, punctuated by the waves crashing against the side of the ship. The sight knocks the air out of my chest. I begin walking toward the bow, eyeing the landmass, when a hand catches my wrist.

Claudette shakes her head. "Sorry, Cap. I cannot let you do that. It is not safe traveling on the island at night."

I pause, letting her hand rest on my wrist, my eyes straying back to the island.

So close. We are *so close* my sister's perfume dances on the wind, as if she's calling to me.

I always imagined Brevlyra would be dark, devoid of anything tangible, but it's not. The spires of the kingdom's ancient walls shine against the stars, patches of light glowing like fresh embers on a dying fire.

"We're here," I whisper, and she lets go.

I back away from the bow and walk across the deck. My hands find purchase on the thick edge of the ship.

Cyrus's fingers brush against mine. "Issa..."

A fire lights within me, and I yank away. "By the sea, we're here. Don't you understand? We're *here*. We don't have time for parties or dancing."

All eyes turn toward me.

"We're losing focus," I say, louder and harsher than I intended. "If you're not needed on deck, you need your rest for tomorrow. Beasts of unknown size and origin might await us there, which means we have to be prepared for anything."

"It's night, Captain," Cyrus says.

I snap my head in his direction. "A night wasted," I snap. "A night we could have gone faster and surer to our heading."

His jaw clenches, and a hard look passes over his face.

"My apologies, Captain," he whispers and walks away.

The moment my back is turned, Britta orders everyone to their stations. I stomp across the ship, my hand hovering near the door to the captain's quarters.

Cyrus waits inside.

"Did you ever stop to think," he starts, pausing and rubbing his hand along the stubble at his chin. "That maybe I had a reason for this party?"

"A reason?" I scoff, and all my worries come crashing down. "Why are you even here? Why did you *let* me take your a ship? *Why*?"

He leans over the table, staring at the map. "My mother, her last words to me, were...complicated. She said she did it all for me." His eyes flash upward. "Gave up Brevlyra, ran to the Hills. But she also said there would be someone who would save me—who would help me get what I had lost."

"You think I'm that person?"

He walks over to me, brushing a loose strand of hair behind my ear, his fingers leaving a trail of heat where they graze my skin.

"I'm here for you," he whispers, truth echoes through his emotions, laced with guilt. "Even if you are or aren't, *you* are enough."

My emotions soften toward him before my words drop. "Never trust a pirate, that's what the Acquisitioner told me. I'm sure he was talking about you, wasn't he?"

When he doesn't answer, I demand, "Wasn't he?"

He doesn't even flinch. At this moment, I can't distinguish the difference between him and me, the emotions warring in my chest.

Cyrus's eyes glaze over. "He was." His hand falls away, leaving me cold.

"So how can I be the one you've been searching for if you're the one who he meant?"

We remain silent for an eternity.

I want to trust Crow.

But I can't.

Yet still I do.

The ship bobs and sways in the chilly night air, picking up a course closer to the island, closer to the Light-forsaken destination I've worked two years to reach.

"I can't fail," I say, my voice catching on each word. "I can't. I can't leave Lucia again. She has to know I will always come after her—that I have always loved her, even when she didn't love herself."

It doesn't matter why he let me take his ship—all that matters is Lucia. I don't care why he needs Brevlyra, and I don't care why he needs me.

Tears trace down my cheeks, and then his arms wrap around me, putting all the crumbling pieces back into place.

He doesn't matter.

*Until he does.*

I look up at him, leaning my forehead against his and breathing in the salt. His lips find mine in the fading candlelight. The touch is tentative at first, a question I never knew I wanted him to ask. My arms wrap around his neck, and he pulls me against him, the heat from our bodies becoming an inferno. He clutches me tighter, dragging my feet off the ground and pressing his lips to mine.

Confusion wars in my gut, bitter in my mouth. It's quickly washed away by his lips moving against mine. Hesitancy weighs heavily on his shoulders, but the moment he lets his guard down, my muscles relax, too.

Cyrus leans me against the drawing table. It digs into my back, and his hands find my face. He trails a line of kisses from the edge of my mouth to my collarbone, and a surprised sigh escapes my lips. I bury my hands in his hair, the locks slipping through my fingers like silk, catching on my palms. My pulse thrums in my ears, my hands roving over and around his shoulders, fisting in his shirt. I clench my eyes tighter and lean into his touch—his soft caress not matching his rough edges.

My lips find his once more.

*By the sea,* I could escape into this moment forever.

Maybe I'm not the one his mother meant—and maybe I won't be the girl from the prophecy in the end. It's all in what we believe, and I believe that this feels right. This with him makes sense; even when the waves crash against me, he is like the tide, constant and true.

A throat clears behind us, and I push Cyrus away. My heart pounds as I curl my fingers into fists and stare at Claudette. Words form against my lips, but it takes a minute for me to even manage, "Yes?" breathlessly.

She sucks in her lips, nodding once before saying, "We're as far as we can go, Cap. We'll have to take the dinghy the rest of the way."

I open my mouth to respond, but at once the ship shifts beneath us. I grab Cyrus, while another gust of wind shakes the ship. Claudette falls to the floor. Lanterns breaking, the screeching of crows, and screams from the crew raise the hair on my arms.

"What's happening?" I yell, clasping the legs of the table.

Before she can answer, the ship tilts, and Claudette and Cyrus slide out the open doors. A scream breaks free, and I hold on tighter to the table as the door slams itself shut behind them. I grapple for *Liehtan,* yanking the blade from its spot on the edge of the table moments before it tumbles to the floor. My hand wraps around the hilt as the ship shifts again. My fingers lose their grip on the table, and I slide toward the exit. I fumble to hold *Liehtan* steady, barely managing to slide it in its sheath before my feet hit the wood, teeth rattling in my head.

I fumble with the knob before finally working it free. Once I'm through, another gust of wind slams it shut behind me. Sea spray pelts my skin, and I can hardly see, reaching for anything to anchor me to the ship. My hand grazes a rope, and I grab hold as the crew slides and stumbles across the deck, fighting the monstrous waves on either side of us. The sea cyclones around us, the eye darker than midnight.

Cyrus yells, but the roaring wind devours his words.

"Cyrus!" I scream over the screeching wind, but my voice doesn't even reach my ears.

I raise a trembling hand, trying to find the sea, but it won't listen. The now-familiar tug is absent. Instead, debris flies through the air, cutting into my upraised arm. A hot pain shoots through me, wet and sticky.

My heart races in my chest, distanced from the sea—though the waves swell toward the ship, spraying water across the deck, the salt sharp against my tongue. This isn't the sea. She's not here.

*The island. It has to be the island.*

A wave caps the side of the ship, and the screams of the crew, my friends, fall to the ocean. I manage to stand, but my muscles burn with the effort. My hands grip the rail of the ship. Leaning over, I catch sight of Claudette fighting in the waves.

My feet slip, and I fight to stay standing on the slick wood.

Another wave crashes against the deck, and more terrified screams fill the air. Suddenly, the entire ship is on top of a wave, riding in the middle of a cyclone of water, barely visible through my curtain of hair and the salt stinging my eyes. My hands lose purchase, and I slide across the ship. Calloused hands grab me, and I look into Bec's eyes, her arms straining against my weight. I grit my teeth and reach for Britta as she falls past us.

She grabs on to my waist, knocking the air from my lungs. I can't find Cyrus through the thick sea mist, and I struggle to yell his name over the howling wind. The cat slams into my chest, silencing my already pathetic cry. I wrap my arm around her, the low growl in her chest erratic against the beating of my heart.

It's over as quickly as it began. The clouds part in the sky, and the moon peeks out from behind the willowy mist. We huddle together, shivering and soaked through, waiting for the next round to hit. After precious minutes, we unclasp ourselves from each other and look around.

"What the glitz was that?" Bec pants.

I stumble to my feet and rush over to the side of the ship. I peer into the water, looking for any sign of Claudette or Cyrus. Duncan stumbles behind me, calling out his captain's name in a raspy voice, his words crackling in the night air.

I search the ship's side for the spare dinghy and notice it's nowhere in sight.

The ship begins to creak.

The clouds shift overhead, turning from wisps of white to thick spools of darkness more complete than the night. An invisible force hits the ship and flings me against the deck. A crack louder than thunder sounds around us as the main mast splinters down the middle. Someone screams, but it doesn't allow those standing beneath its trajectory to move in time before they're crushed beneath it.

"We have to get off this ship!" I yell as members of the crew go overboard.

Bec runs up to me and grabs my arm. "Nerissa, you have to jump. *Now.*"

"Not until everyone else has gone—" I grab on to the side of the ship as it begins to quake once more. The wood at the center of the ship starts to splinter, creating a giant maw of deadly spikes. Britta holds on at the opposite side.

"Go!" I yell to my cousin, waving the hand not hanging onto the rail of the deck, and she scrambles over the side, diving into the waves.

Bec grabs me again. "Ner—"

"Becci!" Duncan screams. "*Go!*"

She glances at him, holding on not far from where Britta was. One of the mercenaries is barely dangling from his hand, the ship's broken middle threatening to swallow him whole. Duncan muscles strain against the weight.

"Please," he whispers, tears rimming his eyes as he tries to save both the man's and his love's life.

Bec turns back to me with tears in her eyes before climbing over. I haul myself up. Duncan screams in defeat, the man slipping through his fingers and into the carnage instead of the waves.

I take a deep breath and jump.

# CHAPTER
## TWENTY-FIVE
### CYRUS

*Brevlyra*

The sun beats down on the small, half-destroyed dinghy Claudette and I are using as shelter against the sun on the hot, rocky beach. I try to reach Issa through our shared connection but come up empty, her absence burning a hole inside me. I turn toward Claudette and try to rub the knot out of my chest.

She shakes her head. "We have been in this heat for two days already. It is not good for either of us."

Memories of Issa's lips on mine fog my mind. If she knew the truth, she would slit my throat as I was supposed to hers. I clench my fist, rubbing the sweat off my brow with the bottom of my shirt. "We have some of the rain left from the first night. We haven't seen the *Red Dawn* yet. We have to stay on the beach."

"Cyrus," Claudette whispers in her lilting accent. "We need to go inland. It's hotter here than Mechelonia. That is saying a lot." She sighs when I shake my head. "Crow, we will die if we stay here—and what good are we to her dead?"

*Cursed.* This place, these forgotten people. Everything about Brevlyra screams it wants to be left alone to rot into inexistence, but it can't. Issa's mission is tied to it, though I don't understand why. Then there's Weylan's insatiable need to conquer the land she cursed. Her reign will never cease if she takes this land. I stare out at the rushing waves, remembering what once was: life with my mother, safety, even when so much had already been taken, including my home and my father. My heart squeezes in my chest, wishing I could claim the land as my own.

But I can't break this curse—only Issa can bring Brevlyra to its past glory.

Spots form at the edge of my vision, and for a moment, it is consumed by brilliant blue and the sharp white of the cresting waves in the distance.

"Crow?"

I reach for my birds once more—nothing.

Nothing.

Nothing.

*Nothing.*

*Where are you, Besnick?*

"One more day," I say.

She glances at the cloudless sky. "We need to find a water source. We have no way to boil out the salt, no pots, no pans. The fire! The fire will not even start! All this Light-forsaken heat, and we cannot even get a fire going."

"At least we have shelter," I say, shooting her a smirk, and she rolls her eyes.

"You should get some rest. Your lips are starting to peel. You might be tanned, but you grew up in the North. I'm made for this weather. You should visit Mechelonia in the summer." She takes off her jacket and tries to hand it to me, though I refuse it.

We're quiet as I continue to search the horizon.

"We need to go inland," Claudette finally repeats.

"All of this water, and we can drink none of it. How poetic," I reply, chuckling in a way that makes me question my sanity.

"The curse of a pirate's life," she replies. She drapes the jacket over my shoulders, the fabric rubbing against my skin. "It is only a few hours until dark. We could find shelter inside the walls of Brevlyra if we hurry."

"It appears we're closer than we are," I say, thinking of the stories my mother would tell me of the fortress being built. "The walls are huge, but we're a few leagues away at best. There's no point running toward it now."

Weylan's cruel voice echoes in my mind, *Even your towering fortress wasn't enough to protect you.*

Claudette's eyes narrow, a question of how exactly I know so much about this cursed land.

"Crow—" She sighs, staring at the waves. "We will die out here."

"One more night," I whisper, putting my head on my knees as I search for Issa with my mind and fail to find her once again. "Let's wait for them for one more night."

"Tell me," she says, tilting her head. "If you are going to be so stubborn about looking for the ship, even though it could be closer to Mechelonia than here, why did you throw the party? It wasn't about Duncan."

"I want what Issa wants," I say, the truth of the words settling in my bones. "I didn't at first, but I do now. Someone on the ship doesn't."

While Issa and I danced, I noticed something—I noticed the one person who watched everyone else as I did. She walked to one of my crows and slid a small note on the bird's ankle while the rest of the crew got lost in laughter. Even family cannot be trusted, but I warned Issa. My stomach rolls.

For once, I did not want to be right.

Issa's question for me—*why was I there*? It was one Britta should've answered, too.

Neither one of us could tell Issa the truth.

My reason had changed by the time she asked me, but apparently, for her cousin it had not.

Claudette looks away and stares at the horizon, squinting against the forming sunset. "Who then?" she asks. "Who was the one?"

"Who would you guess?"

She doesn't turn to look at me, her shoulders sagging. "I never did like her cousin. I have always been a good judge of character. It is a shame Nerissa does not know her blood betrayed her."

"Tossed her to the highest bidder," I mumble.

"Crow," Claudette says suddenly, pointing toward a ship in the distance.

I squint, getting to my feet and swaying from the rush and dehydration.

"That's not the *Red Dawn*," I say, swallowing the anxiety bubbling in my chest.

"We have two choices. Die here when that boat arrives or risk our chances in there." She eyes the ruins. "Which is it?"

"We'll do it your way," I say.

She sheaths her sword and begins packing up our camp.

# TWO
# YEARS
# AGO

# CHAPTER
## TWENTY-SIX
### NERISSA

*Island of Helene*

Lucia rarely speaks to anyone, walking around the house and the island as if she's the one who's a ghost now.

All she does is stare.

She stares at her plate of food at dinner.

Stares and doesn't eat.

Matilda, the Browns' daughter, laughs with her mother, holding the baby in her arms and rocking her to sleep. One of their servants, a small girl with bright red hair, asks to take the baby from her so she can eat, but she says the Light blessed her with two working hands and tells her to take the rest of the evening off.

The servant tries not to look too excited as she runs back into the kitchens with her friend, another girl with long black curls and bronzed, brown skin. They giggle, the door swinging shut behind them. They're roughly sixteen, like me, yet so different—so carefree, another day, going home early. I thought Lucia would be comfortable here, but she wants to go back to the life she was promised with Nathaniel.

Her...deformity has made her callous; when she speaks it is to take her pain out on the world around her.

She and I don't live in the same world anymore. My feet are still rooted in the sand, commitment doubled by my responsibility to our family. She's slipping and sliding in the rising tide, unable to stand straight, stumbling faster into the waiting waves. She doesn't appear to care, either.

I've donned the black of mourning, still raw from Father's death after over a month, but Lucia doesn't appear any different. When I told her of his passing, she looked at me as if the words meant nothing.

I grip my fork, the metal digging into my palm.

"Eat," I hiss, my voice drowned by the surrounding chaos.

Kip glances in our direction, his eyes meeting mine across the table. They flash for a second toward my sister, and a twinge of jealousy rears its ugly head. I haven't felt anything besides friendship for Kip in over a year, but his devotion to Lucia boils my blood. She doesn't deserve the look in his eyes.

She picks up the fork and holds it in her hand, her eyes moving to me, nothing behind her blue gaze. Half of her face will never heal, and it's the side I see now. The scars burned into her flesh stretch into a permanent frown, traveling from below her chin up to her hairline. Though the flames missed her hair, Mrs. Chastain had to cut it short to her scalp to ensure she got salve on every inch. Months later, it's growing back, but slower than it had in the past.

"I'm not hungry," she mumbles. Her bony hands tremble, and her collarbone stands out starkly above what little cleavage she has left. The short hair accentuates the severity of her cheekbones, and the blue bags under her eyes match the color of the tablecloth.

"You haven't eaten all day, Lucia," I say, softening my tone despite my frustration. "Do you want something else—"

She slams down her fork, and the conversation hiccups. Matilda turns her watery grin in my direction, bouncing her sleeping daughter in her arms. She turns to her mother and whispers, rising from the table and walking into the hall.

Lucia throws her napkin on her abandoned meal and slides out from the table, nearly pulling the entire tablecloth with her. She storms from the room, and her sobs rip through me as the door swings shut behind her.

I mutter a quick apology and dash after her, my dress in my hands, my necklace bouncing against my throat. The Browns' front door falls shut behind her as I run into the entryway, almost knocking over a maid on my way out. Tossing an apology over my shoulder, I hurry down the steps after Lucia, not bothering to grab my shawl.

The crowd bends around her but slows my path. By the time I reach the beach, my breaths come in huge gulps of air, my hair falling from my braid and framing my face.

Lucia stands at the edge of the water, the bottom of her dark navy dress soaked through to her knees. Her arms wrap tightly around her waist, the wings of her shoulder blades straining against her skin. I walk to her, the sea bleeding into the bottom of my gown and soaking into my shoes.

"Father is dead," she states, and I dig my nails in my palms. "You no longer have to pretend you want to be here. Go find a better life, Issa."

Her words sting. I push away the tears welling in my eyes and take a sloppy step toward her. The sea bends around my feet, the sand sinking beneath my toes. I grab her arm to steady myself, and she shrugs me off as soon as I'm stable.

"I heard what she said to you," she whispers. "Taavi. Don't give me that look, Issa. I don't need your pity on top of everyone else's. Besides, they look at you that way now, too." Her eyes pierce me, sad—guilty. A flash of the sister I knew appears for a moment before washing away with the waves. "I'm sorry," she whispers. "I'm sorry I'm like this."

The tears fall down her cheeks, and I brush her shoulder. She winces, and I draw back. "Lucia, don't apologize. You did nothing wrong."

Lucia's watery gaze drifts toward the horizon. "You think I don't see the way the whispers follow me in town. If it weren't for the suffocating tension in the Browns' home, I would never go outside."

"There's no tension," I say before I can process the words.

She snorts indignantly, wiping her tears with the back of her hand. "You're fooling yourself. Did Kip follow you or me?" she asks, glancing back once. He waits near the dunes, his hands stuffed in his pockets, arms bulging through his sleeveless tunic.

"You."

She laughs, but there's no mirth behind it. "Surely you deceive yourself, sister."

"I think the only one lying is you."

She faces me. Her eyes are bright with tears, and one corner of her mouth rises. "Lying about what? People look at me with disgust or worse—pity. They look at you, and they see a girl burdened by her sister. Orphans. We're orphans. Penniless. Pathetic. At least with Nathaniel, I had a chance."

"They know nothing about you, Lucia."

"And you do?" she asks with such vehemence I take a step back. "You know nothing, Nerissa. You can't even speak of Mother without your words laced with anger. You don't even know who we *are*. What *you* are. If you did, you truly would pity me. If you knew anything at all, you'd understand why I can never forgive you for this."

I clench my fists. "Forgive me for what, Lucia? The reason you look like this? Or for Nathaniel? I didn't do anything—"

"Exactly! You did nothing to stop him!" she shouts, grabbing my arm as if trying to shake the truth into me. "You let Father go, again and again. You let him leave us here, *alone*. You didn't care as Mother laid there dying!"

"I'm the one who was able to be in the same room as she suffered!" I snap, shaking off her hands. "You want me to be all these things, Lucia, but you're supposed to by *my* big sister. Everyone expects me to be so much more than I can give, and it's not fair."

"Because you are the one who got it all! You hated Mother, and she still gave every part of herself to *you*," she says, her words landing on me like a punch in the stomach. "To *protect you*.

"She still loved you most even though you hated her. Even when you defied her and picked up a sword, when you read all those stories and spoke out of turn at every chance, she still protected *you*. And I will never forgive you for that," she says, voice cracking.

I grab her arm and force her to look at me. "Mother forced me to hide who I am—"

"Because it's who she was! She wanted you to hide your connection to the sea like she hid her magic."

I take a step back, nearly collapsing in the waves.

A humorless laugh builds in her throat. "Yes, Mother had magic. That's how she sensed it in you," she whispers. "She gave you so much of her time, and you curse her memory. I would have done anything for her attention, but she only had eyes for you. Because you are *exactly like her*." Lucia goes back to staring at the waves. The words stick in my throat, so I turn around and walk to Kip.

"Is she—" he starts to say, but I cut him off with a look.

"Ask her yourself, Mr. Brown," I say and walk up the dunes and back toward the center of town, my dress dripping on the cobblestones. My mind spins with the knowledge that my mother had magic, that she hid it for years. She told Lucia, but not me. I can still remember her sobs as she lay dying. She never did anything to save herself. She never called on her supposed magic.

What had she given up to live this life?

I stay up most of the night worrying over what Lucia said and understanding none of it. I close my eyes and think back to my mother when she started getting sick. We found her wholly submerged in the tub and rushed to pull her out.

*"Let me go," she whimpered near the end, soaked through. "Let me go. It burns. Let me go."*

Her magic. It comes to me suddenly. Her magic burning—trying to get out. The thought leaves me cold. Why did she ignore who she was? *Why?*

Lucia had come home well after sunset. Instead of coming to our shared room, she had climbed into the newly renovated attic and locked the door behind her. Thinking of her, I get out of bed and go to my trunk. Mother's journals had survived the fire. I had thrown them in my small bag of things salvaged from the house. They've sat abandoned ever since. I've never built up the courage to read them.

Lucia and I didn't speak of Mother after she died. We barely talked at all. Her death and our growing resentment toward one another built a wall between us, only allowing our individual pain to fester.

My eyes fly through the pages until I find a journal entry with my name over and over again.

*I ran to give my girls a chance at something greater than the words of the prophecy spoken by the witch in Teraceron. I wanted to curse the witch as soon as they fell from her lips. Curse her like she cursed my girls. My Issa.*

*Cursed.*

*My Issa is cursed.*

*She called the water to her, and it listened. I've seen it before in my home. I remember it myself when the fire called to me. I turned my back for one moment, and Lucia was under the waves, Nerissa was sobbing, and the water swirled around my youngest. I ran to them, but I couldn't touch Issa. The water had claimed her, as the flame had claimed me so long ago.*

*I thought my heart would stop—that both of my girls were gone, one consumed by the waves and the other drowned by her sister. Once Lucia took another breath on that beach, my world finally righted again. Nerissa had stopped crying. Her eyes were wide and wet, but every other part of her was bone dry.*

*I trusted only Mrs. Chastain. When I took the girls to her, she told me about the witch.*

*Pirate's Bay, that forsaken place.*

*But*

Whatever the next words were, Mother scratched them out, the page practically bleeding ink, and wrote beneath them. I struggle to process the words as I skim the page for words not ruined by indecision. My breath catches in my throat at the sight of my father's name, and tears burn behind my gaze as I read.

*Ranulf disapproves. "Self-fulfilling," he thinks. If I play into the words spoken, I will fulfill the prophecy before figuring out what it means. If I don't—*

More hurried scratches cover the page, and I search for the rest.

*I can fix this. It was one incident, not—*

A blot of ink, suggesting her pause, makes one of the words difficult to read. I hold the page up to the light.

*—not a whole childhood. Not eighteen revolutions, not eighteen years. I still have time.*

My mind reels as I flip through the pages. I don't remember that trip to the beach—I barely remember Lucia and I arguing before I was thirteen. The arguments began when I realized Kip loved her and not me.

I fly through the pages, cutting my finger on the edge. I pop it in my mouth, tasting the blood welling on my skin, and peer at the journal entry. The sharp tang of copper heightens my focus, the salty aftertaste adding to the foreboding words on the page.

*Mrs. Chastain can't help, so she sent me to the witch.*

*"Destiny," she told me, her blind eyes staring into the depths of my being.*

*Destiny. I wanted to spit in her face. Destiny doesn't subject my daughter to the Darkness.*

*Nothing is set, she added. But I don't believe prophecies are the future defined—a Light-blessed prophecy that my daughter—my Nerissa—will control the sea. Not only will she hold the magic of our line—but she will fall to the Darkness.*

*The Light gives us a choice; I wanted to yell at her. I left.*

She crossed out the words. I hold the page closer, trying to peer through the ink to no avail.

*—to find my will, to find my freedom, and this is what I get? A daughter bound back to the lands from whence I came? To both of those dangerous lands?*

*The world I used to know is gone, mixed with the ashes of my parents and sisters and brother. To go back is to welcome death. Our lands were dying, no matter what—*

More words are crossed out, and I go to the next legible line.

*I can't get those words out of my head. I still can't. Writing them down means I believe they're true, but if I don't, they will haunt my dreams.*

In wobbly script, Mother's words curl on the page. My hands tremble as I mouth the words.

*Eighteen revolutions around the sun,*

*Will reveal the chosen ones.*

*The power of the sea,*

*Shall either tempt or make Him flee.*

*Eighteen years. I have time. To fix Issa, my darling girl. I don't care what that witch says. Her prophecy will not come true, and I will do whatever I can to save my girls.*

My fingers trace Father's name, smearing the tears falling from my cheeks with the blood still welling from the cut on my finger.

*I will do whatever I can to save my girls.*

*Whatever it takes.*

I stare at my hands. They quiver slightly in the fading light. No matter how many times I re-read the entry, I can't make sense of it. I'm terrified of returning to the healer on the hill, so I sit with this knowledge, a history I don't understand. If I did, maybe the power of the water flooding through me would make sense.

A noise from down the hall startles me out of her journals. I stuff my hands under my thighs as if I've been caught doing something I shouldn't. My heart beats erratically in my chest, and I listen for the sound of footsteps.

I grab what's left of my candle and slowly open my bedroom door. My sister hurries down the stairs, and I don't hesitate to follow after her. The front door of the Browns' house shuts with a soft click as she exits. I chase after her, barefoot and in nothing but my nightgown.

Mother's journals haunt me as I follow Lucia under the cloak of darkness. For years, Mother was the enforcer, a constant presence over my shoulder, waiting for me to make a mistake. And she was. The entire time, she waited for a sign of the girl she glimpsed on the beach, and when she rose up, she hid her away. She forced me to ignore the sea, and now I don't know what to do with it.

Worse—what did I do to Lucia? What did I do that terrified my mother so much? Did I do anything at all?

I wrack my brain with every step, but the memory is gone. Mother said she would do whatever it took to stop the inevitable.

What had she done?

Someone slams a door nearby. I stop and hug the wall closest to me. Lucia turns around, searching the streets before starting up again.

She keeps to the shadows, and I almost lose her a few times before we make it to the docks on the far side of the island. She walks out to the edge where a man sits, his feet dangling off the pier. Another man, possibly a guard, hovers behind him. I sneak between the boats and go as close as I dare.

His breeches are rolled up to his knees, and he wears a tunic more suited to a man from New Kingdom, since men from the islands rarely cover their arms and always wear shorter, looser breeches. The silver shirt hugs his chest and wraps around him, showing off thick shoulders in sleeves that disappear into a pair of black leather gloves. He turns toward my sister, and I duck down, but not before the moonlight catches on the buckles lining the left side of his shirt. The outfit isn't suited for this weather or any weather in Easterly.

It isn't his unusual attire that knocks the breath out of my chest but his face. Scars travel from his hairline to the bottom of his chin, puckering the skin on his cheek. Soulless, silver eyes reflect in the moonlight like those of a cat hunting in the night.

The wind drowns out their conversation, and I tiptoe around the crates and boxes crowding the pier, crawling to hide behind one of the boats anchored nearby. As I walk, I keep my eyes on the other man, his hand on the hilt of his sword. A slight breeze ruffles the bottom of my nightgown, and goosebumps pepper my flesh.

Whereas his master is eerie, the guard is a patchwork quilt of body parts, his face more scarred than his master's. He's shirtless, and the moon catches the black veins running through his skin in sharp angular patterns. When he turns, inky black seeps into his eyes, creating pools of endless ebony. Strands of loose silver hair fly back from his head while the rest sits at the nape of his neck in a low ponytail.

"There is no going back, Lucia Eliott," the man in charge says, his voice deep and rich like thick velvet.

My fingers itch to scratch his words from my flesh.

"I want revenge," she replies, her voice thick with tears. "I want him to know the pain I have felt. He left me because of *this*." She motions to her face. "His choices told everyone I wasn't worthy of his time—his love."

"Revenge is an insidious thing, Lucia," he says. "You survived the fire. If the boy was worthy of you, he would've stayed. The price for what you ask is not cheap. It will take more than a simple bargain."

"I'll give anything," she says, almost before he's finished speaking.

"*Anything* is a strong word."

"I will give you *anything*." She turns to look at the man, and I catch a glimpse of her scarred cheek. The man raises his hand and runs it down the damaged flesh, and her eyes flutter shut as she relaxes into his touch.

"Even your life here?" He tilts his head, a birdlike movement that swirls my stomach.

"This isn't living!" she yells.

The man behind him glances back, his sword echoing a chilling hiss as he pulls it farther out of the sheath. "You will come to me once the deed is complete."

The man on the edge of the pier raises his hand but doesn't turn around.

Lucia nods. "There is nothing for me here."

"What of your sister?"

"Nerissa"—her voice shakes around my name—"knows nothing."

He chuckles once, sharp and chilling. "Pity."

He takes my sister's face between his gloved hands and kisses her. I stifle a scream as deep mist curls around them. When they're gone from view, I jump to my feet and run across the pier, screaming Lucia's name.

"It is done," the man says, the words echoing around me as I fight through the mist.

"Lucia!" I bellow, but a harsh wind drowns out the sound and knocks me to my knees. A rough board cuts through my gown and pierces my skin. A cry of pain escapes my lips, and I sit back and inspect the deep cut.

The mist clears, and the man and his guard are gone. Lucia stands over me, her eyes hollow.

"Hello, Issa," she whispers into the night.

"What have you done, Lucia?" I ask, scrambling to my feet and digging my fingers into her arms. I don't care if I bruise her—I want her to look at me, to *see* me.

She looks at the sky.

"Lucia, *what have you done?*"

Her voice is hollow. "Found another way."

# NOW

# CHAPTER
## TWENTY-SEVEN
### NERISSA

*Brevlyra*

I reach for my connection with Cyrus yet again.

Nothing.

He and Claudette have disappeared together.

*What a way to spend your birthday, Nerissa.*

We've been walking the beach for hours after coming ashore with no sign of them. My gut twists at the thought of them dead because of me. Unshed tears burn at the back of my eyes, but the heat pushes them away. All the liquid in my body needs to stay in its place. There aren't many of us left. Only two of the hired deckhands remain, along with myself, Britta, Bec, and Duncan. I envision the wide-eyed fear of the one Duncan wasn't able to save as he slipped through his fingers.

Tall cliffs jut into the clear blue sky. Most likely, they stand between us and the rest of our crew.

Cyrus.

My parched lips prickle as an onslaught of memories thunder through my mind. Our stolen kisses, the heat of his body through his clothes. I may not feel him now, but deep down I know he's alive...for now. Cyrus and Claudette are somewhere on this forsaken land.

The heat breaks through every layer of clothing covering our bodies, scorching even hidden skin. Waves assault the cliffs in the distance, and I head toward them, the final destination on the map, leading me to Lucia. Bubbling foam rolls from the crashing current and wets our feet as we move along the beach, but it does nothing to penetrate the severe heat.

"Why's it so Light-blessedly hot?" Duncan asks.

"The curse, newk," Becci responds, pushing him nearer the forest. "The magic surrounding the island—the *thing* that destroyed our ship. It didn't kill us, but this heat might."

Bec stares at the cliffs, her eyes wandering to the forest and back to the shore. Duncan jogs ahead, striking the brush with his sword and making a path through fallen branches, sand, and the pine needles sticking to our shoes. Britta's eyes rove the landscape, her cheeks already red from the sun. It's as if she's searching for something, and an unease I can't shake sinks into my bones.

"You should've covered your face more," I say, taking off the shirt shielding my head and ripping it in two. I wrap the piece under my eyes and across my nose. It's tough to breathe, but the relief from the sun helps.

I hand her the other half, and she copies me. "Where do you think Cyrus's birds went?" she asks, eyes studying the sky.

I adjust the bandana I found in the wreckage on my head and tuck my braid inside my shirt. The heat hits my spine, and I recoil. "With him, hopefully."

Britta looks toward the Northern walls on the outer ranges of Brevlyra, a curious glint in her eye. "We're close to Teraceron—to Queen Weylan's land. Maybe we should go there, Issa. Don't you think?"

"Go to New Kingdom?" Britta knows why we're here. My chest tightens as I stare at my cousin, her eyes never meeting mine. "What we came for isn't there. *You* know this. We have to find Lucia—"

Bec's laughter cuts through my words. She takes a stumbling step forward with a crazed look in her eye. "We've lost Cyrus—not to mention your first mate! And you're *still* worried about your sister."

"I am worried—" I start.

"I thought you cared for him—them," Bec says, her words piercing my skin. "We lost them because of you, and you act like you don't even care. Or is this all a part of your plan?"

Hurt slices through me, but I hold my tongue and continue walking, keeping my cousin in front of me.

Bec's on my heels, the words hitting me like embers in a flame. "Honestly, what kind of captain are you? How did you manage to get anyone to follow you anywhere, much less to the end of the world?"

One of the remaining mercenary's arms appears to form a wedge between us as the man glares down at Bec. Duncan takes a step forward, his mouth opening to say something, but Bec pushes her hand into his chest. "Not now, Duncan." She turns to the mercenary who blocked her. "Why did you follow her?"

I look up at the mercenary.

He purses his lips, and he glances down at me. "The pay."

She laughs and takes a step closer. "There's no money in this for me. I need a good reason to stay—a good reason for why we're not going to save my cousin *now!*"

"Because I have to save my sister. If I don't save her, then the Darkness wins. But she can be saved," I interject.

Britta's eyes twinkle as she turns, crossing her arms. Her voice is sing-song sweet as she intones, *"Eighteen revolutions around the sun, Will reveal the chosen ones. The power of the sea, Shall either tempt or make Him flee."*

Bec reels back as if slapped. "What? Light-bless him. He knew, didn't he? I *knew* there was something he was holding back. You're not just *a* girl, but *the* girl. Even Weylan believes you can defeat the Darkness. That's why she wants you here." She shakes her head. "He should have told me."

I exhale slowly, about to answer when Britta says, "Who's the newk now?"

Bec ignores her. "You want to fight the Darkness," she continues.

"The Darkness needs her—needs me. She'll be nineteen tomorrow, an adult. After that, her choice can't be reversed. She'll belong to the Darkness. But I can reverse it. This place—this place is her prison, but I can set her free."

"The Darkness and Weylan stole everything from Cyrus and me—our people, gone without a trace." Bec sweeps her arms out wide. "Made our home this insufferable land."

"That's why—"

"No! You don't get it. The Light couldn't keep out the Darkness, and you think you can defeat it because of what some witch said in a prophecy? No wonder Cyrus was able to trick you."

"Trick me?" I ask, stepping toward her.

"Why do you think we're here?" she shouts, her tears seeping into the cloth around her face. She pounds a fist against her chest as if trying to clear away the cobweb of memories trapped inside.

"Don't you get it? Queen Weylan is desperate. She can't touch this land until the Light falls—and *if* you managed it, Cyrus was to *kill* you. And then she'd break his bond to her and free us. She wants this land, but she can't touch it, not while she's consumed by the Darkness. Brevlyra is protected by the Light. No one as evil as Weylan can step foot on this land."

I'm rooted in the sand.

*Kill you, kill you, kill you.*

The words ring in my ears, over and over again, even if I knew—the Acquisitioner had told me as much. I didn't believe it until now.

Bec steps up to me, her gaze locked on mine. "Yes! Why do you think it was so *easy* to get our ship? But he changed his mind! I could tell. He looks at you...like you are home, and he's been lost for over half his life. He would have done it already, but instead, he's trying to protect *you*. And you're leaving him to rot. Right, Duncan? Don't look at me like that! You shouldn't have kept things from me."

Duncan nods. "Aye, I'm sorry, Becci. The captain didn't want you to worry. He told me when I brought her on the ship in Pirate's Bay, when she was pretending to be a *maiden in distress*."

"Well, too late!" she screeches, throwing her hands in the air.

"Well—" Duncan begins, but she stops him with a look.

"Careful, Duncan, before you lose your other eye," she snaps. Realization lights her eyes as my thoughts spin.

"Your sister—she's trapped here. The Light trapped Brevlyra so the Darkness couldn't infiltrate it. Only the ones He lets in can enter this land," Bec says. "Somehow, she got through and the Light trapped her..." Her words trail off.

"Trapped her until you could come and save her. It's protecting her like it protected the people of Brevlyra. Ugh! Why me? Why did I have to be related to a Crow?"

Duncan raises his hands in surrender. "Captain Eliott had to bring us here, Bec. Cyrus needed the map, but it would only work if the other person trying to reach Brevlyra agreed. Remember? Cyrus couldn't read the map, not without her. She had to lead us to Brevlyra, but she needed him as much as he needed her."

"You have a decision to make," he replies, smiling humorlessly. "You're eighteen today, if the prophecy is right, aye? You choose to release the curse on Brevlyra and open the borders to the rest of Penreine, or you choose the Darkness and it falls. Your sister, if she can be saved, will be forced to make the same choice as you. Am I right, lass?"

Everyone is silent.

The connection Cyrus and I have causes me to pause, to want to go looking for him and the rest of the crew members we've lost. I've started to care for them like family, even more than family in some cases. I'm terrified Lucia won't need me when I find her—or that I'll be too late.

The trees rustle around us, and Bec lets out a surprised gasp. I spin around. Britta holds a knife to the mercenary's throat. Strangers, soaked through, bloodied, and bruised, come out of the forest, swords drawn.

"One move, and I slit his throat," Britta says, her eyes trained on me.

Half a step ahead, Duncan has already thrown his sword and dagger and hit two of the strangers in the chest. The men collapse, dead.

Britta hesitates long enough for the man in her grasp to grab her from the side. He yanks her toward the thin line of trees leading to New Kingdom, twisting back her wrist. Her knife falls to the ground with a cry, and she continues to struggle. Betrayal is tight in my chest, but I have no time to ask why as I'm charged by another intruder. I unsheath *Liehtan,* and our swords collide, the metal singing. The sea comes to life behind me, and his eyes widen in shock as the waves beat against the sand. The power emanates between my bones, the air electric with my power.

There's a sudden yell, and the fighting stops. Britta grapples with Bec, her hair locked in her hand. Another one stands off with Duncan, who drops his blade at the sight of Becci on her knees, the blade at her throat.

"One more move, and she dies," Britta says, a wicked grin on her face.

"Why?" I ask, shaking my head.

"I told you, my father spent a lot of time on the Queen's court—"

"We're family!" I say, pain lacing my tone.

"Your father abandoned us. Made us look foolish." She spits on the ground. "Queen Weylan has promised me a title—a true place in the court. A title your father gave up without a thought.

"So, let's find your sister, and you can break this curse for us. But first, we need to straighten a few things up."

My cousin signals for us to lead the way, the queen's puppets dragging us along the shoreline as we draw closer to the cliffs.

# CHAPTER
## TWENTY-EIGHT
### CYRUS

**Brevlyra**

"I was a little disappointed they brought so few with them," Claudette says.

When the boat appeared on the horizon, I truly thought my life had ended. In the masts, Weylan's family flag, the Chimera mid-roar was more than an omen. It was the last nail in my coffin. "If they wanted us dead, we would be," I whisper.

The small rock building we're tucked in used to be a home outside the Kingdom of Brevlyra, one of the few that didn't sit inside the gates, yet still close enough to watch the sun sink beneath the castle's spires. Voices of our captors carry through the night. "We did not have any luck. Maybe they will not be able to find them either," Claudette says, listening to the arguing outside. "What about your birds?"

*Besnick?* I called out once more with no success.

I shake my head. "I haven't heard anything since we landed ashore."

"Does that usually happen?"

I shake my head. She curses under her breath and fights against her restraints once more.

"Could be they got lost in the storm, or— What are you doing?" I ask.

Claudette lets out a laugh. "One more...moment..." She whips out one hand and wriggles the wrist from side to side. "I think they're coming back, but—"

"How'd you do that?" I demand, a smile tugging at the corner of my mouth.

"They didn't tie me up properly. They used a clove hitch when everyone knows those usually work free with a little bit of help from the rock jutting out of the wall. Should have used a bowline."

After she's free, she unties my wrists. I rub the raw skin and study the room, looking for any way out.

Claudette silently walks to the door and inspects it. "Locked, of course." She pulls something out of her hair and jiggles it in the lock. "I think I can....Crow," Claudette hisses. "Someone is coming."

*Issa.*

Her pain radiates through me like a whip. "Claudette—"

She throws me a look.

"Nerissa," I hope.

Her eyes widen, but the sound of boots scuffling outside snaps us into action. We dash back to our spots and bundle the ropes behind our backs. Claudette and I share a look, and she snaps the rope. I do the same. Whoever is on the other side of the door won't make it long if we can overpower him.

The door creaks open. A body is flung through the door and hits the floor with a thud. As soon as one lands, another follows, the person hitting the wall with a crack. A low moan escapes the girl's lips.

"Bec," I whisper. Her right eye is swollen shut, and a trail of blood streaks down her cheek from her open lips.

She whispers something, and I rush over, moving her out of the way before someone else flies through the door.

Claudette jumps to her feet and goes to Duncan. "Where is she, Duncan?" she asks. "Where is the captain?"

He looks even worse than Bec, his eye patch gone, both his sockets swollen, and there's a large gash on his forehead. "They won't stop until she gives it to them," he says, his voice thick and drowsy. "They won't stop until she gives them all the pieces. They want Brevlyra—" he stops, shoulder convulsing with a bloody cough. "They're working with Queen Weylan. They're doing what she didn't think Cyrus could."

Claudette freezes, her entire back contracting at the words. "What were you supposed to do, Crow?" she asks.

"Kill her," Becci says through a cough. The sharp tang of blood coats the air. "Weylan sent him to kill Nerissa after she defeated the Darkness. She is the only one who can, and the queen wants this land. She is trying to expand her empire."

Claudette stands, turning a steely glare on me. I get to my feet, glancing at my cousin, who stares at us both with worry in her eyes.

"I wasn't—"

Claudette slaps me. "Like keels you were not," she hisses. "What did she give you in return for my captain's life?"

"Mine," I whisper. "She was going to give me my life back."

Her mouth twitches with a sneer. "You forget where I am from, Crow. I know of Weylan and her dealings with Mechelonian aristocracy. I know of the lies she feeds them all—I know of her *cats*. If you cross her, she will tear you apart, limb by limb, tooth by tooth, until there is nothing left but your broken bones that her beasts will suck on for the marrow," she whispers. "You give her what she wants, and she kills you to keep you quiet. If you do not, you will wish you were dead."

"I'm not going to let anything happen to her, Claudette," I say, my body shaking with emotion. "Even if it kills me. I will not let anything happen to Nerissa. I promise."

"Nerissa does not deserve to fall victim to your problems with the queen."

"You're right," I say. "And I will do everything in my power to stop her."

A tap on the miniscule window gets my attention, and Besnick's presence soothes the anxiety burning in my chest. I try to enter his mind, but I can't break through. Still, my bird cocks his head to the side, the words between us not needing to be spoken. Magic is more than power. It's something softer, purer. It's connection.

"Don't worry, crew. I've got a plan."

# CHAPTER
## TWENTY-NINE ·
### NERISSA

*Brevlyra*

I glare at Britta as she leans back against the rock wall. She smirks as if waiting for me to continue fighting the gag in my mouth and bless her with a response. Instead, I bite down harder on the fabric and turn away from her, not giving her the satisfaction of watching me squirm. My wrists bleed through the rope, coating my hands in the sticky blood.

The screams of my crew carry over the trees, magnified as they lap at the cliffs. At first, I fought behind the gag, cursing Britta, calling her every foul name I've ever learned. But my wails didn't sway her or the rest of her crew—not like my stare. My cold gaze kept them at bay.

"Captain!" one of her men shouts. "We're ready for her!"

She yanks me upright and brings me to the clearing, throwing me to the ground. I fall onto a broken branch, searing pain radiating up my jaw. She reaches toward me and yanks the gag down.

Duncan, Bec, Cyrus, and Claudette stand before me, all in various bloodied and bruised states.

Disgust coats the back of my throat, at this girl I treated as my family—her true colors shining through.

I push away the anger and find my voice. "Britta—"

"No," she says, her voice thick, her distaste twitching her lip. "I did everything for you—contacted the witch, had your back when we stole Crow's ship. Then you got rid of me in favor of *her*. It was how I knew I'd made the right decision. You didn't see me as family any more than your father saw my mother." Her hatred-filled eyes flash toward Claudette. *Keels.*

"You *love* the sound of your own voice. Don't you have something to say?" Britta goads me.

I spit in her face.

She wipes my saliva away with the back of her hand, anger rising in her cheeks. "We're related to Weylan, you know, even if your magic is different than hers. Stronger, as much as she hates to admit it."

The thought of being *related* to the monster who tortured Cyrus makes my stomach turn.

*Distraction.* She's trying to distract me. "You're lying," I say.

She harrumphs. "If only."

Nausea coats the back of my throat. "What does this have to do with anything—"

Laughter bubbles from her chest. "Because I didn't want to do it, at first. I didn't want to spy for her—I didn't even want to meet you." Her jaw quivers. "Your family is a blight on our line, even more so than my mother's reckless choices in husbands. Even still, I love my mother, and I would do anything to protect her.

"Weylan promised a raise in our status and payment for your father's transgressions. Ranulf and my mother are Weylan's first cousins—brother and sister, and he left her with her horrible husband. You're here to save your sister, but where was your father when his sister—my mother—needed him? Your father abandoned us—turned his back on those who needed him. There are consequences, and sometimes *the children* must pay for the sins of the father."

I grit my teeth and force my eyes to meet Britta's. "My father was a good man, and you can't blame him for doing what he needed to do to escape the toxicity of the court."

Britta gives a spiteful chuckle before grabbing my hair and pulling me up to her face. "Where is it, *cousin*?"

I lazily roll my eyes upward, ignoring the pain radiating from my skull. "I have no idea what you're talking about."

She scowls at me. "The map! I would have taken it myself, but you never let it out of your sight. Then when the ship nearly sank, I thought it was lost for good. Something as priceless as that map gone"—she snaps her fingers—"like that. But then, I could tell you had a purpose—knew where we were going."

"What's so special about it?" I asked through clenched teeth.

Her gaze narrows. "It's as old as time itself, created before the great divide between Light and Dark. That's why it needs two masters. Because one person can't wield so much power—a map that can lead us to our heart's desire."

"It's a stupid map—"

"It's no such thing. Tell me where it is, Nerissa, or we'll feed you to the sharks. Besides, Cyrus was meant to kill you. Might as well help him out."

The words ring in my ears, and my gaze lands on Cyrus.

His gaze never lingers, and his guilt pierces my chest, rising from the pit of my stomach and up into my throat. The connection isn't there, not like before. It's smaller, humming beneath my skin. But I don't need our connection to know the truth. There's a difference between hearing the truth and seeing it in the arch of Cyrus's brows, the tilt of his chin. Someone I've started to measure as my equal—as my friend—lying to me.

*As something more.*

"Ask him," Britta whispers.

My silence beckons her closer. "Ask him," she repeats.

I look at him, but I keep the words hidden in my chest. "No," I say. "I already knew. Unlike you, he didn't follow through with his plan. I'm not dead, but I was betrayed—by *you*."

She nods at one of her men, dropping me. He hands her *Liehtan*, and she holds it up to the sun. "So, what's so special about this sword, hmm?"

She turns it in the air, the blade whirring stiffly. It shines in the sunlight, the tip of the blade sparkling.

"It's only a blade," I say, clenching my jaw.

She brings it down on me, slicing the sharp end against my face. My crew screams out in horror, but the blade doesn't pierce my skin. I fall to my back on a blunt rock, the air rapidly escaping my lungs.

"Inventive," she says. "The stories don't do *Liehtan* justice. What an honor to behold it. A blade incapable of hurting its owner and able to break through the Darkness. That's why you need it, right? To fight the Darkness holding Lucia? I wonder, could it hurt anyone else on your crew?" She grabs Claudette from the pile, and I roll over on my side, my shoulder digging into the ground, still wheezing and gasping for air.

She brings Claudette's face down to mine, the blade at her throat. Her eyes are clenched shut, but her breathing is even. She opens her eyes and looks at me, shaking her head so tightly, I almost don't notice it.

"Where's the map?" Britta whispers.

"Bec...Bec has it..." I pant. I gave it to her as soon as we touched land. "Don't...hurt...her...please."

Britta's lackey searches Bec's jacket and pulls out the crinkled parchment. She kicks Claudette aside, and a small whimper escapes her mouth as she lands on the ground next to me. I meet her gaze, her lips barely moving as she tries mouthing something to me, but I can't understand her. I shake my head, and Britta nods toward our crew, her words muffled from the pain in my head. One of the deckhands grabs Claudette by the shirt and throws her back with the others before I can figure out what she was trying to tell me.

"Read it, then."

She spreads the map out in front of me, ordering one of her men to hold down my head, forcing my eyes on the map.

"Can't," I say, the lie tasting like ashes in my mouth. "Cyrus and I have to work together—Ahh!"

A sharp pain slices the back of my skull, sending me sprawling across the map. "What about now?"

My eyes blur in and out of focus, but I squint at the map. It moves, but not because Cyrus and I aren't in agreement—it shifts because of the throbbing pain and the blood oozing from the fresh wound. Nothing is clear.

"You bumbling idiot—she might not be able to see anything if you keep hitting her over the head," Duncan yells.

Cyrus's gaze pierces my skin, and I look up. He gives a small nod. The map leads me to my sister—I have to believe that—but we don't know what truly waits at the end of this journey.

"The castle," I mumble. "In the center of the city."

Britta leans down closer. "What was that, *Captain*?"

I meet her gaze, forcing power behind my words. "The castle."

She smiles. "Lovely. Get a move on it, crew." Britta jerks my elbow and drags me to my feet. When we get back to the small stone building, they throw us inside.

"This isn't necessary," I say, hoping she'll see reason. "Look at what you've already done."

Britta turns a steely gaze in my direction. "I'm done with you. Talking, caring—done. You lose, Nerissa. We have the blade. We have our heading. And soon the queen can have this land." She walks away, shoulders taut, and stomps back into the sunlight.

Anger simmers in my chest, threatening to burn through my fingers. The waves crash against the cliffs outside, and my entire body sings, wanting to let my emotions take control and end this right now. So close—I'm so close to saving Lucia.

"Calm down, Nerissa," Duncan mutters. "We have a plan. Don't create waves just yet."

I breathe in and out, fiddling with the rope around my wrist. It rubs against my skin, a new pain creating a welcome distraction.

"So, you aren't going to kill me anymore?" I ask Cyrus.

He snorts. "Yeah, I think you're safe with me, milady," he says, but his eyes are unfocused, his neck stretching.

"Anyone want to inform me of this plan, or—"

A rush of urgency hits me in the gut, and I turn to Cyrus. Our eyes meet. He motions to Duncan, who has been wiggling like he has a fish down his breeches for the last few minutes. He looks at Cyrus and shakes his head.

My eyes search the space as I fiddle with the bindings. Cyrus does the same. As the rope starts to dig into the flesh on my wrist, a small pecking starts. The waves swallow the sound. But—

Again. More urgent.

It grows louder, and the sound of screaming pierces through the door.

It flies open, and Britta stumbles inside. A murder of crows bolts into the room, knocking her to the floor. The crows flock toward Cyrus first. Feathers fly around us, tickling exposed skin as they rush to their master. Britta covers her head as some of the birds swoop down, nipping at her. She shrieks with every bite and peck, curling in on herself.

The birds move away from Cyrus, and he rips his hands from behind his back. They rest their beady black gazes on us, and I jerk away as the first bird lands on my shoulder.

"Be still," he orders over the flapping of their wings, getting lost amongst the murder as they begin to swarm once more. "They'll do the rest."

My wrists break free, and the birds flee, escaping back to the outside world, mixing with the screams until even those fall silent. We stand in the room, staring at one another.

"We're the same," I whisper, my chest tightening—in what? Wonder? Awe? A mixture of emotions I can't quite define, but I'm not afraid of him. I've seen him with his crows before, but it hits me how similar it is to my connection with the sea—how much we are alike. Maybe because I've come to accept the sea, and now I can recognize the acceptance in his eyes. Warmth spreads through my body, and it shines in his eyes.

"Besnick is my familiar. Like the sea calls to you, I call to him. He even took care of the bird Weylan snuck into our ranks," he says as the crow lands on his shoulder, nipping at his ear before flying away. "Our connection is deeper than words. He told them what to do because he knew we needed saving."

"Thank you," I say.

He smiles once. "What did the map say? Where are we, Issa?"

I shake my head. "I have to get to the castle. Somehow. But I don't even know where we are. It's not like there's many maps of Brevlyra to study."

"You *know*. It's here," he says, his voice low as he pounds his fist to the spot where his heart lies. "We have the tools we need to get to your sister, but you're running out of time. Today is your birthday—and the sun is getting ready to set—"

His hand brushes mine, sending heat up my arm. The connection between us pulses with life. His blue eyes stare deeply into mine, asking a question as much as giving me determination. I quickly move my hand away, looking at my crew.

"Lucia doesn't have much longer," I say.

I close my eyes and reach out, searching for my sister. Connection—Cyrus said he and Besnick had a connection. Maybe my magic is more than a call to the sea, but a call to all I am. My sister is part of me, so maybe I can call to her, too.

At first, nothing happens. The sound of the waves crashing against the cliffs overwhelms my senses, and I cover my ears, listening to the steady rhythm of my breathing. Then, like blowing out a candle in the night, the noise falls away. I lower my hands and wrap myself in the silence. Eyes still closed, the steady drumming of a heartbeat, asynchronous with my own, fills my ears.

*Lucia.*

My eyes snap open, and my lips curve into a smile.

"I know how to find her," I say and take off into the forest.

# part five

The heart an arrow

Must always land true

The mind a barrier

For what our arrow aims to do.


— *"Arrow, a Love Poem" found in the lost*

*texts of Brevlyra*

# CHAPTER
# THIRTY
### CYRUS

*Brevlyra*

The world outside lays in ruins. The crows attacked with a vengeance, bearing down on Britta's crew with a sick ferocity. Most of the men ran, while the bodies of those who attempted to fight back are hidden in the trees. Only Britta remains, the birds circling her as she cries.

"What are you?" Britta asks, shrinking into the rock.

My heart beats faster as my gaze meets Issa's, a new understanding that shakes me to my bones. Even with the magic of Brevlyra thick in the air, our connection pulsates—softer yet more certain. I turn back to her cousin.

"Someone tired of the lies. That's all Weylan is good for. You should've considered that before choosing her over your cousin."

"We have one day, one sword, and one chance," Issa says, as the rest of our crew comes up behind us, having ensured there is no one alive waiting in the bushes. Issa picks up the abandoned blade of lore and sheaths it. She turns to Bec, Claudette, Duncan and the one remaining mercenary. "If you want to stop here, I don't blame you. In fact, please do. I don't know what to expect when we get to the castle. If it's anything like this heat," she brushes damp strands of hair behind her ears, letting loose a laugh. "We might be in for the fight of the five kingdoms."

"Please!" Britta squeaks. "You can't leave me to die in this heat. We're fam—"

A wave crests over the cliffs, slamming into her and soaking the grass. It dies down, and she sputters. A crow lands on Britta's shoulder, cawing loudly in her ear. She releases a high-pitched yelp.

I smirk, and Duncan lets out a hearty laugh.

"I-I can help you," Britta sputters.

"What can you offer me, my dearest *cousin*? Why shouldn't we leave you tied on that ship? You are a traitor, a scoundrel who sides with whoever is winning at the time. You can't be trusted. You calculated this from the beginning, earning my trust because you knew how deep the hurt went."

All eyes stare at Britta as she squirms. Bec leans over and whispers something in Duncan's ear, nodding toward Britta's shifty gaze. Claudette goes and stands behind Issa, her hand on the hilt of her sword.

Issa smiles at her first mate, her gaze moving over each of us before returning to her cousin. "But you miscalculated. Family isn't always *blood*. It's loyalty and the unwavering belief in one another—knowing we're stronger together. And you, cousin, will always be alone."

Britta charges Issa but gets stopped by Duncan's outstretched arm, the equivalent of running into a brick wall. I bite my lip to keep from laughing as she falls to her backside, cursing.

I step forward, hovering over her with my arms crossed. My crows circle above, and fear widens her eyes. "You might have cost everyone here and in all of Easterly, maybe even Penreine, something we can't get back if Issa doesn't reach her sister in time. The Darkness seeks to destroy Penreine, corrupting every soul it can until there is no Light left, and if you help Weylan, you're helping it. Why do you think Weylan ordered me to kill *her*?"

"Welp, there it is, aye," Duncan says.

"Not the time, Duncan," Becci whispers.

Issa's shoulders tighten, the harsh wind whipping her hair off her shoulders. One of my crows caws, waiting for me to tell it what to do next. Issa slowly lifts her head and studies the birds around her.

"We don't need you, cous—" Issa starts.

"Do you know why this place is cursed?" Britta cuts her off. The waves settle behind her, though her jaw clenches in anger. "Yes, the three days of Light—"

"But why?" Issa pushes, eyes twinkling as if she has found a hole in our armor. "Who gave this land over to the Darkness? How did it happen?"

"My mother," I say, crossing my arms. "There was an arranged marriage between Weylan and me. Meant to unite the lands but allow us to be our own people. But my mother wouldn't have it. She hid me in the Hills, right under Weylan's nose. Until she found us...and when she killed my mother—the Light came for the Darkness."

"You're the reason for all of this," Issa says, and her understanding pulses through her. It knocks the breath from my lungs—she's not angry. It's another puzzle piece falling into place.

"It started a war, fifteen years ago—my mother's death—between the Darkness and the Light. I'm why the land is cursed."

Issa reaches her hand out, weaving her fingers between mine. "And together, we'll make it right."

# TWO
# YEARS
# AGO

# CHAPTER
## THIRTY-ONE
### NERISSA

*Island of Helene*

I haven't seen Lucia in over a week. I didn't think she would show up today. She locked herself in the attic bedroom at the Browns' home and refused to let anyone inside. I almost climbed onto the roof to make sure she was still alive. "I'm fine, Issa," she whispered when I threatened the door with an ax. "Don't cause the Browns any more hardship by destroying the wood."

Still, I regularly reminded her of our uncle and cousin's arrival today. She never responded, and she rarely ate the food I left outside.

I stand on the dock next to Lucia, a hint of a smile on her lips.

I wear an island-fashioned dress in muted gray, the loose outfit hanging by cloth straps on my shoulders. My sister shrouds herself in a fierce black, her arms covered in netted sleeves. She loops her arm through mine, and I jump at the contact.

"Sorry," she whispers and goes to pull away.

I grab her hand and pull her close, watching her become the sister from before—before Nathaniel, before Mother, before our childhoods separated us. No matter what she thinks, even with her marred features, she still has an elegance only years of practice can create. However, a brisk breeze whisks away the almost-smile along with the wrinkles in her face covering.

The waves bob against the ship, shining in the sun. I shelter my eyes from the glare with a hand to my brow.

"Is that them?" I ask no one in particular.

"Well, who else would it be, Issa? It has to be someone high born enough to think an umbrella is going to help with this weather. And the dress. Keeling color, truly. By the sea, I'm about to die in these *netted* sleeves. Imagine *that* thing in this heat."

A smile quirks at the corner of my mouth. The jokes are starting to return.

"Why don't they wait until the ship is closer to the docks to come ashore?" she asks. "Do you have any idea? All those nights you stole away to the docks, to learn all the ropes you could think of—don't look at me like that, Issa. Of course, I knew. Everyone but Mother and Father knew, or else they would have stopped you. You did stop, though."

She turns to look at me, though I don't meet her gaze.

"Why?" she asks.

Ignoring her, I let go of her hand and walk down the steps without answering, moving closer to the water as the dinghy glides over the waves. My uncle, who was once married to my father's sister, holds firmly to the side of the boat.

"Nerissa!" He beams, extending a hand. His graying hair flies in the breeze dancing over the waves. "It has been years since I've seen you, child. Let me get a better look at you."

The words mean nothing to me. If it weren't for a letter arriving a few months ago, we wouldn't even know we had an uncle, someone we didn't remember. After a few shared correspondences, he told us he would visit us on the island.

Family we didn't even know existed.

I help him out of the boat. He stands before me, taking my face between his hands.

"Hello, Uncle Wesley," I say, smiling broadly, my grin squished between his palms.

My cousin stands behind him, her umbrella protecting her fair skin and hair from the harsh sun. I try to find something to remind me of Father in her features—anything to connect us as family.

Maybe her nose? The tilt of her head as she stares at us?

"You look exactly like her," he says, drawing my attention away from the girl behind me. "Except for your eyes. Those are his eyes. And you!" He moves to my sister. "As regal as you were when you stood beside your mother's chair as she rocked this one to sleep. I've heard what happened, heard you were scarred—"

She removes her face covering, and I don't recognize the face behind it. It's been months since I've seen the Lucia from *before*. Her skin is flawless—like her scars never existed. No lines, blemishes, or puckering, almost as if she's wearing a mask. But her face is different. She looks like our mother. She looks like me.

Except—

Older, matured, alien.

*Wrong.*

"I thought you wrote her face had been badly burned," Uncle Wesley says, looking at me curiously. "Surely you have a marvelous healer hidden on this island, unless Issa, with her wordy letters, was mistaken."

My jaw hangs unhinged, so Lucia steps between our uncle and myself and takes his hands in hers.

"Hello, Uncle," she says, kissing him on both cheeks. "Are we still able to call you that since you're on wife number two after leaving our aunt?"

Instead of taking offense, his gut shakes with laughter. My cousin does not. She flinches beneath the shadow of her umbrella, looking away as soon as our eyes meet.

"You have your mother's sense of humor, as well as her eyes, then!" he says, taking my sister's stolen face in his hands and kissing her forehead. "Come, Britta, and let's experience this island life we've been craving! I knew your father was a saver, but I didn't understand *how much*. Well, even so, it is nice to know my nieces are safe."

*Since you had been* so *concerned before you learned of the money.* I smile tightly.

Lucia's appearance overwhelms me, but she hooks her arm through our uncle's, making it impossible to get a word in. They walk across the cobblestones toward our reconstructed home, a pair of strangers. Lucia glides like Mother used to, her head thrown back in delight at something ridiculous Uncle Wesley tells her.

"She's quite beautiful," Britta whispers to me. "Nothing like I imagined, but also exactly as I would've imagined."

I glance at her. If not for her blue eyes, I wouldn't know Uncle Wesley was her father. Her hair is fair and fine, and her willowy frame doesn't match the staunch belly rolling with laughter up ahead.

"Yes, well." I don't know what else to say. The words won't pass over my lips.

"You mentioned the fire in your letters."

"Yes," I say slowly, wondering where this conversation is going. I used to have to talk about the fire all the time, retelling the story multiple times a day to people I've known my entire life as often as the pitying strangers new to the island. Eventually, Kip suggested he accompany me. With him as my shadow, the questions stopped.

"Her scars—they must be"—she clicks her tongue—"not visible to the naked eye. I've learned the worst scars are invisible."

"What scars do you have, then?" I ask, even though I don't know this girl. The only connection we have to each other is our parents. My parents are gone, and we know little to nothing about the family walking with us now. I can hardly remember our aunt's name—Lorelai? Lullette?

"I'm to live here, aren't I?" she calls out to Uncle Wesley. "Correct, Father?"

I study his anxious gaze. "I want you to see it first, darling, since it's to be your home."

She shares a look with me and walks ahead.

"You'll have to buy her a new wardrobe. Quite necessary, Uncle," I say.

She smirks, fanning herself. "Certainly, Father. The heat isn't like this in Teraceron," she responds, waving a manicured hand in the direction of my dress.

Her father mumbles something under his breath, and I bite my bottom lip to stifle my laughter.

"At least I get something out of this," Britta adds. She winks and speeds up to him, talking about the new outfits she'll need. They've almost reached the gate of our reconstructed home when my sister falls back, the smile on her face hovering toward a frown.

"Don't say anything," Lucia hisses through her teeth, grabbing my arm, her nails digging into my skin.

I pull away from her. "What happened to your face?"

She walks ahead, grabbing the skirt of her dress and hurrying to catch up with our uncle. "Nothing," she says. "Absolutely nothing."

"What do you mean nothing—"

"I mean nothing, Issa!" she hisses. "Nothing is wrong with my face. I'm perfect. *It's* perfect. Don't you think I look like Mother?" She tilts her face from side to side. "I can't stop looking at my reflection. I'm sure I'm going to wake up one day, and everything will go back to the way it was supposed to be instead of the way it is now—"

"The way it's supposed to be? You can't control how things are or how they change. What happened to you was an accident, Lucia, but it was an accident that showed who cares about us. We wouldn't have anything if it weren't for the Browns, and you want to forget any of this ever happened? You want to go back to the way we were—"

"Yes!" she shouts, earning us a few looks. "That's what I want. I want to look like this and have a life I love again."

"That *thing* said you belong to him—how long will this last?"

She stares at me, crossing her arms over her chest and jutting out her chin. Her eyes slice through me, cold and stoic.

"You know nothing," she says, her hands tightening into fists. "You have no idea what I did."

"Because you won't talk to me!"

Her eyes turn cold, and her face hardens. Suddenly, she looks nothing like Mother. Even when I couldn't stand to be in the same room as her, there was a passion in her gaze, an urgency for me to learn to ignore my magic. After reading her journals, I realized how she had been misguided and obsessive. She didn't know how to love that part of me, but she did love me. Her secrets ripped us apart. That's the burden I have to bear now that she's gone, but she never would have looked at me the way my sister stares at me now.

There isn't love in my sister's gaze. No matter how misguided my mother's actions were, she loved me. I know her fear pushed her to force my magic into submission. Lucia isn't fearful—she's emotionless.

The sea races into my veins. The sky follows the direction of the waves, bringing forth the wind. It whips my hair from the pins holding it back, and I swipe it out of my eyes. Lucia glances up at the sky and then back at me, a look of mild curiosity on her face.

*Calm down, Nerissa,* I tell myself, digging my nails into my flesh.

"It's not about beauty," Lucia says. "This was a surprising plus I wasn't expecting."

"Nathaniel? He's married," I say, trying to hide the sympathy pressing its way into my voice.

She barks out a laugh. "Not even close, Issa. That fantasy died a long time ago. I have other ideas in mind. Something that doesn't involve fickle proclamations of love and a ridiculous sense of hope."

"What ideas, Lucia? What can you possibly want more than love and at least a little bit of hope? You have Kip—"

"Mr. Brown," she interjects, her jaw tightening even more. "Is not what I want, nor has he ever been."

"The token in your pocket suggests otherwise."

She digs into the pocket of her dress. The wooden trinket lands in the dirt with a hollow thud.

"Take it, Nerissa. You wished he had given it to you, anyway," she snaps, turning around. She walks toward the gate of our old home being made new. Her gaze wanders in the direction of the Lord's estate.

She only ever wanted Nathaniel—her fantasy, she called it—a life of promise and status. Without her scars, she can have that—but that man said she had to go with him after this deal was through. What will her decision cost her? Cost me?

I lean down and pick up the small wooden trinket. The size of a children's toy, but too intricate and detailed to be wasted on dirty, sticky hands and dips in the bathtub. The wooden mermaid's head is lifted in song, her arms stretched toward the sky. I look up at the sun, sweat coating my brow as I squint against the light, then back down at the mermaid. I stuff her in my pocket and go after Lucia.

The sound of cursing wakes me.

Uncle Wesley insisted we stay with him and Britta in the new house.

I had returned to my old bedroom. The walls are no longer a light sea foam green but a soft blue. They replaced the bed with something much more garish than I would have picked, with a canopy and too many pillows. It was the last thing the carpenter had on such short notice, a canceled order from a family in New Kingdom.

My feet glide over the chilled wood floors, and I tip-toe toward the noise. I find my sister hurriedly cleaning up a mess she made in the entryway, a vase of fresh flowers sprawled on the carpet near the door.

"What are we looking at?" Britta whispers from behind me, and I manage to hold in my yelp.

"What are you doing, Britta?" I whisper-hiss.

She smirks, her eyes twinkling with the light of the moon coming through the windows. "I'm a light sleeper, too. Father wouldn't wake for the end of the world, though, which explains a lot about him."

I arch a brow at her.

She sighs, but Lucia is too busy cleaning up her mess to notice. "Selfish and completely oblivious. He always drowns out his current wife's complaints. Never loses a bit of sleep. My siblings and I know more about his private goings on than he does." Britta nods to my sister. "What do you suppose she's doing?"

Lucia stuffs the flowers back into the vase and grabs her shawl. She walks through the forgotten puddle of water, her footprints the only evidence she was there at all.

"Let's find out," I say, grabbing my cloak.

Britta and I stick to the shadows, following Lucia as she goes toward the one place I knew she would go—the Lord of Helene's house. Nathaniel never offered her an explanation before he found a replacement to marry. The coldness in my sister's gaze terrifies me.

What will she do? What revenge is she wishing to enact?

We shelter behind a bush as she bypasses the gate and climbs the stairs. I expect her to knock, even if it is a Light-forsaken hour for a lady to be out, but she doesn't. She fiddles with the door for a few moments before quietly slipping inside.

I glance at Britta, but she's already staring at me.

"She certainly demands a presence, doesn't she?" she mumbles.

We wait.

And wait.

We sit with our legs hidden beneath our nightgowns as the cool night breeze brushes against our cheeks.

Lucia finally runs down Lord Wood's front steps and back in our direction. I push Britta farther into the bushes and hold my breath as my sister speeds past us, her feet barely making a sound against the cobblestones.

"What do you think—"

"I don't think I want to know," I interrupt before she can finish her question.

# NOW

# CHAPTER
## THIRTY-TWO
### NERISSA

*Brevlyra*

We walk through the forest, the unforgiving heat growing more intense the farther inland we travel. Cyrus and Claudette drag Britta behind our group. We weren't going to bring her, but who knows where Weylan is hiding.

The farther we walk, the steeper the land grows.

"What does the map say, Cap?" Claudette asks. "I do not know how much longer we can take this heat without stopping for water."

I pull the parchment out of my pocket and spread it on a rock nearby. The lines dart this way and that as sweat drips down my spine. Once it's settled, I trace the line leading us to the castle.

"We should be close," I say, wiping the sweat off my brow. "The closer we get, the worse the conditions grow. There should be a water source close by, and it appears to be on the way. You can stop here, any of you." I look at my crew, sweating and miserable. We've walked for what feels like years, yet we still have at least a quarter league until we get to the castle.

"We can do it, lass," Duncan says, his endless positive attitude grating on every nerve. "Which way is the water?" His cheeks burn red beneath his light brown skin, already peeling from the harsh sun. His eyes are bright with determination.

I point in the direction of the water. "Should be a couple hundred feet that way."

"Come on, Bec, beat you to it." Duncan challenges.

Her eyes roll toward the heavens, but she trails after him. I glance back at Britta, who is busy staring at the sun glinting through the trees as it becomes more challenging to navigate the terrain. Claudette arches a brow in my direction, but I give a firm shake of my head.

"Cyrus!" Bec calls out to her cousin, a hint of urgency underlying her tone. "*Glitz.* Guys! I can't find Duncan!"

We break out into a run, Britta cursing at Claudette as she drags her along, following Bec's voice farther into the forest.

The quiet river is not much more than mud with a few puddles of water, and Bec steps into them, the mud splashing on her boots. "I've looked everywhere. His trail ends here." She points to the stream.

The air ripples around the river, and I squint my eyes at the shift in light. "What—"

Cyrus looks at me, but I shake my head. "I thought I saw something," I say. "It's nothing—the heat getting to me."

"We'll split up," Cyrus says, not convinced. "It shouldn't take us long to find him. It's going to be dark soon, and he knows we have to keep moving. He wouldn't have left you, Becci."

The urgency of getting to the castle and the duty to stay and look for Duncan wars in my chest as Cyrus and Claudette tie Britta to a nearby tree. Claudette comes over to me, but before she can ask the question, I say, "We have to find him."

"We came all this way. The others can find him. You do not have time to search," she replies.

Cyrus meets my eyes over her head and walks over.

"You don't have time, Issa," he whispers.

I look at Bec, and she cocks a brow.

"I have to find my sister," I whisper.

Her lips tighten, but she nods. She opens her mouth to respond, but I whip my head around at a noise tickling my ears.

A whisper carries on the wind, and I nearly weep at the familiar sound of my sister's voice.

*Nerissa.*

"Lucia," I breathe out.

No reply comes.

I close my eyes and clench my jaw tight, digging my nails into my palms before heading back toward the others.

*Nerissa.*

My back tenses, but this time I don't turn around.

"Issa!" Cyrus yells, voice urgent.

I run for the clearing. When I break through the trees, he's nowhere to be seen—the entire clearing is empty. "Cyrus?" I say.

No one answers. Panic slams in my chest.

"Claudette!"

My voice echoes in the dry heat before a harsh wind whips my hair.

*Nerissa.*

"What do you want?" I scream, whirling around. "Cyrus? Claudette? Bec?" I shout into the noiseless forest, wrapped in the intense silence and relentless heat. "What have you done with them?"

*Finish it, Nerissa.*

A shadow passes over me, and I turn back toward the forest. The shadow disappears behind the trees like the whooshing of dresses and coattails, followed by mocking laughter. I run after the shadow, following the echo of my sister's voice among the trees.

# CHAPTER
## THIRTY-THREE
### CYRUS

*Brevlyra*

"Issa? *Issa?* Issa, can you hear me?" I reach for her but hit an invisible wall—around her, behind her, when I run in front of her. It ripples as my voice hits it, and I rest my palm against the invisible force.

"Cap?" Claudette asks, taking a tentative step forward, her hand extended.

Issa's screams pierce the undulating silence, and Claudette jerks back.

"Cyrus?" Issa calls. "*Cyrus?* Claudette? Becci?"

"Issa!" I yell, but Becci grabs my arms.

"She can't hear you," she says, breathless.

Claudette mutters something in Mechelonian under her breath and takes a step back.

"What's wrong?" Duncan asks, breaking through the trees.

"Where were you?" Claudette asks.

A veil shimmers, and the once empty river now rushes with water. Is Nerissa doing this? It's almost like we have one foot in and one foot out of the curse on this land, and my brow furrows as I study the world around me. Something is off, not quite solid. Duncan must have slipped into the other side of it. Now we're partly there, the heat still strong—but is it a little less so?

Duncan points over his shoulder, his words dragging me out of my thoughts. "Just over there. The river has water—"

Becci barrels into him and grabs his face, her lips smashing so hard against his that their teeth clack against one another. She pulls back and smacks him. "Don't you *ever* do that again!"

Duncan stares at her stunned, his fingers hovering over his lips. All he can do is nod, and I bite back a grin.

My eyes find Issa. Her head whips back around, shoulders tensing before she dashes into the trees. The crunch of the leaves and pine needles under her feet dies beneath the beating of my heart.

"Go," Claudette says, pushing me after her.

I break into a run. The trees bend and shape around me, tugging at my clothes and ripping into my flesh. This halfway place where we are, in the middle of a curse, electrifies the air. It sizzles around us, keeping Nerissa far enough away from me to send an ache into my chest.

Is it her? I don't trust myself or the magic of this place. But I follow her anyway.

I stumble through the foliage, keeping an eye on Issa's back as she weaves effortlessly through the brambles, the forest moving out of her way.

I chase after her and would certainly lose her if not for the fading sunlight glinting across her hair. Time passes slowly, though we travel no more than a quarter league. She breaks through the trees a few moments before I do and faces the high walls of the city—*my city*. My breath catches in my throat, and I study the crumbling gray stones, pockets of dying sunlight piercing the holes in the city's armor. The air tastes of heat but also something sweet, like the steam wafting from freshly made bread. The charge in the air brings the city alive, and I half-expect people to appear.

My eyes flutter shut, breathing in the scorching yet comforting warmth, only to be brought back by the thorns cutting into my flesh. The same vines that snake up the side of the walls, reach for me. I wrench free from their hold, a hiss of pain passing over my lips as blood drips warmly over my wrists. I jerk my attention back to Issa. She jogs alongside the wall until she finds an opening. I rush after her, fighting through the vines as they come to life, and barely manage to squeeze through the small hole in the wall.

My feet crackle against the cobblestones with each hurried step, echoing through the abandoned streets. A harsh, hot wind whips my hair back and stings my eyes. I squint against the pain, keeping one eye on her.

"Issa!" I call, but she never turns.

She weaves in and out of alleys, heading toward the high spires of the castle. When I can't see her, the melody of her boots brushing over the cobblestones and her labored breaths determine my path.

I break into the center of Brevlyra, my chest aching and sweat dripping down my face. Issa stands in front of what used to be the back of the castle.

*My home.*

I study her, this girl I've come to know and still can't figure out. Her name rests on my tongue, but no sound comes out. I reach out and brush my hand over her cheek, but she doesn't so much as flinch.

"Where did you go?" she whispers, looking from side to side, her brow furrowed as she gnaws on her bottom lip.

A slight breeze ruffles her hair, and I turn at the same moment she jumps in front of me and takes off sprinting.

I don't understand what's happening.

"Wait. Issa!" I dash after her as she continues to wind in and out of the dilapidated buildings, unaware of the fallen debris covering her path.

We stop in front of the castle doors. She stares up at the aged wooden door before stepping inside.

Up close, the size of the castle is dizzying. My mother died when I was barely five, and I remember more about her death than the place she used to call home. The spires stretch impossibly high, reaching for the arriving stars as twilight descends on the city. I trail after Issa, my breath stolen. Even in ruins, the great room stands more regal than the one in Teraceron.

Faded tapestries, ripped and hanging by threads, cover the walls. Great columns brush the gold, white, and black ceiling with flecks of silver spread throughout like stars. The floor shows a map of the kingdoms in Penreine. The ceiling has a crow crest mingled with the other houses present in Brevlyra, the lineage of my ancestry—the sixth kingdom in Penreine if it hadn't been destroyed.

The crunch of the crumbled floor beneath Issa's feet brings me back. Instead of the oppressive heat, the air is damp and tastes slightly of salt. She walks toward where the throne used to stand, a chair made of golden crow feathers and forged by dragon fire in the Dragonlands. She stands at the top of the dais and studies the room, a furrow in her brow.

"Where are you?" she whispers.

She walks down from the throne and begins searching the castle. Her turns have no pattern yet still a specific purpose. We find ourselves in the dungeons with glowing blue orbs filling the dilapidated cells. A bouquet of decay and rot burns my nostrils, bringing everything into sharp focus. Nerissa ignores the crumbling ruins around her and the orbs of light pulsing behind the bars. Her eyes are fixed on one at the end of the hall.

Rock crunches beneath her feet as she steps up to the light.

"Lucia?" she whispers, eyes trained on the glowing orb.

She circles it slowly, bending down to peer eye level with the orb, her brown gaze shining in the light. "What are you?" she asks.

"Issa," I say, the words falling on deaf ears.

Then, her hand wraps around the orb. As soon as her fingers pierce the light, she collapses on the floor.

I run to her as she begins to seize. "Nerissa. Answer me, Issa. Please. You can't—" Her eyes roll back in her head. "No, Issa. Wake up, Nerissa. Wake up!"

I don't know how long I scream her name, begging her to wake up, when I'm suddenly aware of voices traveling through the castle. I pull my sword, nearly chopping off the head of my cousin.

"Whoa! Watch the blade!" Becci says, and Duncan yanks her back in time for me to miss my mark.

"What happened?" Claudette demands, charging down the steps after them. I can't recall how long I've been here trying to shake Issa awake. Claudette takes Nerissa's free hand, but the other has a clawed grip around the blue light.

"She fell as soon as she touched it," I reply, holding her head in my lap and studying her face as she continues to twitch. "Keels! Where's her sister? What is that thing?"

"Should we try to take it from her?" Becci asks, but when I reach for it, a shock of lightning flashes up my arm.

"Glitz!" I curse. "What are we going to do?"

"Well? Any ideas? How did you get here? How did you find us?" I demand. They all share a look.

"As soon as you left..." Bec says, glancing around the dungeon. The blue light from the orbs casts an eerie glow on the faces, and my skin prickles with anxiety.

"Go on?" I yell.

"Issa dropped the map when she ran. It cleared when you left as if it didn't need you anymore. It led us straight to you," Bec says, her voice measured and low.

"Or you didn't need it, mate," Duncan adds.

"A regular map," Claudette says.

Nerissa stops seizing, her eyes moving frantically behind her lids, hand clenched around the glowing orb. I brush her hair out of her face.

"What a lovely picture," says a voice behind us.

We all turn to gape at a woman with silver hair cascading over her shoulders. Her bare feet peek from beneath her dress, sand and debris covering her skin. The light from the orb focuses on the veins running beneath her skin, giving her an otherworldly glow.

I tense, pulling Issa onto my lap.

I know this woman—this witch who works for Weylan.

The witch they call her, the same woman who gave the map to Issa.

"You've done quite well, Captain Crow. Too bad it's not enough."

# CHAPTER
## THIRTY-FOUR
### NERISSA

I'm falling, twisting and turning in on myself, until I slam against cobblestones. The world around me blurs as if the Island of Helene is on fire, and I'm pushing through the smoke.

I sit up, gasping for breath, *Liehtan* a few inches away on the ground. I crawl toward it, my chest still heaving, and wrap my fingers around the hilt. A swift wind blows, taking a wall of mist with it.

This blade—able to cut through the Darkness holding Lucia hostage—is the only thing I recognize. I'm in my dirt-covered clothes, hair mussed and ratty, cold and shivering from the blur that slammed me here.

I try to speak, but my voice won't come. I touch my throat, glancing around, and notice that no one *sees* me. Strangers and friends walk around me but not quite through. Suddenly, I'm running behind my sister on the street at dusk, the new November sky a bright orange. My heart falls to my feet, and my blood runs cold.

"No." My lips form the words.

*No,* I scream inwardly. I can't do this. I can't *watch* this—not again.

My thoughts resound like my voice cannot. *Remember*—my memory taken from the Acquisitioner hovers at the edge of my mind in a haze. But like the smoke, it clears and I remember. My sister, scorning the attention from the boy I loved. The wedge between us that started years before this awful moment. The painful memory torn from me is restored and consumes me with grief.

I run toward myself, wanting to plead with her—to beg her to stop, but time—it's a thief, and now I've forced myself to watch as it steals from me once again.

*"Lucia, you can't pretend like—" I said.*

*Lucia turned on me—the old me. "I'm not pretending," she replied calmly.*

*"You're not admitting what you've done," I hissed through my teeth, chest heaving.*

I want to yell at myself to stop, to let it go.

No one is dead.

Not yet.

Lucia tilts her head to the side, a specter of the past, and my stomach rolls. I don't think I will ever forget the look on her face, the apathy painting her features. I'd seen it once already, witnessing it for a second time drives the pain deeper than I knew was possible. She doesn't care. The girl I grew up with hadn't died in the fire; she hadn't even wasted away in the Browns' home. She died on the docks, behind the mist, the night she made a deal with the Darkness.

*"I've done nothing wrong," she said calmly and turned around and headed toward the Brown's home, her coin purse dangling on her wrist.*

"Don't go," I mouth to my past self, even though I know it's useless. Even though I know she's me, and I've already done this. I've already followed my sister—now, I know what happens next.

When my past self breaks off into a run, I follow, pulled by an unknown force to this horror again. Even the hair on my past self reflects the distress, whipping behind me like a golden-brown curtain in the fading sunlight, loosed from the braid I hurriedly plaited the morning before I went to look for Lucia.

*"Lucia," I screamed.*

*She didn't turn to look at me. She walked faster, breaking into the fence surrounding the Brown's home.*

*"They nearly died, Lucia. You've been gone for a week, and you almost killed someone!" The last few words came out a whisper.*

I clench my fist, wanting to slap my past self and my sister, to snap us out of it.

*"Are you insinuating I had something to do with the fire at Nathaniel's home? You can't honestly think that?" she asked, hand wrapped around the door handle. But her gaze was cold, measured. The fire had mirrored the one that destroyed our home months before.*

*Too much of a coincidence.*

*"I'm leaving the island, and you'll be rid of me."*

*"Leaving?" I breathed.*

*Lucia wouldn't look at me, fiddling with the knife at her waist. She never carried a blade—it was unladylike, as she constantly reminded me when I began to adorn myself with the one Kip gifted me on my birthday.*

My stomach twists now, as it did then, wondering why she needed a weapon.

*"Let me go, Nerissa," she said, shaking her head and walking out.*

I flex my fingers around *Liehtan* and follow myself out into the street.

*"You can't leave, not after what you did. I can't protect you anymore, Lucia. You need to tell someone, even if it's Uncle Wesley. You can't—"*

*"Protect myself?" she interrupted, whirling on me, her fingers wrapping around the hilt of the knife. I took it as an idle threat. "You did a pathetic job if that's what you thought you were doing, little sister."*

It cut through me then, but her words nearly eviscerate me now. My past face crumbles, and I can almost remember what I thought to myself: *You're stronger than she is.*

Tears form in my eyes while the younger me faces Lucia as twilight descends on the island. The mask of indifference falls over my features, and I barely recognize myself, fuller and well-fed, having not yet turned to the sea. My dress, a loose, strappy thing, brushing the cobblestones, still reeks of my family's money and prestige, which I will drop mere days after this night. The night I will never want to turn back toward again. A wind brushes over us, ruffling the purple fabric, while I can do nothing. The scent of Lucia's perfume, fresh lilacs, brings tears to my eyes.

*I didn't know.*

"Stop this," I say, but no one hears me. The words belong to the present, and this has happened already—no matter how much my fingers itch to rip out the threads of the bloodied tapestry.

As the past unfolds before me, Lucia runs at the other me, where I have barely enough time to grab my own weapon from my side. Our blades meet halfway and ring through the Browns' front yard. I raise *Liehtan* to stop the past from merging with the now, but I hit a wall, falling back on the cobblestones. I sit up, unable to do anything as Lucia and I fight in the street, no one coming out of their houses as the fight unfolds. We don't speak. Fresh tears drip down my past self's cheeks, flowing down my neck, and pooling in the collar of my dress. Every time my blade hits the mark, I wince. My side, hands, and face ache with every blow I felt at the time, even though it is nothing but a phantom.

The old me knocks Lucia's blade from her hand. It skitters across the cobblestones and thuds against an empty barrel. My sister scowls and grabs a rope, swinging it violently at me, and it lassos it around the wrist holding the weapon. I let out a cry, rubbing my skin as if the burn is fresh. The knife clatters to the ground, and Lucia grabs the hilt, raising the blade. My past self takes a step back, pulling a small knife from the holster on her ankle. It's deadly sharp—even more dangerous than the one Lucia stole from me.

*"Give up, sister,"she panted.*

*"Where—"I began to say, but Lucia cut me off.*

Even now, her laugh chills my core.

*"Where did I learn to fight?"she asks with a sneer. "Everyone has secrets. A girl with a face like mine has to learn to protect herself."*

*"I can't let you leave,"I said.*

I want to scream at her to do exactly that, to let this go.

I don't need this moment—we should have never had this argument to begin with. I know now I would have gone after her anyway, even if this hadn't happened.

Lucia lunges for me, and my past self throws back my arm, the knife loosening from my palm and going straight toward the Browns' front door. It creaks open, and I notice the figure step out.

When he shouldn't.

Past me scrambles to her feet, Kip's name stuck in her throat then, and mine, now. *This* is the moment, the one I haven't been able to face. I run toward him, but then—and now—I'm not fast enough.

*"No!" I screamed. "Christopher!"*

The words break through my chest.

*His mouth opened to form words—words I would never hear, never know—when the knife sank into his neck. Blood blossomed at his throat, and he fell.*

My past and present screams echo in the wind.

*I dropped to the ground in a pile of purple fabric as Kip's blood pooled around him like a macabre scarf and soaked into the dress.*

Lucia spins around, her face a mask of indifference, and present me charges her, knowing I'll probably hit the invisible wall separating us again, unable to stop this replay.

Not fast enough.

Not powerful enough.

Never enough—to stop her, stop Kip from dying.

I'm angry she let me fight her, that she wouldn't listen. But I can't escape it. Never will.

The present me sinks the blade into my sister's chest. But the girl in front of me is not my sister—this figure is the Darkness disguised as someone I love.

Lucia looks at me, her lips forming a silent "o," even though this shouldn't happen—the past mingling with the present. She's supposed to leave—to be gone when I turn to scream at her. Water flows around the blade in my sister's chest as the sea swells around the island, controlled by the girl I used to be. The cries of my past self echo around me as the water overtakes us all, salty mist swirling like a hurricane through the buildings. I dig my blade deeper, wanting this to end.

The first time I was overwhelmed by the sea—the first time I remember the pain and euphoria overwhelming me all at once. The heartbreak envelops me in the salt and spray of the tide coming to shore.

I cry out as Lucia crumbles under the blade, her fingers wrapping around the hilt, her cuts bleeding inky black blood as the Darkness leaves her body. My legs give way, and we both fall as the tides rise above us.

The next day half the island would be wondering why the waves crashed so far inland, what curse had come to the Island of Helene.

Now, I embrace it, shock running through my veins when Lucia's hand grabs my wrist.

*"Thank you,"* she says, and my world fades to black.

# TWO
# YEARS
# AGO

# CHAPTER
## THIRTY-FIVE
### NERISSA

***Island of Helene***

*Kip is dead.*

Tears burn the back of my eyes, and I can't think—can't process all that has happened. First Nathaniel—scarred for the rest of his life, burned in his own home with his wife sleeping next to him.

Now...the thought knocks the breath from my lungs. I grab my stomach as I struggle to breathe. The recent events leave a gaping wound in my chest, and I push them out of my mind. If I don't, I worry I'll crack into a million pieces. I inhale slowly, making my way up the walkway. Mrs. Chastain had arrived on the scene as Kip bled out in my arms. It's been hours since our encounter. Since she said those words that marked me a murderer. It doesn't matter that it was an accident.

No one blames me, but I know what happened. I know it was my knife.

It took a long time for me to clean the blood from my body, the stench of copper having seeped into my soul. My hand shakes as I lift it to the door, my fingers raw from how I rubbed the nails with the brush to get the last of the dried crimson from them.

Mrs. Chastain stands on the threshold, and a sad smile comes to her face. "My dear girl, how are you holding up?"

I shake my head as she leads me into the warmth of her home. "Lucia. Did she come to you after...?"

"Lucia has not been back in quite some time," she says, shaking her head as her assistant comes into the room.

I step toward her, my chest heaving as I point my finger at her. "You told me about the Darkness. You told her, too! She made a deal with him. Because of you!"

Taavi sets her tea down, her eyes flashing toward Mrs. Chastain.

"My sister is gone! Not simply gone, but has *disappeared*." My voice cracks, the grief heavy on my chest. "She was there when...but I have spent hours looking for her, and she's...gone. It's like she was never here."

The women share a look.

I look back to Taavi, standing with her hands on her elbows and shifting from foot to foot.

"What did you tell her?" My heart thunders in my ears, and I glare at her.

"I told her the stories she wanted to hear," Taavi says, her voice filled with sick wonder. "The Darkness can give you whatever you want, but for a price. Once the price is paid, his followers never discuss what they traded."

"She's not a *follower*." I close my eyes, clenching my fist tightly enough to draw blood. The Darkness's words echo in my ears, *Even your life here.* "Do you know anyone who has asked a favor of Him?" I ask her.

When I open my eyes again, she's staring straight at me. "Not personally," she says, "But he's been said to start and end wars. His hand is always in something. It's a constant battle between the Darkness and Light, but the difference is you pray to the Light and wait for your miracle. The Darkness grants your desire as soon as you wish it, in return for a trade."

"The Light doesn't ask us to give anything up—"

"Doesn't He?" she asks, tilting her head.

My jaw clenches. "I suppose you follow the Darkness?"

"I do what is best for me," she says slowly, finally taking a seat across from me. "The Light and Darkness are real, but I believe they only have as much power as we give them. Knowledge is true power. Look at you. Light-blessed, what have you had to give up for the sea?"

I clench my teeth. "How do His bargains work? Has she given up her humanity?"

*She didn't even stay. She ran as he fell to the ground and his blood soaked through my dress.*

"If a woman were to ask for a child," Taavi says, bringing me back. "She would have to give up something big—something meaningful. Your sister wanted something back. It might have required nothing more than a blood bargain. It might have required something else. Her beauty might have been a symptom of her deal, not the actual prize." She stands and pulls the kettle from the fire, refreshing her drink. "Either way. She can't get out of whatever their trade was, even if she wanted to. Her soul—"

I jump up, the aroma of fresh tea bitter in my nose. "What about her soul?"

Taavi settles back in her chair, smoothing the wrinkles in her dress.

"Taavi," Mrs. Chastain says, her voice commanding without issuing the demand.

"It's His. Well, almost. There is time, since she is so young, not yet an adult. Our young minds are malleable. Adulthood hardens us. She has until she's nineteen to change her mind. Theoretically, she could change her mind after that, but it would require strength she does not possess."

I fall back to the chair. "How do you know she couldn't overcome him?"

She hesitates and then her eyes lift to mine. "I know your sister, Nerissa Eliott. She is not *you*. She does not have your will. When she turns nineteen, she will be his forever."

A cry I didn't know lived inside my chest falls from my lips. It's all too much. My sister gone, Father dead, and Kip—I hold in the sob for him. He would not want me to mourn this way. He and Father would want me to do something.

To save Lucia.

"How do I find her?" I whisper, strength I did not know I possessed steadying my voice.

"There are rumors of a map that leads to your truest desire. If your sister is to be saved, it would lead you to her." Taavi studies me. "But those texts are written in the lost language, so the translation may be slightly off. A map like that, so old—"

"Where can I get this map?" I ask, standing.

"Oh, darling," she says, a smirk on her lips. "Are you sure you're ready for that adventure?"

"Tell me," I demand.

"First, you're going to need a crew."

# NOW

# CHAPTER
# THIRTY-SIX
CYRUS

*Brevlyra*

The air ripples around us, and the entire castle shifts. Dust flies into the air, clogging my lungs as the ground shakes, and the stone rebuilds itself into what it used to be. Nerissa awakens with a jolt, the world still spinning as it rights itself.

"Cyrus," she whispers, eyelashes fluttering against her cheeks as she looks up at me.

"Issa." I take her face between my hands and press my lips against hers in relief. The taste of the sea on her lips is salty yet sweet. It's a reminder of everything we've gone through the past few weeks, washing away the worry of what we'll face next.

She cups my cheek as rocks and broken pieces of the castle fly around us, missing us as if we are the center of it all. I press my forehead against hers, my heart falling back into rhythm, able to beat properly with her so near. The warmth of her skin against mine tells me she's here, alive.

Suddenly, everything stops. The dungeon grows brighter, and instead of blue orbs, each cell is filled with a person. Our connection snaps back into place, and her joy cascades through her, colliding with my own. Nerissa's lips tip up in a smile that falters as her gaze lands on something behind me. The mixture of elation, sadness, and guilt quickly recedes, knocking the breath from my lungs. She rushes to her feet and pushes past me to a girl huddled in the corner of the room.

"Lucia," Issa cries as she pulls her into her arms. The girl's face is badly scarred, her dark brown hair dull and tangled.

"Nerissa," Lucia whispers, tears filling her eyes as she embraces her sister. "You came."

"What a lovely reunion," the witch says, her hollow gaze suddenly clear. "You broke the curse! I appreciate my sight, so thank you for returning it to me."

"I don't understand," Nerissa says, gripping the girl's hand.

The girl grabs her arm, nails burrowing into the fabric of her shirt, and I step in front of them, half blocking them from the witch.

"This land was in a holding place, protected by the Light but cursed to be without the other king– and queendoms in Penreine. When the light protected its chosen land, it trapped the Darkness. The only way it could spread through Penreine was through people like your sister. But now, it's free."

"That means—" Nerissa begins, but the witch cuts her off with a bone-chilling cackle.

"Precisely, lovely. That means the Darkness can spread through Penreine once more. Thanks for that."

My body tenses as the witch lifts her staff. *BLOOD. KILL HER. KILL HER. KILL HER*. All that's left is to kill the girl in front of me. Issa senses my panic, and our eyes lock as a blinding ball of light shoots from the witch's hands and engulfs us all.

# CHAPTER
## THIRTY-SEVEN
### NERISSA

*Brevlyra*

The witch transports us right outside the city—a city teeming with life. Her power knocked us out, and when we awoke, our hands were bound. *Liehtan* was ripped from my side, tearing the sheath nearly in two.

Now, as we walk through Brevlyra, echoes of joy fill the air, electrifying it with light and happiness. The witch waves her hand over us, deafening the sound and hiding us from view. People raise their hands to the sky and dance, finally free from the curse that has held them in the Darkness for so long. No longer are they prisoners inside Brevlyra; instead, they can walk free—travel through all of Penreine. It's like the weather—what used to be an unbearable heat is now heading toward winter. A bitter chill settles over my skin and cuts through my clothes.

Here at the edge of the forest, I'm consumed by the intense dread wafting from Cyrus. The rope tying us together burns our wrists, and my side feels empty without *Liehtan* resting against my hip. Cyrus flanks one side, my sister on the other. We're surrounded by our slim crew, each of us tied to one another. An eerie laugh fills the air, happy and cruel at the same time, and the hair on the back of my neck stands on end.

"No," he says, his voice shaking. The dread has turned to anger and determination. "The curse may be lifted, but Weylan has no right to this land—despite whatever deal you made with the both of them. This land is *mine.*"

"Tsk, tsk. Did you think Weylan would let you have it quite so easily, little crow?" the witch replies before tapping her staff in an odd rhythm that makes my teeth clench. There's a flash of light, like the one that transported us here, and we find ourselves in a frigid abyss, surrounded by heavily armored guards bearing Queen Weylan's seal. Gone is the excessive heat. In its place, a sharp, piercing winter wind cuts through us. The clothes we wore on the ship don't protect us from the November air.

"Come along now," the witch practically sings, pointing us in the direction she wants us to go. "We're almost there!"

The sea is out of my reach, still a quarter of a league away, at least—but I can smell it, taste it. I grip my sister's hand tighter, unable to let her go.

"Thank you, Issa," she whispers, and I turn to her, tears shining in her eyes. "You didn't have to come for me—"

"Lucia." I stop her before she can say anything else. "I will always come for you. I know we had our...disagreements—"

She silences me by wrapping her arm around my neck and burying me in a hug, stopping our group's progress. The sister I knew is back, scars and all, though a smile touches her lips.

"I knew you'd come for me," she says, tears shining in her eyes. "I fought every day, the Darkness telling me lies and the Light shining in with His truth—the truth. He told me that you would come—you would save not only me but this place." She wraps me in her arms once more, and I fight back tears, holding her close.

"I'm so sorry, Lucia," I whisper into her hair. "Sorry for it all—"

"Stop." She presses her forehead against mine. "It's been two years, Nerissa. We are both different people, better people. You don't need to apologize."

"Now is not the time for a family reunion," the witch snaps, yanking us apart with a flick of her wrist.

We begin moving once more. The trees start to thin, still towering high above us, but no longer a thick blanket of black. The full moon illuminates the rest of our way, and the stars blink in and out of sight behind wispy gray clouds. Cyrus's voice sounds in my head, nothing short of a whisper. Our bond has never been more concrete.

*She's taking us to the New Kingdom. Weylan still can't set foot on this land. Not without spilling blood of the Light-blessed.*

We break through the forest into a barren field that rises into a steep hill. The forest is merely a barrier between the hill and New Kingdom—Teraceron.

I glance up at Cyrus.

"So. Now's the time," I say. "Weylan wanted you to kill me as soon as the curse is lifted. So what will it be, Crow?"

His smile curls humorlessly on his face. "You know, I never have been one to listen to orders."

A tinge of anxiety rolls over him, and I see a flash of razor sharp claws of a cat. A memory shared between us.

I breathe in what I can of the salt and moisture in the air. The sea expands in my lungs and invigorates me. I glance at my crew and my sister, passion swirling in my gut and driving me forward, no matter what awaits us over the crest of the hill. We have conquered the Darkness—done what others said could not be done, and Weylan—the one who caused this all—must pay.

*The Light will prevail.* His eyes bore into mine, echoing the sentiment.

A bitter breeze settles in the air as more than thirty soldiers in full-body armor ride in. The Queen of Easterly is in the midst of them. Her inky black hair flies in the wind, and a gown of navy cascades behind her, threads of silver and gold shining in the moonlight.

"The queen requests your presence, Nerissa Eliott," the guard announces once they're a small distance away. "Witch." He gives a slight nod. "Please release her to my custody."

The witch unties me from the rest of the group, but I don't want to leave my sister or my crew.

"Why me?" I ask.

"The queen doesn't have to explain herself to you."

"Do as the guard says, Nerissa," the witch says, yanking the ropes and bringing Cyrus closer to her. "Wouldn't want me to hurt your boy here, would you?"

My eyes flicker to my sister. The guard canters up to me on his horse and grabs me by the arm, swinging me up behind him.

"Not a word," he says.

I glance toward Lucia, and she gives me a trusting smile. My gaze lands on Cyrus, and his emotions wash over me, filling me with warmth and the knowledge of what he will do to save me—to save *our* crew. I want to call upon the sea to take us away from here and engulf Weylan into its dark depths.

"Hello, Miss Eliott," the queen says when we arrive, the guard sliding me to the ground so I have to look up at her. "You and your sister look nothing alike, if I might say so. If it weren't for those eyes, I wouldn't even know you were your father's daughter. You are the image of your mother."

I clench my fist, staring at her with my chin held high. "You have no idea who you are up against."

The queen slides off her horse and saunters closer. Members of her guard follow suit, swords releasing from scabbards with resounding zings. She raises her hand to stop them from coming any closer. An arrogant smirk paints her elegant face.

"What do *you* know of your abilities?" she asks, looking down at the ground with her next step.

I study the grass, noticing the slight discoloration, a near perfect line separating one land from the other. Even at the cusp of winter, it's almost as if there's a physical mark between New Kingdom and Old Kingdom.

"I know enough," I say, the words sour.

"Do you know where your mother is from?" she asks, crossing her arms in front of her.

"She's from New Kingdom. Teraceron," I lie, thinking of the name in her journal I could never decode. I'll play her game.

"She lived here for many years, but she's not *from* here." She glances behind her at the land she claims as her own. "Your mother was from the Dragonlands, was she not? However, your father is the one I know the most about." She pauses, tilting her head and allowing a soft but cruel smile to lift her thin lips. "Cousin."

I blink at her, swallowing the emotions swirling through me. Cyrus's mind whirs with a plan, lighting a fire inside me. I have to distract the queen a little bit longer.

The queen's bottom lip protrudes in a childish pout. "Britta told you."

I snort. "Please, if you had anything of consequence to say, you would have already said it. Tell me, *Your Majesty*, why are you stalling?"

"I had to wait on my cats," she says as three monstrous beasts appear between the horses. Her smile turns calculated.

I take a tentative step back. A black panther, muscles straining underneath a sleek coat, stares at me with its one eye, fangs dripping saliva as it pulls back its lips and growls. A black and white striped tiger, like I read about in storybooks, sniffs the air, throws back its head. Finally, a spotted leopard, the biggest of the three, rubs against the queen's stomach. Its shoulders reach past her middle, large legs flexing with every movement.

"You..." Weylan says. "You're a girl of prophecy. In a way, it makes you nothing special, another note in the history books. Will she, won't she live up to her destiny? All of that." She flutters her hands as if amused by the thought. "However, you have done something *most* egregious: you stole something of mine."

*Cyrus.*

His emotions nearly knock me flat. Fear floods my veins, his and mine. The thing Cyrus fears the most is not the queen but the beasts at her side.

Queen Weylan threads the fingers of one hand through the tiger's fur, petting the leopard on the head with the other and staring lovingly at the one-eyed panther. It comes up to me, sniffing every inch of my skin. My body pulls taut, and the ringing in my ears drowns out the sound of yelling from down the hill. The hair on my neck rises.

Cyrus's panic rushes through me, piercing my chest. He tries to reach for me, both physically and mentally, but the fear coating my tongue distracts me from the words he tries to push into my mind.

I swallow the bitter taste, letting the cat continue to rub its damp nose on my skin to distract me as the noise behind me escalates.

The queen rubs a cat between the ears, and a pout forms as the feline's eyes rise to hers. "Oh dear, they're hungry." She looks up at me.

"Brevlyra belongs to the Crows," she says. "Cyrus was promised to me—I should rule beside him. His mother wasn't too keen on the idea, and she hid him away, casting this place into darkness with her foolishness. Hidden from all but two: the heir and the Light-blessed heart of the sea—the one purest of heart that could defeat the Darkness." Weylan's hand digs into the animal's fur, and a whine passes over his maw. "And now you've broken the curse *and* the bond that guaranteed me this land."

"What do you want from me?" I ask, sweat dripping down my spine.

"Leverage. Without the bond, I have two options—Cyrus will either hand me the throne in exchange for your life, or he will die."

# CHAPTER
## THIRTY-EIGHT
### CYRUS

**Brevlyra**

"No!" I scream as Weylan's cats come out. This is Weylan's cruel game at the front lines. She wants me to suffer, to witness the woman I love torn limb from limb like all the others—

The servant girl who gave me my first kiss.

The commoner delivering packages to the palace who accidentally met me in the kitchen—and came back for a second visit.

My personal guard's sister who cornered me at a dance, sharing a kiss tasting of strawberries and honey.

The queen doesn't care for me, but I'm not allowed to care for anyone else. This time will be worse because we share everything through the bond. Issa's heartbeat rings in my ears, racing with fear we share. My birds rise out of the forest, flocking toward us like a hurricane. The caws of the murder carries in the wind, and a spark of hope lights inside me.

*I'm coming, Issa.*

"Lift your hands up!" I yell.

We throw our bound hands in the air. The birds swoop down, slicing through the ropes. Besnick finds his place on my shoulder, his claws biting into my flesh.

"Crow—" Claudette starts, but the witch's blade blocks them from view.

"Shouldn't have done that, little Crow," the witch hisses.

I duck as she swings her blade, Besnick flying from my shoulder and attacking the witch. She screeches angrily as the bird flies toward her face, dropping my stolen blade. I lunge for it, charging her. She reaches for the other blade at her side in time to meet mine in the air. At least thirty soldiers run down the hill, and Duncan yanks his bow and quiver of arrows free from his shoulder, hidden in his thick leathers. He shoots down two horses as they storm down the hill. The animals' death cries echo in the wind.

Bec picks up a fallen blade and fights with two guards who made it past Duncan's arrows, her red hair flying.

"You're outnumbered, little Crow!" the witch screams, as our blades meet in the air. She holds Nerissa's stolen sword in her hands, leaning her weight into it.

"You underestimate my crew and my crows," I say, spittle hitting her cheeks.

I shove her back, causing her to stumble. She glares at me, taking another step back and lifting her arm out to her side. The clouds race above us, swirling gray and black in the sky, and a harsh, piercing wind knocks the whole crew to the ground. I crash onto the hard packed earth, the air escaping my lungs in one sharp gasp. My muscles strain as I turn over and claw toward the witch, my nails digging into the loose soil. Weylan's threats tumble down the hill.

Issa yells, and I whip around as Lucia steals a horse from a fallen guard, running to her sister. Lucia grabs Issa's hand and yanks her on the back of the horse, taking a turn so tight it's more reaction than thought. They draw nearer to the forest, the cats charging after them.

But it won't be enough. A horse, no matter how well-bred, cannot outrun the queen's beasts.

Issa's cry carries through the harsh storm. I squint in the fierce rain and wind but lose her through the harsh weather pelting my skin.

Sharp whinnies pierce the air, and my ears ring as I struggle to my feet.

*Too late.*

Hot pain sears my back, and my body arches. *Liehtan* slices through my shirt and buries itself in my skin. The ground rushes to meet me as warm wetness oozes from my wound. My vision fogs, my birds swarming around those left on the battlefield.

"Issa," I whisper.

The witch suddenly screams, and I catch a glimpse of crow feathers clawing at the witch's face.

*Take* Liehtan *to Nerissa...* I tell Besnick through our connection, the words slurred in my mind. He takes to the skies, a glint of steel in his grasp.

The bitter salt of the sea drips onto my tongue, mingling with the acrid tang of blood in my nostrils.

*Issa.*

My eyes droop as tentative fingers touch my skin.

"Ah!" I scream.

"The blade cut too deep. We need...By the Light, Cy," Becci whispers.

"Get Bec out of here, aye. She's going to be sick," Duncan says to someone.

A ringing in my ears rises over their voices as the world grows dark.

# CHAPTER
## THIRTY-NINE
### NERISSA

*Brevlyra*

I race toward my sister as she grabs the reins of a fallen guard's horse and throws herself on the saddle. The sun begins its slow ascent on the horizon, hints of dawn casting the world in hues of red and gold. As soon as I reach her, she grabs my hand, and I put all my weight into swinging onto the back of the horse. The cat's hot breath laps at our heels as we take a sharp turn and race across the field, shortening the distance between us and the forest.

"We're not going to make it," Lucia whispers.

"Like keels we aren't," I mumble, wrapping my arms around her and grabbing the reins. I squeeze my thighs into the horse.

We're a blur of white as we race forward. I yank at the sea, bringing it to me from over half a league away, calling on it with every fiber of my being. Magic prickles at my skin, but not my own. I glance back at the witch, the mix of our powers calling forth gray and black clouds, the moon and stars blinking out of existence. She tugs at the storm and I call for the sea, the two colliding to create a catastrophic distraction. The rain wraps around us, and the air tastes of salt as I lean into my sister's back. She wraps her arms around the horse's neck, so we're nearly lying down as we go through the forest.

"It's not enough," Lucia cries.

A break in the trees looms ahead. Genuine hope spreads through my core. "We're going to make it," I whisper.

But Lucia's right. It's not fast enough. The leopard pounces, grabbing the back leg of the horse inches before we reach the end of the forest. We fly through the air, the horrifying scream of the horse splintering around us like broken glass.

Lucia and I stumble to our feet, taking off in a run through the trees.

Large paws knock me from behind, and I hit the ground. Lucia screams my name, and I fumble for the dagger on my waist. I yank it free in time to stab in the general direction of the beast's face. A roar rumbles the ground as my blade connects, but the black cat still moves. I have enough room to scramble out from under it. Lucia works her hands under my arms, helping me along.

"What are you doing?" I shout. "By the sea, *run!*"

She stubbornly grabs my hand and yanks me with her. "No! I'm not leaving you!"

Her eyes are bright as the cats circle us. My emotions swell—Lucia is back. My sister is *here* with me like when we were children. Fear ices my veins, but the strength of her back to mine calms it down. The queen screams her orders through the pelting rain.

My fingers tighten around Lucia's, but I know we'll never make it past the cats. They snarl at me. Suddenly, through the thick onslaught of rain, something splashes in the mud at my feet.

I look up as a streak of black and white rushes back to his master—Besnick.

I snatch up *Liehtan* and point it at the nearest cat.

*Yes, they'll never expect that.* Cyrus's voice echoes in my mind.

My sister grabs the blade from my hand and slashes the horse in the chest. The cats' eyes turn in the direction of my blade, and they leap over us and tear into the horse, thirsty for blood.

"What was that?" I ask as she hands me back my soiled blade.

"Surviving."

I shake my head, rising to my feet. The cats are distracted now, but they won't be for long. Without a horse, there's no way we can outrun them.

"Issa—"

"We need another blade!" I call out to Cyrus, forcing the thought in my mind, praying one of his crows can follow through.

It takes a moment, but suddenly, a sword falls from the sky, followed by the screeching of a murder of crows. Lucia picks up the blade and weighs it in her hands.

"Neck, eyes, gut—can you remember that?" I say, now gripping *Liehtan* with two hands.

"I did learn a thing or two on my own, you know," she says, and I can hear—even at this moment—the smile in her voice.

I clench my jaw tight and fight the stinging in my eyes. I go for the guards, who have closed in on us with my sister at my back. I block out all other sounds, focusing on the man in front of me. His blade slices in the air, and I duck, slide face-first underneath him, mud spraying my face. My blade slips from my hand because of the rain, and I fumble for the hilt. I scarcely have enough time to arch it upward and into the gut of the nearest guard. He falls to the ground, and the white tiger jumps over me for its meal after destroying the other slain guard.

Power runs through me, salty like the sea and fiercer than a monsoon. *Liehtan's* ability makes me unstoppable. The first guard gets a sampling of my new strength. Though he's seas better and fights harder, he's missing something I have.

A reason.

A purpose—family to protect.

I use his exhaustion and hesitant motions to my advantage and press my sword at his throat.

"Drop it," I say, breathing heavily.

He tilts his head back, exposing more of his neck, challenging me to do what he doesn't think I will. He stares fiercely down at me, the rain leaving tracks down his face.

"Drop. It," I repeat, the salt water dripping onto my tongue.

He does, and I grab his sword from the ground. Turning around, my sister swings the dagger at the panther as it pounces. Its cries ricochet into the rain as the blade hits its mark, and I run toward her, calling her name and tossing the sword in the air. She spins and catches it, throwing her dagger at the leopard. It misses, and the beast growls, stalking nearer.

I yank her to me, and we spin so that we're back-to-back, the heavy rain obscuring my view.

"Give it up, Miss Eliott." Queen Weylan's voice rings through the rain. Her cats are less regal than before, not the unstoppable beasts Weylan believes they are. Blood drips from the tiger's jaws and oozes from the wounds on the panther, while foam slides down the leopard's teeth as it pants. "My cats are trained for this, even if my guards disappoint."

"If you want to lose your cats, so be it," I shout back, voice barely audible through the fighting around us.

I let go of my sister's hand and charge the panther as it pounces. My blade misses, and the cat pushes me to the ground, blood flying over my clothes. I slice through the beast's throat, and a tortured cry falls from its mouth as its dead weight sags on top of me.

My muscles scream as I push the body away and pivot toward the slowly stalking leopard, but my sister's screams cut me short. I lean forward on my knees, struggling for breath, searching the field for my sister.

"Lucia!" Her name falls from my lips at the sight of the leopard and tiger standing between us.

I force my body into a run, heading for the spotted cat. My muscles burn as I arc my sword through the sinew and bone, not sparing a glance as its head rolls cleanly away. Somewhere in the distance the queen's rage reaches a crescendo, her scream piercing through all sound on the battlefield. The shock of my strength—no, the sword's strength—halts me for a second. My arms tremble and struggle to keep hold of the blade as I run to my sister, her gaze still fixed on the tiger.

But I'm not quick enough. The tiger bites down on my sister's shoulder before I can reach it. I let loose another cry and charge. I bury the blade in the tiger's chest, and it releases her with a death cry.

As soon as the beast falls dead on the ground, I drop to the ground beside Lucia.

"Lucia," I say, the tears falling down my cheeks. I study the gaping wound, my heart rising in my throat.

At first, I think she's crying, her body shaking in fear, but when I turn to her, she's grinning like I haven't seen in years. Our tears mix with the salty downpour, and her laughter rings through the angered screech of the queen as she takes in her fallen pets. Lucia fumbles for my hands, her shoulders still shaking.

Then laughter bubbles over my lips amidst the tears. I bite down to quiet the sobs that follow soon after, a split on my bottom lip stinging.

She turns weary eyes toward me, and this time the tears pooling in her eyes are from something else. I pull her close. Her blood seeps into my clothes as the rain starts to subside. We shiver from the cold and wet, shaking in each other's arms and letting the tears fall.

When we pull back from each other, she places her forehead against mine, closing her eyes.

"I'm sorry," she whispers, voice dissipating in the rain.

"Me, too. Lucia, please—"

"No," she whispers. "Don't say anything. Please." Her cheeks are white, her blood a bright red pool beneath us. The blue of her eyes shines in the moonlit minutes of dawn, and I want to stop this—beg for this to not be real. I've traveled to find her—for her to live the life she deserves—but it came to a gruesome end. "This is how it should be, sister. It had to be me. The world isn't ready for you to leave yet. If one of us has to go, I'd rather it be me. I know what..." Pain laces her features. "I know what it must have cost to come find me, to release me from the hold the Darkness had on me."

She winces in pain, and I wipe the tears from her cheek with a swipe of my thumb. She coughs, and blood trickles down the side of her lip, mixing with the rain.

"The queen—" I begin, but she isn't finished.

"You're the best—" She stops, gasping in pain. "You are the best sister anyone could have asked for, and I'm sorry." She grabs my hand, and her grip is so tight the pain is like a harsh stab. "Thank you. There isn't enough time on this side of forever—" She coughs again, blood seeping from her mouth. "To show you how much I appreciate you. How much I love you." Tears pool in her eyes. "I don't want to leave you, especially after your birthday." A sob rips from her chest.

"Stop talking like this, Lucia! You're going to be fine!" I pull her hand close to me, my heartbeat thundering against her palm.

She smiles. "Light be with you, sister," she finishes, her hand falling slack as the rain suddenly stops.

The hardest thing I have ever had to do is turn my back on my sister and pick up *Liehtan*. The witch sits tied up and gagged, knocked out from the fight. Someone has strung rosemary around her neck, most likely Claudette, so she won't be able to use magic when she wakes.

The queen has recovered from the loss of her cats, knowing part of the prophecy is complete.

Lucia is dead; the blood spilled.

Weylan relishes it, walking down the hill, her head tilted back, breathing in the coming winter. "The land almost smells differently here," she says, extending her hands. She closes her eyes against the brightness of an imminent sunrise, the fading moon and starlight shining in her hair. Turning away from us, her entire body shakes with laughter. My heart pounds against my ribs, lungs tightening from the icy air in my chest.

"It's mine now," she says.

Pain and loneliness rip a gaping wound in my chest.

Lucia, but also—

*Cyrus.*

A guard rushes toward me, but Claudette steps in front of me, striking him down in a splash of blood. I inhale, bringing my sword up as I start up the hill, screaming a death wail.

Bec and Duncan work on one guard together, and Claudette calls their names as she runs toward me. "What are you doing, Cap?"

She grabs my wrist, and I jerk away. She shakes her head, eyes flashing with fear. The fight intensifies around us. The storm has stopped, but the sea is too far. Sunrise peeks through the diminishing clouds. The sky is brighter than it has ever been—an ethereal light not connected to this plane of existence. My path is clearer than ever, unbidden by the darkness.

"Nerissa—"

"Let me do this!" I snap, and she hesitates once more before returning to the fight.

I sprint the rest of the way up the hill, raising my sword against the pain in my legs and arms. I keep my eyes on the queen. She's ready for me, and one of her guards releases an arrow, grazing my shoulder. The pain should be sharp, insistent, but fire swells in my core. I stumble but continue, dodging the next one aimed at my head.

Weylan's guards step in front of her, swords at the ready. She settles her gaze on me and takes out her blade, walking closer, the protectors around her still a few steps ahead. Fresh tears mix with rain dripping down her cheeks. Mud covers my trousers and spots my shirt, my hair sticking to my face in stringy strands. The queen's eyes are bright with fury.

The guards closest to her try to hold her back, but she doesn't care. She continues forward, almost running.

The queen raises her dagger, and it meets my upraised sword. Our blades ring in the night, and I yank back. The light of the full moon is lost as the sun rises, and Weylan's smile goes impossibly white as we circle one another. A guard runs up, and she raises her hand.

"No," she says, oozing fake consideration. "She's *mourning*. Let her come at me. Maybe she will understand the pain I felt when she cut through my sweet babies. I don't need her anymore—the blood of prophecy has been spilled. *Light-blessed.* What's more Light-blessed than a sister saved by the heart of the sea?"

An arrow shoots into the air and lands in the guard's throat. I spin as Duncan lowers a stolen bow. The queen breaks into a run, grabbing a fallen sword from the ground. Claudette fights one of the queen's guards, and Duncan knocks down another three as Bec fights two more.

"You will *never* control the entire kingdom," I say, spitting the words as we circle one another.

The queen smiles. "I don't want *the* kingdom. I'd prefer all of Penreine."

*The five kingdoms.*

Our blades meet again. I yank back and aim for her face. She leans back, and it barely grazes her cheek. She pushes me off, touching the spot with her gloved hand.

"Even you bleed, *my queen*," I say, sneering.

Her lips pull back in a snarl, and we drop the pretenses, fighting blade for blade. Her long dagger slices at my arm, and the sharp cold laces through my clothes. She smiles, spitting in an un-queenly way in the grass. My muscles burn with every continued blow. It goes on forever, but the ache of my sister's death is fresh in my bones and keeps driving me forward.

A scream rips through me, and I swing my blade, aiming for her head. She ducks, but I'm fueled by something inhuman. Going at her again, the hilt of my blade crashes against her fingers. The blade falls from her hand with a cry of pain, and she drops to her knees to avoid my next blow. I sense the motion coming, slowing my sword enough to rest it at the base of her throat. The sharp metal tip rests in the spot where her head and neck meet. Her pulse vibrates up the blade.

"This blade can't hurt me, my queen," I whisper, my words dripping from my tongue. "But what can it do to you?"

The sounds of the others fighting falls away. Their eyes bore into me.

"Did you ever think we'd be here, Your Majesty? With you bending the knee?" I ask, chest heaving and the emotions swirling bitterly in my gut.

Her smile widens, her cheek dripping blood onto the ground as a frigid wind whips her hair. She closes her eyes and tilts back her head. Her mouth opens in a laugh as rainwater runs down her cheeks and onto her tongue.

"Cap, would you not agree—" Claudette begins, but I silence her with a look.

I glance at my crew. Cyrus lies motionless in the grass. His absence captures my breath, widening the wound already created by my sister's death. A lump forms in my throat, tears burning behind my eyes. The few remaining guards hover at the edge of our group, arms raised in surrender. Duncan raises his bow, and even in her worried state, Claudette doesn't drop her blade.

I snap my attention back to the queen in front of me.

"I will kill you," I whisper.

Weylan winks. I press the blade farther into her throat. A prick of blood slides down her skin. "You won't," she says.

"My sister is dead." My voice cracks. "Cyrus is—"

"Forever mine, Miss Eliott."

She throws her arm into the sword to push it away from her neck, lunging from the ground and screaming as the blade slices into her skin. With a cry, she charges at me with her sword raised. I swing my sword at her but miss, ducking to avoid her next blow. I right myself, ready to swing, but suddenly, an arrow pierces her chest. She falls to her knees, and I stare down at her as she stares up at me.

"I wouldn't have killed you," she croaks. "It would've been a waste."

"You can't have this land," I say.

"If not me, then who? Brevlyra will never be free. Land demands to be taken," she says and falls the rest of the way, her eyes lifeless.

Claudette grabs my arm to stop me from crumpling to the ground. My weight is too much, and I fall to the grass. The last guard sprints toward New Kingdom, the others having run back from where they came. Duncan raises his bow, but I croak out, "Let him go. The people need to know what happened to their queen."

I stare for a moment before struggling to my feet and running to Cyrus. My fingers graze the gash that spreads from his side to his back, fingers coming back sticky with his blood.

"Cyrus," I whisper. "Wake up."

*I can't lose you, too.*

*I can't lose someone else.*

Suddenly, I'm sobbing, my middle ripping in two. I fall next to Cyrus, my fingers digging into his shirt, begging him to wake up. His heartbeat is weak, barely there under my palm. Someone touches me from behind, and I scream in agony, my heart breaking into a million pieces. A faint blue glow emanates from my hands, melting into Cyrus. Magic—something I've never experienced before. Spots fill my vision as the scream continues to claw its way out of my throat. I pass out to the sound of hooves in the rain and the cawing of crows.

# CHAPTER
# FORTY
### CYRUS

*Brevlyra*

A fire crackles in the corner. I blink, and the room spins. Becci rushes to my side, her mouth forming whispered words drowned by the blood pounding in my ears.

"Let him rest," says a deep voice. "The more he rests, the better for his recovery."

"And the faster we can leave," Becci mumbles under her breath.

A low laugh rumbles in the direction of the speaker. "You're in quite a hurry to leave," he says.

"We've outstayed our welcome," she says, sarcasm thick in her voice.

"Hardly. This is your home, milady. Plus, you have no ship."

"I am no lady," Becci says.

I try to sit up, and— "By the sea," I groan.

Becci catapults from her chair and wraps her arms around my neck.

A hiss of pain escapes my lips. "Keels, Becci. That hurts."

She jerks back. "Sorry. It's—I can't believe it worked. Nerissa did something to you, and you—you healed."

I reach for Nerissa, listening for her thoughts. I can't find her past the buzzing in my head.

"Careful," the deep voice says. "He's still pretty battered."

"What happened?" I ask, looking around the ornate room and catching sight of the man in question. He's huge, with long black hair tied in a ponytail and a beard resting near the top of his chest. His eyes wrinkle around the edges, bright with sincerity.

I'm in the castle—in a room fit for a prince. It's larger than even my room in Weylan's castle, and while outdated, elegant tapestries hang on the walls, representing the different houses. The House of Crow is the largest of them all, hanging on the wall across from the bed and over the fireplace.

"The group that found you recognized you by the crows. They brought you to the castle," a new voice says, this one belonging to a woman. My eyes slide to the open door, a slight woman in both height and weight.

"What about Issa?" I ask, anxiety rolling in my gut. "Where is she? They found her, too, didn't they?"

Becci forces a smile on her face. "Issa is...fine."

I try to throw my legs over the side of the bed to go—well, I'm not sure where. Maybe to Issa, wherever she may be. The world tilts, and I fall back on the pillows.

"You shouldn't do that," the man says.

He can't be much older than we are, but there's something different about him, less weary. A smile curves easily on his face, and he rushes to help Becci settle me back on the pillows.

He reaches over me and presses a cup to my lips. "Drink this."

I push his hand away. "I don't want anything to drink. I'm fine—" I go to stand, but I end in a crumpled heap on the floor, my head spinning.

"Stubborn newk," Becci snaps, getting to my level.

I push up off the floor, and the man catches me as the ground rushes up to meet me. He helps me stumble back onto the sheets, head spinning.

The woman tilts her head. "We're happy to have you here in the castle. My name is Colette Elrod, the Speaker of the Octadus in Brevlyra. We're a group of eight individuals who make the political and financial decisions for Brevlyra. We would like to thank you for your efforts to lift the curse. You are welcome here as long as you choose, and in due time, I would like to discuss your future here. But first, you must rest." She winks at me. "That's an order."

"Sleep, by the Light," Becci says. "We need you at your best."

I wonder if '*we*' means an entire kingdom now.

"Brevlyra will be waiting when you wake," the man says.

I bite back a groan and close my eyes.

It's been nearly two weeks since our ship was destroyed off the coast of Brevlyra, and how those around the castle treat me—as someone with words they should listen to—unnerves me.

The workers in the castle offer me timid grins and "Do you need anything?" so often that I've taken to hiding in the shadows. It rarely works, and never with my crew. Becci stays glued to me, and Claudette constantly checks on me whenever my cousin isn't around. Duncan wreaks havoc with the guards situated across the city, challenging them to endless battles. Even he's easier to smile.

I've barely had the chance to speak to Issa. She mainly stays in her rooms, mourning in the only way she knows how. The bond still tugs at my core, but a hollowness awaits on the other end of it. I finally find the courage to follow it, finding Nerissa in an abandoned tower, sitting on a window ledge and staring at the rain as it falls down the windowpane.

"Light reading?" I ask, her hand stuck between the pages of a book.

She jerks in surprise, wiping her cheeks.

"Stories." She shrugs. "My father used to have a copy. He took it with him when he sailed to Halivaris. Actually, I snuck it in his luggage. I thought he might want to read it while away—to remember us."

The cushion bends beneath my weight as I take a seat, and Nerissa hugs her legs tighter to her chest. Sorrow rolls off her in waves, and I choke on the cloudy taste of it.

"Have you read the story about the girl who discovers she's living in a story?" I ask.

She swallows and shakes her head.

"My mother used to tell it to me. It was about a girl whose life was being written by fairy tale characters. They were so happy, they wanted to read something that didn't end happily ever after."

She snorts, sounding like herself again. "So we read fairy tales because they give us hope, and they write tragedies to break their hearts?"

"There's nothing wrong with having a heart, even if it does break," I whisper, clenching my fist. If I don't, I'll reach out for her, and I'm not sure that's something she needs or wants.

So I'll wait for her.

"I wish it didn't hurt so much," she says, crawling over to me and laying her head on my shoulder.

When she falls asleep in my lap, I carry her as far as my healing body allows. A guard meets me at the bottom of the tower, rushing over to catch her before I crumple under her weight.

"You shouldn't be carrying her," he says.

"It's good exercise."

"It's how you'll open your stitches," says a wizened voice behind him.

I peer around the guard, my gaze locking with Colette's. "Hello, Cyrus Crow," she says. "It's almost like you've been avoiding me. Which is hard considering our residence is the same."

"I'll take her from here," the guard says, disappearing from sight with Nerissa wrapped in his arms. Jealousy burns warmly in my gut, but I push it down and focus on the Speaker.

She wears a winter cloak of the richest black with a corseted top and pair of flowing breeches beneath. Rain pelts the window near my head, off beat with the thump of her boots against the carpeted walkway.

My eyes flash to the patch on the right side of her cloak, recognizing the sigil by the feather surrounded by a circle of stars, an arrow shooting through the middle.

The words, "For flight or battle, Brevlyra," in a semi-circle around the bottom.

"How are you faring?" she asks.

"It's been a lot to take in," I say.

She winks. "All in due time, but I do believe it has come. I would like to discuss something with you. Do you fancy a stroll?"

I raise a brow, curiosity churning in my mind. "In the rain?"

She waves her finger around her face. "Less eyes in the rain. They'll have to peek through the shutters."

On our way through the castle, the servants stop and bow their heads, mumbling whispered "hellos" in our direction. Before we go out, one of them hands me a cloak, and I shrug it on before stepping into the cold, misting rain.

We're a few blocks down the street before she speaks. "First, what questions do *you* have?"

I shrug my shoulders under the cloak, resituating it over my body as rain slips through. Her feet are light over the cobblestones, not even the puddles acknowledging her.

"You call yourself the Octadus, correct?" I ask.

She nods. "We do."

"Why eight?"

"Most would think an odd number would be wiser, someone to always break a tie." Our eyes meet. "The ninth spot is for you."

I purse my lips, biting the inside of my cheek and considering her words. She leads me past a small alcove and down an alley, the streets almost empty in the rain the harder it falls. Her pace increases, and she walks up a hill with a gazebo resting at the top. My feet slip on the cobblestones, struggling to gain purchase. Once we reach the top, she settles into a seat on the far left side and looks over her shoulder.

"Come look," she says, voice nearly drowned out by the rain.

I take a seat beside her, breath hitching in my throat at the sight before me. Brevlyra spreads around us, towering buildings thinning into small houses before thickening into a forest of pines. Beyond our vision, the sea waits, but I can't see it.

"When Brevlyra was given another chance, we wanted to change things."

"Why?" I ask.

Colette leans back to face me. "We have nothing against your family, and your father and mother brought us many prosperous years. However, our people needed protecting, and we had learned putting our entire world in the hands of one family wasn't what we desired anymore." She pauses for a heartbeat before continuing. "Have you ever read 'Arrow, a Love Poem'?"

My brow furrows, and I shake my head.

She recites,

*"'The heart an arrow*

*Must always land true*

*The mind a barrier*

*For what our arrow aims to do.'"*

"We always believed we needed a type of government to hold us accountable, all of us. Our hearts are with the land, but not always our heads. It's why we have an arrow on our sigil. The monarchy didn't need to fade away, but it needed to become something different. So when you finally returned, as many believed you would, we wanted you to have a spot among us."

"You want my involvement?" I ask.

"Do you desire your crown, Cyrus Crow?" she asks.

Her question surprises me. Whenever I think of Brevlyra, it's a home I never got to enjoy. My mother whisked me away before I was old enough to appreciate the land—before I was even old enough to consider myself a prince. Going back has always been about righting the wrong done to the land by Weylan and her hunt for power. It was never about getting back my crown.

"Is that what you want of me?" I ask, looking out on the lands free of strife.

"The government you have in place has made this—my first home—flourish.

I know nothing of ruling aside from Weylan's reign. You would be better off without me."

"It's because you have lived in that environment that we welcome you back home. Why would someone who suffered as you have do that to a people you love? You certainly know what *not* to do."

We laugh for a moment before it fades into the squall around us.

"I don't think I'm made to live on land for long. I'm a Crow," I say, shrugging. "We fly."

She studies my face for a long moment, a smile hovering on the edge of her lips. "You do," she says. "But sometimes they need a place to land. This will always be your home, my king."

"I'm no king. I'm a pirate, and my heart is elsewhere," I say, with complete conviction.

"And so it is." Colette rises and shrugs on the hood of her cloak. "As I said, an odd number would be beneficial to the council. Perhaps as an advisor on all things..." She flutters her hands, "Abroad. While you are a bird who wants to fly, I fear many of us, myself included, have become fond of our cage. We could use your expertise and eyes in the sky."

My chest tightens, and she stops me, looking up into my eyes. "You will be free to do as you please. We need your mind, not your body. In exchange, you'll have room and board when you require. A ship and a place to stock your helm when needed. A contract you can cancel at any time..."

"I'll consider it," I say, thinking of the freedom it would give me, my crew, and Issa, if she wanted.

We walk through the rain back to the castle, a weight lifting from my shoulders. For the first time, I can breathe.

"Have you seen Issa?" I ask Becci the next day when I exit my bedroom, a tray of food laid out before her.

With her mouth full, she says, "I changed my mind. I don't know where this cook was a few days ago. Are you sure we can't stay a little longer?"

I roll my eyes and tap the hilt of my sword. "No."

"Try this bacon. Seriously."

I shake my head. "Not hungry."

"Are you all right?" she asks, wiping her greasy fingers on her pants.

"I'm worried about her. I haven't been able to find her—" Not since our conversation a few days ago.

"She's been hiding," she says, unable to meet my gaze. "She's good at it, too."

I bite the inside of my cheek and go over the castle layout in my head, what I can remember of it from the few times I've walked down the halls. "Maybe she's in the library again—"

"Cyrus."

Something in her voice draws my attention back to her. "What?"

"You're better now, so I'm not afraid to mention it, but when you find Nerissa, you should..." She stops, shaking her head. "You were—well, you're alive because of Issa and that blue light of hers. She did something and saved you."

"What?" I ask.

Becci shakes her head. "Whatever Issa did wasn't natural. I guess...I don't know. The seas are calmer, the queen and Lucia are dead, and you aren't. Her magic saved you, and now the seas are calm around Brevlyra—because of her."

Pain laces through me, not fully my own. The tug of it almost takes me back to Issa, and I want to run through the halls until the cord connecting us has no more line.

"There was no saving Lucia. Instead, she saved you. But—" She stops, shaking her head.

"What, Becci?"

"We went back for her sister's body," she whispers. "After you both passed out, we used the carriage to take you to a cottage in the woods, but when Nerissa woke, she insisted we go back. The others took you to the castle. And..."

"And," I say, taking a seat across from her, pain flooding through me. Nerissa's pain. "Had they done something to...her sister?"

She swallows, fear lacing her features. "She was gone, Cyrus. They took her—someone. The witch was gone, too, and no one can remember, you know, what happened during the fight. Nerissa didn't...handle it well. She finally wore herself out screaming and crying around sunrise the next morning. Some of the scholars think—this is just a theory—the Light took her body. The shock of it surprised her."

"So—what should I do? How can I help her?" I ask.

Becci gets up and walks over to me, ruffling my hair. "Some things can't be helped," she says. "Simply be there for her. I think she's better. Last I saw, anyway."

My chest constricts, and I look in the mirror on the wall across from us. Bruises cover my face, though faded to a sickly green and yellow around the edges. There's a new scar taking shape near the corner of my mouth. I touch it, and scowl at the man looking back at me.

"She shouldn't have saved me," I whisper.

"Right? Of all the lives to save." Becci tries to smirk, but it turns into more of a grimace.

I glare at her, but I can't hold it at the sight of the tears in her eyes.

"She was here for her sister," I say. "She should have saved her—"

"Cyrus," she interrupts. "You need to accept that you are alive when Lucia is not. Nerissa is having a hard time, and she needs you. We all need you. Get over your problem with still being alive, and do what a good captain does—lead."

I straighten my spine and give a stiff nod. Becci's shoulders relax, and a timid grin tugs at the corner of her lip.

# CHAPTER
## FORTY-ONE
### CYRUS

*Brevlyra*

I rap my knuckles on the door to Nerissa's chambers. I wait for the sound of her footsteps on the other side, seconds dragging on for a lifetime. The door creaks open, and she leans her head out, face relaxing and shoulders slumping in relief when she sees me.

"I was thinking you were—" She stops and shakes her head. Irritation floods through her, before being pushed gently aside with grief. Grief is never gentle. It's faster than a flood or the tide, coming hard and yanking you under.

It dances over my skin like a fine mist. Nerissa steps aside and lets me in. She carries her sadness with every step as I follow her into the room. She slides onto the couch and pulls a blanket onto her lap, lips pursed on a cup of tea.

"Are you falling back into your life as a lady?"

The irritation returns, this time aimed at me. I flash her a smile, and a reluctant one slides onto her face.

"The council has asked me to assist them at Britta's trial." Her eyes flash over to me. "Justice here is so different—objective and less cruel. Though they never want her out of their sight."

I take a seat across from her, hands itching to caress her cheek, to try to lift some of the sadness from her shoulders.

Our eyes lock. "I'm not sure I should weigh in. She's my cousin, but she did betray me, too." She rubs her temples, eyes clenched shut. "What do you think I should do?"

"Nerissa Eliott," I say slowly, getting up and sitting on the opposite side of the couch. She opens her eyes, and I take her hands in mine. "When have you ever asked me what to do?"

She chews her bottom lip, and the grief rushes through, coloring her cheeks. "I don't know what to do. My decisions don't end well."

"Nerissa—"

"She's gone," she says, no longer speaking about her cousin. "And I have no tears left. Now, I'm here, and I don't know where to go next. I don't know what to *do* next now that she's gone. I need someone to tell me what to do now." She looks to me, eyes pleading. Grief covers her like a blanket, practically darkening the room around us. "What do I do?"

I slowly place my hand on hers. "You don't need me to tell you what to do," I whisper.

She shakes her head. "She's gone. I've lost her all over again, and now—I have to decide what to do with Britta, and it's tearing me apart. I can't decide. Why can't I decide? Father would know what to do."

I wrap her in my arms, her heart beating in rhythm with my own. Her breathing steadies as I hold her close. "And what is that?"

Pain begins to ebb from her and becomes a dull reminder, something she'll carry for the rest of her life. I also notice the acceptance layered beneath it.

"He would say," Her words are warm as they hit the center of my chest where her face rests. "To forgive Britta, but to be on guard. Those who hurt us can always hurt us again, but it is not in us to decide whether or not they are worthy of forgiveness."

I wrap her tightly in my arms. "And how does that align with the options the council has laid out?"

"They didn't say much, but they did tell me they value my opinion. Her hearing is tomorrow. I think I should go."

"And what do you think should happen to Britta?"

"I think there is more than one kingdom, and keeping her here would be its own kind of punishment. It's not one she would learn from."

"Sounds to me you know what to do."

A smile curls onto her face. I lean over, pressing my lips to the spot where her hairline begins, breathing in her scent.

"Thank you," she says. "And I appreciate you not killing me."

A laugh bursts from my chest, and then she joins in, pulling back and showing me the full control she has over me with a simple grin.

"But I can't stay here," she says, face falling. Uncertainty wars within her, hot and sticky. "I can't be *here*. I was never made for this." She waves a hand around the room. "And if we are still talking about my...sister." She pauses. "She wouldn't want this for me either."

I grit the back of my teeth and nod. "That's why I'm here," I reply. "I wanted to talk with you about what to do about us—me—here."

The words tumble from my lips as I explain Colette's offer. Her face remains neutral, though curiosity sparks inside her as more understanding takes root. She begins to nod her head, and I watch the gears moving behind her eyes.

"So what would we do on the sea?" she asks, a gentleness in her tone when she says the word 'sea,' speaking as if it's a person. I think back to all the times she's spoken of it and can hardly remember a time she said the word without a trace of fear. But now, she has something closer to kinship in her tone.

"Exploring," I say. "Working with Brevlyra and discovering new opportunities. We're on no timeline, and I have full control of the ship."

She barks out a laugh. "I don't think that'll work, Crow, not with me on your ship."

My smile widens, and excitement grows in my core. "Are you saying you want to join my crew?" I want to kiss her, to brush my lips over hers to know she's alive, here before me and ready to take on the sea and the monsters and beasts that come with it. But I hold back and give her a wicked grin.

"Your crew?" She snorts and reaches for her tea. "We'll see about who they call Captain."

"Captain, eh? You stole my ship. *This* will be my ship."

Issa smirks at me and holds out her hand. We shake, and she grabs on tight, her nails digging into my skin. "I saved your life, Crow. The least you can do is give me your ship."

"*Our ship,*" I say, taking a step closer. "Co-captains."

The golden flecks in her eyes sparkle. "We'll discuss it."

# CHAPTER
## FORTY-TWO
### NERISSA

*Brevlyra*

The next morning, I wear a loose black skirt that exposes my legging-covered thigh when I walk, a flowing white top, and a gray jacket. Cyrus comes to my room at fifteen past nine, dressed in his own version of the outfit with fitted black pants tucked into his leather boots and an off-white shirt that exposes the top of his chest. His black hair is a mess on top of his head, and Besnick rests on his shoulder, beady black eyes staring at me.

I look at the bird, and he squawks, bringing a laugh to Cyrus's lips.

"You two will get used to each other," he says.

"Hm," I mumble. "If you say so."

His face turns serious, a deep ridge forming between his brow. "Are you ready?" he asks.

I nod, unable to form the words and follow him through the halls of the castle and to the meeting hall on the west side. It's a smaller room, a set of double doors opening to a table situated under a stained-glass window with eight chairs. Besnick extends his wings and takes to the sky, flying through the crack in the door before it closes behind us.

One feather floats to the ground, and I stare at it a moment too long before turning my focus back on the room in front of me. The picture in the window is twenty golden stars in a circle with a feather in the center, an arrow shooting through it. The words, "For flight or battle, Brevlyra," are below it in a banner made of golden glass.

A woman with white hair sits at the center.

"Welcome," she says. "We're pleased you decided to come today, Miss Eliott. We value your opinion on this matter." She extends her hand and two servants place chairs behind us. "Please, take a seat."

There's a slight clicking sound wafting to the ceiling, but it calms me. We do as we're asked, and Cyrus reaches over, placing his hand on my knee. I realize the sound is coming from me and stop jiggling my booted foot against the marble floor. The expansive space between the Octadus and where we sit narrows as they drag in Britta.

She wears the same clothes she had on when we stepped foot on Brevlyra, her ensemble covered in blood and dirt. A stale, bitter perfume of fear wafts from her. Her eyes widen when she catches sight of me, knees cracking on the floor.

"Cousin," she pleads, crawling to me. "Please, cousin. I did what I thought was best—"

"You did what was best for you," I say, and she jerks back as if slapped.

Red blossoms on her cheeks, and a scowl tugs at the corners of her mouth. Her pleading gaze turns sharper than steel. "I did what had to be done to protect those I love. The same thing you would have done."

"How is raising your status protection?" I say, voice sharp.

"Some of us don't have the privilege of living behind daddy's lies," she snaps back. "Your father hid the cruelty of Weylan's father—and then her—reign. Not all of us are lucky enough to be raised by cowards."

I rise from my seat, and Cyrus jumps up, restraining me with his hand wrapped around my forearm. "She's baiting you, Issa," he whispers.

Britta's laughter fills the room. "Now you have another coward to protect you. You haven't donned your crown yet, young king."

I glance back at Cyrus, taking in his clenched jaw and his sharp gaze. Questions rise within me, and his pain cuts through me sharper than a blade. The pain is accompanied by acceptance. Whatever decisions he's had to make since being here have been for the greater good.

"While I think this conversation will help you make a decision similar to ours," the woman at the center says, drawing our attention back to her. "It is time for us to tell you what we have decided."

A guard comes over to Britta and yanks her to her feet. Cyrus and I stay standing, and he loops his fingers through mine. To her left, a man with curly salt and pepper hair and skin a shade or two lighter than Claudette's stands. He clears his throat and crosses his hands in front of him.

"Good afternoon," he says. "Thank you for joining us. As Colette mentioned, we value your opinion on this matter, so we have come up with three solutions, all of which will properly represent an appropriate punishment for Britta of Teraceron's actions."

A woman with straight black hair and almond eyes stands. "The first decision was a suggestion made by me," she says. "My name is Augustina of Halivaris. I relocated to Brevlyra, originally as an ambassador for my queendom prior to the Three Days of the Light. It protected Brevlyra, but it also trapped those of us not from here. However, the past fifteen years here has made this my home as much as Halivaris, which is why this solution was approved by me."

She smiles at us, not sparing Britta a glance.

"Your cousin, Miss Eliott, has not been completely honest with you. When she escaped Teraceron under the guise of helping Queen Weylan, she sent her mother and her sisters away—to Halivaris. We became privy to this knowledge when I contacted my queen and told her of Brevlyra's new state."

I glance at Britta, but she doesn't spare me her attention. Cyrus squeezes my hand and Augustina continues.

"My suggestion is she be sent to live in Halivaris with her family, though she will not be treated as a visitor of their queendom. She will face the consequences set by my queen, which include a life of servitude and a deduction in status. She will never be allowed to step foot in Easterly again."

The breath hitches in my throat. I might never see my cousin again. While I know she betrayed me, and I struggle to forgive her for what she's done, the abruptness of the truth knots my stomach.

"I suggested," Colette says. "That she remain here in Brevlyra, as a prisoner, to serve a sentence for her crimes. The most severe punishment is death, though we will make an exception because her actions brought Brevlyra back into the world of the living. While we enjoyed our time away from the outside world, increasing our trade now that we have an established system of government will be beneficial. She would serve a maximum of twenty years and a minimum of five in our prison."

My mouth goes dry at the thought, thinking of how different the world might be when she joins us again.

"She will remain in Brevlyra," Colette continues. "For the rest of her life. What happens after she is released is dependent on many things."

"Finally," another member of the group says, a short man with hair the color of silver and lines telling his age. "I suggested sending her to the Dragonlands."

"But isn't it impenetrable?" I ask, finding my voice.

The man turns to me, but the reply does not come from him. "Elisha has a way to transport her there," Colette says. "But we'd like your input."

"Why?" I ask. "Why does it matter what I have to say?"

Colette smiles. "You are one of the reasons we are eight, not nine."

My brow furrows at her words.

"I turned down their offer to remain here," Cyrus says.

I look at him, words on the tip of my tongue, but he stops me with another squeeze of my hand. "I will still be a part of Brevlyra, but I'm not meant to remain still. My crows will help me communicate with the country as I continue to travel. As your co-captain."

"They wanted you to stay," I say.

He nods.

"And you said no?"

He nods again. Anxiety wars inside him, and it's bitter on my tongue. I try to give him the smallest of smiles. His relief pushes away the worry. We've hardly known each other for a few weeks, but sharing the sea with Cyrus makes sense. It feels like what I'm supposed to do on the next journey. This time, I'm the one squeezing his hand for reassurance.

"Well, Miss Eliott? What do you suggest we do with your cousin?"

I think of the options they gave me, chewing on the consequences for Britta each one holds. When my decision has been made, Cyrus's pride wells inside me, even though he might not know exactly what I'm about to say. Either way, he supports the decision, and that's the most important part of being co-captains, trying to understand what the other wants and doing what is best for the crew.

"I agree with Augustina. I think my cousin should be stripped of all titles and sent to Halivaris."

The Octadus nods their approval. Colette says, "Let us discuss for one moment—"

"But," I interrupt, "I want to be the one to take her there."

A heavy silence falls over the room, and a surprised laugh comes from my cousin's lips. "You've got to be kidding," she says.

"Miss Eliott, I don't think—" Augustina begins.

"It's the best option," I say before she can dissuade the others. "Even if we had a member of the Octadus on our ship, I need to be the one to take my cousin. She betrayed Brevlyra, and she also betrayed me. However..." I glance at Britta, and her brow furrows, unsure of how to take this new revelation. "She's my family. I deserve the right to stand by her when her fate is handed to the Queen of Halivaris."

They stare at me a long moment, my hand growing clammy in Cyrus's grip. His reassurance floods me, but he doesn't speak—I don't need him to. This decision is mine and mine alone.

"I think it's a wonderful idea," Elisha says.

"I disagree," Augustina says. "She's not from Halivaris. She doesn't know what to expect—"

"Then you can go with her," Colette says.

And the silent members turn their eyes to the Speaker of the group.

"You want me to go?" Augustina asks.

Colette shakes her head. "I want us to vote on this, but you used to be an ambassador before you pledged your allegiance to Brevlyra. We've even given you citizenship. Are you afraid to go back to your home queendom?"

The woman pauses before saying, "No, of course not."

"Very well. Thank you for your input, Miss Eliott. We will have a decision by nightfall. You may go."

The doors creak open behind us, and Cyrus and I walk out of the room as they carry a struggling Britta back to her cell.

Once we're out in the hall, Cyrus turns to me. "That was brave of you."

I release his hand. "It was what needed to be done."

"And selfless," he adds.

My cheeks warm, and I cross my arms over my chest, thinking of my sister. I meant what I said. Family is important, even the family we cannot trust. We don't pick who we're related to, but we do pick how we treat them and how we choose to love them. If this is the little slice of grace I can show Britta, then maybe it will be the first step to change.

I tell Cyrus as much, and he leans over and presses a kiss on my forehead. "You're a better person than me," he says.

I laugh. "I wouldn't say that. Besides, I would like to visit the place my father went before his death. Now that..." My throat tightens, and tears burn behind my eyes. "Now that Lucia is gone, I can. She would want me to—would want answers as much as I do."

He brushes a strand of hair behind my ear. "About Lucia...there's something I want to do. For you, and for her."

"What—"

"Trust me, okay?"

I nod. "Okay."

"I'll come by your room after dinner. Wear something warm. It's supposed to be cold tonight."

Cyrus knocks rhythmically on my door around eight o'clock. A winter wind rushes the side of the castle, and I grab my cloak and throw it over the long dress I picked from my closet, a pair of leggings and my trusted boots hidden beneath it. With every step, my shoes flash leather to anyone walking near, adding a level of intrigue to the dark gray fabric.

"Nice dress," he says when I open the door.

I fiddle with the chain hanging around my neck. Lucia's ring dangles at the end. The cuts and bruises from the fight forced me to slide it from my hand. Since then, I've kept it on the chain, unable to place it back on my finger. If I do, it's like admitting she'll never wear it again. I never meant to keep it forever, only keep it safe for her.

"I found it in the back of my closet," I tell Cyrus, forcing myself out of my thoughts and patting down the dress with my other hand. "No unnecessary undergarments. It's not an islander dress..." I trail off thinking of the thin, soft dresses we wear on Helene. "But it'll do."

He smirks and extends a hand. "Come on. I have something I want to show you."

We walk hand in hand through the castle and down the streets of Brevlyra. It's new to me, this level of affection. Before him, my first and last kisses had been messy, at best. The boys I kissed were barely older and as experienced as me. This is sweet—comfortable.

We leave the city as the moon rises even higher in the sky, casting its waning light down on us. Our feet dance over the rocky path leading to a small clearing in the woods, and my heart clenches in my chest. Claudette, Becci, and Duncan wait for us, each holding a candle in their hands. Duncan goes around the small group with a match, lighting the wicks.

"What is this?" I ask.

Cyrus's crows flap their wings as they land in the trees above. Besnick flies down and lands on his master's shoulder. He extends his wing, and Cyrus reaches up and plucks a feather from the crook. As soon as it's in his hand, the bird takes into the air and goes back into the trees.

"When my mother passed, and I was taken prisoner in Weylan's court, a man lost his life to do this with me. He knew my mother, and he knew of the Crow line. When one of our own dies, we take a feather from our crow and light it aflame, letting it fly in the wind." He rolls the feather between his fingers, eyes studying it instead of being focused on me. "I know you're not one of us—not a Crow—but we're your family now. Your crew. And if we're co-captains, then my crows are yours, and your sea is mine."

He extends the feather toward me, and I take it from him, the tips of our fingers brushing.

"You don't have to—" he begins.

I reach up and wrap my hand around the back of his neck, melding his lips to mine. The kiss is soft and sure, and I don't even mind the eyes of the others that burn past the fabric of my dress and straight into my skin. His surprise stops him for a breath before he responds, wrapping his arm around my waist and pulling me close.

I draw back and gaze into his eyes, leaning my forehead against his. My words come out in white clouds as I say, "Thank you."

We hold the feather together as Duncan brings over the matches, lighting one on the side of the box and touching the flame to the tip of the crow's gift. The black grabs onto the orange and red, creating a burst of light. We hold it to the sky, watching as it dwindles down as far as it will go before we set it free, nothing more than a memory, the ashes dancing among the stars.

# CHAPTER
## FORTY-THREE
### NERISSA

**Abhors Sea**

"How are you?" Cyrus asks, coming to stand next to me in the moonlight. Bec and Claudette argue at the stern, and I can almost count the seconds until Claudette either pulls her sword or stomps away. Before I can respond to Cyrus, Claudette does the latter and storms past us.

"We cannot go due west. The wind is blowing north-east. If we go west..." she mumbles to herself, with Bec not far behind her.

"Don't you dare!" she yells. "Duncan, don't *you* dare."

Duncan raises his hands off the wheel and shakes his head. "I can leave you both to decide our fate if you want to take my shift," he says.

"Duncan!" Bec screeches, running.

Cyrus chuckles under his breath. "We might never make it to the shore again," he says.

Some of the new deckhands wrestle between looking fearful or smirking. The hierarchy of our ship is ever changing, and the new members of the crew will need more than a day to figure out our system.

I smile, closing my eyes once again and letting the sea breeze brush against my cheeks. "I could live like this," I state. "Our adventures aren't over yet."

"You don't say?" he teases, and I look at him. His eyes are soft, gentle as he wraps my hand in his. "I would ask how you are after the ceremony for Lucia—"

"But that's not us. We don't talk about our emotions. We know, don't we?" I wrap my free hand around the edge of the ship, the wood digging into my palm. "But thank you," I say, clearing my throat. "I was able to tell her goodbye."

Tears burn behind my eyes, and he reaches over, placing his calloused hand over mine. Warmth spreads through his touch, and I lean into him. The absence of her body haunts me, and I don't think I'm done wondering what happened to her—who took her from me. But right now, we have a mission, taking my cousin to the Queendom of Halivaris. While there, who knows what other mysteries I'll solve? Lucia's body was taken. The scholars believe by the Light, but I'm not sure. Either way, her spirit is with the Light.

The sea will soften my heart, in time. Accepting my connection, my Light-given ability, makes everything right. No longer are we fighting one another—we're working together, the Light flooding through my power with the sea.

My eyes drift upward to meet Cyrus's. I have to stop myself from getting lost in the deep blue depths. I lift my fingers and brush back the lock of black hair that tugged free of the bandana wrapped around his head.

"What were you thinking, Crow? Any rumored treasures?" I ask. "Not sure this one," I nod to the woman pacing the deck, Augustina, the member of the Octadus, "will let us have any fun."

I pull back my hand, but he grabs it again, twining our fingers together.

"As your captain—" he starts.

"You're pushing it," I say, a smile taking over.

"Co-captain," he corrects. "Either way, doesn't that mean she has to listen to us?"

"Still pushing it with the co-captain thing, but I'll let it slide." I risk a glance in Augustina's direction. "I'm not sure *she's* used to taking orders."

His laughter rolls up my side, warming me to my core. "I think you might be right."

"Well, we have a long journey to find out."

He steals a quick kiss, drawing a smile on my face. "You're right, milady."

I scrunch up my nose. "Don't call me that. Ever, please."

He winks. "No promises. What do you say we flaunt that upper class up-bringing in Halivaris?"

"Oh, yeah?" I ask, putting our hands on the ship between us and looking out at the sea—my home—my birthright.

He leans down, angling his mouth against mine. My eyes flutter shut as his lips meet mine, soft and perfect. I thread my fingers through the hair at the nape of his neck, tugging him close. He smiles against my mouth before drawing his tongue slowly over my bottom lip. I wrap my other arm around his shoulders, pressing into him until there's barely any space left. He pulls back and leans his forehead against mine. His blue eyes stare into mine, intense and asking a million questions only a million years can answer. I lean my head against his chest, and our breathing falls into a rhythm as our hearts frantically beat against each other.

"You ready for an adventure, milady?" he asks, his voice rumbling in my chest.

*First stop, taking Britta home.*

*Forgiveness.*

*Let's start this journey off right.*

"Lead the way," I say, the waves rushing against the side of the ship with my co-captain by my side.

# Acknowledgements

First and foremost, to my Lord and Savior, Jesus Christ, who has supplied me with His endless blessings and mercies. This book is evidence of patience and prayer, and I truly am blessed to get to write the stories and characters I love.

If you've made it this far, THANK YOU. I wouldn't be able to do this if it weren't for readers like you. Readers are the best people in the world because they live in many. I hope you loved escaping into this world of my creation.

When they say it takes a village, they mean it. This book is many years, many tears, and many drafts in the making. First, to April Skelly for believing in this story, even in its roughest form. Thank you so much for bringing me into the Quill & Flame family. And also to all the Q&F ladies! Thanks for bringing me into the fold, reading this story and sharing it with your friends, and I'm so excited my book is among such wonderful company.

Second, to Cassie Giovanni, my critique partner and, more importantly, my friend. This book would still be sitting on my laptop if it weren't for you. Your editing skills and honest feedback are why Nerissa and Cyrus are more than an untold story.

Next, to my editor Meghan Kleinschmidt, for seeing all of *Heart of the Sea's* pieces and helping it become the story it is now.

To my proofreaders, Ava Lauren Greyson, for finding the little mistakes, and to Sarah Harmon for discovering every little comma, grammatical error, and sentence that didn't make sense—all while sipping champagne in Champagne.

And I still won't get over the pictures you sent me of my book being edited in Paris. And to Ty, my Beta reader. You read this book many times and helped make it shine!

I can't believe I have such a beautiful book to hold in my hands, all thanks to Emilie Haney for her beautiful cover design, Celene Reese for her interior design help and handwritten Part One, Two, Three, Four, and Five, and Haleigh DeRocher for the hand-drawn map. You each listened to my vision for the inside and outside of this book, and it turned out stunning. Thank you so much!

Sometimes you don't know you need a friend until you slide into each other's DMs. Thank you, Amanda, for being the friend I didn't think I needed. I'm grateful to have found a fellow writer so close by with whom I can share my faith, my words, and my worries over a cup of coffee. Your prayers and your friendship mean the world to me.

Finally, to my family.

I wouldn't have written my first story if it weren't for the constant encouragement from my parents and family. My mom handed me my first copy of *Twilight* at twelve, and from then on, I had to read everything I could. When I realized I could write my own stories, you encouraged me every step of the way, reading all the good and bad stories, listening to my constant ideas, and believing in me when I didn't believe in myself. To my dad, who only reads non-fiction and his Bible, but takes time for my stories, too. To my grandma for reading all of my short stories out loud to my papa because he can't read them on his own anymore---and then reading them a second time, so you didn't miss anything the first go around.

To my in-laws, even though you aren't readers, you own every anthology I've been in and supported my cover reveals, shared my posts on social media, and talked about my writing to your friends.

Lastly, to my husband: through every storm, on any ship, I wouldn't want to be a passenger with anyone but you. I love you.

# About the Author

Moriah is the author of the young adult fantasy *Heart of the Sea* and various short stories. She is a two-time graduate from the University of South Carolina with a Bachelor's in Liberal Arts and a Master's in Library and Information Science. It's been said you can find perusing bookstores, attempting to persuade strangers to read her favorite books, oscillating between watching the *Lord of the Rings* trilogy (her husband's favorite) or *Harry Potter* (hers), and keeping her books from the clutches of her two feisty cats.

# IF YOU WANT TO READ MORE BOOKS LIKE

Heart
OF THE
Sea

# QUILL & FLAME PUBLISHING HOUSE
# HAS YOU COVERED

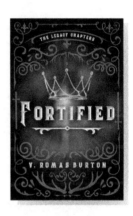

# HEAT WITHOUT THE SCORCH

Quill & Flame
PUBLISHING HOUSE

www.quillandflame.com